Ramsey Campbell wa[...]
lived in Liverpool fo[...]
Wallasey, Merseyside [...]
he was 18, and he wo[...]
before becoming a f[...]
author of the novels *The Doll Who A[...]*
The Face That Must Die, *The Nameless*, *The Parasite*,
Incarnate and *Obsession* as well as five collections of
short stories: *The Inhabitant of the Lake*, *Demons by*
Daylight, *The Height of the Scream*, *Dark Companions*
and *Cold Print*. He has won the World Fantasy Award
twice (for best short story of the year) and the British
Fantasy Award twice (once for best short story, once for
best novel) – more than any other writer in the field.
Ramsey Campbell has also edited several anthologies of
horror fiction, broadcasts frequently on Radio Merseyside
as a film critic, and is President of the British Fantasy
Society.

By the same author

Novels

The Parasite (To Wake the Dead)
The Doll Who Ate His Mother
The Face That Must Die
Incarnate
Obsession
The Nameless

Short Stories

The Inhabitant of the Lake
Demons by Daylight
The Height of the Scream
Dark Companions

Anthologies (as Editor)

Superhorror (The Far Reaches of Fear)
New Terrors
New Tales of the Cthulhu Mythos
The Gruesome Book

RAMSEY CAMPBELL

Cold Print

GRAFTON BOOKS

A Division of the Collins Publishing Group

LONDON GLASGOW
TORONTO SYDNEY AUCKLAND

Grafton Books
A Division of the Collins Publishing Group
8 Grafton Street, London W1X 3LA

A Grafton UK Paperback Original 1987

Copyright © Ramsey Campbell 1985

ISBN 0-586-06364-1

Printed and bound in Great Britain by
Collins, Glasgow

Set in Times

For Fritz Leiber and Bob Bloch
who were there before me, and did it better

Contents

Acknowledgements

'The Church in High Street,' copyright © 1962 by August Derleth. From *Dark Mind, Dark Heart*.

'The Room in the Castle,' 'The Horror from the Bridge,' 'The Insects from Shaggai,' 'The Render of the Veils,' 'The Inhabitant of the Lake,' 'The Will of Stanley Brooke,' 'The Moon-Lens,' copyright © 1964 by Ramsey Campbell. From *The Inhabitant of the Lake*.

'Before the Storm,' copyright © 1980 by Ramsey Campbell. From *Fantasy Readers Guide 2*, March 1980.

'Cold Print,' copyright © 1969 by August Derleth. From *Tales of the Cthulhu Mythos*.

'Among the pictures are these:,' copyright © 1980 by Harry O. Morris, Jr. From *Nyctalops* 16, March 1981.

'The Tugging,' copyright © 1976 by Edward P. Berglund. From *The Disciples of Cthulhu*.

'The Faces at Pine Dunes,' copyright © 1980 by Arkham House Publishers, Inc. From *New Tales of the Cthulhu Mythos*.

'Blacked Out,' copyright © 1984 by Ramsey Campbell. Original to this collection.

'The Voice of the Beach,' copyright © 1982 by Fantasy Tales. From *Fantasy Tales* 10, Summer 1982.

INTRODUCTION
Chasing the Unknown

The first book of Lovecraft's I read made me into a writer. I found it in the window of a Liverpool sweetshop called Bascombe's. I was fourteen years old then, and went there every Saturday to search through the second-hand paperbacks at the rear of the shop once I'd made sure there was nothing in the window. Sometimes, among the covers faded like unpreserved Technicolor in the window, there would be a bright new book on which to spend my pocket money: an issue of *Supernatural Stories* written by R. L. Fanthorpe under innumerable pseudonyms (Pel Torro, Othello Baron, Peter O'Flinn, Oben Lerteth, Rene Rolant, Deutero Spartacus, Elton T. Neef were just some of them), a Gerald G. Swan *Weird and Occult Miscellany* whose back cover advertised studies of torture and flagellation and execution 'for the nature student.' But that Saturday, among the yellowing molls and dusty cowboys, I saw a skeletal fungoid creature, the title *Cry Horror*, the author's name I'd been yearning for years to see on a book. For a panicky moment I thought I hadn't half a crown to buy the book, dreaded that it would be gone when I came back with the money. I read it in a single malingering day off school; for a year or more I thought H.P. Lovecraft was not merely the greatest horror writer of all time, but the greatest writer I had ever read.

Some (Stephen King and Charles L. Grant among them) would take that to prove that Lovecraft is an adolescent phase one goes through – certainly a writer best read when one is that age. I can only say that I find his best work more rewarding now than I did then. Grant claims that 'when you grow up you discover that what attracted you when you were fourteen was his rococo style and very little else,' but I don't think it was so in my case; certainly I don't agree that 'the style makes the stories.' Indeed, I think that's precisely the trap into which too many imitators of Lovecraft fall.

I was one of them, of course, having already done my best to imitate Machen and John Dickson Carr. If I avoided the trap to some extent, I did so unconsciously – did so because I didn't merely admire Lovecraft, I was steeped in his work and his vision throughout the writing of my first published book. I began it as a way of paying back some of the pleasure his work had given me, some of the sense of awesome expectation that even reading some of his titles – 'The Colour out of Space,' 'The Whisperer in Darkness' – could conjure up. No other writer had given me that so far. I wrote my Lovecraftian tales for my own pleasure: the pleasure of convincing myself that they were almost as good as the originals. It was only on the suggestion of two fantasy fans, the Londoner Pat Kearney and the American Betty Kujawa, that I showed them to August Derleth at Arkham House.

'There are myriad unspeakable terrors in the cosmos in which our universe is but an atom; and the two gates of agony, life and death, gape to pour forth infinities of abominations. And the other gates which spew forth their broods are, thank God, little known to most of us. Few can have seen the spawn of ultimate corruption, or known that centre of insane chaos where Azathoth, the blind idiot god, bubbles mindlessly; I myself have never seen these things – but God knows that what I saw in those

cataclysmic moments in the church at Kingsport tran-
scends the ultimate earthly knowledge.'

So began 'The Tomb-Herd,' one of the stories I sent
Derleth. Since his death, a regrettable element of fantasy
fandom has devoted a good deal of energy to defaming
him. The honesty and courage of these people may be
gauged by their having waited until Derleth was unable
to defend himself and by the way they often conceal their
smears in essays ostensibly on other subjects. For myself,
not only did I find him unfailingly helpful and patient and
encouraging when I most needed this support, but in
retrospect I'm doubly impressed that he could find anything worth encouraging among the second-hand Lovecraft I sent him. Here are a few more choice passages
from 'The Tomb-Herd':

'The house which I knew as my friend's, set well back
from the road, overgrown with ivy that twisted in myriad
grotesque shapes, was locked and shuttered. No sign of
life was discernible inside it, and outside the garden was
filled with a brooding quiet, while my shadow on the
fungus-overgrown lawn appeared eldritch and distorted,
like that of some ghoul-born being from nether pits.

'Upon inquiring of this anomaly from the strangely
reticent neighbours, I learned that my friend had visited
the deserted church in the centre of Kingsport after dark,
and that this must have called the vengeance of *those
from outside* upon him.'

I suspect most of us would be strangely reticent if a
stranger came knocking at our door to ask why his
shadow resembled that of a ghoul-born being, but let's go
on:

'In that stomach-wrenching moment of horrible knowledge, realization of the abnormal ghastlinesses after which
my friend had been searching and which, perhaps, he had

stirred out of aeon-long sleep in the Kingsport church, I closed the book. But I soon opened it again . . .'

Best of all:

'(Now followed the section which horrified me more than anything else. My friend must have been preparing the telegram by writing it on the page while outside unspeakable shamblers made their way towards him – as became hideously evident as the writing progressed.)

'*To Richard Dexter. Come at once to Kingsport. You are needed urgently by me here for protection from agencies which may kill me – or worse – if you do not come immediately. Will explain as soon as you reach me* . . . But what is this thing that flops unspeakably down the passage towards this room? It cannot be that abomination which I met in the nitrous vaults below Asquith Place . . . IA! YOG-SOTHOTH! CTHULHU FHTAGN!'

Behold the trap I mentioned earlier – the fallacy by which one can persuade oneself that if one imitates or, more probably, exceeds the worst excesses of Lovecraft's style, one is achieving what he achieved. (One reason Lovecraft and Hitchcock are so often imitated is that both display their technique fully rather than concealing it.) But the hyperbolic passages in Lovecraft's writing (by no means as numerous as his detractors claim) are built up to; as Fritz Leiber puts it perfectly, they're orchestrated. It's easy to imitate Lovecraft's style, or at least to convince oneself that one has done so; it's far more difficult to imitate his sense of structure, based on a study of Poe, Machen (in particular 'The Great God Pan'), and the best of Blackwood. I think that's the point Charlie Grant misses: Lovecraft's style would be nothing without the painstaking structure of his stories.

Derleth told me to abandon my attempts to set my work in Massachusetts and in general advised me in no uncertain terms how to improve the stories. I suspect he would have been gentler if he'd realized I was only fifteen years old, but on the other hand, if you can't take that kind of forthright editorial response you aren't likely to survive as a writer. I was still in the process of adopting his suggestions when he asked me to send him a story for an anthology he was editing (then called *Dark of Mind, Dark of Heart*). Delighted beyond words, I sent him the rewritten 'Tomb-Herd,' which he accepted under certain conditions: that the title should be changed to 'The Church in the High Street' (though he later dropped the latter article, along with the prepositions from the title of his book) and that he should be able to edit the story as he saw fit. The story as published, there and here, therefore contains several passages that are Derleth's paraphrases of what I wrote. Quite right too: as I think he realized, it was the most direct way to show me how to improve my writing, and selling the story was so encouraging that I completed my first book a little over a year later.

I've included here a selection of tales from that book, *The Inhabitant of the Lake*. Though prior publication never deters me from revising my stories – revised editions of my novels *The Doll Who Ate His Mother* and *The Nameless* are soon to appear, and some of the stories in my collection *Dark Companions* were revised for that book – I've resisted the temptation to improve these earlier tales, partly because I feel too distant from them. Here they are, flaws and all.

'The Room in the Castle' expands Lovecraft's reference to 'snake-bearded Byatis' (am I remembering it accurately?) – Bob Bloch's originally, I believe. 'The Horror from the Bridge' is based, like several of these stories, on Lovecraft's Commonplace Book as it appeared in the

Arkham House anthology *The Shuttered Room*. It's based on two entries: 'Man in strange subterranean chamber – seeks to force door of bronze – overwhelmed by influx of waters' and 'Ancient (Roman? pre-historic?) stone bridge washed away by a (sudden & curious?) storm. *Something* liberated which had been sealed up in the masonry thousands of years ago. Things happen.'

The story is based to some extent on the chronology of events in Lovecraft's 'The Dunwich Horror,' but towards the end I found I hadn't the patience to build as minutely as Lovecraft would have.

'The Insects from Shaggai' is based on another entry in the Commonplace Book, or rather on my misreading of it. Lovecraft wrote 'Insects or some other entities from space attack and penetrate a man's head & cause him to *remember* alien and exotic things – possible displacement of personality,' a superb idea I rushed at so hastily that I failed to notice he hadn't meant giant insects at all. (An account of the dream which gave him the idea can be found in the *Selected Letters*, volume V, page 159.) Of all my stories this is probably the pulpiest. As such it has some energy, I think, but I wish I'd left the note alone until I was equipped to do it justice.

I wrote the first page of 'The Inhabitant of the Lake' and developed writer's block. What released me weeks later was writing 'The Render of the Veils' in the garden on a summer morning. It's based on a Lovecraft note ('Disturbing conviction that all life is only a deceptive dream with some dismal or sinister horror lurking behind') but it began my liberation from Lovecraft's style, in the sense that it's told largely through dialogue. I was pleased enough with it to want to name my first book after it, but Derleth felt – rightly, I think – that it sounded mystical rather than frightening. I returned to 'The

Inhabitant of the Lake' (again rooted in the Commonplace Book: 'Visit to someone in wild & remote house – ride from station through the night into the haunted hills. House by forest or water. Terrible things live there') with renewed enthusiasm.

Four stories followed that are not included here. 'The Plain of Sound' may be read in the small press journal *Crypt of Cthulhu*, in an issue devoted to my work. 'The Return of the Witch' was suggested by two Lovecraft notes: 'Live man buried in bridge masonry according to superstition – or black cat' and 'Salem story. The cottage of an aged witch, wherein after her death are found sundry terrible things' but it developed as a rewrite, virtually scene by scene, of a Henry Kuttner story I had never read and didn't encounter until several years after my story was published.

My story contains a moderately evocative dream sequence: 'He dreamed of wanderings through space to dead cities on other planets, of lakes bordered by twisted trees which moved and creaked in no wind, and finally of a strange curved rim beyond which he passed into utter darkness – a darkness in which he sensed nothing living. Less clear dreams occurred, too, and he often felt a clutching terror at glimpses of the shuttered room amid bizarre landscapes, and of rotting things which scrabbled out of graves at an echoing, sourceless call' and a sudden outburst of paranoia that points rather disconcertingly forward to fiction of mine such as *The Face That Must Die*: '(Look at the bastard! He tells you you're possessed, but you know what he really means, don't you? That you're schizophrenic. Push him out, quick! Don't let him come poking round your mind!)' but otherwise I think the story can be allowed to rest in peace.

'The Mine on Yuggoth' was a thorough rewrite of one

of the first tales I showed Derleth, 'The Tower from Yuggoth.' I got one of the ideas for the rewrite in church, during mass, and I suspect that was when Catholicism lost its grip on me, though probably never entirely. 'The Will of Stanley Brooke' was my first punning title; the story attempted to tell its tale wholly through dialogue, with no Lovecraftian adjectives at all, but I remember congratulating myself on the originality of a theme which in fact was Lovecraft's, from 'The Festival.' The next story here, 'The Moon-Lens,' has its basis in a Lovecraft note ('Ancient necropolis – bronze door in hillside which opens as the moonlight strikes it – focused by ancient lens in pylon opposite'), as did 'The Face in the Desert,' a poorly imagined Arabian tale Derleth rejected from the book and I for this one. More background on the book can be found in *Horrors and Unpleasantries*, Sheldon Jaffery's anecdotal history of Arkham House.

While Derleth was looking at the manuscript of my collection I wrote another story, 'The Stone on the Island.' For a change, this was based on one of M. R. James's 'Stories I Have Tried to Write':

'The man, for instance (naturally a man with *something* on his mind), who, sitting in his study one evening, was startled by a slight sound, turned hastily, and saw a certain dead face looking out from between the window curtains: a dead face, but with living eyes. He made a dash at the curtains and tore them apart. A pasteboard mask fell to the floor. But there was no one there, and the eyes of the mask were but eye-holes. What (James wonders) was to be done about that?'

My solution was that it wasn't a mask. The tale may be technically superior to any of the *Inhabitant* stories, and it reads more like me than Lovecraft, I think. However, I find its adolescent sadism excessive, and so I haven't included it here.

Now began my struggle to leave Lovecraft behind and write like myself – a struggle that caused me to write an article, 'Lovecraft in Retrospect,' condemning his work outright (when what I was really condemning was my own dependence on him). I suspect that writing about his creations had been a way to avoid dealing with my own fears. My impatience with trying to imitate the Lovecraftian structure led to the extreme compression of some of the stories in *Demons by Daylight*, my second book. One story in that collection, 'The Franklyn Paragraphs,' is based on two notes from the Commonplace Book, and two stories written during that period belong to the Lovecraft Mythos. One, 'Before the Storm,' I didn't feel was worth rewriting in order to fit into *Demons by Daylight*; it appears here for the first time between hard covers. By contrast, 'Cold Print' was fully rewritten in 1966. Both show my struggles to be myself, I think, and in 'Cold Print' the struggle has pretty well been won.

I had nothing more to do with the Lovecraft Mythos until 1971, when Meade and Penny Frierson asked me to contribute to their extraordinarily ambitious (and, on the whole, impressively successful) small press anthology, *HPL*. I offered them 'A Madness from the Vaults,' written in 1962 but, I'd felt, too fantastic to fit into my first book. When I turned up the fanzine in which it had eventually appeared I was dismayed to find that its sadism far exceeded that of 'The Stone on the Island.' All I could do for the Friersons was write what was virtually a new story under the same title.

'The Tugging' was written three years later, in response to a request for a story for a DAW Books anthology, *The Disciples of Cthulhu*. That anthology set me thinking of

editing one of my own. Just before his death Derleth had
told me that he planned to edit *New Tales of the Cthulhu
Mythos*. Arkham House agreed that I should, and I
contributed the story 'The Faces at Pine Dunes.'

Editing that book helped me organize my thoughts
about the followers of Lovecraft. The great merit of
Lovecraft's mythos was always that however much it
showed, it suggested more: it was a way of sketching the
unknown in terms that fed the reader's imagination –
mine, certainly. Perhaps it was inevitable that writers
such as myself would attempt to fill in the gaps. I think
the most important question to be asked about any story
based on Lovecraft is whether it conveys any of the awe
and terror Lovecraft's stories did. I've little time for the
kind of story which purports to discover yet another
genealogical link among Lovecraft's entities – this kind of
nitpicking may be all right for the fanzines, but hardly a
basis for fiction – and much less time for stories that rob
Lovecraft's concepts of awe by explaining them away. On
the other hand, I admire such disparate stories as Bloch's
'Notebook Found in a Deserted House' (surely the most
frightening Mythos tale by anyone other than Lovecraft),
Wandrei's 'The Tree-Men of M'Bwa' and *The Web of
Easter Island*, Frank Belknap Long's 'The Space-Eaters'
(an oddly moving as well as awesome story about the
pupil confounding the teacher), Henry Kuttner's 'The
Graveyard Rats,' T.E.D. Klein's 'Black Man with a
Horn,' among quite a few others.

My doubts about the overpopulation and overexplan-
ation of the Mythos prompted me to write 'The Voice of
the Beach.' Lovecraft regarded Blackwood's 'The Wil-
lows' – in which, as he often pointed out, nothing is
shown or stated directly – as the finest of all weird
tales. The closest he came to achieving what Blackwood

achieved was in 'The Colour out of Space,' which contains none of the paraphernalia of the later mythos. 'The Voice of the Beach' was my attempt to return to Lovecraft's first principles, to see how close I could get to his aims without the encumbrances of the mythos. Lin Carter looked at the story when he was editing *Weird Tales*, but rejected it as insufficiently Lovecraftian. For my part, I believe it's the most successful of these stories.

Whether I shall return to Lovecraft as an influence I don't know. Some may feel I've never shaken it off. 'Blacked Out,' the most recent story in this book, is clearly indebted to Lovecraft, though it wasn't written with that intention. (In a sense 'Among the pictures are these' is the earliest piece, a literal description written in 1973 of some drawings I executed in my early teens.) One Edna Stumpf (a name on which I can scarcely improve) rounded off a review of my novel *Incarnate*, which she very kindly described as 'surprisingly good,' with the words 'My dream is that Campbell take ten years to flush the Lovecraft out of his typewriter. And rewriter (sic) it.' I hope she and any others of like mind will not be too distressed if I don't take ten years off from writing. If some of Lovecraft's sense of wonder remains in my work, so much the better. I hope that at least my attempts to repay the pleasure his work still gives me have not lessened his power.

Merseyside, England
6 July, 1984

THE CHURCH IN HIGH STREET

'. . . the Herd that stand watch at the secret portal each tomb is known to have, and that thrive on that which groweth out of the inhabitants thereof . . .'

ABDUL ALHAZRED: *Necronomicon*

If I had not been a victim of circumstances, I would never have gone to ancient Temphill. But I had very little money in those days, and when I recalled the invitation of a friend who lived in Temphill to become his secretary, I began to hope that this post – open some months before – might still be available. I knew that my friend would not easily find someone to stay with him long; not many would relish a stay in such a place of ill repute as Temphill.

Thinking thus, I gathered into a trunk what few belongings I had, loaded it into a small car which I had borrowed from another friend gone on a sea voyage, and drove out of London at an hour too early for the clamorous traffic of the city to have risen, away from the cell-like room where I had stayed in a tottering, blackened backstreet house.

I had heard much from my friend, Albert Young, about Temphill and the customs of that decaying Cotswold town where he had lived for months during his research into incredibly superstitious beliefs for a chapter in his forthcoming book on witchcraft and witchcraft lore. Not being superstitious myself, I was curious at the way in which apparently sane people seemed to avoid entering Temphill whenever possible – as reported by Young – not so much because they disliked the route, as because they were disturbed by the strange tales which constantly filtered out of the region.

Perhaps because I had been dwelling upon these tales, the country seemed to grow disquieting as I neared my destination. Instead of the gently undulating Cotswold hills, with villages and half-timbered thatched houses, the area was one of grim, brooding plains, sparsely habited, where the only vegetation was a grey, diseased grass and an infrequent bloated oak. A few places filled me with a strong unease – the path the road took beside a sluggish stream, for instance, where the reflection of the passing vehicle was oddly distorted by the green, scum-covered water; the diversion which forced me to take a route straight through the middle of a marsh, where trees closed overhead so that the ooze all around me could barely be seen; and the densely wooded hillside which rose almost vertically above the road at one point, with trees reaching towards the road like myriad gnarled hands, all wearing the aspect of a primeval forest.

Young had written often of certain things he had learned from reading in various antique volumes; he wrote of 'a forgotten cycle of superstitious lore which would have been better unknown'; he mentioned strange and alien names, and towards the last of his letters – which had ceased to come some weeks before – he had hinted of actual worship of trans-spatial beings still practised in such towns as Camside, Brichester, Severnford, Goatswood and Temphill. In his very last letter he had written of a temple of 'Yog-Sothoth' which existed conterminously with an actual church in Temphill where monstrous rituals had been performed. This eldritch temple had been, it was thought, the origin of the town's name – a corruption of the original 'Temple Hill' – which had been built around the hill-set church, where 'gates', if opened by now long forgotten alien incantations, would gape to let elder demons pass from other spheres. There was a particularly hideous legend, he wrote, concerning the errand on which these demons came, but he forebore to recount this, at least until he had visited the alien temple's earthly location.

On my entrance into the first of Temphill's archaic streets, I began to feel qualms about my impulsive action. If Young had meanwhile found a secretary, I would find it difficult, in my indigence, to return to London. I had hardly enough funds to find lodging here, and the hotel repelled me the moment I saw it in passing – with its leaning porch, the peeling bricks of the walls, and the decayed old men who stood in front of the porch and seemed to stare mindlessly at something beyond me as I drove by. The other sections of the town were not reassuring, either, particularly the steps which rose between green ruins of brick walls to the black steeple of a church among pallid gravestones.

The worse part of Temphill, however, seemed to be the south end. On Wood Street, which entered the town on the northwest side, and on Manor Street, where the forested hillside on the left of the first street ended, the houses were square stone buildings in fairly good repair; but around the blackened hotel at the centre of Temphill, the buildings were often greatly dilapidated, and the roof of one three-storey building – the lower floor of which was used as a shop, with a sign – *Poole's General Store* – in the mud-spattered windows – had completely collapsed. Across the bridge beyond the central Market Square lay Cloth Street, and beyond the tall, uninhabited buildings of Wool Place at the end of it could be found South

Street, where Young lived in a three-storey house which he had bought cheaply and been able to renovate.

The state of the buildings across the skeletal river bridge was even more disturbing than that of those on the north side. Bridge Lane's grey warehouses soon gave way to gabled dwellings, often with broken windows and patchily unpainted fronts, but still inhabited. Here scattered unkempt children stared resignedly from dusty front steps or played in pools of orange mud on a patch of waste ground, while the older tenants sat in twilit rooms, and the atmosphere of the place depressed me as might a shade-inhabited city ruin.

I entered into South Street between two gabled three-storey houses. Number 11, Young's house, was at the far end of the street. The sight of it, however, filled me with forebodings – for it was shuttered, and the door stood open, laced with cobwebs. I drove the car up the driveway at the side and got out. I crossed the grey, fungus-overgrown lawn and went up the steps. The door swung inward at my touch, opening upon a dimly-lit hall. My knocks and calls brought no answer, and I stood for a few moments undecided, hesitant to enter. There was a total absence of footprints anywhere on the dusty floor of the hall. Remembering that Young had written about conversations he had had with the owner of Number 8, across the road, I decided to apply to him for information about my friend.

I crossed the street to Number 8 and knocked on the door. It was opened almost immediately, though in such silence as to startle me. The owner of Number 8 was a tall man with white hair and luminously dark eyes. He wore a frayed tweed suit. But his most startling attribute was a singular air of antiquity, giving him the impression of having been left behind by some past age. He looked very much like my friend's description of the pedantic John Clothier, a man possessed of an extraordinary amount of ancient knowledge.

When I introduced myself and told him that I was looking for Albert Young, he paled and was briefly hesitant before inviting me to enter his house, muttering that he knew where Albert Young had gone, but that I probably wouldn't believe him. He led me down a dark hall into a large room lit only by an oil lamp in one corner. There he motioned me to a chair beside the fireplace. He got out his pipe, lit it, and sat down opposite me, beginning to talk with an abrupt rush.

'I took an oath to say nothing of this to anyone,' he said. 'That's why I could only warn Young to leave and keep away from – that place. He wouldn't listen – and you won't find him now. Don't look so – it's the truth! I'll have to tell you more than I told him, or you'll try to find him and find – *something else*. God knows what will happen to me now – once you've joined *Them*, you must never speak of their place to any outsider. But I can't see another go the way Young went. I should let you go there – according to the oath – but *They'll* take me sooner or later, anyway. You get away before it's too late. Do you know the church in High Street?'

It took me some seconds to regain my composure enough to reply. 'If you mean the one near the central square – yes, I know it.'

'It isn't used – as a church, now,' Clothier went on. 'But there were certain rites practised there long ago. They left their mark. Perhaps Young wrote you about the legend of the temple existing in the same place as the church, but in another dimension? Yes, I see by your expression that he did. But do you know that rites can still be used at the proper season to open the gates and

let through *those from the other side*? It's true. I've stood
in that church myself and watched the gates open in the
centre of empty air to show visions that made me shriek
in horror. I've taken part in acts of worship that would
drive the uninitiated insane. You see, Mr Dodd, the
majority of the people in Temphill still visit the church
on the right nights.'

More than half convinced that Clothier's mind was
affected, I asked impatiently, 'What does all this have to
do with Young's whereabouts?'

'It has everything to do with it,' Clothier continued. 'I
warned him not to go to the church, but he went one
night in the same year when Yule rite had been consum-
mated, and *They* must have been watching when he got
there. He was held in Temphill after that. *They* have a
way of turning space back to a point – I can't explain it.
He couldn't get away. He waited in that house for days
before *They* came. I heard his screams – and saw the
colour of the sky over the roof. *They* took him. That's
why you'll never find him. And that's why you'd better
leave town altogether while there's still time.'

'Did you look for him at the house?' I asked,
incredulous.

'I wouldn't go into that house for any reason whatever,'
confessed Clothier. 'Nor would anyone else. The house
has become theirs now. *They* have taken him *Outside* –
and who knows what hideous things may still lurk there?'

He got up to indicate that he had no more to say. I got
to my feet, too, glad to escape the dimly-lit room and the
house itself. Clothier ushered me to the door, and stood
briefly at the threshold glancing fearfully up and down
the street, as if he expected some dreadful visitation.
Then he vanished inside his house without waiting to see
where I went.

I crossed to Number 11. As I entered the curiously-shadowed hall, I remembered my friend's account of his life here. It was in the lower part of the house that Young had been wont to peruse certain archaic and terrible volumes, to set down his notes concerning his discoveries, and to pursue sundry other researches. I found the room which had been his study without trouble; the desk covered with sheets of notepaper – the bookcases filled with leather- and skin-bound volumes – the incongruous desk-lamp – all these bespoke the room's onetime use.

I brushed the thick dust from the desk and the chair beside it, and turned on the light. The glow was reassuring. I sat down and took up my friend's papers. The stack which first fell under my eye bore the heading *Corroborative Evidence*, and the very first page was typical of the lot, as I soon discovered. It consisted of what seemed to be unrelated notes referring to the Mayan culture of Central America. The notes, unfortunately, seemed to be random and meaningless. 'Rain gods (water elementals?). Trunk-proboscis (ref. Old Ones). Kukulkan (Cthulhu?)' – Such was their general tenor. Nevertheless, I persisted, and presently a hideously suggestive pattern became evident.

It began to appear that Young had been attempting to unify and correlate various cycles of legend with one central cycle, which was, if recurrent references were to be believed, far older than the human race. Whence Young's information had been gathered if not from the antique volumes set around the walls of the room, I did not venture to guess. I pored for hours over Young's synopsis of the monstrous and alien myth-cycle – the legends of how Cthulhu came from an indescribable milieu beyond the furthest bounds of this universe – of the polar civilizations and abominably unhuman races

from black Yuggoth on the rim – of hideous Leng and its
monastery-prisoned high priest who had to cover what
should be its face – and of a multitude of blasphemies
only rumoured to exist, save in certain forgotten places
of the world. I read what Azathoth had resembled *before*
that monstrous nuclear chaos had been bereft of mind
and will – of many-featured Nyarlathotep – of shapes
which the crawling chaos could assume, shapes which
men have never before dared to relate – of how one
might glimpse a dhole, and what one would see.

I was shocked to think that such hideous beliefs could
be thought true in any corner of a sane world. Yet
Young's treatment of his material hinted that he, too,
was not entirely sceptical concerning them. I pushed aside
a bulky stack of papers. In so doing, I dislodged the desk
blotter, revealing a thin sheaf of notes headed *On the
legend of the High Street Church*. Recalling Clothier's
warning, I drew it forth.

Two photographs were stapled to the first page. One
was captioned *Section of tesselated Roman pavement,
Goatswood*, the other *Reproduction engraving p. 594
'Necronomicon.'* The former represented a group of what
seemed to be acolytes or hooded priests depositing a body
before a squatting monster; the later a representation of
that creature in somewhat greater detail. The being itself
was so hysterically alien as to be indescribable; it was a
glistening, pallid oval, with no facial features whatsoever,
except for a vertical, slit-like mouth, surrounded by a
horny ridge. There were no visible members, but there
was that which suggested that the creature could shape
any organ at will. The creature was certainly only a
product of some morbid artist's diseased mind – but the
pictures were nevertheless oddly disturbing.

The second page set forth in Young's all too familiar

script a local legend to the effect that Romans who had laid the Goatswood pavement had, in fact, practised decadent worship of some kind, and hinting that certain rites lingered in the customs of the more primitive present-day inhabitants of the area. There followed a paragraph translated from the *Necronomicon*. 'The tomb-herd confer no benefits upon their worshippers. Their powers are few, for they can but disarrange space in small regions and make tangible that which cometh forth from the dead in other dimensions. They have power wherever the chants of Yog-Sothoth have been cried out at their seasons, and can draw to them those who will open their gates in the charnel-houses. They have no substance in this dimension, but enter earthly tenants to feed through them while they await the time when the stars become fixed and the gate of infinite sides open to free That Which Claws at the Barrier.' To this Young had appended some cryptic notes of his own – 'Cf. legends in Hungary, among aborigines Australia. – Clothier on High Church, Dec. 17,' which impelled me to turn to Young's diary, pushed aside in my eagerness to examine Young's papers.

I turned the pages, glancing at entries which seemed to be unrelated to the subject I sought, until I came to the entry for December 17. 'More about the High Street Church legend from Clothier. He spoke of past days when it was a meeting-place for worshippers of morbid, alien gods. Subterranean tunnels supposedly burrowed down to onyx temples, etc. Rumours that all who crawled down those tunnels to worship were not human. References to passages to other spheres.' So much, no more. This was scarcely illuminating. I pressed on through the diary.

Under date of December 23, I found a further reference: 'Christmas brought more legends to Clothier's memory today. He said something about a curious Yule rite practised in the High Street Church – something to do with evoked beings in the buried necropolis beneath the church. Said it still happened on the eve of Christmas, but he had never actually seen it.'

Next evening, according to Young's account, he had gone to the church. 'A crowd had gathered on the steps leading off the street. They carried no light, but the scene was illuminated by floating globular objects which gave off a phosphorescence and floated away at my approach. I could not identify them. The crowd presently, realizing I had not come to join them, threatened me and came for me. I fled. I was followed, but I could not be sure *what* followed me.'

There was not another pertinent entry for several days. Then, under date of January 13, Young wrote: 'Clothier has finally confessed that he has been drawn into certain Temphill rites. He warned me to leave Temphill, said I must not visit the church in High Street after dark or I might awaken *them*, after which I might be *visited* – and not by people! His mind appears to be in the balance.'

For nine months thereafter, no pertinent entry had been made. Then, on September 30, Young had written of his intention to visit the church in High Street that night, following which, on October 1, certain jottings, evidently written in great haste. 'What abnormalities – what cosmic perversions! Almost too monstrous for sanity! I cannot yet believe what I saw when I went down those onyx steps to the vaults – that herd of horrors! . . . I tried to leave Temphill, but all the streets turn back to the church. Is my mind, too, going?' Then, the following day, a desperate scrawl – 'I cannot seem to leave Temphill. All roads return to No 11 today – the power of those from *outside*. Perhaps Dodd can help.' And then, finally, the frantic beginnings of a telegram set down under my name and address and evidently intended to be sent. *Come Temphill immediately. Need your help* . . . There the writing ended in a line of ink running to the edge of the page, as if the writer had allowed his pen to be dragged off the paper.

Thereafter nothing more. Nothing save that Young was gone, vanished, and the only suggestion in his notes seemed to point to the church in High Street. Could he have gone there, found some concealed room, been trapped in it? I might yet then be the instrument of freeing him. Impulsively, I left the room and the house, went out to my car, and started away.

Turning right, I drove up South Street towards Wool Place. There were no other cars on the roads, and I did not notice the usual pavement loafers; curiously, too, the houses I passed were unlit, and the overgrown patch in the centre, guarded by its flaking railing and blanched in the light of the moon over the white gables, seemed desolate and disquieting. The decaying quarter of Cloth Street was even less inviting. Once or twice I seemed to see forms starting out of doorways I passed, but they were unclear, like the figments of a distorted imagination. Over all, the feeling of desolation was morbidly strong, particularly in the region of those dark alleys undulating between unlit, boarded houses. In High Street at last, the moon hung over the steeple of the hill-set church like some lunar diadem, and as I moved the car into a depression at the bottom of the steps the orb sank behind the black spire as if the church were dragging the satellite out of the sky.

As I climbed the steps, I saw that the walls around me had iron rails set into them and were made of rough stone, so pitted that beaded spiders' webs glistened in the fissures, while the steps were covered with a slimy green moss which made climbing unpleasant. Denuded trees overhung the passage. The church itself was lit by the gibbous moon which swung high in the gulfs of space, and the tottering gravestones, overgrown with repulsively decaying vegetation, cast curious shadows over the fungus-strewn grass. Strangely, though the church was so manifestly unused, an air of habitation clung to it, and I entered it almost with the expectation of finding someone – caretaker or worshipper – beyond the door.

I had brought a flashlight with me to help me in my search of the nighted church, but a certain glow – a kind of iridescence – lay within its walls, as of moonlight reflected from the mullioned windows. I went down the central aisle, flashing my light into one row of pews after the other, but there was no evidence in the mounded dust that anyone had ever been there. Piles of yellowed hymnals squatted against a pillar like grotesque huddled shapes of crouching beings, long forsaken – here and there the pews were broken with age – and the air in that enclosed place was thick with a kind of charnel musk.

I came at last towards the altar and saw that the first pew on the left before the altar was tilted abnormally in my direction. I had noted earlier that several of the pews were angled with disuse, but now I saw that the floor beneath the first pew was also angled upward, revealing an unlit abyss below. I pushed the pew back all the way – for the second pew had been set at a suitably greater distance – thus exposing the black depths below the rectangular aperture. The flickering yellow glow from my flashlight disclosed a flight of steps, twisting down between dripping walls.

I hesitated at the edge of the abyss, flashing an uneasy glance around the darkened church. Then I began the descent, walking as quietly as possible. The only sound in the core-seeking passage was the dripping of water in the lightless area beyond the beam of my flashlight. Droplets of water gleamed at me from the walls as I spiralled downward, and crawling black things scuttled into crevices as though the light could destroy them. As my quest led me further into the earth, I noticed that the steps were no longer of stone, but of earth itself, out of which grew repulsively bloated, dappled fungi, and saw that the roof of the tunnel was disquietingly supported only by the flimsiest of arches.

How long I slithered under those uncertain arches I could not tell, but at last one of them became a grey tunnel over strangely-coloured steps, uneroded by time, the edges of which were still sharp, though the flight was discoloured with mud from the passage of feet from above. My flashlight showed that the curve of the descending steps had now become less pronounced, as if its terminus was near, and as I saw this I grew conscious of a mounting wave of uncertainty and disquiet. I paused once more and listened.

There was no sound from beneath, no sound from above. Pushing back the tension I felt, I hastened forward, slipped on a step, and rolled down the last few stairs to come up against a grotesque statue, life-sized, leering blindly at me in the glow of my flashlight. It was but one of six in a row, opposite which was an identical, equally repulsive sextet, so wrought by the skill of some unknown sculptor as to seem terrifyingly real. I tore my gaze away, picked myself up, and flashed my light into the darkness before me.

Would that a merciful oblivion could wipe away forever what I saw there! – the rows of grey stone slabs reaching limitlessly away into darkness in claustrophobic aisles, on

each of them shrouded corpses staring sightlessly at the
ebon roof above. And nearby were archways marking the
beginning of black winding staircases leading *downward*
into inconceivable depths; sight of them filled me with an
explicable chill superimposed upon my horror at the
charnel vision before me. I shuddered away from the
thought of searching among the slabs for Young's remains
– if he were there, and I felt intuitively that he lay
somewhere among them. I tried to nerve myself to move
forward, and was just timidly moving to enter the aisle at
the entrance of which I stood, when a sudden sound
paralysed me.

It was a whistling rising slowly out of the darkness
before me, augmented presently by explosive sounds
which seemed to increase in volume, as were the source
of it approaching. As I stared affrightedly at the point
whence the sound seemed to rise, there came a prolonged
explosion and the sudden glowing of a pale, sourceless
green light, beginning as a circular illumination, hardly
larger than a hand. Even as I strained my eyes at it, it
vanished. In a few seconds, however, it reappeared,
three times its previous diameter – and for one dreadful
moment I glimpsed through it a hellish, alien landscape,
as were I looking through a window opening upon
another, utterly foreign dimension! It blinked out even as
I fell back – then returned with even greater brilliance –
and I found myself gazing against my will upon a scene
being seared indelibly on my memory.

It was a strange landscape dominated by a trembling
star hanging in a sky across which drifted elliptical clouds.
The star, which was the source of the green glowing,
shed its light upon a landscape where great, black triangular rocks were scattered among vast metal buildings,
globular in shape. Most of these seemed to be in ruins,

for whole segmentary plates were torn from the lower walls, revealing twisted, peeling girders which had been partially melted by some unimaginable force. Ice glittered greenly in crevices of the girders, and great flakes of vermilion-tinted snow settled towards the ground or slanted through the cracks in the walls, drifting out of the depths of that black sky.

For but a few moments the scene held – then abruptly it sprang to life as horrible white, gelatinous shapes flopped across the landscape towards the forefront of the scene. I counted thirteen of them, and watched them – with cold terror – as they came forward to the edge of the opening – and *across it*, to flop hideously into the vault where I stood!

I backed towards the steps, and as in a dream saw those frightful shapes move upon the statues nearby, and watched the outlines of those statues blur and begin to move. Then, swiftly, one of those dreadful beings rolled and flopped towards me. I felt something cold as ice touch my ankle. I screamed – and a merciful unconsciousness carried me into my own night . . .

When I awoke at last I found myself on the stones between two slabs some distance from the place on the steps where I had fallen – a horrible, bitter, furry taste in my mouth, and my face hot with fever. How long I had lain unconscious I could not tell. My light lay where it had fallen, still glowing with enough illumination to permit a dim view of my surroundings. The green light was gone – the nightmarish opening had vanished. Had I but fainted at the nauseating odours, at the terrible suggestiveness of this charnel crypt? But the sight of a singularly frightening fungus in scattered patches on my clothing and on the floor – a fungus I had not seen before, dropped from what source I could not tell and about which I did not want to speculate – filled me with such awful dread that I started up, seized my light, and fled, plunging for the dark archway beyond the steps down which I had come into this eldritch pit.

I ran feverishly upward, frequently colliding with the wall and tripping on the steps and on obstacles which seemed to materialize out of the shadows. Somehow I reached the church. I fled down the central aisle, pushed open the creaking door, and raced down the shadowed steps to the car. I tugged frantically at the door before I remembered that I had locked my car. Then I tore at my pockets – in vain! The key-ring carrying all my keys was gone – lost in that hellish crypt I had so miraculously escaped. The car was useless to me – nothing would have induced me to return, to enter again the haunted church in High Street.

I abandoned it. I ran out into the street, bound for Wood Street and, beyond it, the next town – open country – any place but accursed Temphill. Down High Street, into Market Square, where the wan moonlight shared with one high lamp standard the only illumination, across the Square into Manor Street. In the distance lay the forests about Wood Street, beyond a curve, at the end of which Temphill would be left behind me. I raced down the nightmarish streets, heedless of the mists that began to rise and obscure the wooded country slopes that were my goal, the blurring of the landscape beyond the looming houses.

I ran blindly, wildly – but the hills of the open country came no nearer – and suddenly, horribly, I recognized the unlit intersections and dilapidated gables of Cloth Street – which should have been far behind me, on the other side of the river – and in a moment I found myself again in High Street, and there before me were the worn steps of that repellent church, with the car still before them! I tottered, clung to a roadside tree for a moment, my mind in chaos. Then I turned and started out again, sobbing with terror and dread, racing with pounding heart back to Market Square, back across the river, aware of a horrible vibration, a shocking, muted whistling sound I had come to know only too well, aware of fearful pursuit . . .

I failed to see the approaching car and had time only to throw myself backward so that the full force of its striking me was avoided. Even so, I was flung to the pavement and into blackness.

I woke in the hospital at Camside. A doctor returning to Camside through Temphill had been driving the car that struck me. He had taken me, unconscious and with a contusion and a broken arm, taken me from that accursed city. He listened to my story, as much as I dared tell, and went to Temphill for my car. It could not be found. And he could find no one who had seen me or the car. Nor could he find books, papers, or diary at No 8 South Street where Albert Young had lived. And of Clothier there was no trace – the owner of the adjacent house said he had been gone for a long time.

Perhaps they were right in telling me I had suffered a progressive hallucination. Perhaps it was an illusion, too, that I heard the doctors whispering when I was coming out of anaesthesia – whispering of the frantic way in which I had burst into the path of the car – and worse, of the strange fungus that clung to my clothes, even to my face at my lips, as if it grew there!

Perhaps. But can they explain how now, months afterward, though the very thought of Temphill fills me with loathing and dread, I feel myself irresistibly drawn to it, as if that accursed, haunted town were the mecca towards which I must make my way? I had begged them to confine me – to prison me – anything – and they only smile and try to soothe me and assure me that everything will 'work itself out' – the glib, self-reassuring words that do not deceive me, the words that have a hollow sound against the magnet of Temphill and the ghostly whistling echoes that invade not only my dreams but my waking hours!

I will do what I must. Better death than that unspeakable horror . . .

Filed with the report of PC Villars on the disappearance of Richard Dodd, 9 Gayton Terrace, W.7. Manuscript in Dodd's script, found in his room after his disappearance.

THE ROOM IN THE CASTLE

Is it some lurking remnant of the elder world in each of us that draws us towards the beings which survive from other aeons? Surely there must be such a remnant in me, for there can be no sane or wholesome reason why I should have strayed that day to the old, legend-infected ruin on the hill, nor can any commonplace reason be deduced for my finding the secret underground room there, and still less for my opening of the door of horror which I discovered.

It was on a visit to the British Museum that I first heard of the legend which suggested a reason for the general avoidance of a hill outside Brichester. I had come to the Museum in search of certain volumes preserved there – not books of demonic lore, but extremely scarce tomes dealing with the local history of the Severn valley, as visualized in retrospect by an 18th-century clergyman. A friend who lived in the Camside region near Berkeley had asked me to look up some historical facts for his forthcoming article in the *Camside Observer*, which I could impart to him when I began my stay with him that weekend, since he was ill and would not be capable of a London visit for some time. I reached the Museum library with no thoughts other than that I would quickly check through the requisite volumes, note down the appropriate quotations and leave in my car for my destination straight from the Museum.

Upon entering the lofty-ceilinged room of carefully tended books, I found from the librarian that the volumes

I wished to study were at that moment in use, but should soon be returned, if I cared to wait a short time. To spend this time, I was not interested in referring to any historical book, but instead asked the keeper of the volumes to allow me to glance through the Museum's copy of the almost unobtainable *Necronomicon*. More than an hour passed in reading it, as best I could. Such suggestions concerning what may lie behind the tranquil façade of normality are not easily dismissed from the mind; and I confess that as I read of the alien beings which, according to the author, lurk in dark and shunned places of the world, I found myself accepting what I read as reality. As I pressed deeper into the dark mythos which surrounds those terrors from beyond – bloated Cthulhu, indescribable Shub-Niggurath, vast batrachian Dagon – I might have been sucked into the whirlpool of absolute belief, had my engrossment not been interrupted by the librarian, bearing an armful of yellowed volumes.

I surrendered the copy of the *Necronomicon* to him, and so great was the lurking terror that had been aroused in me that I watched to be certain that the book of horror had been locked securely away. Then I turned to the historical volumes I had requested, and began to take notes from the passages in which my friend had expressed interest. As was inevitable, I could not help reading a large proportion of useless matter in my quest for connected material; and it was in a section I had considered useless that my eye noted in passing a reference which was in some way reminiscent of the book I had been reading. At first I thought that my concentration on alien cult-practices had metamorphosed a harmless and quaint country legend into something abnormal and disturbing; but on reading further I realized that this was indeed a rather unconventional legend.

'Yet be it not thought,' the Berkeley clergyman had written, 'that *Satan* does not send Trouble betimes to put Fear in those who lived by *God*. I have heard that Mr *Norton* was sorely troubl'd by Cries and horrid Roars from the Woods when he liv'd nearby, and that one Night the Drums were so loud that he could not return to his Farming for a Month from then. But, not to burden my Reader, I will recount the Tale of what a Farmer told me not two Years ago.

'One Night, when I was walking the Road outside *Berkeley*, Farmer *Cooper* came upon me out of the Field upon the left Side, much begrimed and filled with Fear at what he had seen. He spoke at first as if his Mind was unsettl'd, as does poor *Tom Cooper* when he is overcome by his Sickness; but I took him into the Church, and the Presence of *God* heal'd his Mind. He ask'd if I were willing to hear of the Blasphemous Vision which had come upon him, for he thought that indeed the Divell must have sent a Daemon to turn him from good *Christian* Ways.

'He swore that he had chas'd a Fox which had troubl'd his Livestock, hoping that he could end its Nuisance; but it had led him such a Dance around the Properties of Farmers *King* and *Cook* that he had lost it, and coming near the River he turn'd homeward. Upon coming to the Crossing over *Cambrook* Stream which he us'd to take homeward, he was dismay'd to find it smash'd in the Middle. While he was making for the Ford near *Corn Lane*, he saw upon a Hill a Figure of no little *Strangeness*. It seem'd to Glow with a Light that did not stay one Colour, but did indeed act like a veritable Kaleidoscope which the Children use in their Play. Farmer *Cooper* did not like it, but he drew near to the Hill and climb'd until he was nigh unto the horrid object. It was of a clear

Mineral, the like of which Farmer *Cooper* has not seen. When I pray'd him to Tell me of its Appearance, he star'd at me strangely and said that so Evill a *Monster* was not to be talk'd of by *Christian* Men. When I press'd him that I must be arm'd against such Daemons by full Knowledge, he said that it had but one Eye like the *Cyclops*, and had Claws like unto a Crab. He said also that it had a Nose like the Elephants that 'tis said can be seen in *Africa*, and great Serpent-like Growths which hung from its Face like a Beard, in the Fashion of some Sea Monster.

'He calls upon the *Redeemer* to witness that *Satan* must have taken his Soul then, for he could not stop touching the Claw of the pestilential Image, though he said angelic Voices bade him draw back. Then a huge Shadow cross'd the Moon, and though he determin'd not to look above he saw the horrid Shape cast upon the Ground. I do not Think he blasphem'd in saying that *Heaven* would not protect me if I heard the Relation of the Shape of that Shadow, for he says that he felt as if *God* had forgotten his Welfare when he saw it. That was when he fled the Hill, swimming through the *Cambrook* Stream to escape; and he says that some Thing pursu'd him part of the Way, for he heard the clatter of great Claws on the Ground behind. But he repeat'd the Prayers as he is Wont to do when he fears some Evill, and the Scuttling soon fad'd away. So he had come upon me as I walk'd on the *Berkeley* Road.

'I told him to go home and comfort his Wife, and to pray the good *Lord* would help him against Evills which the Divell might Plan against him to turn him from the Proper Way. That night I pray'd that these terrible Dealings of *Satan* might soon quit my Parish, and that the Pit might not take the wretch'd Farmer *Cooper*.'

Reaching the bottom of this page, I immediately continued on the opposite leaf. But I quickly realized that something was amiss, for the next paragraph treated of something entirely different. Noting the page numbers, I discovered that the page between the two was missing, so that any further references to the alien figure on the hill were unobtainable so far as I was concerned. Since nothing could now be done to rectify this – and, after all, I had come to the Museum originally to look up quite different information – I could only return to my original research. However, a few pages on I noticed an irregularity in the edges of the pages, and on turning to that point I discovered the missing leaf. With a strange feeling of jubilation, I fitted it back into place and continued my interrupted reading.

'But this is not the end of the Tale of Farmer *Cooper*. Two months from then, Farmer *Norton* came to me sorely troubl'd, saying that the Drums in the Woods beat louder than ever before. I could not Console him further than by saying that he must keep his Doors clos'd, and watch for Signs of the Works of *Satan*. Then came the Wife of *Cooper*, saying that her Husband had on a sudden been Took ill, for he leap'd up with a Shriek most horrid to hear, and ran away towards the Woods. I did not like to send Men into the Woods when the Drums beat so fierce, but I call'd a Party of the Farmers to go through the Woods, watching for signs of the Divell, and seek Farmer *Cooper*. This they did, but soon came back and arous'd me, telling a very curious and horrid Tale of why they could not bring poor *Cooper* back, and why he was assuredly Took by the Divell.

'Where the Woods grew thickest, they began to hear Drums beating among the Trees, and approached the Sound fearfully, for they knew what the Drums had herald'd before now. When they came upon the Source, they found Farmer *Cooper* sitting before a huge black Drum, staring as if Mesmeriz'd and beating upon it in a most savage Way, as 'tis said the natives do in *Africa*. One of the Party, Farmer *King*, made to speak to *Cooper*, but look'd behind him and shew'd to the Others what he saw. They swore that behind *Cooper* was a great Monster, more Horrid even than the toad of *Berkeley* is relat'd to be, and most Blasphemous in its Shape. It must have been the Monster which serv'd to model the Figure on the Hill, for they say it was somewhat like a Spider, somewhat like a Crab, and somewhat like a Horrour in Dreams. Now, seeing the Daemon among the Trees, Farmer *King* fled, and the Others follow'd him. They had not gone far when they heard a Shriek of great Agony in the voice of Farmer *Cooper*, and another Sound which was like the Roaring of some great Beast, while the Beating of the black Drum was ceas'd. A few Minutes after then, they heard a Sound of Wings, like the Flapping of a great Bat, which died away in the Distance. They managed to get to *Camside Lane*, and soon return'd to the Village to tell of the Fate of the wretch'd *Cooper*.

'Though this was two Years ago, I do not Doubt that the Daemon still lives, and must roam the Woods in wait for the Unwary. Perhaps it still comes into the Village; for all those who went seeking Farmer *Cooper* have dream'd of the Monster ever after, and one died not long ago, swearing that some Thing peer'd at the Window and drew his Soul from him. What it is, I do not know. I think it is a Daemon sent from Hell by *Satan*; but Mr *Daniel Jenner*, who reads many books of the History of the Region, says it must be what the *Romans* found behind a stone Door in a Camp which was here long before the Invasion. At any rate, Prayers against *Satan* seem to have little Effect on it, so that it must be some Thing far different from the Monsters which are Wont to trouble good *Christian* Communities. Perhaps it will die if my Flock keep away from the Woods. But I hear strange Rumors that Sir *Gilbert Morley*, who came to live near *Severn Ford* some Years ago, counts himself able to Subdue the Divell by Black Arts, and is said to hope that his Blasphemous Dealings may give him Control of the Monster of the Woods.'

This ended the references to the legendary haunter of the woods, but to me it did not seem likely that this was the only probable legend concerning it. The mention at the last of the attempts of some 18th-century warlock to subdue the being sounded like an indication of some tale of the actual outcome of Morley's experiments, and I could easily spare an hour to search for references for the further myth. Not, of course, that my reading of the *Necronomicon* had made me credulous about fictitious monsters; but it would be a topic of conversation for when I visited my Camside friend, and perhaps I could even visit the home of Sir Gilbert Morley, if anything remained of the building – and if, indeed, such a person had ever existed.

Determined to make a search for the legend which, I felt sure, would be recounted somewhere, I had the librarian select all the volumes which might be of interest to me in my quest. The final selection included Wilshire's *The Vale Of Berkeley,* Hill's *Legendry and Customs of the Severn Valley*, and Sangster's *Notes on Witchcraft in Monmouthshire, Gloucestershire and the Berkeley Region*. My original research forgotten, I began to peruse the books, not without a shudder at certain passages and illustrations.

The Wilshire volume I soon dispensed with. Apart

from the usual stories about female apparitions and earthbound monks, the only legends which touched on the supernatural were those of the Witch of Berkeley and the Berkeley Toad. This last, though a hideous one dealing with an inhuman monstrosity which was kept in a dungeon and which fed on human corpses, did not appear to help me in my search. The Hill and Sangster volumes were more productive, however. Various passages, some occupying over one complete page, told of strange things glimpsed by unwary travellers in the Severn region. Still, I could not think that everything reputed to exist in the surrounding countryside could bear on my present quest. Then I chanced upon a passage in Sangster's work which could be nothing but a reference to the case with which I was concerned. It began by describing almost exactly the occurrences of which I had already read, and continued in the following manner:

'What this being actually was, whence it originally came, and why no legends concerning it are heard before this point, are questions which the reader will ask. There are vague answers for all. The being was supposedly Byatis, a pre-human being which was worshipped as a deity. It was released, according to the legend, by Roman soldiers, from behind a stone door in a camp of indeterminate origin, built long before the advent of the Romans in Britain. As to why there are no legends antedating that of Farmer Cooper's discovery – it is said that there were indeed legends, but in a form so unrecognizable that they were not connected with the later tales. Apparently the terrifying Berkeley Toad was the same being as the deity Byatis; indeed, though the being has only one eye, it does, when its proboscis is retracted occasionally, resemble the general shape of the toad. How it was imprisoned in the Berkeley dungeon, and how it eventually escaped, is not told in the legend. It had some hypnotic power, so that it may have hypnotized someone to open the cell door, though it is likely that this power was used only to render its victims helpless.

'After its encounter with the farmer, it had finally been called from its place in the woods by one Sir Gilbert Morley, who owned a Norman castle, long uninhabited, outside Severnford. The said Morley had been shunned for quite a time by all those living nearby. There was no specific reason why; but he was reputed to have made a pact with Satan, and people did not like the way bats seemed to cluster at the window of one particular tower room, nor the strange shapes which formed in the mist which often settled into the valley.

'At any rate, Morley had stirred the horror in the woods out of its festering sleep, and imprisoned it in a cellar room in his great mansion off the Berkeley Road, no trace of which remains nowadays. As long as it was under his power, he could tap its inherent cosmic vitality and communicate with the sendings of Cthulhu, Glaaki, Daoloth and Shub-Niggurath.

'He was supposed to lure travellers to his homestead, where he would manage to bring them near the cellar and lock them inside; when no victims were forthcoming he would send the thing out to feed. Once or twice late homecomers would be struck speechless with terror by the spectacle of Morley in flight, with a frightful winged thing flying ahead of him. Before long he was forced to remove it and imprison it in a hidden underground room at the castle; forced to do this because, according to the legend, *it had grown too vast for the cellar room*, growing out of all proportion to the food it ate. Here it remained in the daytime, while after dark he would open the secret door and let it free to feast. It returned before dawn, and he would also return and re-imprison it. If the door were closed, the creature would not be free to roam, by virtue of some seal on the door. One day, after Morley had closed the door on the horror inside (his closing door was apparent, since searchers found no trace of an open door) he disappeared and did not return. The castle, now unattended, is slowly decaying, but the secret portal has apparently remained intact. According to the legend, Byatis yet lurks in the hidden room, ready to wake and be released if someone should open the hidden lock.'

This I read in the Sangster volume. Before proceeding any further, I had the librarian search for data on the being Byatis in the various books in the locked bookcase. Finally he brought forth the following, which he discovered in Prinn's *De Vermis Mysteriis*:

'Byatis, the serpent-bearded, the god of forgetfulness, came with the Great Old Ones from the stars, called by obeisances made to his image, which was brought by the Deep Ones to Earth. He may be called by the touching of his image by a living being. His gaze brings darkness on the mind; and it is told that those who look upon his eye will be forced to walk to his clutches. He feasts upon those who stray to him, and from those upon whom he feasts he draws a part of their vitality, and so grows vaster.'

So I read in Ludvig Prinn's volume of horrifying blasphemies, and I was not slow in shutting it and returning it to the librarian when I was sure that nothing more on Byatis could be found in the book. This was also the last reference to this terrifying enigma that I could discover in any volume I had selected, and I handed them back to the custodian. I happened to look at the clock at that moment, and saw that I had spent far more time in my researches than intended. Returning to the original volume by the Berkeley clergyman, I quickly noted down the points named by my friend which I had not already copied, and then left the Museum.

It was about noon, and I intended to drive from the Museum straight to Camside, covering as much distance as possible during daylight. Dropping my notebook in the dashboard pocket, I started the engine and moved out into the traffic. Less vehicles were driving in the direction I took than in the opposite direction, but some time passed before I found myself on the outskirts of London. After that, I drove without giving much thought to the landscape flashing past the windscreen, nor did I particularly notice the approach of darkness, until I realized, upon leaving a roadside café where I had drawn up for a meal, that night had fallen. The landscape following my stop at the café became merely a view of two discs of yellow hurrying along the road ahead or sliding across the hedge at each bend. But as I neared Berkeley I began to be haunted by thoughts of the unholy practices which had been carried out in this region in olden times. As I passed through Berkeley, I remembered the horrible stories which were told about the town – about the leprous, bloated toad-monster which had been kept in a dungeon, and about the Witch of Berkeley, off whose coffin the chains had inexplicably fallen before the corpse stepped forth. Of course, they were merely superstitious fancies, and I was not really troubled by them, even though the books I had read that afternoon had mentioned them with such credulity; but the glimpses which the headlights now gave of the surroundings, of unlit black houses and moistly peeling walls, were not reassuring.

When I finally drew into the driveway of my friend's

house, he was there to guide me in with a flashlight, my headlamps having given out between Camside and Brichester. He ushered me into the house, remarking that I must have had a difficult journey towards the last along the lanes without lights, while I could only agree with him. It was quite late – later than I had intended to arrive, but the unallowed-for research at the Museum had taken some time – and, after a light meal and a conversation over it, I went to my room to sleep off the effects of the somewhat hectic day.

The next morning I took from my car the notebook containing the information I had acquired at the Museum, and this reminded me of my intention to visit the ruin of Morley's castle. My friend, though able to move about the house, was not fit to leave it for long periods; and since he would be working on his forthcoming article that afternoon, I would have a chance to seek out the castle. After I had given him the notebook, I mentioned casually that I intended to take a stroll through the nearby countryside after dinner, and asked him whether he could suggest any localities that might interest me.

'You might drive down to Berkeley and take a walk round there,' he advised. 'Plenty of survivals from earlier times there – only I wouldn't stay too long, because of the mists. We'll probably have one tonight, and they're really bad – I certainly wouldn't want to drive in a mist like we get.'

'I had thought,' I said tentatively, 'of going along to Severnford to try and find this castle where a warlock's familiar was supposed to have been sealed up. I wonder if you know where it is? It was owned by someone named Morley – Sir Gilbert Morley, who was apparently in league with the devil, or something of the sort.'

He seemed rather shocked, and looked strangely disturbed by my mentioning the place. 'Listen, Parry,' he said, 'I think I may have heard of this Morley – there's a horrible tale which connects him with the disappearance of new-born babies around here in the 1700s – but I'd rather not say anything more about him. When you've lived down here a bit, and seen them all locking their doors on certain nights and putting signs in the earth beneath the windows because the devil's supposed to walk on those nights – and when you've *heard* things flying over the houses when everyone's locked in, *and there's nothing there* – then you won't be interested in tracking down things like that. We've got a home help who believes in such things, and she always makes the signs for our house – so I suppose that's why it always flies over. But I wouldn't go searching out places that have been polluted by witchcraft, even protected as I may be.'

'Good God, Scott,' I rebuked – laughing, but rather disturbed by the way he had changed since coming to live in the country, 'surely *you* don't believe that these star signs they make around here can have any effect, for good or for evil? Well, if you're so set on preserving my neck, I'll just have to ask one of the villagers – I don't suppose they'll have such a misplaced protective instinct as you seem to have.'

Scott remained unconvinced. 'You know I used to be as sceptical as you are now,' he reminded me. 'Can't you realize that it must have been something drastic that changed my outlook? For God's sake believe me – don't go looking for something to convince you!'

'I repeat,' I said, annoyed that my intended pleasant afternoon should provoke an argument, 'I'll just have to ask one of the villagers.'

'All right, all *right*,' Scott interrupted, irritated. 'There *is* a castle on the outskirts of Severnford, supposed to have belonged to Morley, where he kept some sort of monster. Apparently he left it locked away one day and never returned to let it out again – got carried off by an elemental he called up, I believe. It's still waiting, so they say, for some imbecile to come along looking for trouble and let it out again.'

Not missing the last remark's significance, I asked, 'How do I get to the castle from Severnford?'

'Oh, *look*, Parry, isn't that enough?' he said, frowning. 'You know the legend of the castle's true, so why go any further?'

'I know the story that the *castle* exists is true,' I pointed out, 'but I *don't* know if the underground room exists. Still, I suppose the people at Severnford would know . . .'

'If you *have* to go and sell yourself to the devil,' Scott finally said, 'the castle is on the other side of Severnford from the river, on a rise – a small hill, I suppose you'd call it – not far from Cotton Row. But look, Parry, I don't know why you're going to this place at all. You may not believe in this thing, but the villagers wouldn't go near that castle, and neither would I. That being is supposed to have some unbelievable attributes – if you just glance at its eye, you have to offer yourself to it – not that I believe all this literally, but I'm sure there's something in the castle that haunts it horribly.'

It was quite obvious that he sincerely believed all he was saying, which only strengthened my resolve to visit the castle and make a thorough search. After the end of our argument, the conversation became somewhat strained, and before dinner was served we were both reading books. As soon as I had finished dinner, I collected a flashlight from my room, and, after making other preparations for the journey, drove off in the direction of Severnford.

After a short drive along the A38 and the Berkeley Road, I found that I would have to pass through Severnford itself and double back if the car were to be parked near the castle. As I was driving through Severnford I noticed, over the church porch, a stone carving depicting an angel holding a large star-shaped object in front of a cowering toad-like gargoyle. Curious, I braked the car and walked along the moss-covered path between two blackened pillars to speak to the vicar. He was pleased to see a stranger in his church, but became wary when I told him why I had approached him.

'Could you tell me,' I asked, 'the meaning of that peculiar group of carvings over your porch – the one depicting the toad-monster and the angel?'

He seemed slightly worried by my question. 'Obviously the triumph of good over evil,' he suggested.

'But why is the angel holding a star? Surely a cross would be more appropriate.'

The vicar nodded. 'That disturbs me, too,' he confessed, 'because it seems to be a concession to the superstitions round here. They say it was originally not part of the church, but was brought here by one of the early parish priests, who never revealed where he found it. They say that the star is the same one they have to use on All Hallows' Eve, and that the angel isn't an angel at all, but a – being – from some other world. And as for the toad – they say it represents the so-called Berkeley Toad, which is still waiting to be released! I've tried to take the thing off the porch, but they won't have it – threaten not to attend church at all if I remove it! Was there ever a priest in my position?'

I left the church, feeling rather unsettled. I did not like
the reference to the carving's not being part of the church,
for this would surely mean that the legend was more
widespread than I had thought. But, of course, the relief
was part of the building, and it was only a distortion of
the legend that spoke of its once being separate. I did not
look back at the carven scene as the car moved away, nor
at the vicar who had left the building and was staring up
at the top of the porch.

Turning off Mill Lane, I cruised down Cotton Row.
The castle came into view as I turned the corner and left
behind me a row of untenanted cottages. It was set on
the crest of the hill, three walls still standing, though the
roof had long ago collapsed. A lone tower stood like a
charred finger against the pale sky, and I momentarily
wondered if this were the tower around whose window
bats had clustered so long ago. Then the car stopped and
I withdrew the key, slammed the door and began to
climb the slope.

The grass was covered with droplets of water, and the
horizon was very vague from the oncoming mist. The
moistness of the ground made progress uphill difficult,
but after a few yards a series of stone stairs led to the
castle, which I ascended. The stairs were covered with
greenish moss, and in scattered places I seemed to detect
faint marks, so indistinct that I could not determine their
shape, but only have the feeling that there was something
vaguely wrong about them. What could have made them,
I had no idea; for the absence of life near the castle was
extremely noticeable, the only moving object being an
occasional bloated bird which flapped up out of the ruins,
startled by my entry into the castle.

There was surprisingly little left of the castle. Most of
the floor was covered with the debris of the fallen roof,

and what could be seen under the fragments of stone
gave no indication of the location of any secret room. As
a possibility struck me, I climbed the stairway which led
into the tower and examined the surface at the bottom of
the circular staircase; but the steps were mere slabs of
stone. The thought of the tower suggested another idea –
perhaps the legend lied when it spoke of the monster's
prison as being underground? But the door of the upper
tower room swung open easily enough, revealing a
narrow, empty chamber. My heart gave an unpleasant
lurch when, moving further in to survey the entire room,
I saw, in place of a bed under the window, a coffin. With
some trepidation, I moved closer and peered into the
coffin – and I think I must have given a sigh of relief
when I saw that the coffin, whose bottom was spread
with earth, was empty. It must have been some bizarre
kind of burial vault, even though it was certainly unortho-
doxly situated. But I could not help remembering that
clouds of bats used to collect at the window of some
tower in this castle, and there seemed to be a subconscious
connection which I could not quite place.

Leaving the tower room rather quickly, I descended
the stairs and examined the ground on all sides of the
castle. Nothing but rubble met my gaze, though once I
did see an odd sign scratched on a slab of rock. Unless
the door to the secret room lay under the remains of the
collapsed roof, it presumably did not exist at all; and
after ten minutes of dragging the fragments of stone to
other positions, the only effects of which were to tear my
fingernails and cover me with dust, I realized that there
was no way of discovering whether the door did, in fact,
lie beneath the debris. At any rate, I could return to the
house and point out to Scott that no malevolent entity
had dragged me off to its lair; and, as far as I was able, I

had proved that there was no evidence of a hidden room at the castle.

I started back down the stone stairs which led to the road, looking out across the gently curving green fields, now fast becoming vague through the approaching mist. Suddenly I tripped and fell down one step. I put my hand on the step above me to help me rise – and almost toppled into a yawning pit. I was tottering on the brink of an open trapdoor, the step forming the door and the stone which I had kicked out of place forming the lock. A stone ladder thrust into the darkness below, leading down to the unseen floor of a room of indeterminate extent.

Drawing out my flashlight, I switched it on. The room now revealed was completely bare, except for a small black cube of some metal at the foot of the ladder. Square in shape, the room measured approximately 20′ × 20′, the walls being of a dull grey stone, which was covered with pits out of which grew the fronds of pallid ferns. There was absolutely no evidence of any sort of animal life in the room, nor, indeed, that an animal of any kind had ever inhabited it – except, perhaps, for a peculiar odour, like a mixture of the scents of reptiles and decay, which rose chokingly for a minute from the newly-opened aperture.

There appeared to be nothing to interest me in the entire room, barring the small black cube which lay in the centre of the floor. First ensuring that the ladder would bear my weight, I descended it and reached the cube. Kneeling beside it on the pock-marked grey floor, I examined the piece of black metal. When scratched with a penknife it revealed a strange violet lustre which suggested that it was merely covered with a black coating. Inscribed hieroglyphics had been incised upon its upper surface, one of which I recognized from the *Necronomicon*, where it was given as a protection against demons. Rolling it over, I saw that the underside of the cube was carved with one of those star-shaped symbols which were so prevalent in the village. This cube would make an excellent piece of evidence to show that I actually had visited the supposedly haunted castle. I picked it up, finding it surprisingly heavy – about the weight of a piece of lead the same size – and held it in my hand.

And in doing so, I released the abomination which sent me leaping up the creaking ladder and racing madly down the hill, on to Cotton Row and into my car. Fumbling at the ignition key which I had inserted upside down, I looked back to see an obscene reaching member protruding from the gulf against the fast-misting sky. Finally the key slipped into its socket, and I drove away from the nightmare I had seen with a violence that brought a scream from the gears. The landscape flashed by at a nerve-wrenching pace, each shadow in the dim headlights seeming a hurtling demon, until the car swung into the driveway at Scott's house, barely stopping before smashing into the garage doors.

The front door opened hurriedly at my violent entry. Scott hastened out of the rectangle of light from the hall lamp. By that time I was half-faint from the hideous sight in the pit and the frantic journey after it, so that he had to support me as I reeled into the hallway. Once in the living-room and fortified with a long drink of brandy, I began to recount the events of that afternoon. Before I had reached the terrors of the castle he was leaning forward with a disturbed air, and he uttered a groan of horror when I spoke of the coffin in the tower room. When I described the horrible revelation which had burst upon me in the underground room, his eyes dilated with terror.

'But that's monstrous!' he gasped. 'You mean to say – the legend spoke of Byatis growing with every victim – and it must have taken Morley at the last – but that what you say could be possible – '

'I saw it long enough before I realized what it was to take in all the details,' I told him. 'Now I can only wait until tomorrow, when I can get some explosives and destroy the thing.'

'Parry, you don't mean you're going to the castle *again*?' he demanded incredulously. 'My God, after all you've seen, surely you must have enough evidence without going back to that place for more!'

'You've only heard about all the horrors I saw,' I reminded him. 'I saw them so that if I don't wipe them out now they're going to haunt me with knowledge that one day that toad-creature may smash out of its prison. I'm not going back there for pleasure this time, but for a real purpose. We know it can't escape yet – but if it's left it might manage to lure victims to it again, and get back its strength. I don't have to look at its eye for what I'm going to do. I know nobody around here would go near – even the cottages nearby are empty – but suppose someone else like me hears of the legend and decides to follow it up? This time the door will be open, you know.'

The next morning I had to drive for some miles before discovering that there was nowhere I could buy explosives. I finally bought several tins of petrol and hoped that the inflammable liquid would destroy the alien monster. Calling in at Scott's house for my luggage – I was returning to London after finishing my task at the castle, for I did not want to be connected when the local police made their inquiries – I was accosted by the home help, who pressed upon me a curiously-figured star-shaped stone, which, she said, would keep off the power of Byatis while I used the petrol. Thanking her, I took my leave of Scott and went out to the car, which I turned out into the roadway. On looking back, I saw both Scott and the woman watching me anxiously from the living-room window.

The petrol cans on the back seat jangled together abominably, unnerving me as I tried to think of my best plan of action at the castle. I drove in the opposite direction on this journey, for I did not want to pass through Severnford; for one thing, I wanted to reach the castle as soon as possible and end the abnormality which scratched at my mind, and, besides, I disliked passing that carving of the toad-horror over the church porch again. The journey was shorter, and I soon was lifting the petrol cans on to the grass at the side of the road.

Lifting the cans near the gaping pit under the lifted stone slab took a great deal of labour and no little time. Placing my cigarette lighter at the edge of the stairway, I prised the caps off the petrol cans. I had taken them around the pit to the next higher step, and now I dipped a piece of plywood from Scott's garage into the petrol in one tin and placed it on the step above. Then, lighting the wood with my cigarette lighter, I hurriedly kicked the tins over the edge of the gulf and dropped the blazing wood in after them.

I think I was only just in time, for as I pushed the open cans into the pit a huge black object rose over the edge, drawing back as the petrol and wood hit it, as a snail retracts its eye organs at a touch of salt. Then came a protracted hissing sound from below, coupled with a terrible bass roaring, which rose in intensity and pitch before changing to a repulsive bubbling. I did not dare to look down into what must be seething in fluid agony at the bottom of the pit, but what rose above the trapdoor was dreadful enough. Thin greenish spirals of gas whirled out of the aperture and collected in a thick cloud about fifty feet above. Perhaps it was merely the effect of some anaesthetic quality of the gas which augmented my imagination, but the cloud seemed to congeal at one point of its ascent into a great swollen toad-like shape, which flapped away on vast bat-wings towards the west.

That was my last sight of the castle and its morbidly distorted surroundings. I did not look back as I descended the stone stairs, nor did I glance away from the road ahead until I had left the glistening of the Severn far above the horizon. Not until the London traffic was pressing around me did I think of the monster as behind me, and even now I cannot stop thinking of what I saw after I lifted the metal cube from the floor of the castle room.

As I had picked up the cube from the floor a strange stirring had begun beneath my feet. Looking down, I saw that the join of floor and wall on one side of the room was ascending the stone, and I managed to clutch a stone rung just before the floor slid away altogether, revealing itself to be a balanced door into a yet vaster room below. Climbing until I was halfway up the hanging ladder, I peered warily into the complete darkness below. No sound came from the blackness, and as yet there was no movement; not until I attempted to get a firmer grip on the ladder and, in so doing, dropped the metal block with a moist thud on something in that blackness, did anything occur.

A slithering sound began below me, mixed with a rubbery suction, and as I watched in paralytic terror a black object slid from underneath the edge of a wall and began to expand upward, slapping itself blindly against the sides of the smaller room. It resembled a gigantic snake more than anything else, but it was eyeless, and had no other facial features. And I was confused by the connections this colossal abnormality could have with Byatis. Was this the haven of some other entity from another sphere, or had Morley called up other demons from beyond forbidden gates?

Then I understood, and gave one shriek of horror-fraught realization as I plunged out of the room of malignancy. I heard the thing dash itself flabbily against its prison walls, but I knew the ghastly reason why it could not escape. I looked back once. The obscene black member was reaching frantically around the edge of the pit, searching for the prey it had sensed in its lair a moment before, and at this I laughed in lunatic glee, for I knew that the thing would search mindlessly until it found that it could reach nothing. 'It had grown too vast for the cellar room,' Sangster had written – but had not mentioned just what growth had taken place with each living sacrifice . . .

For the snake-like thing that had reached for me, that thing as wide as a human body and impossibly long, had been merely the face-tentacle of the abomination Byatis.

THE HORROR FROM THE BRIDGE

I

Clotton, Gloucestershire, is not a name which can be found on any map, and of the inhabitants of the few leaning red-brick houses which remain of the uptown section of the once-prosperous town, there is not one person who can remember anything of that period of horror in the town in 1931. Those in Brichester who heard the rumours that filtered out of the terror-clutched town deliberately refrain from recounting what they learned, and they hope that the monstrous series of events will never become generally known. Nobody, in fact, knows quite why that twenty-foot-high concrete building was erected on the bank of the Ton, the tributary of the Severn which flows near what used to be the riverside section of Clotton. Nor can they tell why a band of men tore down all the buildings which lay anywhere near the river, leaving only that sparse remnant of uptown Clotton. And of the eldritch sign which was clumsily engraved in each wall of the concrete riverside building, Brichester folk do not like to think. If one asks the professors at the University, they will answer vaguely that it is an extremely ancient cabalistic symbol, but one is never told exactly what the symbol is supposed to invoke, or against what it may be intended as a protection. The whole affair, in fact, is a curious conglomeration of hints and avoidances; and perhaps it would never have been known what actually took place in Clotton in 1931, had not a typed document been found in the house of a deceased Brichester recluse. It seems that this recluse had recently been preparing the document for publication, and possibly it may be better that such a document was never published. For, in fact, the document is a description of the horror, by one of those who tore down the riverside buildings; in view of what he recounts, it is understandable that he became reclusive.

The writer, Philip Chesterton, obviously intended his document to be as scholarly a document as possible. His reclusiveness, stemming, for reasons not to be conjectured, from 1931, allowed him a great deal of time to investigate the historical aspects of the affair through his large stock of volumes on the Roman occupation of Britain and following events. Other tomes, indeed, made it possible for him to include a good deal of historical and genealogical data about the people of Clotton, though this does not give more than a composite picture of the small population of the town, and does not add any information for those seeking to learn all factors affecting what erupted at the beginning of that cataclysmic period. Admittedly, however, certain legends and quasi-historical tales about some of the people of Clotton may be taken as hints of the eventual explanation of that problematic flood of 1931, but it is undeniably difficult to assess the true worth of various peculiar tales which Chesterton seems to have believed. The intrinsic value and veracity of several pivotal descriptions in the following transcription, which is a version, in some places severely cut, of the document found in the Brichester house, must therefore be considered carefully by the reader.

In 1800, according to the manuscript, a strange visitor moved into an empty house on Riverside Alley, a little-tenanted street within sight of a bridge over the Ton. The townsfolk could learn little about him, save that his name was James Phipps, and that he had come from Camside because his unorthodox scientific researches were distasteful to the inhabitants. Of course this was when the Reverend Jenner's witch-hunts were at their height, so that these 'researches' may have been taken for witchcraft. People living near the riverside street noticed the anomalous instruments and cases which were carried into the house by two furtive-looking rustics. Phipps seemed to direct operations with singular care, and came near to fury when one of the men almost slipped while carrying something which appeared to be a statue wrapped in thick canvas. The gaunt, pallid-faced man, with his jet-black hair and long bony hands, must have affected the watchers with strange feelings.

After some days had elapsed since his arrival, Phipps began to haunt taverns near the river. It was noticed that he never drank anything, and was once overheard to remark that he was averse to alcohol. It seemed, in fact, that he came there solely to discuss affairs with the less reputable inhabitants of Clotton – in particular, to learn of the prevalent legends of the countryside. In time, of course, he heard of the legend that a demon had once lurked nearby, and showed great interest in the story. The inevitable elaborations reached his ears – the belief of one or two people that a whole race of abominations was entombed somewhere in the vicinity, and the idea that a monstrous underground city could be discovered if one found the entrance which was reputed to lie submerged under the turbulent river waters. Phipps showed unaccountable interest in the further idea that the alien monster or race had been sealed up in some manner and could be released if the prisoning talisman were removed. He apparently held much stock by these curious legends, for he rewarded his informants very highly. To one or two he even suggested that they should send their sons to him for education in the sciences, but those approached were not interested in offers of this sort.

It was in the spring of 1805 that Phipps left his home one night. At least, he must have moved in darkness, for nobody knew of his temporary removal until the silence and lightlessness of the building on Riverside Alley made them aware of it. The strange tenant, it seemed, did not deem it necessary to set any guard upon his house, beyond locking the doors and shuttering the windows; and, indeed, nobody was sufficiently curious to investigate, for the barred house near the river remained silent and untouched.

Some months later, in early November, Phipps returned to take up tenancy again. This time, however, he was not alone, for during his absence he had taken a wife – a woman with a similar corpse-like pallor, who was heard to speak little and walked with a peculiarly stiff gait. What information could be gathered about her was sparse, only revealing that her husband had met her in Temphill, a nearby town in the Cotswolds, where he had journeyed to procure some extremely rare chemicals. They had met at some unnamed gathering, and Phipps showed strange caution in speaking of this mysterious gathering.

Nothing more need be noted about the curious couple in the house bordering the river for some time after this. In late 1806 a son was born in that darkly brooding house, and some consider that this was the actual beginning of a series of events to reach so devastating a climax in 1931. The child, who was named Lionel by his science-seeking father, was born on a day in November, of lashing rain and skies ripped by lightning. The people living near Riverside Alley used to say that a throaty and muffled rumbling had seemed to come from *below the ground* rather than from the throbbing sky; a few would even insist querulously that the lightning, often striking near the river, had once struck, in the form of a scintillating pillar of energy, directly through the roof of the Phipps homestead, even though no marks of such a phenomenon were afterwards found. The son was, at any rate, born of strange parents, and no such superstitious accounting for his abnormal inclinations in later life need be believed.

It was in 1822, when Lionel Phipps would have been seventeen or eighteen years of age, that his rumoured instruction by his father commenced. Definitely passersby would see faint gleams of light through the shutters which nearly always now were closed over the windows, and frequently muttered discussions or arguments between father and son were overheard. Once or twice these low-voiced conclaves took on a faintly ritualistic flavour, and those hearing the words would experience a vague sense of unease. A few passersby would become sufficiently interested to peer through a crack in the shutter, upon which they might see the younger Phipps poring over some large and ancient tome, or assisting at some unknown and vaguely sinister-looking apparatus. It seemed obvious that the boy was passing through a period of initiation or instruction in some branch of knowledge, of a definitely outré kind, if one were to judge from reports.

This period, it appears, continued well into the late months of 1823, and at its latter end a change was noted by the neighbours of the antique building on Riverside Alley. For one thing, whereas before only the woman of the household had been seen to leave the house, a series of nocturnal journeys now commenced. These were made by father and son with what seemed an extreme degree of caution, and the usual destination was thought to lie near the river. At one time the two were followed by a puzzled passerby, who returned to report that they had been engaged in some sort of survey of the ancient, moss-grown river bridge. They had even clambered down the banks to balance precariously above the swirling ebon waters, and at one time the father, examining one of the supports by the light of a lantern, let out a cry of what sounded like realization. His son seemed equally surprised when he joined the seeker, and both disappeared under the bridge. The watcher could not view the proceedings without revealing himself, and he made his way home with a turbulent mind.

Then came that particularly anomalous occurrence which may explain a seemingly inexplicable accident which befell a visitor later. The younger Phipps was seen to leave the house following the strange visit to the bridge, and those who took interest in the actions of this family soon discovered that the young man had visited the local general supplier's to purchase pickaxes and spades – for what purpose he would not tell. Those expecting to see the two secretive tenants of the river-bordering lane engaged in some form of excavation were puzzled when no such occupation was noticed.

While no excavation was visible anywhere on the surface, the peculiar evidence of some occupation of the men and the woman was soon evident. The nearby residents began to hear muffled sounds of digging and the noise of metal striking stone from somewhere adjoining the cellar of that much-discussed house in the alley. This series of sounds was not static in its location, for the sounds of excavating metal moved slowly, it seemed, in the direction of the river. These noises continued for some weeks, during which neither of the men was seen at all outside the house, and the woman only seldom. Finally, one night perhaps two months later, a party of men entered the Riverside Alley building, carrying, among other things, doors and frames and an unaccountable amount of material apparently intended for reinforcing the doors. A great noise of working came from below the ground, mostly located near the house and later near the archaic river bridge. After the cessation of the sounds, lights were seen in the room thought to be the laboratory or room where the men carried out their secretive experiments. Next came a reverberation which suggested that the party was returning to the underground region, following which there was a silence lasting some moments, and finally a sound of rushing waters somewhere below the earth. Shouts of amazement and terror were borne to the ears of those listening above, and a few minutes later a sound of something wooden crashing against stone, while an unpleasant reptilian odour rose to the shimmering stars. In an hour or so the party of men departed singly as stealthily as they had come.

Early in 1825, the escape of a criminal from the nearby prison on Mercy Hill led a party of searchers from Brichester to come to Clotton, antedating seekers after something much more hideous by over a century. Despite James Phipps' insistence that no refugee was hidden in his house, one of the group would not be satisfied by this reiteration. He went alone into the forbidding house while the others searched nearby, but when the man had still not joined the main party over an hour later they returned precipitously to Riverside Alley. They discovered him lying by the side of the road outside the house, unconscious and covered with water and slime.

Upon regaining consciousness the searcher recounted a strange tale. According to Chesterton's research, his tale ran:

'When you all left, this man Phipps waited till you were out of sight, and then he showed me in. Upstairs there's only bedrooms, and so bare that I didn't even need to go over the threshold to see that there was nobody hiding. Almost too bare – Phipps seems wealthy enough; where's all his money spent, then? Downstairs there's the usual sort of thing, except facing on the street there's some sort of laboratory. He wouldn't show me in there at first, but I insisted. The place was full of machinery and bookcases, and over in one corner there was a glass tank full of liquid, with a – well, something like a green sponge covered with bubbles – floating in it. I don't know what it was, but looking at it almost made me sick.

'I thought I'd seen all the house, and then I heard footsteps coming up from below. A woman appeared in the kitchen – Phipps' wife – and I went in to ask her where she'd been. He gave her a sort of warning look, but she'd already blurted out that she'd been down in the cellar. Phipps didn't seem to want me to go down, but finally he opened a trapdoor in the kitchen floor and we went down some steps. The cellar's quite large and bare. Tools and panes of glass, and what looked like a row of veiled statues; nowhere you could hide.

'I was just making for the stairs when I noticed a door in the wall to the left. There was a lot of carving on it, and a glass window in the top half, but it was too dark for me to see through the glass; anyway, it looked like a good hiding place. When Phipps saw where I was going he yelled out something about its being dangerous, and started down the steps. At first I didn't see how it opened, because there was no doorknob – then I noticed a brick

in the wall just to the right of it which looked loose, and I
pushed it in. There was a sort of grating noise, and
another I couldn't place at the time, but now I think it
was Phipps running back upstairs.

'The rest of what happened I don't understand. The
door swung open as I expected when I pushed the brick
into position – and then a flood of water poured into the
cellar! I don't know what was behind that door – the
water threw me backwards too quickly for me to see
anything – but for one minute I thought a figure was
standing in the open before it floundered into the cellar
with the water. I only saw it as a shadow, but it was like
something out of a nightmare – towering – neckless –
deformed – ugh! It couldn't have been anything like that
really, of course. Probably one of those statues I was
telling you about. I didn't see it again, and I can't
remember anything else till you revived me outside the
house. But what sort of man is it who has doors in his
house leading to underground rivers?'

No amount of pounding on the door of the house
could elicit a response, and those in the party did not
particularly like to enter that building of brooding secrets.
They went away intending to return later with a warrant,
but somehow this intention was forgotten on their return
to Brichester. Their later capture of the escaped criminal
restored a kind of sanity, and the peculiar rumours of
demon-haunted catacombs were almost forgotten.

II

The death of James Phipps came in 1898, on a day of howling wind, on which the hills in the distance muttered subterraneously in curious rhythms; the people of the country spoke of invisible primal mountain presences which chanted in nighted caverns, even though professors at the university in Brichester told them of the probability of underground rivers. The nightjars which now and then skimmed over the hills cried in peculiarly expectant tones, almost as if they expected to capture the soul of the dying man, as the legends told in that countryside hinted. For a long time through that May afternoon Phipps' voice could be heard, strangely distorted, from a shuttered upper-floor window; at times it seemed to address someone, while at others the voice would wail nonsensical fragments in unknown languages. It was not until after the rise of the miasma-distorted moon that an anguished groan came from the dying man, followed by a united rising of affrighted nightjars, from where they perched lengthwise in the trees and watched the house from across the river with glinting eyes. They flew as if escaping from some pursuing horror, which some believe these psychopomps to have attempted to capture. Close upon this came faintly-heard footsteps upon the stairs in the house, followed by the sound of creaking hinges and muffled splash rumoured to have been heard in the lower regions of that house.

Nothing was ever heard concerning the burial of any remains of James Phipps, although the son said he preferred to dispose of the corpse himself. The Clotton people could understand this, since the corpse of a man who had apparently lived decades over a century, and practised unknown sciences and experiments in secret, might necessarily be hidden from the eyes of the curious. It is very probably fanciful superstition which leads to scattered references to late travellers glimpsing someone very like Phipps in appearance near various hills topped by rings of monolithic stones, long after his death; but these same stone-capped hills often bore a nauseating reptilian odour which is not so easily explicable when linked with ensuing events.

Lionel Phipps and the unnamed Temphill woman were left in sole possession of the house, and evidently a rift began to open at once between them. For some days a light burned at most times behind the shutters of the laboratory, where the son was thought to be studying whatever books he now inherited. This attracted the attention of the owner of the adjoining house, Mary Allen; and as she could easily hear the conversations from next door through the thin wall when she was interested, her discoveries supplied Philip Chesterton with very useful information. Some days after Phipps' death, for instance, Mrs Allen overheard an interesting altercation. She heard only part of it, actually entering her own house just as Lionel Phipps began to shout angrily.

'I need the tables for the positions of the orbits, I tell you,' he was shouting. 'He must have copied it down somewhere, but there's nothing about it here. If he left it in the laboratory, it's certainly not in there now – are you sure you haven't . . . ?'

'I haven't seen them,' came the terrified answer. 'You know I wouldn't go near them. Maybe I was in the Temphill gathering, but this sort of thing terrifies me more than what I learned – down there . . . Why do you have to carry on this meddling? Whoever shut away *that from outside* must have known what they were doing, so why do you have to be so bent on setting it free?'

'You've taken the chart, haven't you!' threatened Lionel Phipps. 'You've taken it so I can't let them back in!'

'No, no, I haven't,' his mother protested. 'Don't jump to conclusions until you've been through the whole house, at least.'

This temporarily satisfied Phipps, who presumably went to the laboratory, for the lamp in there was lighted again a few minutes later. The search of the house proved unavailing, however, and another furious argument took place. The mother still insisted that she neither knew of the hiding-place of the notes nor did she know the actual information which he sought.

'Well,' Phipps conceded, 'perhaps you don't but anyway it makes no difference now. Before the time comes I'll go down to London and look up the British Museum copy of the *Necronomicon*; that's bound to have the chart. And don't try to persuade me not to go ahead with Father's work! Of course, you don't have to stay around – it might be better if you went back to your coven in Temphill. Satanism is so much healthier, isn't it?'

'You know I need – ' began his listener.

'Oh, of course, I forgot,' admitted Lionel Phipps satirically. 'Well, just don't interfere in my business here – I won't stand for it.'

The expected trip to London and the British Museum came in early 1899, and Lionel Phipps found little difficulty in gaining access to that section of the library which contains the rarer books. The librarian did not like the pallid face and leanness of the visitor, but he unlocked the bookcases containing the restricted volumes readily enough. The seeker speedily realized that the monstrous work of Abdul Alhazred would be useless to him in his quest; while it did contain an astrological table, this was very incomplete and long outdated. The even older tome, the *Book of Eibon*, appeared to him a possible source, with its records of the knowledge of an elder civilization. The librarian discovered that Phipps was attempting to find the position of some sphere Glyu'uho in an obscure relationship with a system of orbits on a certain autumn night – Glyu'uho, translated from that terrible primal tongue, being Betelguese. That little-known table in the complete *Book of Eibon* which gives positions of suggestive far worlds was quickly found by Phipps, from which he copied down parts of the table. The keeper of the books shuddered as he peered over the visitor's shoulder and translated the names of Aldebaran and the Hyades in Phipps' notations. He disliked, too, the walk of the seeker as he left the echoing room, for it appeared that he had some slight difficulty in using his limbs. The librarian might have shivered more had he known of the forthcoming results of this visit.

The return of Phipps, late in the evening, to the house on Riverside Alley, brought the most serious, and last, quarrel between the two remaining inhabitants of the building. Towards its end both were screaming at each other, and the listening Mrs Allen found their remarks terrifying.

Phipps was yelling something which first brought Mrs Allen to listen closely. 'All right, you try and stop me,' he told his mother, 'and I'll forget to operate next time you need it. You have to keep in my good books, or else you *won't last out*. You wouldn't even be here on this earth if it wasn't for that meeting in Temphill. You'll tell them about my plans, will you? If the people in this town knew what they found in Temphill in 1805 just after the day *they* met, you might be disposed of quickly . . .'

She shrieked back: 'The people in this town won't be able to do anything if you go on with your father's work – there'll be other tenants in Clotton. Wasn't the tunnel from the gate to the cellar enough?'

'You know I wouldn't be able to protect myself if I let them though the cellar entrance.' Phipps sounded defensive.

'So just because you're a coward, do you have to let them through *the other way*?' she inquired. 'Once the sign's removed there'll be no way to keep them in check – they'll just multiply until they let the Old Ones back on the earth. Is that what you want?'

'Why not?' suggested her son. 'We both worship the Old Ones; the river-creatures won't harm me. We'll exist side by side as *Their* priests, until They return to rule the world.'

'Side by side – you're naïve,' Phipps' mother scoffed. 'Still, perhaps the juxtaposition of Fomalhaut and the Hyades won't be enough; even you may get tired when you have to wait more than thirty years . . . I'm not staying to see what happens. I'll go back to Temphill and chance what should have come years ago – perhaps it'll be the best thing.'

At about eleven o'clock that night the front door opened, and the strange woman began to walk down the street. A vaguely terrible picture was presented to the warily watching Mary Allen, as James Phipps' widow made her way with that half-paralytic gait which seemed to be a characteristic of all the Phipps family, between the dark houses under a lich-pale moon. Nothing more was ever heard of her, though a woman was seen walking very slowly, and with some difficulty, along a road some miles away in the direction of Temphill. Daylight showed a strange horror; for a little way further on a woman's skeleton was found, as though it had fallen at the side of the road. Body-snatching seemed the most plausible explanation, and the matter was discussed little. Others to whose ears it came, however, linked it indefinitely with references to something that 'should have come a century ago.'

After this breach Lionel Phipps began to make an increasing number of journeys to that immemorially-constructed river bridge, and was noticed to go underneath to peer into the water frequently. At night he would step into the street at various hours and examine the sky with an excessive degree of impatience. At such times he appeared to be interested in a portion of the sky where, from directions given, Fomalhaut would have risen. Towards the end of March 1899, his impatience began to ease, and a light would be seen more often in the library. He seemed to be preparing for something extremely important, and those who heard the sounds which emanated from the shuttered laboratory disliked to consider just what he might be awaiting.

Early that Autumn came the night concerning which the Brichester people begin to grow reticent. Fomalhaut now glared like the eye of some spatial lurker above the horizon, and many tales began to be whispered abroad about the increasingly frequent happenings around Gloucestershire and the Severn. The hill rumblings were louder and more coherent, and more than once people forced to take forest routes had sensed vast and invisible presences rushing past them. Monstrous shapes had been glimpsed scuttling through the trees or flapping above the stone circles on the hills, and once a woman had come fleeing into Brichester, shrieking a tale of something which had looked very like a tree but had suddenly changed shape. On a night at the peak of these bizarre occurrences, Phipps made his first experiment.

He was seen leaving the house on an evening of late October, 1899, and seemed to be carrying a long metal bar of some sort. He arrived on the river-bank near the bridge at about midnight, and immediately began to chant in ritual tones. A few minutes later the hill noises redoubled in intensity, and a peculiar sound started up close at hand, near the bridge – a monstrous bass croaking which resounded across the countryside. What appeared to be a minor earthquake followed closely on the beginning of the croaking, shaking the river-bank and causing slight turbulence in the water, though nothing more. Phipps then disappeared under the bridge, and through his continued chanting rang the sound of metal scraping on stone. Upon this sound came a subterranean commotion, with a rising chorus of voiceless croaking and a sound as if of Cyclopean bodies slithering against one another in some charnel pit, with a nauseating rise of that alien reptilian odour. But nothing came into view, even though the scrape of metal against stone continued with greater ferocity. Finally Phipps appeared above the bridge's shadow again, with an expression of resignation on his face. He made his way back to the house in the alley, as that abominable commotion died out behind him, and entered, closing the door stealthily. Almost at once the light filtered out from the shuttered laboratory where, presumably, he was again studying the inherited documents.

Seemingly, Phipps was becoming unsure whether he was using the right chant, for that was what he told the British Museum librarian, Philip Chesterton, this now being the year of 1900. Phipps preferred not to say which incantation he needed, or what he hoped to invoke by its use. He made use of the *Necronomicon* this time in his search, and Chesterton noted that the seeker appeared interested in those pages which dealt with the commission of beings in tampering with the elements. The reader copied down a passage and continued to another section of the volume. Chesterton, reading over the other's shoulder, noticed that he showed considerable interest in the following passage, and shuddered to think of possible reasons.

'As in the days of the seas' covering all the earth, when Cthulhu walked in power across the world and others flew in the gulfs of space, so in certain places of the earth shall be found a great race which came from Outside and lived in cities and worshipped in dark fanes in the depths. Their cities remain under the land, but rarely do They come up from Their subterranean places. They have been sealed in certain locations by the seal of the Elder Gods, but They may be released by words not known to many. What made its home in water shall be released by water, and when Glyu'uho is rightly placed, the words shall cause a flood to rise and remove at last the seal of those from Glyu'uho.'

Phipps admitted to his listener that he would have a considerable wait before anything could be done towards the release of what he knew to exist, 'But,' he continued, 'it won't be too long before those in Clotton will see shapes striding down their streets in broad daylight that would drive them insane at night! In the old days the shoggoths used to avoid those places where They peered out of the depths at unwary passers-by – what do you think will be the effect on a man who sees Their great heads break the surface – and sees what they use to view him instead of eyes?'

Then he left, possibly conjecturing that he had said too much; and Chesterton was alone, with various speculations. As time went by, he began to investigate the doings of this eldritch being on Riverside Alley; and as a horrible idea began to form concerning the woman from Temphill, he contacted an acquaintance in that town. Legends, he was told, existed of a monstrous coven in the 1800s, which convened in artificial caverns beneath the graveyards. Often vaults would be opened, and newly buried corpses might be dug forth and reanimated by certain horrendous formulae. There were even hints that these living cadavers were taken as wives or husbands by favoured members of the cult, for the children resulting from such charnel betrothals would have primal powers which properly belonged only to alien deities.

So horrified was Chesterton by what he learned and suspected that he apparently decided to do something about it. In 1901 he resigned from his post at the British Museum and moved into a house on Bold Street in Brichester, working as a librarian at Brichester University. He was bent on preventing Lionel Phipps' intentions; and those who visited Chesterton at his home in Brichester, where he lived alone among his vast collection of books, left oddly disturbed by his outré, half-incoherent ramblings. During library hours at the University he showed no signs of any such aberration as manifested itself in his free conversation, beyond a strange nervousness and preoccupation. But in his free time he tended to speak of nameless things in a frightful manner, half-describing hideous things in a way which promised cosmic revelations if the listener would only be patient.

'God help us – what alien powers has Lionel Phipps

got, lying dormant in that mad brain? That woman James brought back from the Temphill meeting of which he never spoke – was she merely one of the coven, or something which they raised from the tomb by their awful rites? Lionel was overheard to say that he had to perform operations so that she *would last out* – maybe he meant that she would decay away if he didn't preserve her ghastly half-life . . . And now he's got the information he was after, there's no telling *what* he may do. What lurking terror is he going to release from wherever he knows it is hidden? He said there would be a considerable wait, though – if one knew the right words, one might be able to seal up whatever is lying in wait . . . Or perhaps Phipps himself could be destroyed – after all, a being which has been born out of such an abnormal union must be prone to arcane influences . . .'

As might be expected, those who heard his odd ravings did not act upon them. Such things might happen in Temphill or Goatswood, but they could not affect sane Brichester folk, where witchcraft was not, at least, practised openly.

The period of more than thirty years passed; and nothing occurred which could shake the complacency of those who dismissed Chesterton's theories with such assurance. To be sure, the staff at the University often met with terrors which they had never thought could exist, for they were sometimes called by the frantic inhabitants of various localities to quell phenomena which were rising from hiding. 1928 was a particular year of horror, with inexplicable occurrences in many places, both around the Severn and far beyond; and the professors were more inclined to credit the wild tales of beings from another plane of existence which impinged on this universe. But Chesterton was always very reticent in the presence of authority, and he mistakenly thought they would explain any unnatural situation in a supposedly scientific manner. He read astrological tables and arcane books more and more, and shivered when he noticed how closely the stars were approaching certain positions. Perhaps he was even then formulating a plan for the destruction of the legendary threat which Phipps was to release; his narrative is not specific on this point.

Terror, meanwhile, was increasing among the more credulous Clotton inhabitants. They noted the loudness of the hill noises, and were quick to remark the frequent visits of Phipps to the bridge over the sluggish river, and the way the lights flashed far into the night in his laboratory. The importance attached to a seemingly trivial find by a child on Riverside Alley was startling; for all that had been found was a hurried sketch on a scrap of paper. The frantic search for this paper made by Chesterton, when he heard of it, startled the more enlightened men who knew him; though those at Brichester University might have been less inclined to scoff, for they were familiar with things whose existence is not recognized by science.

When Chesterton managed to acquire the paper and compare it with an illustration in the *Necronomicon*, he found that these depicted the same species of incarnate hideousness, though in markedly different postures. The only plausible explanation for the sketch seemed to be that it had been drawn frantically by an eavesdropper outside the Phipps house, copied from some picture glimpsed through the shutters; at least, that was what Mrs Allen suggested when she gave him the paper. From comparison with the sketch, Chesterton used the other picture to form a composite portrayal of the being, though the details of both pictures were vague. The thing had

eight major arm-like appendages protruding from an
elliptical body, six of which were tipped with flipper-like
protrusions, the other two being tentacular. Four of the
web-tipped legs were located at the lower end of the
body, and used for walking upright. The other two were
near the head, and could be used for walking near the
ground. The head joined directly to the body; it was oval
and eyeless. In place of eyes, there was an abominable
sponge-like circular organ about the centre of the head;
over it grew something hideously like a spider's web.
Below this was a mouth-like slit which extended at least
halfway round the head, bordered at each side by a
tentacle-like appendage with a cupped tip, obviously used
for carrying food to the mouth. The whole thing was
more than a simply alien and horrific monstrosity; it was
surrounded by an aura of incredible, aeons-lost evil.

The finding of this only roused the fear of the Clotton
people to a more hysterical pitch. And they were quick in
their perception of Phipps' growing stealth in his nocturnal ventures – the way he took devious routes in his ever-
increasing visits to the river. At the same time, though
nobody else was aware of it, Philip Chesterton was noting
the approaching conjunction of stars and clusters, said to
portend terrific influences. More – he was fighting against
the urge to destroy the being in the house on Riverside
Alley before the hidden primal race could be released.
For Chesterton had pieced together a powerful formula
from various pages of Alhazred, and he felt it might both
destroy the surviving Phipps and seal the subterranean
entities back into their prison. But dared he chance
releasing elemental forces, even to prevent such impending hideousness as he suspected? Thinking upon the
horribly suggestive illustrations he had acquired, his terror
of the powers with which he was to tamper receded.

So it was that on the night of September 2, 1931, two men were attempting to push back the veils which hold the lurking amorphousnesses outside our plane of existence. As nightjars cried expectantly in the hills, and increasing reports of nameless things seen by travellers terrorized the superstitious, the lights burned in the study of Philip Chesterton far into the night, while he drummed on an oddly-carved black drum which he had procured from the University and began to repeat the dreadful formula he had worked out. At the same time, Lionel Phipps was standing on the bridge over the Severn tributary, staring at Fomalhaut where it glared over the horizon and shrieking words which have not been heard on the earth for aeons.

It can only have been a startling coincidence that a party of young men, carrying rifles which they had lent to a rifle range for the day, was walking along the bank of the Ton. Even less believably, they were making for the bridge just as Phipps completed the shocking evocation. At any rate, they saw what happened as the hysterically screaming voice ceased; and they recount things of such horror that one can only be thankful for Chesterton's remote intervention. 'What made its home in water shall be released by water,' Alhazred had said, and the words of the long-dead sorcerer were proved in that chaotic scene.

A bolt of lightning seemed to crash directly on the bridge, and the shattered stonework of a support momentarily revealed a circular seal, carven with an immense star, before the waters rushed to conceal it. Then the flood began, and the watching group had time only to leap back before a torrent of water shattered the banks and thundered repeatedly and with incredible force upon the spot where the carven circle had appeared. There came a shifting sound from under the throbbing waters, and as the three men in the party watching moved backwards, a huge circular disc of stone rumbled through the liquid and smashed against the lower bank. It had been the seal over the legendary entrance to the hidden alien city.

What happened after this transcended in shocking terror everything which had gone before. Chesterton was nearing the completion of his own invocation at this point; otherwise the thing which was found dead on the riverbank could never have been destroyed by the men. It is surprising, indeed, that they could have retained enough sanity to try.

As the waters began to slow their torrential rush, the watching three saw a dark object break the uniformity of the surface. Then a titanic, shadowy thing rose from the water and rushed across the bank with a revolting sucking noise towards the town nearby. The three did not have a great deal of time, however, to concentrate upon that looming figure, for at that moment Phipps turned towards them. In the dim moonlight they saw him sneer dreadfully, and a look of fearful evil started up in his eyes. He began to move towards them, his eyes seeming to stare at each of them; and they noticed him beckoning behind him, after which there came a sound as of something huge splashing out of the river. But they could not see what was behind Phipps.

'So,' sneered that half-human being before them, 'this is the total of the strength which can be mustered by the great Elder Gods!' Apparently he misunderstood the true intentions of the terrified three men. 'What do you know of the Great Old Ones – the ones who seeped down from the stars, of whom those I have released are only servitors? You and your *Celaeno Fragments* and your puerile star-signs – what can you guess of the realities which those half-veiled revelations hint? You ought to be thankful, you imbeciles,that I'm going to kill you now, before the race below gets back into sway on the earth and lets Those outside back in!' And he moved towards them with the same dreadful look in his eyes.

But it was not upon Phipps that the watchers fixed their eyes in stark terror. For the moonlight, weak as it was, showed them what towered beside him, two feet taller than himself, shambling silently towards them. They saw the shining network of fibres over the one eye-organ, the waving tentacles about the gaping mouth-slash, the shocking alienness of the eight members – and then the two things were upon them.

At that minute, however, in a house in Brichester, Philip Chesterton spoke the last word of his painfully acquired formula. And as the foremost of the men turned his rifle blindly on the two abominations before him, forces must have moved into operation. It can be only this that could account for the bullets' actually penetrating the alien amphibian which Phipps had released; for the thing fell backwards and croaked horribly for some seconds before it writhed and lay still. As Phipps saw this, he launched himself at the foremost of the party, who fired again. The change which took place in Lionel Phipps must indeed have been swift, for the man with the rifle, braced against the impact of the leaping figure, was struck by a skeleton, clothed with rags of flesh, which shattered upon contact.

The half hysterical three turned towards the river, where a greater miracle was taking place. Perhaps moved by Chesterton's invocation, the pieces of the shattered seal were recomposing in their original shape and location. It may only have been imagination which caused the men to think they saw a shape thrust back into the concealed entrance; it is at any rate certain that whatever lay below in its aeons-forgotten prison was now once again sealed into that sunken hideaway.

The nightjars were quietening their expectantly vibrating cries, and the turbulence of the waters had almost ceased. Not just yet could the men bring themselves to look at the monstrosity which they had shot, to ascertain that it was dead. Instead, they stared towards nearby Clotton, towards which they had seen a dim shape plunge some time before. The monster from beyond was at last loose on the world.

III

By the time that Philip Chesterton had reached the bank of the river outside Clotton, some time had elapsed, and during it several events had occurred. Chesterton, hastening to view the effects of his interference, had been delayed by the necessity of buying petrol, and also by his uncertainty where the sorcerer might be; though he knew the man would be somewhere near water, it was some time before the bobbing lights and commotion of the crowd of evacuees who had come from the nearby town attracted him to the bridge. There he found more things than he had expected.

The crowd would in any case have congregated near the bridge, no doubt, since the noise of shots and other things would have drawn them; but actually they had been forced to evacuate from Clotton. Built above the normal flood-plain of the Ton, the town had been partially inundated by the abnormally-provoked flood; the section near the river had become a morass of submerged streets and basements. Those so driven from their homes had made for the bridge – the banks of the river were actually higher land than the low-lying downtown quarter of Clotton, and the hills which lay on the other side of the town were precarious at night if one wanted to hurry for help to Brichester. At the bridge, of course, the already frenzied townsfolk met with a scene which only aggravated their hysteria; and this was not alleviated by the tales of several people. Chesterton heard clearly the wails of one woman as he came up. She was telling the bystanders:

'I was just goin' up to bed w'en I 'eard these shots an' yells down be the river. I came downstairs an' peeped out o' the front door down the street, but I didn't see anythin'. Anyway, all this runnin' up an' down 'ad woken me up, so I went into the kitchen an' got a sleepin' tablet. Just as I was goin' back through the front room I 'eard this sort o' – well, I don't know; it sounded like someone runnin', but bare feet, an' sort o' *wet*-soundin'. Looked out o' the winder, but there wasn't anythin'. An' then somethin' went past the winder – big an' black an' shiny, like a fish. But God knows wot 'eight it was! Its 'ead was level with mine, an' the 'winder's seven foot off the ground!'

Nor was this all Chesterton heard recounted when he arrived. He had not yet seen the horribly incomplete remains of Phipps, nor that other object which lay in shadow some distance away, for the crowd was being skilfully directed away from the two monstrosities by a surprisingly sane three men – the same ones who had been partly responsible for their destruction. Now, however, the three, sensing his instinctive authoritative bearing, converged on him and began to recount their terrible

experience, supplementing their account by pointing out
the remains of Phipps and his dreadful companion. Even
though Chesterton had formed a good idea of the appearance of the river creatures, he could not suppress a gasp
of revulsion as the being was revealed. The sketch and
the *Necronomicon* illustration had not reproduced everything; they had not shown the transparency of the half-
gelatinous flesh, revealing the *mobile* organs beneath the
skin. Nor had they shown the globular organ above
the brain, at whose use Chesterton could only guess
shudderingly. And as the mouth fell open when they
stirred the body, he saw that the being possessed no
teeth, but six rows of powerful tentacles interlaced across
the opening of the throat.

Chesterton turned away, nauseated by this concrete
symbol of cosmic alienage, to move back and speak to
one or two of the affrighted crowd, who had no idea of
what lay nearby. He twisted around again as a choking
cry of horror came behind him; and, under the fast-
sinking moon, he saw one of the three men struggling
with the tentacles of the river monster. It stood semi-
erect on its four lower legs, and was dragging the man
towards the yearning members about the mouth. The
globular device in the head was pulsing and passing
through shocking metamorphoses, and even in this position, Chesterton noticed that the river had momentarily
washed almost to the edge of the crowd, and the water
was being levitated into an orifice in the head above the
globe.

The distance between the wide-gaping mouth and the
victim was momently lessening, while the companions of
the man were standing seemingly paralysed with terror.
Chesterton snatched a rifle from the hands of one of

them, aimed it, and stood temporarily uncertain. Recollecting that the being had only been put out of action by the other bullet because of his own incantation, Chesterton doubted whether another shot would harm it. Then, as he saw that pulsing sphere in the head, a conjecture formed in his mind; and he aimed the weapon at the organ, hesitating, and pulled the trigger.

There was a moist explosion, and the watchers were spattered with a noisome pulp. They saw the being sink to the ground, its legs jerking in spasmodic agony. And then came an occurrence which Chesterton would not write about, saying only that very soon almost no remains of the monstrosity existed.

And, as if they had reacted in delayed fashion to the destruction of the being, the crowd now shrieked in unity of terror. Chesterton saw before he turned that the intended victim was indeed dead, whether from pure terror or from the embrace of the tentacles – for where these had gripped, the man's flesh was exposed. Then he turned to look where the mob was staring, and as they too stared in that direction, his two companions remembered what they had seen heading for the town in those recent lunatic minutes.

The moon had sunk nearly to the horizon, and its pallid rays lit up the roofs of the Clotton houses behind which it hung. The chimneys stood up like black rooftop monoliths, and so did something else on one of the nearer roofs – something which moved. It stumbled on the insecure surface, and, raising its head to the moon, seemed to be staring defiantly at the watchers. Then it leapt down on the opposite side, and was gone.

The action was a signal to the waiting crowd. They had seen enough horrors for one night, and they fled along the riverside path which, dangerous as it was, seemed more secure than any other means of escape. Chesterton watched as the lights faded along the black river, and then a hand touched his arm.

He turned. The two remaining members of the party which had killed Phipps stood there, and one awkwardly said: 'Look, you said you wanted t' destroy them things from the river, an' there's still one left. It was them did for Frank here, an' we think it's our – duty – to get 'em for 'im. We don't know what *they* are, but they went an' killed Frank, so we're bloody well goin' to try an' kill them. So we thought that if you needed any help with killin' that last one . . .'

'Well, I told you something of what I know,' Chesterton said, 'but – well, I hope I won't offend you, but – you must understand certain things pretty thoroughly, to unite your wills with mine, and I don't know whether you'd – What sort of work do you do anyway?'

'We're at Poole's Builder's Yard in Brichester,' one told him.

Chesterton was silent for so long that they wondered what had occurred to him. When he looked at them again, there was a new expression in his eyes. 'I suppose I could teach you a little of the Yr-Nhhngr basics – it would need weeks to get you to visualize dimensional projections, but maybe that won't be necessary if I can just give you a copy of the incantation, the correct pronunciation, and give you the lenses for the reversed-angle view of matter if I can make any in time – yes, those plain glass spectacles would do if I put a filter over to progress the colours halfway . . . But you don't know what the devil I'm running on about. Come on – I'll drive you to my house.'

When they were driving down the A38, Chesterton broke the silence again: 'I'll be frank – it was really

because you work at Poole's that I accepted your aid.
Not that I wouldn't be glad of help – it's a strain to use
those *other* parts of the brain with only your own vitality
to draw on – but there's so much I have to teach you, and
only tonight to do it in; there wouldn't even be tonight,
but it's crazy to attack while it's dark. No, I think I can
use you more in another way, though perhaps you can
help with the chant. So long as I still have the reproduction of that seal in the river . . . and so long as you
can get used to artificial reversal of matter – I always do
it without artificial help, because then it doesn't seem so
odd.'

And as he drew up the car in the driveway off Bold
Street, he called back: 'Pray it stays near water to
accustom itself to surface conditions. If it doesn't – they're
parthenogenetic, all of them, and pretty soon there'll be
a new race to clear off the earth. Humanity will just
cease to exist.'

IV

The next day was one of sickly-glowing sunlight and
impending winds. Chesterton had copied out the formula
in triplicate and given a copy to each of the men, retaining
one for himself. Now, in mid-morning, the librarian and
one of his helpers were going through the streets of
Clotton, gradually approaching the riverside section. On
the bank waited the third of the party, like his friend
wearing the strange glasses which Chesterton had prepared the night before; his was the crucial part of the
plan. The riverbank was otherwise bare – the human
corpse and the others having been disposed of.

Chesterton concentrated on his formula, awaiting the finding of what he knew lurked somewhere among the deserted red-brick houses. Strangely, he felt little fear at the knowledge that the amphibian terror lurked nearby, as though he were an instrument of greater, more elemental forces. At the conclusion of the affair, upon comparing impressions, he found that his two companions had been affected by very similar feelings; further, he discovered that all three had shared a vision – a strange mental apparition of a luminous star-shaped object, eternally rising from an abyss where living darkness crawled.

Abruptly a gigantic shape flopped out of a side street, giving forth a deafening, half-intelligent croaking at the sight of the two men. It began to retrace its journey as Chesterton's accomplice started to chant the incantation; but Chesterton was already waiting some yards down the side street, and was commencing the formula himself. It gave a gibbering ululation and fled in the direction of the river, where the two followed it, never ceasing their chant. They were slowly driving it towards the riverbank – and what waited there.

That chase must have resembled a nightmare – the slippery cobbles of the watersoaked street flashing beneath their feet, the antique buildings reeling and toppling on either side, and the flopping colossus always fleeing before them. And so the infamous building on Riverside Alley was passed, and the nightmarish procession burst out on the bank of the river.

The third member of the party had been staring fixedly at the point at which they emerged, and so saw them immediately. He let in the clutch of the lorry in whose cab he sat, and watched in the rearview mirror while the two manoeuvred the thing into the right position. Perhaps it sensed their purpose; at any rate, there was a hideous period when the being made rushes in every direction. But finally the man in the truck saw that it was in the correct position. They could not aim for the head-organ of the being, for the flesh of the head was strangely opaque, as if the opacity could be controlled at will; but a bullet in the body paralysed it, as Chesterton had deduced it would. Then the lorry-driver moved a control in the cab, and the crucial act was performed.

Upon the paralysed body of the river-creature poured a stream of fast-hardening concrete. There was a slight convulsive movement below the surface, suppressed as Chesterton recommenced the incantation. Then he snatched an iron bar which had been thoughtfully provided, and as quickly as possible carved a replica of that all-imprisoning seal below the bridge upon the semi-solid concrete surface.

Afterwards, Chesterton put forward enough money to have the building firm erect a twenty-foot tower over the spot, carved with replicas of the seal on each side – one never knew what agencies might later attempt to resurrect what they had buried. When the Clotton inhabitants began to trickle back, a chance remark by one of the two builders that more than one being could have escaped caused them to tear down the buildings in the riverside quarter, with Chesterton's approval and aid. They found nothing living, although Phipps' homestead yielded enough objects to drive one of the searchers insane and turn many of the others into hopeless drunkards. It was not so much the laboratory, for the objects in there were largely meaningless to most of the seekers – although there was a large and detailed photograph on the wall, presumably the original of that sketch Chesterton had acquired. But the cellar was much worse. The noises which came from beyond that door in the cellar wall were bad enough, and so were the things which could be seen through the reinforced-glass partition in it; some of the men were extremely disturbed by the steps beyond it, going down into pitch-black waters of terrifying depth. But the man who went mad always swore that a huge black head rose out of the ebon water just at the limit of vision, and was followed by a blackly shining tentacle which beckoned him down to unimaginable sights.

As time passed, the remaining section of Clotton was repopulated, and those who know anything about the period of terror nowadays tend to treat it as an unpleasant occurrence in the past, better not discussed.

Perhaps it ought not to be so treated. Not so long ago two men were fishing in the Ton for salmon, when they came upon something half-submerged in the water. They dragged it out, and almost immediately afterwards poured kerosene on it and set fire to it. One of them soon after became sufficiently drunk to speak of what they found; but those who heard him have never referred to what they heard.

There is more concrete evidence to support this theory. I myself was in Clotton not so long ago, and discovered a pit on a patch of waste ground on what used to be Canning Road, near the river. It must have been overlooked by the searchers, for surely they would have spoken of the roughly-cut steps, each carrying a carven five-pointed sign, which led down into abysmal darkness. God knows how far down they go; I clambered down a little way, but was stopped by a sound which echoed down there in the blackness. It must have been made by water – and I did not want to be trapped by water; but just then it seemed to resemble inhuman voices croaking far away in chorus, like frogs worshipping some swamp-buried monster.

So it is that Clotton people should be wary still near

the river and the enigmatic tower, and watch for anything which may crawl out of that opening into some subterranean land of star-born abominations. Otherwise – who knows how soon the earth may return through forgotten cycles to a time when cities were built on the surface by things other than man, and horrors from beyond space walked unrestrained?

THE INSECTS FROM SHAGGAI

I: *The Place Of The Cone*

Perhaps it would be better if I enjoyed myself as best as possible in the next few hours, but somehow I feel bound to write down some explanation for my friends, even if they will not believe it. After all, I am not really depressed – it is only because I must not be alive after sunset that I will slit my wrists then. Already, certainly, my reader will feel incredulity, but it is quite true that my continued existence might be a danger to the whole human race. But no more – I will tell my story from the beginning.

When drinking I tend to be boastful and intolerant, so that when I stayed in the hotel in the middle of Brichester I resolved to keep a check on myself; to stay away from the bar, if possible. But one of the residents – a middle-aged teacher who read extensively – had heard of Ronald Shea, and quite liked some of my fantasy stories. So it was that he led me into the bar, with promises that he would tell me all the Severn Valley legends which might form plots for future stories. The first few tales served to get me slightly intoxicated, and then he suddenly started on one which did not sound like the usual witch-story. By the end I was forced to admit that it was at least original.

'In the woods towards Goatswood,' my informant began, 'the trees get very thick towards the centre. Of course not too many people go down there – there are too many stories about Goatswood itself to attract outsiders – but there's a clearing in the middle of the forest. It's supposed to have been cleared by the Romans for a temple to some god of theirs, I think the Magna Mater, but I wouldn't know about that. Anyway, sometime in the 1600s what must have been a meteor fell in the clearing one night. There were quite a few peculiar happenings earlier that night – arcs of light across the sky, and the moon turned red, according to books I've seen. The fall of this meteorite was heard for miles around, but nobody went to investigate; there were attempts to get together a search-party in Brichester and Camside, but that petered out.

'Not long after, people began to go there – but not normal people. The local coven made it their meeting-place; on ritual nights they'd consummate the Black Mass there and make blood sacrifices, and before long the country people began to say that the witches didn't even worship Satan any more; they worshipped the meteorite. Of course, the local clergymen said the thing was probably sent from Hell anyway. Nobody could really say they'd seen these rites in the clearing, but a lot of them still said that something came out of the meteor in answer to the witches' prayers.

'Then someone went down to the clearing, long after Matthew Hopkins had found the coven and had them executed. It was a young man who visited the clearing in daylight on a bet. He didn't come back before dark, and the others began to get worried. He didn't return until after daylight the next morning, and by that time he was completely incoherent – ran screaming into Brichester, and they couldn't get anything out of him.'

'That's where it ends, I suppose,' I interrupted. 'Somebody sees a nameless horror and can never tell anyone what he saw.'

'You're wrong there, Mr Shea,' contradicted the

teacher. 'This man gradually calmed down, though for a few days he was so quiet that they were afraid he'd been struck dumb. Finally he *did* calm down enough to answer questions, but a lot was left unexplained. Of course, as you say . . .

'Apparently he'd been ploughing through the thickest part of the forest when he heard something following him down the path. Very heavy footsteps, he said – with a sort of metallic sound about them. Well, he turned round, but there was a bend in the path that blocked his view. However, the sun was shining down the path, and it cast a shadow of something which must have been just beyond the turning. Nobody knows exactly what it was; the man only said that while it was almost as tall as a tree, it was no tree – and it was moving towards him. I suppose he would have seen it in a moment, but he didn't wait for that. He ran the other way down the path. He must have run for quite some time, I think, because he ended up in the haunted clearing. Quite the last place he'd have chosen.

'This is the part that rather interests me. The sun was near to setting, and maybe that gave an added luridness to the scene. Anyway, in this glade in the forest he saw a metal cone standing in the centre. It was made of grey mineral that didn't reflect, and was more than thirty feet high. There was a kind of circular trapdoor on one side, but on the other side were carved reliefs. Presumably he was frightened to go near it, but finally he approached it. Over at one side of the space, there was a long stone with a rectangular hollow scooped out of the top. It was surrounded by human footprints – and there was dried blood in the hollow.

'Another hiatus, I'm afraid. He never would describe those carvings on the cone, except to say that some represented the thing he had almost seen on the path, and others were of – other things. He didn't look at them long, anyway, but went round the other side to look at the trapdoor. It didn't seem to have any lock or way of opening, and he was studying it. Then a shadow fell across him. He looked up.

'It was only the sun finally setting, but it did attract his attention away from the trapdoor. When he looked back, it was hanging open. And while he watched, he heard a throbbing noise somewhere above him, in the tip of the cone. He said he thought there was a sort of dry rustling inside, getting closer. Then he saw a shape crawling out of the darkness inside the trapdoor. That's about it.'

'What do you mean – that's all there is?' I said incredulously.

'More or less, yes,' the teacher agreed. 'The man became very incoherent after that. All I can learn is that he said it told him about its life and what it wanted. The legend hints something more, actually – speaks of his being dragged off the earth into other universes, but I wouldn't know about that. He's supposed to have learned the history of these beings in the cone, and some of what's passed down in the legend is remarkably unusual. At sunrise the Daytime Guardians – that's what they're called in the story – come out, either to warn people away from the clearing or to drive them in there, I don't know which. These were that species of thing that cast the shadow he saw on the path. On the other hand, after dark the others come out of the cone. There was a lot more told him, but the whole thing's very vague.'

'Yes, it *is* vague, isn't it?' I agreed meaningfully. 'Too vague – horrors that are too horrible for description, eh? More likely whoever thought this up didn't have enough imagination to describe them when the time came. No,

I'm sorry, I won't be able to use it – I'd have to fill in far too much if I did. The thing isn't even based on fact, obviously; it must be the invention of one of the locals. You can see the inconsistencies – if everybody was so scared of this clearing, why did this man suddenly stand up and go into it? Besides, why's the thing so explicit until it reaches any concrete horror?'

'Well, Mr Shea,' remarked my informant, 'don't criticize it to me. Tell Sam, there – he's one of the locals who knows about these things; in fact, he told me the legend.' He indicated an old rustic drinking a pint of beer at the bar, who I had noticed watching us all through the conversation. He now rose from the stool and sat at our table.

'Ah, zur,' remonstrated our new companion, 'you don't want t' sneer at stories as is tole roun' here. 'Im as you was 'earin' about laughed at wot they said t' him. 'E didn't believe in ghosts nor devils, but that was before 'e went t' the woods . . . An' I can't tell yer more about wot 'e got from the thing int' cone 'cos them as knew kep' quiet about it.'

'That's not the only one about the clearing in the woods,' interposed the teacher. 'This witch-cult which held their meetings there had their reasons. I've heard they got some definite benefit from their visits – some sort of ecstatic pleasure, like that one gets from taking drugs. It had something to do with what happened to the man when he went in – you know, when he seemed to enter another universe? – but beyond that, I can't tell you anything.

'There are other tales, but they're still more vague. One traveller who strayed down there one moonlit night saw what looked like a flock of birds rising out of the glade – but he got a second look, and even though these things were the size of large birds, they were something quite different. Then quite a few people have seen lights moving between the trees and heard a kind of pulsation in the distance. And once they found someone dead on a path through the woods. He was an old man, so it wasn't too surprising that he'd died of heart failure. But it was the way he looked that was peculiar. He was staring in absolute horror at something down the path. Something had crossed the path just ahead of the corpse, and whatever it was, it must have been enough to stop a man's heart. It had broken off branches more than fifteen feet from the ground in passing.'

We had all been talking so long that I did not realize how much I had drunk. It was certainly with alcoholic courage that I stood up as my two companions stared in amazement. At the door to the staircase I turned, and unthinkingly declared: 'I've got some days to spare here, and I don't intend to see you all terrified by these silly superstitions. I'm going into the woods tomorrow afternoon, and when I find this rock formation you're all so scared of, I'll chip a bit off and bring it back so it can be exhibited on the bar!'

The next morning brought cloudless skies, and up to midday I was glad that the weather could not be construed an ill omen by the innkeeper or similar persons. But around two o'clock in the afternoon mist began to settle over the district; and by two-thirty the sun had taken on the appearance of a suspended globe of heated metal. I was to leave at three o'clock, for otherwise I would not reach the clearing before dark. I could not back out of my outlined purpose without appearing foolish to those who had heard my boasting; they would certainly think that any argument that the mist would make my progress dangerous was merely an excuse. So I decided to journey a little distance into the forest, then return with the tale that I had been unable to find the clearing.

When I reached the wood after driving as fast as was safe in my sports car, the sun had become merely a lurid circular glow in the amorphously drifting mist. The moistly peeling trees stretched in vague colonnades into the distance on both sides of a rutted road. However, the teacher had directed me explicitly, and without too much hesitation I entered the forest between two dripping trees.

II: *The Thing In The Mist*

There was a path between the tortuous arches, though it was not well defined. Before long the oppressive atmosphere of the tunnel, distorted through the walls of mist, combined with the unfamiliar sounds which occasionally filtered into the ringing silence to produce a disturbing feeling of awed expectancy. What I expected, I could not have said; but my mind was full of hints of some impending occurrence of terrible significance. My eyes were strained by my efforts to pierce the drab wall before me.

It was not long before this persistent conviction became unbearable, and I told myself this was the time to return to the inn with my prepared excuse – before darkness. The path had had no others meeting it, so that I could easily retrace my journey, even through the mist. That was when I turned to go back down the path, and stopped in indecision.

I had almost collided, I thought, with a metallically grey tree. Small in comparison with the average in the forest, this tree was about sixteen feet high with very thick cylindrical branches. Then I noticed that the trunk divided into two cylinders near the ground, and the lower ends of these cylinders further divided into six flat circular extensions. This might merely have been a natural distortion, and such an explanation might also have accounted for the strange arrangement of the branches in a regular circle at the apex of the trunk; but I could not reach for a natural explanation when those branches nearest me suddenly extended clutchingly in my direction, and from the top of what I had taken for a trunk rose a featureless oval, leaning towards me to show an orifice gaping at the top.

The mist eddied around me as I ran blindly down the path, which slid from under my feet and twisted away at unpredictable places. I visualized that giant being clumping in pursuit through the forest, its tentacles waving in anticipation, the mouth in the top of that featureless head opening hungrily. The silence of the forest unnerved me; perhaps the monstrosity was not pursuing me, in which case there must be some yet worse fate ahead. How many of the things might inhabit the forest? Whatever they were, surely they could be no acknowledged species. How could I see if they were waiting in silent ambush? The mist would effectively camouflage them, for a pillar-like blur might merely be another tree.

Despair followed upon my terrified imaginings, and finally I fell against a grey oak and awaited whatever terror might come for me. The exhaustion resulting from my frenzied flight dulled the edge of fear, and quite soon I ceased to glare in horror at every sound among the trees. My muscles ached from that mad chase, and muscular weariness soon combined with the tiredness I suddenly felt to produce a troubled sleep. I was soon awakened by a dream that a forest such as that surrounding me had changed to an army of oval-skulled titans; but the sleep had lasted long enough to refresh me.

I did not feel thankful for the rest, however. The mist had almost lifted; and because of this I could see that the sun was near to setting. I had to leave the forest quickly; sleep had not erased the memory of what I had recently seen, and my mind might not take the strain of being alone at night near such prowling lunacies. But I quickly realized that I no longer knew the way out of this maze of terror, even though the surroundings were easily visible. If I went in the wrong direction, I would not know this until dark, when all the lurking haunters of the forest might close in on me.

However, it was even more obvious that, since no amount of concentration would show me the route, I must waste no more time in futile debate, but go in one direction, praying that it would lead me out of the nightmare into which I had plunged. A vague intuition suggested that the path to the left was my original route, and I hastily began to walk down it, attempting to silence faint premonitions. There was no recognizable landmark anywhere near the route, although once or twice I thought a distorted oak was familiarly shaped; but, considering that the inward journey had been merely a terrified flight, it was not surprising that I remembered nothing. Occasionally despair overtook me, and I was sure that the faceless colossi of the wood never would let me escape; but I shunned such ideas where possible.

Soon my hopes began to rise. Surely the trees were beginning to thin out, and vegetation to become less abundant; as though I were approaching the edge of the forest? It would not be any too soon, either – for, from the position of the sun, night could not be more than a quarter of an hour away. And was that not my car that I saw in the distance among the trees? Certainly something gleamed with a flash of dull metal just where the path seemed to end, though as yet I could not make out any details. I hurried towards the furtive gleam on the road – and reached the clearing I had taken for a road.

The thirty-foot-high metal cone which towered in the clearing reflected the light only because it was covered with moisture, for it was constructed of a dull mineral, pitted and scarred from unimaginable stresses. As yet I could not see the carven side of the cone, and that facing me was bare except for a circular protrusion, surely the trapdoor of the legend. But though those unholy carvings were not then visible, what I could see in the shunned clearing was disturbing enough. There was a roughly rectangular stone at the opposite side, the top surface of which was hollowed out and darkly stained – and the stains appeared fresher than could be healthily explained, although I did not approach to verify the dreadful idea which occurred to me. No marks of feet, nor of anything else, appeared in the muddy earth; what manner of unnatural prints I had expected I do not know, but their absence did not reassure me. I knew that some species of being lurked here in the haunted clearing – and what being made no mark in passing?

Though my fear had been great when I came upon the hidden place in the forest, my curiosity combined with a certain fatalism to impel me to examine the cone. After all, it would soon be night, long before I found my way to the edge of the wood – it was useless to flee the beings of the forest when they would be awaiting my attempted escape. In the few minutes which remained to me, I determined to see what was carved on the opposite side of the cone; and so I circled the object, noting a faint dry rustling sound which came from somewhere in the clearing.

Immediately I saw the images on the pitted grey

expanse, I regretted my wish to view them. I can describe them, and the actions they were shown performing – from which I drew conclusions which were verified dreadfully soon after. But none of these descriptions can convey the sheer abnormality and alienness of those depictions, for the human mind cannot imagine the cosmically unnatural until concrete evidence has been shown undeniably to it.

There were five distinct races of entities pictured in the reliefs. A species of insect appeared most often – an insect with certain alien characteristics marking it as not of this planet. Often these beings would be manipulating peculiar cylindrical appliances, which seemed to project a thin ray disintegrating whatever lay in its path. Another instrument, a box-shaped crystal emitting a scintillating petal-shaped field, was used to subdue the counterparts of that oval-headed faceless being, which apparently were a race of enslaved workers used to perform tasks requiring strength for the relatively weak insect species.

Those were not the only creatures depicted on the surface of the cone – but what use is it to describe them at this point? It was very soon after that I saw such beings in their natural surroundings, and such an experience was infinitely worse than seeing a mere representation of nightmare. It is sufficient to say that the sculptures were so crude as to cloak the more hideous details of the subjects, for more details had been used in the reproduction of the surroundings. The two suns that ceaselessly orbited above the scenes were startlingly realistic, although for sheer alienness even this could not equal the actual scene. The sky-clawing pylons and disturbingly shapen domes of the cities frequently looming in the distance were not shown from the inside; nor was the utter horror of the interior of the cone ever portrayed.

About then I realized that it was becoming increasingly difficult to see the figures on the cone, and I started in terror as I realized the sun had set upon my engrossed contemplation. The glade had become dreadfully quiet, stressing the sound of rustling which still emanated from somewhere nearby. That dry sound seemed to come from above, and abruptly it came to me that it was the noise of something coming down inside the cone.

Abruptly it ceased, and I tensed, waiting for the thing which would appear around the curved metal at any minute. That it was something which figured in the scenes engraved on that metal I did not doubt; probably one of the omnipotent semi-insect race. But what details of it might blast my mind before the thing fell on me?

And it was at that moment that I heard a clanging sound on the opposite side – the sound of the opening of the circular trapdoor.

III: *The Insects From The Cone*

That dull noise of the pitted trapdoor beyond my line of vision echoed for a long time, yet when it ceased nothing had appeared around the curve of the cone. All that could be heard was the rustling of the unseen dweller, now mixed with a scrabbling which steadily approached.

At last a shape appeared, flapping above the ground on leathery wings. The thing which flew whirring towards me was followed by a train of others, wings slapping the air at incredible speed. Even though they flew so fast, I could, with the augmented perception of terror, make out many more details than I wished. Those huge lidless eyes which stared in hate at me, the jointed tendrils which seemed to twist from the head in cosmic rhythms, the ten legs, covered with black shining tentacles and folded into the pallid underbody, and the semi-circular ridged wings covered with triangular scales – all this cannot convey the soul-ripping horror of the shape which darted at me. I saw the *three* mouths of the thing move moistly, and then it was upon me.

I thought it had somehow managed to fly over me, even though the horribly flat face had a moment before been pressed into mine; for I had felt no impact. But when I turned to look behind me, there was no sign of the insect-creature, and the landscape was empty. The others from the cone did not attempt to attack me, but flapped away over the trees. My mind a chaos of speculation, I watched them in their flight, attempting to decide where their companion had gone.

The next moment the whole landscape seemed to ripple and melt, as if the lenses of my eyes had twisted in agonizing distortion. Then I felt it – the thing which was distorting my impulses to such an extent – the thing which, in some hideous way, had become a parasite – the thing which, at the moment when it flew in my face, had entered my body and was crawling around *in my brain*.

Now, as I look back upon my first sensation of something worming through the corridors of my brain, with a slightly higher degree of objectivity, I can only surmise that the being cannot have been strictly material – constructed of some alien matter which allowed its atoms to exist conterminously with those of my body. But then I could think of nothing but the frightful parasite which crawled where my clawing fingers could not reach.

I can only try to speak of the other occurrences of that night with some degree of coherency, for my impressions after that became somewhat confused. It must have been that my mind was growing accustomed to the unholy object in my skull – for, unbelievable as it seems, within a short time I thought of this state as perfectly normal. The being was affecting my very thought-processes – and even as I stood before the cone, the insect-creature was pouring its memories into me. For as the landscape melted about me, I began to experience visions. I seemed to float above scenes like those of a hashish dream – in a body such as that of the horror from the cone. The worlds swam out of darkness for what seemed an eternity; I saw things of indescribable hideousness, and could not flee from the sight of them. And as the thing gained a hold over me, I began to see actual scenes from the life of the being which occupied me.

There was a place of green mists through which I flapped, over a boundless surface of pitching water. At one point the mists began to roll back, and I rose through them, the green, attenuated film billowing round me. In the distance a long, vague cylinder poked towards the invisible sky, and as I drew closer I saw that it was a stone pillar, protruding from the swaying water, grown with hard shell-like plants and with curiously shaped projections on each side at regular intervals. There seemed to be no reason for the terror which boiled up in me at the sight of that pillar, but I purposely flew around the object at a distance. As the mists began to conceal it again, I saw a huge leathery hand, with long boneless fingers, reach out of the water, followed by a many-jointed arm. I saw that arm's muscles tense, as if whatever owned the arm were preparing to pull itself out of the sea. I turned away and flew into the mist – for I did not want to see what would appear above the surface.

The scene melted into another. I crawled down a path which snaked between translucent, diamond-like rocks.

The path entered a valley, at the bottom of which lay a strange black building, inexplicably luminous under the purple night sky of that far planet. The building was of no recognizable architecture, with its deliriously sloping roof and many-sided towers, and I did not know why I was approaching it so purposefully. My claws clattered over the rock-strewn surface which became a black-tiled pavement before the gaping entrance to the ebon building, and I entered. Many passages twisted before I reached that which I sought – that which was spoken of on Shaggai as so powerful – and I did not like what hung from the ceilings in shadowy corners; but at last I came upon the windowless chamber in a high black tower. I took the strangely shaped piece of metal from where it lay on a central slab and turned to leave the chamber. Then a door in the opposite wall crashed open, and I remembered the whispered legend of the guardian of this weapon of a lost race. But I knew how to use the weapon's fullest power, and through it I focused mental waves to blast apart the many-legged furry thing which scuttled from the opened door, its abominably shrunken heads waving on hairy, scrawny necks. Then I flapped from the haunted lightless tower in terror, clutching the metal weapon – for as I looked back I saw the many-headed thing, all the legs on one side of its body burned away, still dragging itself sideways after me.

Again the vision rippled and changed. I stood on a high slab of some beautifully polished plastic, surrounded by lines of the most nauseous beings imaginable. They were oval, two-legged, dwarfed things, scarcely two feet high, without arms or head, but with a gaping moist grey mouth at the centre of their bodies, which were of a spongy white pulp. They were all prostrate in an attitude of worship before me on the fungus which appeared to compose the ground in a solid gelatinous sheet on their side of the slab. My side of that slab was bare rock, covered with huge squat dark-emerald buildings of the same material as the slab. These, I knew, had been constructed by a race other than the pulpy white things, and probably antedating them; the beings that worshipped my hardness could not work such material or even touch it, but lived in repulsively moist burrows in the fungus. Indeed, even as I watched, one of them moved too near to the dais upon which I stood, and in so doing ripped away a sponge-wet portion of itself, which speedily putrefied where it lay.

Yet another scene flashed before me. I skimmed over a plain covered with colossi depicting naked humanoid figures in various bestial attitudes, each statue at least a hundred feet tall; and about them all was some hideous detail which I could not quite place. I disliked the vast footprints which led between the leering figures, and still more disliked the disturbingly *gnawed* bones of huge animals which were strewn across the plain, for I felt that I knew the cause of these horrors, and knew the abnormality of the colossi, if only I could place it. Then came those clumping footsteps behind me, startlingly close; and as I turned and saw what came striding across that field of unholy carvings, I knew the answer to both questions. It was humanoid – almost – as it pounded through the maze of statues; but it towered above the hundred-foot figures. And the atrocious thing which I glimpsed as I fled from that shrine to cosmic accidents was the eyelessness of the living colossus and the way the hair of the scalp grew in the sockets where the eyes should have been.

As the visions began to overtake me in greater quantity, they acquired more definite connection, and it was not long before I realized what was now being put into my brain was a sort of history of the insect-race. Perhaps the most horrible part of the affair was the way I regarded the events and scenes now presented to me, not with the horror and disgust of a sane human being, but with the exact same impersonal observation of the insect-parasite. As the chronicles of the race were passed through my mind, I *was*, to all purposes, the insect which had become part of me. I write this now with more emotion than when I experienced the memories of the being – and that thought fills me with more terror than did the memories themselves.

So it was that I learned the history of the insect-race, and so it is that I write now what I learned. And horror can still be provoked in me by thoughts of what the insects from Shaggai may yet do on this earth.

IV: *The Exodus From The Gulf*

The beings had, I learned, originally come from Shaggai, a globe far beyond the reach of any earthly telescope, which orbited a double sun at the edge of the universe. Upon this planet they built their cities, full of globular domes for their habitations and pylons of that grey metal which composed the cone. The main buildings were almost all globular, entered by a doorless orifice at the top of each, through which the insects could fly – but there was one important building which was not globular, but pyramidical: the temple at the centre of each city. And the thoughts of the being grew oddly reticent on the subject of this temple, whence all the inhabitants would go to worship at ritual times; for never could I tap a memory of what was worshipped inside that grey metal pyramid. The only fact which became apparent was that, incredible as it sounds, the tenant of the temple was one living being, but was somehow the *same* being in each temple.

The life of the beings of the grey cities followed no definite pattern, except for certain observances. They would leave their domes as the blinding emerald light of the two suns rose above the horizon, and while a generally avoided group of priests flew to the temple, the rest went about personal business. None needed to eat – they lived by photo-synthesis of the green rays of the double star – and so they visited other planets, seeking new abnormalities which they, in their perversion, could aesthetically enjoy. At the time of birth of my informant, the race, needing to do no work, had sunk to an abysmal state of decadence. While on Shaggai they would torture slave-races from other worlds for pleasure; and when on other planets, they sought the most terribly haunted localities to view their horrors – with which pastime the early memories of the insect-being had been occupied. There was another practice of the insects which was not then fully revealed – but it was connected, it appeared, with what they practised on the witch-cult at their outpost on earth.

At any rate, the beings had set up outposts and built cities on many of the outer worlds, in case anything should ever make Shaggai uninhabitable; for they had had experience of what might crawl over the rim of the universe and conquer their world before then. So they were to some extent prepared when a catastrophe did indeed devastate their world, many aeons before their advent on earth. Even at the time when I visited their shrine, they had very little idea of what had really destroyed Shaggai; they had seen it happen from the beginning, but could only explain the cause vaguely – and, having viewed a vision of what they saw for myself, I did not wonder at their puzzlement.

It was at the dawning of one of those emerald-lit days that the object was first seen. Above the double disc on the horizon, and slowly approaching their planet, appeared a strange semi-spherical red globe. The edges were indistinct, while the centre was a sharply-defined point of crimson fire. At that time the approach of the sphere was so unnoticeable that few of the city's inhabitants remarked it; but by the third dawn the object was much nearer, so that the race's scientists began to study it. They decided, after much speculation, that it was not a star or planet, but some species of body which was composed of no recognizable substance; the spectrum was completely unknown, and the substance must have come from a region where conditions were unlike those anywhere in this universe. Because of this vagueness of its identity they were uncertain of its probable effects on their planet – for the body was heading directly for Shaggai, and should reach it before the suns had set thrice more.

On the third day the globe was a huge red glow in the sky, blotting out the green suns and lighting everything with a crimson flame; but no heat emanated from it, and no other evidence of its existence met the insects besides the blood-red light. They were uneasy, for the menacing sphere in the heavens was very disturbing, and therefore many of them visited the triangular temple frequently for private worship. The being in my body had been one of those frequent visitors, and owed its life to being in the temple when the cataclysm struck. It had entered under the arched portal, where a portcullis-like sheet of translucent mineral would fall at any external threat, to protect the tenant inside. As the insect made to leave the temple after that act which it must practise before the tenant of the pyramid, it saw a prolonged crimson flash in the sky, speedily approaching the ground, while at the same time the protective shield crashed down in the temple entrance. The forty or so other beings which also were at worship clattered to stare through the shield at what was happening in the city outside.

As the red glow slowly faded, the buildings became again visible, as did the beings in the streets. The creatures and buildings had changed in some way during the cataclysm – for they glowed with that same crimson light, streaming from *inside* each. And the light became every moment brighter, changing from red – orange – blinding yellow to white, as the insect-beings writhed and clawed at themselves in helpless agony.

It was the way in which the temple was fortified that saved those inside. The radiation from the bursting globe was kept from affecting them long enough for them to use certain powers. By some obscure method of teleportation they transported the entire temple, with themselves, to the nearest planet on which they had a colony – the world of the faceless cylindrical beings, called Xiclotl by its inhabitants. As the devastated world of Shaggai faded from outside the shield, the insect-creature saw the buildings reel and the inhabitants burst asunder in momentary incandescence. And its last glimpse was of the globes of light which were now all that remained of the lords of Shaggai, as they sank to fill the ground with crimson radiation.

Upon their arrival on Xiclotl, the insects called the rest of their race from the other planetary colonies to join them. The faceless horrors of the planet were enslaved by the new ruling race, and because of their great strength and little brain-power, were driven to perform all tasks in building the new city of the insects on Xiclotl. These beings, which were subdued by one of the insects' instruments for focusing mind power to promote unpleasant nerve impulses, were naturally carnivorous and, if not enslaved in this way, might have eaten any slow-moving insect. However, it was relatively easy to force them to labour, and under their strivings the city speedily took shape.

The insects did not remain on Xiclotl for more than two hundred years, during which my informant had reached maturity. The reason for their leaving was one about which it would rather not have thought in detail, having to do with the faceless slaves and their somewhat primitive theology. They believed in a legendary plant-race which inhabited the bottom of a sheer-sided pit in the outer regions of the country in which the city lay. The religion of the planet's race demanded that periodic sacrifices be chosen from the race and throw themselves as food to the plant-gods in the pit. The insects did not object to this practice, so long as it did not remove so many beings as to draw on their labour force – at least, not until a group of insects followed one of the sacrifices to the pit. After that, however, the tale which the returning party told caused the more superstitious – including my informant – to teleport the temple again, together with a number of the race from Xiclotl as a means of labour, to a planet at the centre of the next galaxy. The insect-being which was pouring its memories into my brain had not actually seen what had occurred in the pit, so was not so explicit as usual; but what it remembered having heard was certainly disturbing. The returning party had seen the faceless creature leap from the edge of the pit and fall towards the abysmal darkness of the lower regions. Then came a splashing in that darkness, and a huge purple moist blossom rose from it, its petals opening and closing hungrily. But the greatest abnormality of the thing which splashed out of the pit was its green tentacles, tipped with many-fingered hands of unholy beauty, which it held yearningly towards the point where the sacrifices threw themselves off.

The temple was positioned next at the centre of a city on that planet in the next galaxy – an uninhabited planet, it seemed, which the insect colonists named Thuggon. They stayed here less than a year; for before they had been there ten months, they noticed a steady decrease in the number of slaves on the planet, and learned that the beings had been disappearing after dark, though none was ever seen to leave. When two insect-beings disappeared on successive nights, a party left the city next day to search; and some miles beyond the colony they discovered a huge stretch of marshy ground, at the centre of which lay a vast stone tower, from which led suggestively recent-looking footprints to a black object at the edge of the marsh. And when the black object was seen to be a neat pile, composed of the severed heads of the insects together with their bodies, and when they saw that all the flesh had been sucked out through the gaping gash where the heads should have been, the party were not slow in returning to the city and demanding the speedy removal of the temple from Thuggon.

After the quitting of Thuggon, the insects established themselves on a planet which the inhabitants knew as L'gy'hx, and which is called Uranus here on Earth. This world became the home of the insects for many centuries, for the native race of cuboid, many-legged metal beings was not openly hostile, but allowed them to build their usual outpost with the labour of the beings from Xiclotl. They built a new temple – the old one having grown dilapidated with so much travelling – and fashioned it in a conical shape, carefully constructing the multi-dimensional gate which must exist in each temple to allow the entry of that which my informant passed off as 'that from Outside.' The city flourished, and the beings native to L'gy'hx gradually came to accept the insects as a race ruling the planet jointly with themselves. The only thing for which the natives did not care was the insects' worshipping the hideous god Azathoth. They themselves were worshippers of the relatively insignificant deity Lrogg, which conferred benefits on its worshippers and demanded only annual sacrifice, in the shape of the removal of the legs of a conscious native. The cuboid beings disliked the vague tales of atrocities practised on still-living victims in the conical temple of Azathoth, and when a rebellious set of natives began to visit the insects' city to worship there the elders of L'gy'hx felt that steps should be taken to prevent such unwelcome infiltrations into their theology. But while they did not fear the weapons of the insect-race, they did not like to incur the wrath of the idiot god, and finally decided to do nothing.

Some years passed, during which two major sequences of events happened. While a steady hate grew in the majority of the insects for the obscene rites of Azathoth, and a desire for the easy rituals prescribed for Lrogg's worshippers began to rise, the rebel set among the natives grew steadily more fervid in their prostrations before the new god and their hate for their natural god. At last these two feelings publicized themselves at the same time. This double revelation came when a particularly fervent group of native Azathoth-worshippers violated a temple, smashing all the statues of the two-headed bat-deity Lrogg and killing three of the priests. After acid had been poured into the brains of the offenders, the chief priests of Lrogg declared that the temple of Azathoth must be removed altogether from the planet, together with its insect-worshippers, although the insects who would conform to the planetary religion might remain if they wished. The cuboid natives who had become believers in the creed of Azathoth were all treated in the same way as the original offenders, as an example.

Only about thirty of the race from Shaggai left in the temple, but teleporting it in unison they managed to bring it down on a nearby planet – Earth. They made an imperfect materialization in the clearing near Goatswood, leaving the best part of the temple underground, and only thirty feet protruding above the surface. In the top of the cone the insects lived, while in the central portion the beings from Xiclotl were stabled; in the lower forty-foot portion was kept that which they worshipped in the temple. During daylight the insects worshipped the tenant of the secret portion of the fane, but after dark they went forth to carry on an insidious campaign to hypnotize selected subjects and lure them to the clearing.

From these hypnotized subjects was formed that decadent witch-cult which grew up around the temple in the clearing. The members of the coven did not merely visit the clearing to worship and sacrifice persons on the altar there; they went there to experience the obscene pleasure of allowing the insects to inject their memories into their brains, which they enjoyed in the same way a drug addict gains pleasure from his induced delirium. And at that moment, God help me, I was experiencing the same sensations – and doing nothing to shake them off.

As the witch-cult grew, the insects began to form a

plan. Whereas at the beginning they merely lured humans to their haven in order to explore the perversions of their subconscious for pleasure, they gradually came to the conclusion that, if they handled their victims the right way, they would become the new rulers of the planet. First they could overpower the inhabitants of the nearby countryside and then, as they themselves propagated, the whole of the planet. The humans might either be destroyed utterly or retained as a subsidiary labour force, while the newly-revealed insect race would build cities and temples, and finally, perhaps, the huge multi-dimensional gate which alone will let Azathoth into this universe in his original form.

Thus the final purpose of the cult was shaped. It thus came as a great blow when the local coven was persecuted for witchcraft and all members executed. Worse still, the word got round that the clearing was connected in an unholy manner with this witchcraft, so that those who lived anywhere near it quickly moved to more wholesome surroundings. The insects would have been able to teleport, had it not been for some constituent of the atmosphere which prevented this; the same unallowed-for obstacle made it impossible for the beings to fly any great distance. They therefore declined, using the beings from Xiclotl – which, because of their guarding the clearing in daylight while the insects worshipped, they called the equivalent in their language of the 'Daytime Guardians' – to drive unwary wanderers in the woods into the glade. The few they managed to lure to the cone they attempted to use as the foundation of the new cult which they tentatively planned, but without success. That young man of whose visit to the clearing the legend told had been the first in many years, and had been such an unwilling subject that attempts to force him into submission led only to his complete insanity. After his visit, the only person actually to be taken over by one of the insect-parasites had been myself.

And so the history of the insects from Shaggai had been brought into the present. For the minute I wondered what memories the being in my cranium would now let flow into my brain, but almost immediately afterwards I knew what I was next to see. The insect had decided to make the supreme revelation – it was going to unveil one of its hidden memories of a visit to *the lower regions of the temple*.

Immediately the creature was in the tip of the cone, lying on a grey metal slab in its quarters. It was awakening at that moment, sensing the rise of the sun outside, and it then extended its legs and clattered off the slab, over to the sliding door. It inserted its leg tip into one of the pits in the door and slid it back, turning to look back at the bare semi-circular chamber and the flashing light over the slab, set where it would hyponotize the slab's occupant to immediate sleep.

The insect joined the ritual procession of its fellows which were preparing to descend into the lower regions. Those at the head carried long pointed rods of that inevitable grey metal, while the rest held portions of the corpse of a native of Xiclotl. The rods, it seemed, were to drive the secret tenant of the temple back when it became too desirous of sacrifice; the only victim to be offered it would be the dismembered faceless being, a member of the labour force which had grown too weak to be of further use.

Adjusting their weapons, the leaders of the procession moved off down the spiral down-slanting passage. The creature, staring fixedly ahead as prescribed, followed them, carrying a group of severed tentacles as offering.

They passed down the grey corridor, not noting the daily-seen bas-reliefs on the walls, representing the denizens of caves and ruins on far worlds. Nor did they turn in passing the cells of the Xiclotl labour force, even when the beings in them crashed themselves against the doors and extended their tentacles in helpless fury upon sensing the portions of their fellow slave. They did not turn when they clattered through the souvenir room, where they kept the preserved eyeless corpse of one specimen from each race subject to them. The first halt in their ritual march was at the carven door of the inner sanctum of the temple, over which certain representations leered down, at which every member of the procession folded its wing-case and prostrated itself for a moment. Then the foremost insect-creature extended its jointed antenna and gripped a projection on the surface of the door – hesitating a ritual instant, while its three mouths spoke three alien words in unison – and then slid the door open.

The first object which came into view beyond the sliding panel was a squat twenty-foot statue, a hideously detailed figure which resembled nothing remotely humanoid – and the information was immediately injected into my brain that this object represented the god Azathoth – Azathoth as he had been before his exile Outside. But the eyes of my informant speedily swung away from the alien colossus to the vast door behind it – a door bordered with miniature representations of insect-beings, all indicating something beyond that door. And the leaders picked up their pointed weapons and approached the final door, followed by the forward-staring procession.

One of the leaders now raised his rod in a curious gesture, while the others prostrated themselves in a semicircle before the bordered door, writhing their antennae in concerted and vaguely disturbing rhythms. Then, as the prostrate crescent rose again, the other leader put forth his tendrils and clasped a projection on the door. Unhesitatingly he drew the portal open.

V: *Beyond The Final Door*

I was alone in the glade, lying in the dew-wet grass before the cone. There was no sign of any living being in the clearing besides myself, not even of the being which, I felt certain, had just withdrawn from my brain. The whole glade was exactly as it had been when I entered it, except for one important difference – that the sun had not yet risen. For this meant that the inhabitants of the cone would still be absent from it, searching for victims; and it meant that I could enter the untenanted temple and open that bordered door, on whose opening the insect's memory had ended.

If I had been able to think without external hindrance, I would immediately have realized that the memory had ended at that point simply as a subtle method of luring me to the underground sanctum. It is less likely that I would have realized that I was being directed to do this by the being which still inhabited my brain. But I still clung to the possibility that I had been dreaming. There was only one way to find out; I must enter the cone and see what lay behind that final door. So I made for the circular entrance in the grey wall of the cone.

Beyond the foot-long passage inside the trapdoor, a diagonally slanting metal corridor led upward and downward. Upward, I guessed, lay the semicircular quarters of the insect-beings, where I had no wish to go; downward lay the temple proper. I started downward, doing my best to avoid looking at the abnormal bas-reliefs which covered the walls.

The passage was less strongly lit than it had seemed in the being's memory, so that at first I did not notice the point where the bas-reliefs ended and a line of doors, containing heavy grilles, began. Not until a grey metal tentacle whipped through a grille to quiver within an inch of my face did I realize that here was the passage of the Xiclotl labour force cells. I cowered back, trembling, to edge along the opposite wall, jerking at the frequent infuriated crashings of the faceless beings against their cell doors, and yearning for the end of the journey. I finally passed the last locked portal and continued on down the spiralling ramp.

The memory of the injected recollections of the insect-creature was already dimming, so that I could hardly explain the premonition I felt a little further on. I gasped in shock when I rounded a curve and saw an eyeless figure standing with bony arms reaching – all the more hideous because, although the corpse was otherwise human, there were three arms held out. The unwavering posture which the thing held gave me the courage to approach it, as I suddenly remembered the vision of the room where the insects kept preserved specimens of their subjects. What sphere had spawned this object I did not think; nor did I linger to stare at the corpse, but passed by quickly between the others. I attempted not to look aside at what I hurried by, but my eyes persisted in straying to things – a frog-flipper attached to a tendrilled arm in one place, an insanely situated mouth in another – so that I was very relieved to quit that room.

When I came to the temple door and saw that it stood open, I hesitated expectantly. Glancing only once at the metal heads which leered, all joined to one body, over the open portal, I entered. I stopped short, for the memory of that huge image of Azathoth had grown dim. I did not look long at it; I would only have seen worse details with every glimpse, and the first view was bad enough. I will not describe everything about it; but basically it consisted of a bivalvular shell supported on many pairs of flexible legs. From the half-open shell rose several jointed cylinders, tipped with polypous appendages; and in the darkness inside the shell I thought I saw a horrible bestial, mouthless face, with deep-sunk eyes and covered with glistening black hair.

I almost turned and fled from the temple, thinking of the door that lay beyond the statue, and speculating over what the idiot god might *now* resemble. But I had come this far unharmed, and, noticing the sharpened rods propped against the base of the idol, I did not think that whatever lay beyond the bordered door could harm me. And so, conquering my revulsion at what leered frozenly above, I took up one of the weapons and made for that door. As I reached for the protrusion on the sliding grey panel I hesitated, for I heard a curious sound inside the hidden room – like the washing of the sea against black piles. It ceased immediately, but for some minutes I could not bring myself to draw the door open. In what form would Azathoth manifest itself? Might there not be some reason why the being was only worshipped during daylight? But all the while my hand was moving towards the projection, almost as though another will besides my own were directing it; so that when it dragged the sanctum door open, I battled to stop its progress. But by then the door was completely open, and I was standing staring at what lay beyond.

A long passage of the omnipresent grey metal stretched away for ten feet or so, and at its end stood, on first glance, a blank wall. Yet not quite blank – for a little way up there was a triangular metal door with a bar held across it in brackets. The passage was deserted, but from beyond the triangular door came a sound which I had remarked before – a liquid rolling.

I had to know the secret of the temple, and so stealthily approached the door and lifted the bar, which grated slightly. I did not open the door, but backed down the passage and stood at the other end. The wave-sound was rising now, as if something at the other side was approaching. Then the triangular portal began to rattle in its frame, and slowly it moved outward on its hinges.

And as I saw that metal triangle shifting with pressure from the other side, a wave of terror engulfed me. I did not want to see what lay on the other side of the door, and I turned and slammed the outer door without giving myself time to think. Even as I did so, a grating sound reverberated down the pasage and the triangular door crashed open. Through the crack as I slammed the door I saw something ooze into the corridor – a pale grey shape, expanding and crinkling, which glistened and shook gelatinously as still-moving particles dropped free; but it was only a glimpse, and after that it is only in nightmares that I imagine I see the complete shape of Azathoth.

I fled from the pyramid then. It was just daylight, and over the trees black shapes were flapping home. I plunged through the corridors of trees, and at one point one of the beings from Xiclotl started out into my path. What was worse, it *drew back* at my approach.

Though some of my possessions were left in my room there, I never returned to the inn at Brichester, and no doubt they still speak of me there as having died horribly. I thought that in this way I could make sure the insects could not harm me – but the first night after the experience in the clearing, I felt again that crawling in my brain. Since then I have frequently caught myself seeking persons gullible enough to be lured to the clearing, but always I have been able to fight off such impulses. I do not know how long I can continue to fight – and so I am going to use the one method to end this unholy preying on my mind.

The sun has sunk below the horizon now, leaving only a lurid glow which shines on the razor lying on the table before me. Perhaps it is only imagination which makes me seem to feel a restless, blinding stirring in my brain – at any rate, I must hesitate no longer. It may be that the insects will eventually overpower the world; but I will have done all that is possible for me to do to prevent the release of that whose shape I once glimpsed, and which still awaits impatiently the opening of the multi-dimensional gate.

THE RENDER OF THE VEILS

At midnight the last bus to Brichester had gone, and it was raining heavily. Kevin Gillson bitterly considered standing under the marquee of the nearby cinema until morning, but the high wind was driving the rain under it so that it provided no shelter. He turned the collar of his raincoat up as water began to ooze down his neck, and slowly walked up the hill away from the bus stop.

The streets were virtually deserted; a few cars which passed did not respond to his signals. Very few of the houses he passed were even lit; it depressed him to walk along the wet-black pavement which reflected wavering images of street lamps back at him. He met only one other person – a silent figure leaning in the shadow of a doorway. Only the red glow from a cigarette persuaded Gillson that anyone was there at all.

At the corner of Gaunt and Ferrey Streets he saw a vehicle approaching him. Half-dazzled by the reflection of the headlights, he made out that it was a taxi, travelling the streets for a final passenger of the night. He waved the bedraggled *Camside Observer* he was still clutching, and the taxi drew to a stop beside him.

'Are you still taking passengers?' he yelled through the partition.

'I was goin' home,' called back the driver. 'Still – if you've got some way to go – I wouldn't want you walkin' the streets on a night like this. Where to?'

Gillson ordered 'Brichester,' and made to get in. At that moment, however, he heard a voice calling something nearby; and turning, he saw a figure running through the rain towards the taxi. From the cigarette between his fingers and the direction from which he had come, Gillson guessed that this was the man he had noticed in the doorway.

'Wait – please wait!' the man was shouting. He clattered up to the taxi, splashing Gillson in the process. 'Would you mind if I shared your taxi? If you're in a hurry, it doesn't matter – but if I take you out of your way, I'll pay the difference. I don't know how I'll get home otherwise, though I don't live far from here.'

'Where *do* you live?' Gillson asked cautiously. 'I'm not in any hurry, but – '

'On Tudor Drive,' the man replied eagerly.

'Oh, that's on the way to Brichester, isn't it?' said Gillson, relieved. 'Sure, get in – we'll both catch pneumonia if we stand here much longer.'

Once in the taxi, Gillson directed the driver and sat back. He did not feel like talking, and decided to read a book, hoping the other would take a hint. He took out the copy of *Witchcraft Today* he had bought on a bookstall that morning and flipped the pages a little.

He was just beginning a chapter when a voice broke in on him. 'Do you believe in that stuff?'

'This, you mean?' Gillson suggested resignedly, tapping the cover of the book. 'In a way, yes – I suppose these people believed that dancing naked and spitting on crucifixes would benefit them. Rather childish, though – they were all psychopathic, of course.'

'Fit to be consigned to a lurid book like that, I'd say,' agreed the other.

There was silence for a few minutes, and Gillson contemplated returning to the book. He opened it again and read the suitably garish blurb inside the cover, then put it down irritably as a trickle of water ran down his sleeve on to the page. He wiped this, then felt beside him for the book.

'But do you know what was behind all these witch-cults?'

'How do you mean?' Gillson inquired, leaving his book where it was.

'Do you know about the *real* cults?' continued the voice. 'Not the medieval servants of Satan – the ones who worship gods that exist?'

'It depends what you mean by "gods that exist",' replied Gillson.

The man did not appear to notice this remark. 'They formed these cults because they were searching for something. Perhaps you have read some of their books – you won't find them on the stalls like you did that one, but they are preserved in a few museums.'

'Well, I was once down in London, and I took a look at what they had in the British Museum.'

'The *Necronomicon*, I suppose.' He seemed almost amused. 'And what did you think of it?'

'I found it rather disturbing,' Gillson confessed, 'but not as horrifying as I'd been led to expect. But then I couldn't understand all of it.'

'Personally, I thought it was ludicrous,' the other told him, 'so vague . . . But of course if it had described what's only hinted at in there, no museum would touch it. I suppose it's best that only we few know . . . Forgive me, you must think me queer. Come to think of it, you don't even know who I am. I'm Henry Fisher, and I suppose you could call me an occultist.'

'No, please go on,' said Gillson. 'What you were saying there interested me.'

'What, about people searching for things? Why, are you searching for something?'

'Not really, though I have had a sort of persistent conviction since I was young. Nothing to bother about, really – just a kind of idea that nothing is really as we see it: if there were some way of seeing things without using your eyes, everything would look quite different. Weird, isn't it?'

When no answer came, he turned. There was a strange expression in Henry Fisher's eyes; a look of surprised triumph. Noticing Gillson's puzzlement, he seemed to control himself, and remarked:

'It's queer you should say that. I've had the same idea for a long time, and quite often I've been on the brink of finding a way to prove it. You see, there *is* a way to see as you would without using your eyes, even though you're actually using them – but not only can it be dangerous, it needs two people. It might be interesting for us to try . . . But here's where I get out.'

They had drawn up before a block of flats. Behind dripping trees a concrete path stretched to where yellow-and-black-painted windows mounted upward. 'Mine's on the ground floor,' Fisher remarked as he got out and paid the driver.

Gillson rolled the window down. 'Wait a minute,' he said. 'Did you mean it – what you said about seeing things as they really are?'

'Are you interested?' Fisher bent down and peered into the taxi. 'Remember I told you it might be dangerous.'

'I don't mind,' replied Gillson, opening the door and getting out. He waved the driver to leave, and it was not until they were standing and watching the tail-lights dwindle that he remembered he had left his book on the seat.

Although the trees still dripped, it had stopped raining. The two men walked up the concrete path, and the wind eddied around them, seeming to blow down from the frosty stars. Kevin Gillson was glad when they closed the glass doors behind them and entered a flowery-papered hall. Stairs led upward to other flats, but Fisher turned to a door to the left with glass panels.

Gillson had not really expected anything specific, but what he saw beyond that glass-panelled door amazed him. It was a normal living-room, with contemporary furnishings, modernistic wallpaper, an electric fire; but some of the objects in it were not at all normal. Reproductions of paintings by Bosch, Clark Ashton Smith and Dali set the abnormal mood, which was augmented by the esoteric books occupying a case in one corner. But these could at least be found elsewhere; some of the other things he had never seen before. He could make nothing of the egg-shaped object which lay on the table in the centre of the room and emitted a strange, intermittent whistling. Nor did he recognize the outlines of something which stood on a pedestal in a corner, draped with a canvas.

'Perhaps I should have warned you,' Fisher broke in. 'I suppose it's not quite what you'd expect from the outside. Anyway, sit down, and I'll get you some coffee while I explain a little. And let's have the tape-recorder on – I want it running later so it can record our experiment.'

He went into the kitchen, and Gillson heard pans rattling. Over the clanking Fisher called:

'I was a rather peculiar kid, you know – very sensitive but oddly strong-stomached. After I saw a gargoyle once in church I used to dream it was chasing me, but one time when a dog was run over outside our home the neighbours all remarked how avidly I was staring at it.

My parents once called in a doctor, and he said I was "very morbid, and should be kept away from anything likely to affect me." As if they could!

'Well, it was at grammar school that I got this idea – in the Physics class, actually. We were studying the structure of the eye one day, and I got to thinking about it. The more I looked at this diagram of retinas and humors and lenses, the more I was convinced that what we see through such a complicated system must be distorted in some way. It's all very well saying that what forms on the retina is simply an image, no more distorted than it would be through a telescope. That's too glib for me. I almost stood up and told the teacher what I thought, but I knew I'd be laughed down.

'I didn't think much more about it till I got to the University. Then I got talking to one of the students one day – Taylor, his name was – and before I knew it I'd joined a witch-cult. Not your naked decadents, but one that really knew how to tap elemental powers. I could tell you a lot about what we did, but some of the things would take too long to explain. Tonight I want to try the experiment, but perhaps afterwards I'll tell you about the things I know. Things like what the unused part of the brain can be used for, and what's buried in a graveyard not far from here . . .

'Anyway, some time after I joined, the cult was exposed, and everybody was expelled. Luckily I wasn't at the meeting that was spied on, so I stayed on. Even better, though, some of them decided to give sorcery up entirely; and I persuaded one of them to give me all his books. Among them was the *Revelations of Glaaki*, and that was where I read of the process I want to try tonight. I read of this.'

Fisher had entered the living-room, carrying a tray on

which were two cups and a pot of coffee. Now he crossed the room to where the object stood veiled on a pedestal, and as Gillson leaned forward, pulled the canvas off.

Kevin Gillson could only stare. The object was not shapeless, but so complex that the eye could recognize no describable shape. There were hemispheres and shining metal, coupled by long plastic rods. The rods were of a flat grey colour, so that he could not make out which were nearer; they merged into a flat mass from which protruded individual cylinders. As he looked at it, he had a curious feeling that eyes gleamed from between the rods; but wherever he glanced at the construction, he saw only the spaces between them. The strangest part was that he felt this was an image of something *living* – something from a dimension where such an example of abnormal geometry could live. As he turned to speak to Fisher, he saw out of the corner of his eye that the thing had expanded and occupied almost the whole side of the room – but when he swung back, the image, of course, was the same size. At least, he was sure it was – but Gillson could not even be sure how high it had originally been.

'So you're getting illusions of size?' Fisher had noticed his puzzlement. 'That's because it's only the three-dimensional extension of the actual thing – of course in its own dimension it looks nothing like that.'

'But what is it?' asked Gillson impatiently.

'That,' said Fisher, 'is an image of Daoloth – the Render of the Veils.'

He went over to the table where he had placed the tray. Pouring the coffee, he passed a cup to Gillson, who then remarked:

'You'll have to explain that in a minute, but first I thought of something while you were in there. I'd have mentioned it before, only I didn't feel like arguing between rooms. It's all very well saying that what we see is distorted – say this table really isn't rectangular and flat at all. But when I touch it I feel a flat rectangular surface – how do you explain that?'

'Simple tactile hallucination,' explained Fisher. 'That's why I say this might be dangerous. You see, you don't really feel a flat rectangular surface there at all – but because you see it the way you do, your mind deludes you into thinking you feel the counterpart of your vision. Only sometimes I think – why would the mind set up such a system of delusion? Could it be that if we were to see ourselves as we *really* are, it might be too much for us?'

'Look, you want to see the undistorted thing,' Gillson said, 'and so do I. Don't try and put me against it now, for God's sake, just when you've got me interested. You called *that* Daoloth – what's it mean?'

'Well, I'll have to go off at what may seem a tangent,' apologized Fisher. 'You've been looking at that yellow egg-shaped thing there, off and on, ever since you came in – you've read of them in the *Necronomicon*. Remember those references to the Crystallizers of Dream? That's one of them – the device that projects you when asleep into other dimensions. It takes a bit of getting used to, but for some years I've been able to enter nearly every dimension as high as the twenty-fifth. If only I could convey to you the sensations of that last plane, where it is the space which exists and matter can have no existence! Don't ask me where I got the Crystallizer, by the way – until I can be sure its guardian will not follow, I must never speak of it. But never mind that.

'After I read in the *Revelations of Glaaki* about the way to prove this idea of mine, I determined to see for myself what I would be invoking. It was mostly trial and error; but finally, one night, I found myself materializing in a place I'd never been before. There were walls and columns so high I couldn't even see where they ended, and in the middle of the floor was a great fissure running from wall to wall, jagged as if from an earthquake. As I watched, the outlines of the crack seemed to dim and blur, and something rose up out of it. I told you that image looks very different in its own dimension – well, I saw the living counterpart, and you'll understand if I don't try to describe it. It stood there swaying for a moment and then began to expand. It would have engulfed me in a few minutes, but I didn't wait for that. I ran off between the columns.

'I didn't get far before a group of men stepped out in front of me. They were dressed in metallic robes and hoods, and carried small images of what I'd seen, so that I knew they were its priests. The foremost asked me why I had come into their world, and I explained that I hoped to call on Daoloth's aid in seeing beyond the veils. They glanced at each other, and then one of them passed me the image he was carrying. "You'll need this," he told me. "It serves as a link, and you won't come across any on your world." Then the whole scene vanished, and I found myself lying in bed – but I was holding that image you see there.'

'But you haven't really told me – ' began Gillson.

'I'm coming to that now. You know now where I got that image. However, you're wondering what it has to do with tonight's experiment, and what Daoloth is anyway?

'Daoloth is a god – an alien god. He was worshipped in Atlantis, where he was the god of the astrologers. I presume it was there that his mode of worship on Earth was set up: he must never be seen, for the eye tries to follow the convolutions of his shape, and that causes insanity. That's why there must be no light when he is invoked – when we call on him later tonight, we'll have to switch out all the lights. Even that there is a deliberately inaccurate replica of him; it has to be.

'As for why we're invoking Daoloth, on Yuggoth and Tond he's known as the Render of the Veils, and that title has a lot of meaning. There his priests cannot only see the past and future – they can see how objects extend into the last dimension. That's why if we invoke him and hold him by the Pentacle of Planes, we can get his aid in cutting out the distortion. And that's about all the explanation I can give you now. It's almost 2:30 already and we must be ready by 2:45; that's when the openings will align . . . Of course, if you don't feel like going ahead, please tell me now. But I don't want to get everything into place for nothing.'

'I'll stay,' Gillson told him, but he glanced at the image of Daoloth a little uneasily.

'All right. Give me a hand here, will you?'

Fisher opened a cupboard door next to the bookcase. Gillson saw several large crates, set in neat order and marked with painted symbols. He held one up as Fisher slid another from beneath it. As he closed the door, Gillson heard the other lifting the lid; and when he turned, Fisher was already laying the contents out on the floor. An assortment of plastic surfaces came to light, which were assembled into a distorted sem-solid pentagram; and it was followed by two black candles formed into vaguely obscene shapes, a metal rod carrying an icon, and a skull. That skull disturbed Gillson; holes had been bored in its cranium to hold the candles, but even so he could tell from its shape and lack of mouth that it had not been human.

Fisher now began to arrange the objects. First he pushed chairs and tables against the walls, then shoved the pentagram into the centre of the floor. As he placed the skull, now carrying the candles, inside the pentagram, and lit the candles, Gillson asked behind him:

'I thought you said we mustn't have any light – what about those, then?'

'Don't worry – they won't illuminate anything,' Fisher explained. 'When Daoloth comes, he'll draw the light from them – it makes the alignment of the openings easier.'

As he turned to switch the lights out, he remarked over his shoulder: 'He'll appear in the pentacle, and his solid three-dimensional materialization will remain in there all the time. However, he'll put forth two-dimensional extensions into the room, and you may feel these – so don't be afraid. You see, he'll take a little blood from both of us.' His hand moved closer to the switch.

'What? You never said anything – '

'It's all right,' Fisher assured him. 'He takes blood from any that call him; it seems to be his way of testing their intentions. But it won't be much. He'll take more from me, because I'm the priest – you're only here so I can draw on your vitality to open the path through for him. Certainly it won't hurt.' And without waiting for further protests, he switched off the lights.

There was a little light from the neon sign of the garage outside the window, but hardly any filtered through the curtains. The black candles were very dim, too, and Gillson could make out nothing beyond the pentagram, from his position by the bookcase. He was startled when his host slammed the icon-bearing rod on the floor and began to shout hysterically. 'Uthgos plam'f Daoloth asgu'i – come, o Thou who sweepest the veils of sight aside, and showest the realities beyond.' There was much more, but Gillson did not notice it specially. He was watching the luminous mist which appeared to arch from both him and Fisher, and enter the misshapen cranium of the skull in the pentacle. By the end of the incantation there was a definite aura around the two men and the skull. He watched it in fascination; and then Fisher ceased speaking.

For a minute nothing happened. Then the arcs of mist vanished, and there was only the light of the candles; but they glowed brighter now, and a misty aura surrounded them. As Gillson looked at them, the twin flames began to dim, and suddenly winked out. For a moment a *black* flame seemed to replace each – a sort of negative fire – and as quickly it was gone. At the same moment Gillson knew that he and Fisher were not alone in the room.

He heard a dry rustling from the pentacle, and sensed a shape moving there. At once he was surrounded. Dry, impossibly light things touched his face, and something slid between his lips. No spot on his body was touched for long enough for him to snatch at what felt at him; so quickly did they pass that he remembered rather than sensed the touching feelers. But when the rustling returned to the centre of the room, there was a salt taste in his mouth – and he knew that the feeler entering his mouth had tapped his blood.

Above the rustling, Fisher called: 'Now Thou hast tasted of our blood, Thou knowest our intentions. The Pentagram of Planes shall hold Thee until Thou shalt do what we desire – to rend the veil of belief and show us the realities of unveiled existence. Wilt Thou show it, and thus release Thyself?'

The rustling increased. Gillson wished the ritual would end; his eyes were becoming accustomed to the glow from the garage sign, and even now he could almost see a faint writhing in the darkness within the figure.

Suddenly there was a violent outburst of discordant metal scraping, and the entire building shook. The sound whirred into silence, and Gillson knew that the pentacle's tenant had gone. The room was still dark; the candlelight had not returned, and his sight could not yet penetrate the blackness.

Fisher said from his position by the door: 'Well, he's gone – and that figure is constructed so he couldn't go back without doing what I asked. So when I turn on the light you'll see everything as it *really* is. Now if you feel your way, you'll find a pair of eyepatches on top of the bookcase. Put them on and you won't be able to see anything – that's if you don't want to go through with it. Then I can turn the light on and see all I want to see, and then use the icon to nullify the effect. Would you rather do it that way?'

'I've come all this way with you,' Gillson reminded him, 'and it wasn't to get scared at the last moment.'

'Do you want to see now? You know once you've seen, the tactile delusions won't ever operate again – are you sure you can live with it?'

'For God's sake, yes!' Gillson's answer was barely audible.

'All right. I'm turning on the lights – *now*!'

When the police arrived at the flats on Tudor Street, where they had been summoned by a hysterical tenant, they found a scene which horrified the least squeamish among them. The tenant, returning from a late party, had only seen Kevin Gillson's corpse lying on the carpet, stabbed to death. The police were not sickened by this, however, but by what they found on the lawn under the broken front window; for Henry Fisher had died there, with his throat torn out by glass slivers from the pane.

It all seemed very extraordinary, and the tape-recorder did not help. All that it definitely told them was that some kind of black magic ritual had been practised that night, and they guessed that Gillson had been killed with the pointed end of the icon rod. The rest of the tape was full of esoteric references, and towards the end it becomes totally incoherent. The section after the click of the light-switch on the recording is what puzzles listeners most; as yet nobody has found any sane reason for Fisher's murder of his guest.

When curious detectives play the tape, Fisher's voice always comes: 'There – hell, I can't see after all that darkness. Now, what . . .

'My God, where am I? And where are you? Gillson, where are you – *where are you?* No, keep away – Gillson, for Christ's sake move your arm. I can see something moving in all this – but God, *that mustn't be you* . . . Why can't I hear you – but this is enough to strike anyone dumb . . . . Now come towards me – my God, that thing *is* you – expanding – contracting – the primal jelly, forming and changing – and the colour . . . Get away! Don't come any closer – are you mad? If you dare to touch me, I'll let you have the point of this icon – it may feel wet and spongy and look – horrible – but it'll do for you! No, don't touch me – I can't bear to feel that – '

Then comes a scream and a thud. An outburst of insane screaming is cut short by the smashing glass, and a terrible choking sound soon fades to nothing.

It is amazing that two men should have seemingly deluded themselves into thinking they had changed physically; but such is the case, for the two corpses were quite unchanged except for their mutilations. Nothing in the case cannot be explained by the insanity of the two men.

At least, there is one anomaly; but the chief of the Camside police is certain that it is only a fault in the tape which causes the recorder to emit, at certain points, a loud dry rustling sound.

THE INHABITANT OF THE LAKE

After my friend Thomas Cartwright had moved into the Severn valley for suitable surroundings in which to work on his macabre artwork, our only communication was through correspondence. He usually wrote only to inform me of the trivial happenings which occur in a part of the countryside ten miles from the nearest inhabited dwelling, or to tell me how his latest painting was progressing. It was, then, somewhat of a departure from the habitual when he wrote to tell me of certain events – seemingly trivial but admittedly puzzling – which culminated in a series of unexpected revelations.

Cartwright had been interested in the lore of the terrible ever since his youth, and when he began to study art his work immediately exhibited an extremely startling morbid technique. Before long, specimens were shown to dealers, who commended his paintings highly, but doubted that they would appeal to the normal collector, because of their great morbidity. However, Cartwright's work has since been recognized, and many aficionados now seek originals of his powerful studies of the alien, which depict distorted colossi striding across mist-enshrouded jungles or peering round the dripping stones of some druidic circle. When he did begin to achieve recognition, Cartwright decided to settle somewhere which would have a more fitting atmosphere than the clanging London streets, and accordingly set out on a search through the Severn area for likely sites. When I could, I accompanied him; and it was on one of the journeys when we were together that an estate agent at Brichester told him of a lonely row of six houses near a lake some miles to the north of the town, which he might be interested in, since it was supposed to be haunted.

We found the lake easily enough from his directions, and for some minutes we stood gazing at the scene. The ebon depths of the stagnant water were surrounded by forest, which marched down a number of surrounding hills and stood like an army of prehistoric survivals at the edge. On the south side of the lake was a row of black-walled houses, each three storeys high. They stood on a grey cobbled street which began and ended at the extremities of the row, the other edge disappearing into the pitchy depths. A road of sorts circled the lake, branching from that patch of street and joining the road to Brichester at the other side of the lake. Large ferns protruded from the water, while grass grew luxuriantly among the trees and at the edge of the lake. Although it was midday, little light reached the surface of the water or touched the house-fronts, and the whole place brooded in a twilight more depressing because of the recollection of sunlight beyond.

'Looks like the place was stricken with a plague,' Cartwright observed as we set out across the beaded stones of the segment of road. This comparison had occurred to me also, and I wondered if my companion's morbid trait might be affecting me. Certainly the desertion of this forest-guarded hollow did not evoke peaceful images, and I could almost visualize the nearby woods as a primeval jungle where vast horrors stalked and killed. But while I was sympathetic with Cartwright's feelings, I did not feel pleasure at the thought of working there – as he probably did – rather dreading the idea of living in such an uninhabited region, though I could not have said why I found those blank house-fronts so disquieting.

'Might as well start at this end of the row,' I suggested, pointing to the left. 'Makes no difference as far as I can see, anyway – how are you going to decide which one to take? Lucky numbers or what? If you take any, of course . . .'

We had reached the first building on the left, and as we stood at the window I could only stare and repeat 'If any.' There were gaping holes in the bare floorboards in that room, and the stone fireplace was cracked and cobwebbed. Only the opposite wall seemed to be papered, and the yellowed paper had peeled off in great strips. The two wooden steps which led up to the front door with its askew knocker shifted alarmingly as I put my foot on the lower, and I stepped back in disgust.

Cartwright had been trying to clear some of the dust from the window-pane, but now he left the window and approached me, grimacing. 'I told him I was an artist,' he said, 'but that estate agent must think that means I live in the woods or something! My God, how long is it since anyone lived in one of these?'

'Perhaps the others may be better?' I guessed hopefully.

'Look, you can see from here they're all as bad,' complained Cartwright.

His complaint was quite true. The houses were very similar, surprisingly because they seemed to have been added to at various periods, as if they were always treated alike; all had unsightly stone roofs, there were signs that they might once have been half-timbered, they had a kind of bay window facing on to the street, and to the door of each led the creaking wooden steps. Although, now I came to stand back, and look up the row, the third from the left did not look as uninviting as the others. The wooden steps had been replaced by three concrete stairs, and I thought I saw a doorbell in place of the tarnished knocker. The windows were not so grimy, either, even though the walls were still grey and moist. From where I stood the lake's dim reflection prevented me from seeing into the house.

I pointed it out to Cartwright. 'That one doesn't look so bad.'

'I don't see much difference,' he grumbled, but moved boredly towards it.

'Well, the estate agent gave you one key to what he said was the only locked house – that must be the one.'

The house was indeed locked, and the key fitted – opening the door easily, which surprised us because of the rustiness of the other locks. On the other hand, the door did not look unpainted or dirty close up; it was merely the artificial twilight which made everything grey. Still, we were not expecting the clean wallpaper in the hallway, and still less the lampshades and stair carpet. The light went on as Cartwright touched the switch inside the door, destroying the dimness, and as I looked up the stairs I thought something peculiar was visible through the open bedroom door at the top.

'*Look* at this lot!' he was saying from where he peered into the first room off the hall. 'Carpet, table, chairs – what the hell's happened? What could have made anyone leave all this here – or is it included in the price or what?'

'It did say "furnished" in the estate agent's window,' I told him.

'Even so – ' We were in the kitchen now, where a stove stood next to a kitchen cabinet. From there we went upstairs and found, as I had thought, a bed still standing, though bare of blankets, in the bedroom and the landing. The whole house, notwithstanding the outside, was almost as one would expect a Brichester house to be if the occupants had just gone out.

'Of course I'll take it,' Cartwright said as we descended. 'The interior's very nice, and the surroundings are exactly what I need for inspiration. But I *do* intend to get to the bottom of why all this furniture's included first.'

Cartwright had not risked skidding into the lake by driving over the slippery cobbles; the car was parked at the end of the Brichester road where it reached the lakeside street. He turned it and we drove leisurely back to town. Although usually I like to be in the country away from civilization, I was rather glad when we reached the area of telegraph-poles and left behind those roads between sheer rock surfaces or above forested hillsides. Somehow all this had an aura of desolation which was not relieved until we began to descend the hill above Brichester, and I welcomed the sight of red-brick houses and steeples which surround the central white University building.

The estate agent's was among the cluster of similar buildings at the western end of Bold Street. As we entered, I noticed again that the postcard advertising the houses by the lake was almost hidden in the upper corner of the window. I had meant to point this out to Cartwright, but that could wait until later.

'Oh, yes,' the estate agent said, looking up from a pile of brochures on the counter. 'You two gentlemen went to view the lakeside property . . . . Well – does it interest you?' His look made it obvious what answer was expected, and Cartwright's 'Yes – where do I sign?' visibly startled him. In fact, he seemed to suspect a joke.

'£500 is the price on the repaired one, I think,' Cartwright continued. 'If you'd like to fix things up, I'll move in as soon as you give the word. I can't say it looks haunted to me, even if that *does* explain the price – still, so much the better for inspiration if it is, eh, Alan?'

He turned back as the man behind the counter spoke. 'I'll put the deal through for you, and drop you a line when it's done.'

'Thanks. Oh, just one thing – ' a look of resignation crossed the other's face ' – who left all the furniture?'

'The other tenants. They moved out about three weeks ago and left it all.'

'Well, three weeks is a bit long,' conceded Cartwright, 'but mightn't they still come back for it?'

'I had a letter about a week after they left,' explained the estate agent ' – they left during the night, you know – and he said they wouldn't come back even in daylight for the stuff they'd left! They were very well off, anyway – don't really know why they wanted to take a house like that in the first place – '

'Did he say why they went off in such a hurry?' I interrupted.

'Oh, some rigmarole that didn't make sense,' said the agent uncomfortably. 'They had a kid, you know, and there was a lot about how he kept waking them up in the night screaming about something "coming up out of the lake" and "looking in at the window." Well, I suppose that was all a bit harassing, even if he was only dreaming, but that wasn't what scared him off. Apparently the wife found the writer of this letter out about eleven o'clock one night a fortnight after they came – that's as long as they stayed – staring into the water. He didn't see her, and nearly fainted when she touched his arm. Then he just loaded everything there was room for into the car, and drove off without letting her know even why they were going.

'He didn't tell her at all, and didn't really tell me. All he said in the letter was that he saw *something at the bottom of the lake, looking at him and trying to come up* . . . Told me to try to get the lake filled in and the houses pulled down, but of course my job's to sell the place, not destroy it.'

'Then you're not doing it very well,' I remarked.

'But you said you'd rather have a haunted house,' protested the agent, looking hurt as if someone had tricked him.

'Of course I did,' Cartwright reassured him. 'Kearney here's just a bit touchy, that's all. If you let me know when everything's ready, I'll be happy to move in.'

Cartwright was not returning to London, and as I wanted to get back that day, he offered to run me across town to Lower Brichester Station. As we passed between the stores and approached the railway, I was deep in thought – thoughts of my friend's living alone in that twilit clearing ten miles outside Brichester. When we drew up in the taxi-rank, I could not leave him without yelling above the echoes of the station:

'Sure you don't want to look round a bit more before you come to live here? I don't much like the look of that place so far away from everything – might prey on your mind after a few weeks.'

'Good God above, Alan,' he remonstrated, 'you were the one who insisted on looking at all the houses when I wanted to leave. Well, I've got it now – and as for preying on my mind, that sort of place is just what I need for inspiration.' He seemed offended, for he slammed the door and drove away without farewell. I could only enter the station and try to forget that shrine of desolation in the mindless echoes of the terminus.

For some weeks afterwards I did not see Cartwright at

all, and my job at the Inland Revenue was so exacting that I could not spare the time to call at his home. At the end of the third week, however, things slackened at my office, and I drove up from Hoddesdon, where I live, to see if he had yet left. I was only just in time, for two cars were parked outside his house on Elizabeth Street; in one was Cartwright and a number of his paintings while behind it his friend Joseph Bulger was bringing out easels, paints and some furniture. They were ready to move off as I arrived, but Cartwright stopped to talk for a few minutes.

'I've got rid of most of the furniture at this end,' he told me. 'Might as well use what that family left, but there were one or two things I wanted to keep. Well, it's a pity you can't call round at weekends any more – anyway, maybe you could come down at Christmas or sometime like that, and I'll write you when I get settled in.'

Again I heard nothing from him for a few weeks. When I met Bulger on the street he told me that Cartwright had shown every sign of enjoyment when left in the lakeside house, and had announced his intention of beginning to paint that night, if possible. He did not expect to hear from Cartwright for some time, as once he began work on a picture he would let nothing distract him.

It was about a month later that he first wrote. His letter contained nothing extraordinary, yet as I look back on it I can see in almost everything intimations of things to come.

> Thomas Cartwright,
> Lakeside Terrace,
> c/o Bold St Post Office,
> Brichester, Glos.
> 3 October 1960

Dear Alan:

(Notice the address – the postman doesn't come anywhere near here, and I've got to go up to Bold Street every week and collect on a poste restante basis.)

Well, I've settled in here. It's very comfortable, except it's a bit inconvenient having the toilet on the third floor; I may have that altered one day – the place has been altered so much that more won't make any difference. My studio's upstairs, too, but I sleep downstairs as usual. I decided to move the table out to the back room, and between us we managed to get the bed into the front room, facing on to the lake.

After Joe left I went for a walk round. Took a glance into the other houses – you've no idea how inviting mine looks with all the lights on in the middle of those deserted shacks! I can't imagine anyone coming to live in them again. One of these days I really must go in and see what I can find – perhaps the rats which everyone took for 'ghosts.'

But about this business of haunting, something just struck me. Was what that family said they saw the first hint of the supernatural round here – because if it was, *why* are the other houses so dilapidated? It's all very well saying that they're so far away from everything, but they've been altered right and left, as you saw. Certainly at one time they were frequently inhabited, so why did people stop coming? Must tackle the estate agent about this.

When I'd finished peering round the houses, I felt like a walk. I found what looked like a path through the woods behind the house, so I followed it. I won't try *that* again in a hurry! – there was practically no light in there, the trees just went on into the distance as far as I could see, and if I'd gone much farther in I'd certainly have been lost. You could picture it – stumbling on and on into the dark, nothing to see except trees, closing in on every side . . . And to think those people brought a kid here!

Just finished my new painting. It shows these houses, with the lake in the foreground, and the bloated body of a drowned man at the edge of the water – *Relentless Plague*, I think. I hope they like it.

Yours, Thomas

P.S. Been having nightmares lately. Can never remember what they're about, but I always wake up sweating.

I wrote back an inconsequential reply. I deplored the macabre nature of his latest work – as I had always done – although, as I said, 'no doubt it will be appreciated for its technique.' I offered to buy anything he might be unable to get in Brichester, and made a few uninspired observations on life in Hoddesdon. Also, I think, I remarked: 'So you're having nightmares? Remember that the business with the last owners began with their boy having dreams.'

Cartwright replied:

10 October 1960

You don't know how lucky you are, having a post-box almost on your doorstep! My nearest one's nearly four miles away, and I get out there only on my way to Brichester, on Mondays and Saturdays – which means I have to write letters on Monday morning (as I'm doing now) or Sunday, and collect the replies on Saturday up at Bold Street.

Anyway, that's not what I wanted to write to you about. I've gone and left some sketches in a cupboard in the studio of the Elizabeth Street house, and I was wondering if you could drop round there and perhaps drive up with them. If you can't, maybe you could call on Joe Bulger and get him to bring them up here. I'm sorry to be such a hell of a nuisance, but I can't do one of my paintings without them.

Yours, Thomas

My job was again very demanding, and I replied that I could not possibly leave town for some weeks. I could not very well refuse to contact Bulger, and on Wednesday evening on my way home from work I detoured to his house. Luckily, he had not left for his weekly cinema jaunt, and he invited me in, offering me a drink. I would have stayed longer, but my job was consuming even spare time, so I said:

'This isn't really a social call. I'm afraid I'm passing you a job which was detailed to me. You see, Cartwright wanted me to collect some drawings from his London studio in a cupboard, but my job's getting in the way – you know what it can be like. So if you could do it for me, and take a train down there with them . . . ?'

Bulger looked a little reluctant, but he only said: 'All right – I'll try and save your face. I hope he doesn't want them in a desperate hurry – I'll be able to get them to him within the week.'

I got up to leave. At the door I remarked: 'Better you than me. You may have a bit of trouble in Elizabeth Street, because someone new's already moved in there.'

'You didn't tell me *that* before,' he protested. 'No, it's all right, I'll still go – even though I don't much like the idea of going to that lake.'

'How do you mean?' I asked. 'Something you don't like down there?'

Bulger shrugged. 'Nothing I could put my finger on, but I certainly wouldn't like to live down there alone. There's something about those trees growing so close, and that black water – as if there were things watching, and *waiting* . . . but you must think me crazy. There *is* one point, though – why were those houses built so far from everywhere? By that lake, too – I mean, it's hardly the first place you'd think of if you were going to build a row of houses. Who'd be likely to live there?'

As I drove back to Hoddesdon I thought about this. Nobody except someone seeking morbid inspiration, such as Cartwright, would live in such a place – and surely such people were not numerous. I planned to mention this to him in my next letter; perhaps he would discover something thus of why the houses had become untenanted. But as it happened, I was forestalled, as I discovered from his letter of the following Sunday.

16 October 1960

Well, Joe's come and gone. He couldn't get into my studio at first – the new people thought he made it all up so he could get in and steal the silver! Anyway, the Walkers next door knew him, so he finally got my sketches.

He was wondering why these houses were built in the first place. I don't know either – it never struck me before, but now I come to think about it I must find out sometime. Maybe I'll ask that estate agent about it next time I'm up Bold Street way. This may tell me why the places got so dilapidated, too. I get the idea that a band of murderers (or highwaymen, perhaps) could have operated from here, living off the passers-by; sort of *L'Auberge Rouge* stuff.

Joe left this afternoon . . . Sorry for the break, but actually I just broke off writing because I thought I heard a noise outside. Of course it must have been a mistake. Nobody could possibly be out there at this time (11 P.M.) – Joe left about seven hours back – but I could have sworn that somebody was yelling in the distance a few minutes ago; there was a sort of high-pitched throbbing, too, like an engine of some sort. I even thought that there was something white – well, a few white objects – moving on the other side of the lake; but of course it's too dark to see anything so far off. Certainly a lot of splashing began in the water about the same time, and it's only just dying down as I write this.

I'd still like you to come down for a few days. Christmas is getting near – maybe . . . ?

Yours, Thomas

I was rather disturbed that he should imagine sounds in such a lonely area, and said as much. Although I, like Bulger, did not relish the idea of going to that half-lit woodland lake, I thought it might be best for me to visit Cartwright when I could, if only so he could talk to me and forget his pocket of desolation. There was less work for me now at the Inland Revenue, but it would be some weeks before I could visit him. Perhaps Bulger's call had lessened his introspection a little, though from his latest

imaginings it did not seem so. I told him of my proposed
stay with him when I wrote that Thursday.

His reply which I received on the 25th I believe to be
the first real hint of what Cartwright unwittingly brought
on himself.

24 October 1960

Haven't had time to get down to Bold Street yet, but I want
to find out about these houses all the more now.

However, that's not really why I wanted to write to you.
Remember I kept on about these nightmares which I could
never remember? Well, last night I had a series of long dreams,
which I remembered on waking. They were certainly terrifying
– no wonder I kept waking up sweating, and no wonder that kid
kept screaming in the night if he had the same dreams! But
what am I saying – that's hardly likely, is it?

Last night I went to bed around midnight. I left the window
open, and I noticed a lot of splashing and disturbance on the
surface of the lake. Funny, that – there was hardly any wind
after 6 o'clock. Still I think all that noise may have caused my
dreams.

My dream began in the hall. I was going out the front door –
seemed to remember saying goodbye to someone, who I don't
know, and seeing the door close. I went down the steps and
across the pavement round the lake. Why I can't imagine, I
passed the car and began to walk up the Brichester road. I
wanted to get into Brichester, but not in any hurry. I had a
peculiar feeling that someone should have driven me there . . .
Come to think, that's the way Joe must have felt last week! He
had to walk to Brichester, because I was right out of petrol and
the nearest garage is a few miles down the road.

A few yards out of the glade I noticed a footpath leading off
among the trees to the left of the road. That's the direct way to
Brichester – at least, it would be if it kept on in its original
direction – for the motor road curves a good deal. While I
wasn't in a hurry, I didn't see why I should walk further than
necessary, so I turned off the road on to the path. I felt a bit
uneasy, heaven knows why – I wouldn't normally. The trees

were very close and not much light got through, so that might have contributed to the feeling. It was very quiet, too, and when I kicked loose stones out of the way the sound startled me.

I suppose it must have been about fifty yards in that I realized the path wouldn't take me back to Brichester at all if it kept on the way it was tending. In fact, it was curving back to the lake – or at least following the lake shore, I'd guess with about twenty yards of forested ground between the path and the open shore. I went a few yards further to make sure; it was definitely curving round the lake. I turned to go back – and glimpsed a blue glow a little ahead. I didn't know what to make of it, and didn't particularly like the idea of going closer; but I'd time to spare, so I conquered this irrational fear (which normally I'd never feel) and went forward.

The path widened a little, and at the centre of the wider space stood an oblong piece of stone. It was about seven feet long, two wide and three high, and it was cut out of some phosphorescent stone which gave out the blue light. On top were inscribed some words too worn away to be legible, and at the foot of the writing the name 'Thos. Lee' was roughly chipped. I wasn't sure whether it was a solid piece of stone or not – a groove ran round the sides about two inches from the top which might have denoted a lid. I didn't know what it was, but immediately I got the idea that there were others along the path. Determined to see if this were true, I walked away up the path – but with my determination was mixed an odd unaccustomed fear of what I was doing.

Twenty yards on or so I thought I heard a sound behind me – first a hollow sliding, then what sounded like measured footsteps following me. I looked back with a shiver, but the bend in the path blocked my view. The footsteps weren't coming very fast; I began to hurry, for oddly I didn't want to see who was making them.

Seventy or eighty yards, and I came into a second space. As I noticed the glowing stone in the centre a blind terror rose up in me, but I continued to stare at it. There came a muffling shifting sound – and then, as I watched, the lid of that stone box began to slide off, *and a hand came scrabbling out to lever it up!* What was worse, it was the hand of a corpse – bloodless and skeletal, and with impossibly long, cracked nails . . . I turned to run, but the trees were so thick-growing that it would have been impossible to flee through them quickly enough. I began to stumble back up the path, and heard those horribly deliberate footfalls close at hand. When a yellow-nailed hand appeared round a tree, gripping the trunk, I screamed hopelessly and awoke.

For a minute I considered getting up and making some coffee. Dreams don't usually affect me, but this one was terribly realistic. However, before I could attempt to hold my eyes open, I fell asleep again.

Straight into another nightmare. I was just coming on to the lake shore from among the trees – but not voluntarily; I was being led. I looked once at the hands gripping my arms, and afterwards stared straight ahead. Yet this wasn't reassuring, either. There was a litle moonlight coming from behind me, and it cast shadows on the ground where I glanced. That intensified my resolution not to look to the side. There were more figures behind me than my captors, but those two were bad enough – abominably thin and tall; and the one on the right had only one hand, but I don't mean the other arm ended at the wrist.

They shoved me forward to where I could look down into the lake. The ferns and water were unusually mobile tonight, but I didn't realize what was making them move until an eye rose above the surface and stared moistly at me. Two others followed it – and, worst of all, none of them was *in a face*. When the body heaved up behind them I shut my eyes and shrieked for help – to whom I don't know; I had a weird idea that someone was in the house here and could help me. Then I felt a tearing pain in my chest, neutralized by a numbness which spread through my whole body. And I regarded the object I had seen rising from the lake with no horror whatever. And that moment I woke again.

Almost like an echo from my dream, there was still a loud splashing from the lake outside. My nerves must have been on edge, for I could have sworn that there was a faint sound just under the window. I jumped out of bed and shoved the window further open, so I could look out. There was nothing moving in sight – but for a moment I thought I heard something scuttling away along the line of houses. There might even have been a

door closing quietly, but I can't be sure of that. Certainly the
moonlight was wavering on the lake's surface, as if something
had just sunk.

It's all rather queer now I look on it in broad daylight, but
just then everything seemed to have an added significance – I
almost expected the monstrous shape of my dream to rise from
the water and squat before me in the street. I suppose you
rather wonder whether I'm going to describe what I saw. You
can't imagine how difficult that would be – maybe I'll make it
the subject of my next painting. I only got one glimpse, though,
even if it was so terribly detailed. It'll be best if I don't lose
what inspiration there is by describing it now, anyway.

Yours, Thomas

I would not give him the satisfaction of knowing he
had interested me; I did not refer to his vision of the
haunter of the lake. Instead, I advised him to contact the
estate agent and find out the original purpose of the
lakeside property. 'Maybe,' I suggested, 'you'll learn of
some hideous deed which has left a residue.' I did not
add that I hoped he would discover something utterly
prosaic, which would destroy the place's unfortunate hold
over him and get him away from its morbid atmosphere.
I did not expect him to find out anything extraordinary,
and so was startled by his reply.

30 October 1960

Last Friday I made a special journey down to Bold Street,
and found out quite a bit about my lakeside street. The agent
wasn't particularly pleased to see me, and seemed surprised
when I told him I hadn't come for my money back. He still was
wary of saying much, though – went on a bit about the houses
being built 'on the orders of a private group.' It didn't seem as
though I'd get much out of him, and then I happened to
mention that I was having dreams like the earlier tenants.
Before he could think, he blurted out: 'That's going to make
some people a bit happier, then.'

'What do you mean by that?' I asked, sensing a mystery.

Well, he hedged a bit, and finally explained: 'It's to do with the "haunting" of your lake. There's a story among the country people – and it extends to them in the suburbs around Mercy Hill, which is nearest your place – that *something* lives in the lake, and "sends out nightmares" to lure people to it. Even though the nightmares are terrifying, they're said to have a hypnotic effect. Since the place became untenanted, people – children particularly – in the Mercy Hill area have been dreaming, and one or two have been admitted to the Hill hospital. No wonder they have nightmares around there – it used to be the site of a gallows, you know, and the hospital was a prison; only some joker called it "Mercy Hill," and the name stuck. They say the dreams are the work of what's in the lake – *it's* hungry, and casting its net further out. Of course it's all superstition – God knows what they think *it* is. Anyway, if you're dreaming, they'd say *it* won't need to trouble them any more.'

'Well, that's one thing cleared up,' I said, trying to follow up my advantage. 'Now, why were the houses really built? What was this "private group" you're so secretive about?'

'It'll sound crazy to you, no doubt,' he apologized. 'The houses were built around 1790, and renovated or added to several times. They were put up on the instructions of this group of about six or seven people. These people all disappeared around 1860 or 1870, apparently leaving for another town or something – anyway, nobody around here heard of them again. In 1880 or so, since there'd been no word from them, the houses were let again. For many reasons, people never stayed long – you know, the distance from town; and the scenery too, even if that *was* what got you there. I've heard from earlier workers here that the place even seemed to affect some people's minds. I was only here when the last tenant came in. You heard about the family that was here last, but this was something I didn't tell you. Now look – you said when you first came that you were after ghosts. You sure you want to hear about this?'

'Of course I do – this is what I asked for,' I assured him. How did I know it mightn't inspire a new painting? (Which reminds me, I'm working on a painting from my dream; to be called *The Thing In The Lake*.)

'Really, it wasn't too much,' he warned me. 'He came in here at nine o'clock – that's when we open, and he told me he'd been waiting outside in the car half the night. Wouldn't tell me why he was pulling out – just threw the keys on the counter and told me to get the house sold again. While I was fixing some things up, though, he was muttering a lot. I couldn't catch it all, but what I did get was pretty peculiar. Lot of stuff about "the spines" and "you lose your will and become part of it" – and he went on a lot about "the city among the weeds." Somebody "had to keep the boxes in the daytime," because of "the green decay." He kept mentioning someone called – *Glarky*, or something like that – and also he said something about Thomas Lee I didn't catch.'

That name Thomas Lee sounded a bit familiar to me, and I said so. I still don't know where I got it from, though.

'Lee? Why, of course,' he immediately said. 'He was the leader of that group of people who had the houses built – the man who did all the negotiating . . . And that's really about all the facts I can give you.'

'*Facts*, yes,' I agreed. 'But what else can you tell me? I suppose the people round here must have their own stories about the place?'

'I could tell you to go and find out for yourself,' he said – I suppose he was entitled to get a bit tired of me, seeing I wasn't buying anything. However, he went on: 'Still, it's lucky for you Friday is such a slack day . . . Well, they say that the lake was caused by the fall of a meteor. Centuries ago the meteor was wandering through space, and on it there was a city. The beings of the city all died with the passage through space, but *something* in that city still lived – something that guided the meteor to some sort of landing from its home deep under the surface. God knows what the city would've had to be built of to withstand the descent, if it were true!

'Well, the meteor crater filled with water over the centuries. Some people, they say, had ways of knowing there was something alive in the lake, but they didn't know where it had fallen. One of these was Lee, but he used things nobody else dared to touch to find its whereabouts. He brought these other people down to the lake when he got to know what was in there. They all came from Goatswood – and you know what the superstitious say comes out of the hill behind that town for them to worship

. . . As far as I can make out, Lee and his friends are supposed to have met with more than they expected at the lake. They became servants of what they awoke, and, people say, they're there yet.'

That's all I could get out of him. I came back to the house, and I can tell you I viewed it a bit differently from when I left! I bet you didn't expect me to find that out about it, eh? Certainly it's made me more interested in my surroundings – perhaps it'll inspire me.

Yours, Thomas

I confess that I did not write a long reply; I suppose because my plan to break the lake's hold over him had gone awry. It is regrettable that I was so abrupt, for the letter which reached me on the 8th was his last.

6 November 1960

. . . Have you seen Joe around lately? I haven't heard from him since he left here about three weeks ago, and I'm wondering what's happened to him – he used to write as regularly as you. Still, maybe he's too busy.

But that's unimportant, really. So much has been happening down here, and I don't understand all of it yet. Some of it, maybe, doesn't matter at all, but I'm sure now that this place is a focal point of something unexpected.

Working till about 3 A.M. on the 31st, I finished my new painting. I think it's my best yet – never before have I got such a feeling of alienness into my work. I went to bed around 3:30 and didn't wake up till 5 in the afternoon, when it was dark. Something woke me up; a sound from outside the window. Loud noises of any kind are rare around here, and this wasn't like anything I'd ever heard before. A high-pitched throbbing noise – quickening in vibration and rising in pitch till it hit a discord, when it would drop to its original pitch and begin the cycle again. I couldn't see anything, but I got a peculiar idea that it was coming from *in the lake*. There was an odd rippling on the surface, too, where it reflected the light from the window.

Well, on the 1st I did what I kept saying I'd do (and this is where the interesting part begins) – namely, explore the other houses along the street. I went out about three and decided to try the one directly on the left. Did you realize that the front door must have been ajar when we first came? – oh, no, you didn't get that far along the line. It was, and once I'd managed to get over those rickety steps it was easy to get into the hall. Dust everywhere, wallpaper hanging off in strips, and as far as I could see there was no electric light fitting. I went into the front room – the one looking on to the lake – but could see nothing. The floorboards were bare, cobwebs festooned the fireplace, there was no furniture – the room was almost unlit with the grimy windows. Nothing to see at all.

The next room on the left was almost as bad. I don't know what it was used for – it was so bare nobody could have known. But as I turned to leave, I noticed something protruding from between the floorboards, and, going over, I found it was the page of a book; it looked as if it had been torn out and trodden into the niche. It was dirty and crumpled, and hardly seemed worth looking at, but I picked it up anyway. It was covered with handwriting, beginning in the middle of one sentence and ending in the middle of another. I was going to drop it, but a phrase caught my eye. When I looked closer I realized that this was indeed interesting. I took it back to my house where I could see better, and finally got it smoothed out and clean enough for reading. I might as well copy it out for you – see what you make of it.

sundown and the rise of *that from below*. They can't come out in the daytime – the Green Decay would appear on them, and that'd be rather unpleasant – but I couldn't walk far enough for them not to catch me. They can call on the tomb-herd under Temphill and get them to turn the road back to the lake. I wish I hadn't got mixed up with this. A normal person coming here might be able to escape the dream-pull, but since I dabbled in the forbidden practices at Brichester University I don't think it's any use trying to resist. At the time I was so proud that I'd solved that allusion by Alhazred to 'the maze of the seven thousand crystal frames' and 'the faces that peer from the fifth-dimensional gulf.' None of the other cult-members who understood my explanation could get past the three thousand three hundred and thirty-third frame, where the dead mouths gape and gulp. I think it was because I passed that point that the dream-pull has so strong a hold on me.

But if this is being read it means that there must be new tenants. Please believe me when I say that you are in horrible danger. You must leave now, and get the lake filled in before *it* gets strong enough to leave this place. By the time you read this I shall be – not dead, but might as well be. I shall be one of the servants of *it*, and if you look closely enough you might find me in my place among the trees. I wouldn't advise it,though; although they'd get the Green Decay in broad daylight they can come out in the daytime into the almost-darkness between the trees.

You'll no doubt want proof; well, in the cellar

That's where it ended. As you can imagine, I wanted nothing better than to go down to that cellar – I presumed it must mean the cellar of the house I'd been exploring. But I felt particularly hungry, and by the time I'd prepared a meal and eaten it, it was pretty dark. I didn't have a flashlight, and it'd have been useless to go into a cellar after dark to look for anything. So I had to wait until the next day.

That night I had a strange dream. It must have been a dream, but it was very realistic. In it I was lying in bed in my room, as though I'd just woken up. Voices were speaking under the window – strange voices, hoarse and sibilant and somehow *forced*, as if the speakers found it painful to talk. One said: 'Perhaps in the cellar. They will not be needed until the pull is stronger, anyway.' Slowly the answer came, '*His* memory is dimming, but the second new one must remedy that.' It might have been the first voice or another which replied, 'Daylight is too near, but tomorrow night we must go down.' Then I heard deliberate, heavy footsteps receding. In the dream I could not force myself to look and see who had been under the window; and, in a few minutes, the dream ended in uneasy sleep.

The next morning, the second, I visited the house again. The door to the cellar's in the kitchen, like my house, There wasn't much light down there, but some did come in from the garden outside. When I got used to it, I saw a flight of stone steps going down into a large cellar. I saw what I wanted immediately – there wasn't really anything else to see. A small bookcase of the type open at the top and front, full of dusty yellowed books, and with its sides joined by a piece of cord which served as a handle for easier carrying. I picked up the bookcase and went back upstairs. There was one other thing which I thought odd: an archway at the other end of the cellar, beyond which was a steep flight of stairs – but these stairs led *down* as far as I could see.

When I got back to my house I dusted the books off and examined the spines. They were, I found, different volumes of the same book, eleven of them in all; the book was called *The Revelations of Glaaki*. I opened Book 1, and found it was an old type of loose-leaf notebook, the pages covered with an archaic handwriting. I began to read – and by the time I looked up from the fifth book it was already dark.

I can't even begin to tell you what I learned. When you come down at Christmas maybe you can read some of it – well, if you start it, you'll be so fascinated you'll have to finish it. I'd better give you briefly the history of the book, and the fantastic mythos of which it tells.

This *Revelations of Glaaki* has been reprinted elsewhere according to notes, or perhaps I'd better say pirated. This, however, is the only complete edition; the man who managed to copy it down and 'escaped' to get it printed didn't dare to copy it all down for publication. This original handwritten version is completely fragmentary; it's written by the different members of a cult, and where one member leaves off another begins, perhaps on a totally different subject. The cult grew up around 1800, and the members almost certainly were those who ordered the houses built. About 1865 the pirated edition was published, but because it referred frequently to other underground societies they had to be careful where the book was circulated. Most of the copies of the very limited edition found their way into the hands of members of these cults, and nowadays there are very few complete runs of all the nine volumes (as against eleven in the uncut edition) extant.

The cult worships something which lives in the lake, as the agent told me. There's no description of the being; it was made out of some 'living, iridescent metal,' as far as I can make out, but there are no actual pictures. Occasionally footnotes occur, such as 'cf. picture: Thos. Lee pinxit,' but if there ever was a picture it must have been torn out. There are numerous references to 'the sentient spines,' and the writers go into great detail about this. It's to do with the initiation of a novice into the cult of Glaaki, and explains, in its own superstitious way, the legends of the 'witch's mark.'

You've heard of the witch's mark – the place on the body of a witch that wouldn't bleed when cut? Matthew Hopkins and his kind were always trying to find the mark, but not always successfully. Of course they often got hold of innocent people who'd never heard of Glaaki, and then they had to resort to other means to prove they were witches. But those in the cult certainly were supposed to have the real witches' marks. It was the long, thin spines which are supposed to cover the body of their god Glaaki. In the initiation ceremony the novice was held (sometimes willing, sometimes not) on the lake shore while Glaaki rose from the depths. It would drive one of its spines into the chest of the victim, and when a fluid had been injected into the body the spine detached itself from the body of Glaaki. If the victim had been able to snap the spine before the fluid entered his body he would at least have died a human being, but of course his captors didn't allow that. As it was, a network spread right through the body from the point of the spine, which then fell away where it entered the body, leaving an area which would never bleed if something were jabbed into it. Through the emission of impulses, perhaps magnetic, from the brain of Glaaki, the man was kept alive while he was controlled almost completely by the being. He acquired all its memories; he became also a part of it, although he was capable of performing minor individual actions, such as writing the *Revelations*, when Glaaki was not emitting specific impulses. After about sixty years of this half-life this 'Green Decay' would set in if the body was exposed to too-intense light.

There's some confusion about the actual advent of Glaaki on this planet. The cult believes that it didn't reach the earth until the meteor hit and formed the lake. On the other hand, the book does mention 'heretics' who insist that the spines can be found buried in certain hybrid Egyptian mummies, and say that Glaaki came before – through 'the reversed angles of Tagh-Clatur' which the priests of Sebek and Karnak knew. There are suggestions that the zombies of Haiti are the products of a horrible extract from early cult-members who got caught in sunlight, too.

As for what was learned by the initiate – well, there are references to the '48 Aklo unveilings' and a suggestion that 'the 49th shall come when Glaaki takes each to him.' Glaaki seems to have crossed the universe from some outer sphere, stopping on worlds such as Yuggoth, Shaggai and even Tond. On this planet it occasionally draws new members to the cult by the 'dream-pull,' which I've heard about before. These days, however, the lake is so far away from everything that the use of the 'dream-pull' takes time, and without the vitality it's said to draw from the initiation it gets too weak to project the dreams to any great distance. The cultists can't come out in the daylight, so the only thing left is for people to come spontaneously and live in the houses. Like me!

That isn't all that's in the book, by any means; the cult believed a lot of other things, but some of them are so incredible and unconventional that they'd just sound ridiculous if I wrote them down. Somehow they don't seem so idiotic in that simple style of the *Revelations*, perhaps because they're written by an absolute believer. You must read some of them this Christmas. If you could imagine what they suggest causes volcanic eruptions! And their footnote to atomic theory; what the scientist will see who invents a microscope which gives a *really* detailed view of an atom! There are other things, too – the race 'of which Vulthoom is merely a child' – the source of vampires – and the pale, dead things which walk black cities on the dark side of the moon . . .

But there's no use my going on like this. You'll see all this in a few weeks, and until then my hints won't mean much to you. I promised you a quotation, so I'll copy down a passage at random:

Many are the horrors of Tond, the sphere which revolves about the green sun of Yifne and the dead star of Baalblo. Few come near to humanity, for even the ruling race of yarkdao *have retractable ears in humanoid bodies. Their gods are many, and none dares interrupt the priests of Chig in their ritual, which lasts three years and a quarter, or one* puslt. *Great cities of blue metal and black stone are built on Tond, and some* yarkdao *speak of a city of crystal in which things walk unlike anything living. Few men of our planet can see Tond, but those who know the secret of the Crystallizers of Dreams may walk its surface unharmed, if the Crystallizer's hungry guardian does not scent them.*

Actually that isn't the best quotation to take – others are much less vague, but mightn't have so much impact if you read them out of context. Now you really *must* come down at Christmas, if only to read the book.

Yours, Thomas

I did not reply to his letter until the 12th. I had intended to reply sooner, if only to take his mind off this latest focus of his morbidity, but this had been a particularly crowded week at the Inland Revenue. Now, at about ten o'clock, I sat down to write to him. I meant to point out that before he had thought all this mere superstition, and that he had only discovered proof of the superstitious beliefs of a few people.

I was just putting down the date when the telephone rang. I was not expecting anyone to call, and momentarily thought it must be a wrong number. When it had rung three times, I wearily stood up to answer it.

'Alan? Thank God!' said a hysterical voice at the other end. 'Drop everything and come in your car – and for God's sake make it quick!'

'Who is that – who's speaking?' I asked, for I was not sure if I recognized the voice.

'Thomas – Thomas Cartwright!' screamed the voice impatiently. 'Listen, there's positively no time for explanation. You must come down here now in your car, at once – or it'll be dark and I'll never get out. I'm in a phone box on the road some miles from the lake, and I'll stay in here till you get here. You can't miss it – just take the lake road from Brichester; it's not as far, that's all.'

'But *why* have I got to come?' I persisted, exasperated.

'Because *they've* wrecked my car engine.' He was becoming very nervous; I could tell from the noticeable shaking of his voice. 'I've found out a lot more since I wrote, and *they* know I know it all. *They* don't even bother to hide, now.'

'I don't know what the hell you're talking about, but why can't you call a taxi instead of bringing me all this way?'

'I can't call a taxi because I don't know the number!' shrieked Cartwright. 'And why can't I look it up? Because last night *they* must have been here before me – *they've* taken the directory. I'd walk to Brichester – I don't think *their* influence extends any further – but if *they* don't call on the tomb-herd under Temphill to turn space back, the tree-creatures a couple of miles up the road might take their real shapes, and it needs the union of two wills to overcome them. Now, for God's sake, will you get your car down here, or do you want Glaaki to rise from the lake again? Perhaps this will give it the strength to broadcast further.' And immediately there came a click as the receiver was replaced.

For some moments I stood by the telephone table. I could not telephone the police, for it would be useless to send them to Cartwright only to find circumstances which would make them think him mad. Certainly his ravings about *them* were not to be taken seriously. On the other hand, if the lake were having such a pronounced effect on his mind, I should surely drive down to Brichester at once. And so I did.

I had only been to the lake once, and on reaching Brichester I had completely forgotten the route. None of the passers-by could help me; in fact, by their expressions I was almost sure that some of them could help me, but for some reason would not. Finally I asked a policeman to direct me to Bold Street, where the estate agent could tell me the way to the lake.

He looked up as I entered, but did not seem to recognize me. 'Can I help you?' he asked.

'About Lakeside Terrace – ' I began.

'Lakeside Terrace? No, not one of ours, sir.'

'Yes, it is one of yours,' I insisted. 'You sold it to a friend of mine a few weeks back – a Mr Cartwright – it's supposed to be haunted. Look, you *must* remember; I've got to see him as soon as possible.' Some of Cartwright's nervous impatience had affected me, and the estate agent's continued puzzled expression caused me to think he could not help me.

'Will you be at the lake after dark, then?'

His pointless-seeming question infuriated me, particularly as I had no definite answer. 'I don't know yet. Yes, maybe. Damn it, do you know the way to the lake or don't you? I can't waste any more time. It's – what, 3:20 already, and I ought to be there by now.'

As I drove out of Bold Street, I was still surprised by his sudden decision to direct me. I was relieved to drive away from the small building, for I had been strangely worried by the unaccustomed slowness of his speech and the rigidity of his limbs; still more by the way he would finger a spot on his chest and wince. I still could not imagine why should he ask whether I was to be at the lake after dark.

I reached the top of Mercy Hill a few minutes later. As the car slowed at the bend which takes one past the grey hospital building, I had a view both ahead and behind; and I very nearly turned back. The red-brick houses looked far more inviting than the steep hillsides, between which plunged roads bordered by leafless trees. I remembered what the people of Mercy Hill said inhabited the lake. But I had come to rid Cartwright of his superstitious morbidity, and could not do this while I was myself superstitious.

When I rounded the curve which brought me in sight of the telephone box, the door swung open and Cartwright ran into the road. He reached the car as I began to slow and, running alongside, he yelled through the open window: 'Open the door on this side! Keep driving – I can jump in at this speed.'

I did not intend him to be injured, and stopped the car. 'Now will you stop acting like someone in a movie and explain?'

'All right, I'm in,' he assured me. 'Now let's get down to the lake.'

'To the *lake*?' I repeated, surprised. 'The way you were going on, I thought . . . Oh, all right, if you're in such a hurry.'

As I was starting the engine, I heard him muttering beside me. Some of it escaped me, but I caught: ' – tried to phone the police, but I couldn't get through – wires must have been down. Must have been an accident, though. Couldn't have been *their* work – *they* could never get that far in the sunlight. The Green Decay – it's in the *Revelations* . . . Could they?'

I ignored this, not turning to look at him. 'Listen, Thomas, I'd like some explanation. I thought you wanted to get away from the lake before nightfall? What's happened up there that's scared you off so suddenly?'

He left my second question for a moment. 'I certainly must get away before nightfall, but I want to bring the *Revelations* with me. If I leave the house empty tonight and come back tomorrow *they'll* get in and take it. We can get down there before 4 o'clock and grab the bookcase. We'll be well towards Brichester before dark. The tree-creatures up the road may get more active after dark, but there's a ritual which I can repeat to subdue them if I can draw on your consciousness. Once we're in Brichester, we ought to be beyond *their* influence.'

'But you weren't like this before. You may have believed in all this, but you weren't frightened of it. What's happening to change your feelings?'

He fumbled a little, then: 'One of them *might* have been a dream, but the other . . . As for the thing I might have dreamed, it happened about one o'clock this morning. I was only half-asleep – I kept dreaming of strange things: that black city among the weeds down there, with a shape under a crystal trapdoor, and further back to Yuggoth and Tond – and that kept me awake. At the time I'm speaking of I kept half-opening my eyes; I got the feeling that someone was watching me, but I could never see anyone. Then I started noticing something pale which seemed to float at the edge of my vision. I realized it was near the window. I turned quickly and saw a face staring in at me.

'It was the face of a corpse; what was worse, it was the face of Joe Bulger.'

We had reached the last stretch of road towards the lake before he continued. 'He didn't look at me; his eyes were fixed on something at the other side of the room. All that was over there was that bookcase containing the eleven volumes of the *Revelations of Glaaki*. I jumped up and ran over to the window, but he began to move away with that horrible deliberate tread. I'd seen enough, though. His shirt had been torn open, and on his chest was a livid red mark, with a network of lines radiating from it. Then he moved off between the trees.'

I stopped the car at the beginning of the lakeside pavement. As I approached the house, he was still muttering behind me: '*They'd* taken him to Glaaki – that must have been all the splashing that night. But that was at eleven o'clock and Joe left about four. My God, what were *they* doing to him in the other seven hours?'

I stood back to let him open the front door; he had even found a padlock somewhere and augmented the lock's strength with it. As we entered the front room I noticed the canvas-covered painting in one corner. I began to lift the canvas off, but Cartwright stopped me. 'Not yet – that's part of the other. I want to show you something else when you see that.'

He went over to the bookcase which stood on the floor opposite the window, and took out the last book. 'When – Joe – had gone, I finally had a look at these books. I had a good idea of what he'd been looking at, but I wanted to make sure. Somehow I knocked the lot down. No damage, luckily, except to the eleventh book; but that one had fallen so that the cover had been torn off. As I was trying to fit it together again, I noticed the back cover was bulging outward a lot. When I looked closer, this is what I found.'

He passed me the volume he had selected. Opening the cover, I saw that the back had been slit open; a sort of pocket existed, and inside it I found a folded sheet of canvas and a piece of cardboard.

'Don't look at those for the moment,' ordered Cartwright. 'Remember I painted *The Thing In The Lake* from my nightmare? This is it. Now, go ahead and compare it with those two.'

By the time I had unfolded the canvas, he had uncovered the painting. The piece of canvas was also a painting, while the card was a photograph. The background of each was different; Cartwright's depicted the lake as surrounded by a black pavement in the middle of a desolate plain, the painting I held – inscribed 'Thos.

Lee pinxit' – possessed a background of half-fluid demons and many-legged horrors, while the photograph simply showed the lake as it was now. But the focus of each was the same totally alien figure, and the one that disturbed me most was the photograph.

The centre of each picture was, it was obvious, the being known as Glaaki. From an oval body protruded countless thin, pointed spines of multicoloured metal; at the more rounded end of the oval a circular, thick-lipped mouth formed the centre of a spongy face, from which rose three yellow eyes on thin stalks. Around the underside of the body were many white pyramids, presumably used for locomotion. The diameter of the body must have been about ten feet at its least width.

Not only the coincidence of the pictures, but also the total abnormality of the creature, disturbed me. However, I tried to sound unconvinced as I remarked, 'Look, you said yourself that the other business was only a dream. As for the rest – what does it amount to, anyway? A few nightmares and the documents of a superstitious cult whose beliefs happen to coincide with your dreams. The photograph's very realistic, of course, but these days you can do almost anything with special photography.'

'You still think it's my imagination?' he inquired. 'Of course you don't explain why anyone would go to the trouble of faking a photograph like that and then leave it here. Besides, remember I did that painting from my dream *before* I saw those. It's Glaaki sending his image from the lake.'

I was still searching for an answer when Cartwright looked at his watch. 'Good God, it's after four'clock! We'd better get going if we want to leave before dark. You go and start the car while I get the bookcases. I don't think they'll touch my pictures, except the latest one, and I'll bring that one with me. Tomorrow, maybe, we can come back from Brichester and get them.'

As I climbed into the driving seat I saw Cartwright struggling across the pavement with the bookcase-handle over one arm and the picture held in front of him. He slid into the back seat as I turned the ignition key.

There was no sound from the engine.

Cartwright ran and threw up the bonnet. Then he turned to stare at me, his face pale. '*Now* will you bloody well believe!' he screamed. 'I suppose it's my imagination that wrecked your engine!'

I got out to look at the mass of torn wires. He did not notice whether I was listening as he continued:

'*They've* been at it – but how? It's not dark yet out here, and *they* can't come by daylight – but *they* must have done it – ' This seemed to worry him more than the engine's actually been wrecked. Then he slumped against the car. 'My God, of course – Joe only just joined *them*, and the Green Decay doesn't affect *them* for sixty years or so. He can come out in the light – he can follow me – he is part of Glaaki now, so he won't spare me – '

'What do we do now?' I interrupted. 'According to you it's insane to start walking so close to nightfall, so – '

'Yes,' he agreed. 'We must barricade ourselves in. The upper floors aren't so important, but every window and door on the ground floor must be blocked. If you think I'm crazy, humour me for your own sake.'

Once inside, we managed to block the front-room window by upturning the bed. The back-room window was fortified with a wardrobe. When we had moved this into the room from the front, Cartwright left me to position it while he went out the back door. 'There's a hatchet lying around out here,' he explained. 'Best to have it in here – it may be useful as a weapon, and otherwise *they'll* get hold of it.' He brought it in and stood it by the hall table.

He helped me to barricade the back door, which opened out of the kitchen; but when we had shoved the kitchen cabinet against it, he told me to take a rest. 'Go ahead, make some coffee,' he suggested. 'As for me – there's a few minutes of daylight left, and I want to take a look in the lake to see what's down there. I'll take the hatchet in case . . . Joe comes. Anyway, *they* can't move very fast – their limbs soon become half-rigid.' I began to ask what protection I would have, but he had already gone.

He was so long away that I was beginning to worry, when I heard him knocking at the back door. I called, 'You've a short memory – go round the front,' but when no answering footsteps came I began to pull the cabinet out of position. At that moment a shout came from behind me: 'What are you doing?'

I had the kettle ready to throw when I turned and saw Cartwright. As calmly as I could, I said: 'Somebody is knocking at the back door.'

'It's *them*,' he yelled, and smashed the cabinet back into place. 'Quick – maybe it's only Joe, but it may be dark enough for the others to come out. Got to block the front door, anyway – what the hell is there?' The hall was bare of all furniture except a small table. 'Have to get the wardrobe out of my bedroom.'

As we entered a number of noises began. Far off came a sliding sound from several directions. A muffled discordant throbbing was also audible, water was splashing nearby, and round the side of the house someone was slowly approaching. I ran to the crevice between window and upturned bed and looked out. It was already quite dark, but I could see the water rippling alarmingly at the shore near the window.

'Help me, for God's sake!' called Cartwright.

As I turned from the window I glimpsed something moving outside. Perhaps I only imagined that glistening shape which heaved out of the water, with long stalks twisting above it; but certainly that throbbing was much nearer, and a creaking, slithering object was moving across the pavement.

I rushed over and helped shove the wardrobe towards the door. 'There's something living out there!' I gasped.

Cartwright looked half-relieved, half-disgusted. 'It's the thing from the picture,' he said breathlessly. 'I saw it before, when I went outside. You've got to look into the lake at a certain angle, otherwise you can't see anything. Down on the bottom, among the weeds – stagnant water, everything dead, except . . . There's a city down there, all black spiralling steeples and walls at obtuse angles with the streets. Dead things lying on the streets – they died with the journey through space – they're horrible, hard, shiny, all red and covered with bunches of trumpet-shaped things . . . And right at the centre of the city is a transparent trapdoor. Glaaki's under there, pulsing and staring up – I saw the eye-stalks move towards me – ' His voice trailed off.

I followed his gaze. He was looking at the front door; and, as I watched, the door bulged inward from pressure from outside. The hinge-screws were visibly tearing free of the door frame. That alien throbbing cry sounded somehow triumphant.

'Quick, upstairs!' Cartwright shouted. 'Can't get the wardrobe there now – upstairs, I'll follow you.'

I was nearest the stairs, and jumped for them. Halfway up I heard a rending crash behind me, and turning I saw with horror that Cartwright was not behind me. He was standing by the hall table, clutching the hatchet.

Through the front door came the dead servants of Glaaki, skeletal arms outstretched to grab him. And behind them a shape towered, pulsing and shaking with deafening vibration. The dead ones were only a few feet from Cartwright when he ran – straight into their midst. Their arms swung slowly in ineffectual attempts to stop him. He reached the front door, but at that moment one of them stepped in front of him. Cartwright did not stop; he swung the hatchet-blade up between its legs until it cut free.

Now he was beyond the slowly turning corpses, and he plunged towards the pulsing shape of Glaaki. A spine stiffened towards him. As he ran on to the point of the spine Cartwright brought the hatchet down and severed it from the body. The throbbing became a discordant shrieking, and the oval body thrashed in agony back into the lake. The dead creatures made purposeless movements for a while, then shuffled away towards the trees. Cartwright, meanwhile, had fallen on the pavement and did not move. I could stand no more; I rushed into the first upstairs room and locked the door.

The next morning, when I was sure it was daylight, I left the house. Outside I picked up Cartwright's body and left it in the front seat of the car. I did not look back at what lay near the front door; the walking corpse he had destroyed. It had been exposed to daylight. I managed not to vomit until I reached the car. Some time passed before I was able to begin walking to Brichester.

The police did not believe all I told them. The bookcase had gone from the back of the car, and nothing could be seen among the trees – or in the lake, though this was too deep to be dragged. The estate agent on Bold Street could tell them nothing of a 'haunting' of the lake. There was the painting in the car – a painting which has since been pronounced Cartwright's most powerful – but it was only the product of an artist's imagination. Of course, there was that metal spine embedded in his chest, but that could have been an ingeniously contrived murder weapon.

When I had the Brichester University professors examine the spine, however, the results were very different. The case was hushed up in the newspapers, and while the professors have not yet got a permit to fill the lake in, they agree with me that something very strange happened that night in the hollow. For the spine, with its central orifice running through it, was formed not only of a metal completely unknown on this planet; that metal had recently been composed of *living cells*.

THE WILL OF STANLEY BROOKE

As a close acquaintance of Stanley Brooke's rather than a friend, Ernest Bond probably noticed his oddities the more readily.

These oddities became apparent soon after Brooke learned that he was dying of cancer. First he sent out to the libraries for medical books and journals, in an obvious attempt to find some cure the doctors had overlooked. Then, when he found no solace in orthodox medicine, he began to search volumes of faith-healing, and Bond realized how desperate he was becoming. It was not until the final phase that Bond began to worry; but he was disturbed by Brooke's quest through ancient grimoires for some answer. He watched Brooke slide gradually into depression, and knew of nothing he could do to help.

He was all the more surprised, therefore, when he arrived at Brooke's house one afternoon in response to a call, and found the owner sitting up in bed smiling.

Brooke placed a bookmark in the yellowed volume he had been reading, and put it down beside him. 'Sit down, Bond, sit down,' he grinned. 'I'm afraid I didn't ask you round just for your company – there's some business we have to discuss, but I told you that on the 'phone.'

'Yes – well, what can I do for you?'

'I want to dictate a will,' Brooke told him.

Bond wondered if the man's condition had brought on amnesia. 'But you've already made one.'

He had indeed made a will, and at his death five people would receive an appreciable legacy. His three sisters and his brother would come into a few thousand pounds each – while Emily, one of the sisters, and his niece Pamela, who had insisted on being his housekeeper for some years, would also come into possession of the large house. Strangely, Brooke was notoriously mean, and remarked that the vultures could pick up what they liked once he was dead, but he could not afford to be generous while alive.

'I know I've already made one,' he said impatiently. 'My mind hasn't gone yet, you know. I want to make a new one. The people next door are going to act as witnesses – they're probably downstairs now. It's completely different from the old one – you see, I've found out something – '

He reached for the book beside him, hesitated, and left it where it was.

'But first you must promise not to tell anyone any of the terms of the will until after I'm dead . . . All right? Good. Now let's get the witnesses up here.'

As Brooke dictated, the lawyer realized why he had been made to promise. The terms of the will shocked him exceedingly; and for some time he debated whether he should keep that promise – whether he should not at least hint the amendments to Brooke's sister Emily. But she would be bound to have it out with Brooke; and, besides revealing Bond's indiscretion, this was surely not the kind of barrage to which a dying man should be subjected. So the lawyer continued to debate.

The decision was taken out of his hands when, on August 6, 1962, Brooke died.

He was buried four days later in St Mark's churchyard, Brichester, and on the afternoon of that day Bond described the general terms of the will to the expectant relatives.

'Impossible,' said Terence Brooke, the dead man's brother. 'I flatly refuse to believe it.'

'I'm afraid it's true all the same,' the lawyer insisted. 'I can't give you the details until the beneficiary arrives, but I can tell you that under the terms of the new will none of you will benefit – '

'The worm!' Emily said. 'After all I did for him, and what my daughter did too – '

Pamela James, her daughter, was obviously upset by the whole business. 'I wish you wouldn't use that horrible word, mother,' she protested. 'After all, this man's going to get Uncle's money, and there's nothing we can do – '

'Oh, shut up, girl!' snapped Emily. 'I don't know about the rest of you, but *I'll* be here when Mr Bond reads the will – maybe when this man sees how we were all expecting something, he'll give us all some money. I think that's the least he can do.'

'And how are you going to recognize this fellow,' Terence Brooke inquired, 'when nobody's ever seen him before?'

'That's the queerest thing about all this,' Bond replied. 'This man – William Collier, he calls himself – is the exact double of the late Mr Brooke. If that isn't enough, he'll be carrying a letter proving his identity written by Mr Brooke, in an unfranked envelope with his name on it also in Brooke's script.'

'When are you expecting him to arrive?' Joyce, another of the sisters, put in.

'That's odd, too,' said Bond. 'I asked him that – because, as you know, I can't open the will until Collier arrives – and he just said "*he'll be here about a week after the burial.*" What that means I don't know.'

On August 17 the lawyer was invited round to the house on King Edward's Way, into which, in spite of protests, Emily and Pamela James had moved. He arrived just before five o'clock, and joined them at tea. Not long after, Terence, Joyce and Barbara, the third sister, arrived.

Quite soon the real reason for this gathering became apparent.

'Mr Bond,' asked Emily, 'do you think it would be ethical for you to point out to this man how distressed we all are by this new will? We don't want all his legacy – it wouldn't be right to interfere with Stanley's wishes like that – but maybe if the six of us got equal shares – '

'Oh, *please*, mother!' Pamela cried. 'Must you be such a vulture?'

'I must say I agree with the girl,' Terence said. 'We didn't know we were coming to this, you know.'

'Will you all please be *quiet*!' Emily shouted, striking the table. 'Mr Bond, what have you got to say?'

The lawyer was saved from the quarrel he would have caused by a knock at the door.

'Don't get up – I'll go,' he said quickly, and opened the door for William Collier.

Bond recognized him at once, yet for a moment it had been as if the dead had returned. Every detail was reminiscent of the dead man except one, and that only added to the unpleasant illusion; for the man's skin was almost white, and abnormally translucent.

'I'm William Collier,' he introduced himself. 'I heard Stanley Brooke was dead, and came as soon as I could.'

'Yes – won't you come in?' Bond invited. 'Have you had a long journey? Perhaps you'd like something to eat – we're just having tea.'

'Thank you, but first – ' Collier hesitated. 'Well, I *have* had a long journey, and I'd like to, ah – '

'Yes, of course,' said the lawyer. 'It's the door right at the top of the stairs. But here, let me take your coat.'

As he hung up the coat, Terence Brooke appeared in the dining-room doorway. They watched the figure to the top of the stairs.

'I like the way you make him feel at home!' Brooke remarked. 'So that's the new tenant, is it? My God, it's going to be like dining with a corpse!'

'The resemblance certainly is striking,' Bond began, but was interrupted by the arrival of Emily.

'You two can go back inside,' she told them. 'I want to meet him when he comes down, and then introduce everybody.'

As he sat down again at the table the lawyer heard footsteps on the stairs, then an inaudible conversation outside the door. Soon Emily ushered in Collier, and introduced those present, adding: 'We all expect to get something under the will,' at which Collier's face briefly took on an odd expression.

A rather uncomfortable silence ensued. Barbara, who was notoriously fond of macabre humour, took advantage of an offer from Emily of cold meat to remark:

'No, thanks, I don't care for meat very much. I always think that if you eat pieces of animal, you'll get to look like them.'

'How do you make that out?' Pamela prompted.

'Well, you know . . . if you eat too much pork you'll get like a pig, and I suppose you'll get pretty fishy if you eat nothing but fish . . . In fact, if you concentrate on one food, I think pretty soon you'll look exactly like it.'

There was a thud. Everybody looked up.

'It's all right,' Collier said with a curious expression, 'I just dropped my spoon, that's all. If I could have another one – '

'I always like vegetables,' Bond interrupted quickly, 'so what does that make me?'

'Well, Mr Bond,' said Barbara, 'nobody could call you exactly *vital* . . .'

'Here's a spoon, Mr Collier,' Emily said. 'Have all the rest of you finished? – What, don't want any more either, Mr Collier? In that case, we may as well all go into the lounge.'

The lawyer was the last to leave the dining-room, and he found Terence waiting for him in the hall.

'You know, I think there's something wrong about that fellow,' Brooke confided. 'I have a feeling he may be an imposter.'

'But what about his appearance? And the letter, if he has it.'

'As for the letter – ' Brooke lowered his voice. 'Suppose if when we went upstairs, he got it from somewhere Stanley had hidden it?'

'Hardly. Besides,' Bond pointed out, 'surely that proves his claim must be genuine, or he wouldn't have known where to find the letter.'

They entered the lounge. Bond decided to get the night's business over at once.

'Mr Collier,' he asked, 'do you have any proof of your identity?'

'Why, yes. I believe this is what you want.' And the lawyer took from the pale fat hand an envelope which, he found, contained the appropriate document.

'Yes, this seems right enough,' he admitted. 'Well, then, I'd better get the reading over with.'

Collier showed no emotion when Bond reached the relevant passage:

'*To my closest friend, William Collier: the property at 19 King Edward's Way, the furnishings thereof, and any others of my possessions remaining after payment of death duties, &c.'*

'But – is that all?' Emily asked, seemingly incredulous.

'Yes,' replied Bond rather coldly, 'I'm afraid it is.'

'You were his closest friend?' Emily said to Collier. 'Surely you're shocked that he was so mean – I realize it's natural to see your friends are provided for, but we were his family, and we did quite a bit for him too . . .'

'Oh, please don't try to be subtle,' Collier advised her. 'I know what you're after, and I can tell you now that I wouldn't dream of splashing my money about.'

'Why, you worm – ' began Emily

Collier recoiled and collided with the sideboard, over-turning a vase.

'My God,' Bond said tonelessly.

'What's wrong, Mr Bond?' asked Pamela.

'It doesn't matter now – nothing . . . I don't think you need me here any more tonight – I'd better be off . . . But could I just speak to you a minute, Mr Collier? Alone?'

Collier followed him into the hall, and the lawyer remarked:

'I'm afraid they don't feel very friendly towards you at the moment. I'm driving into the town centre, so if you'd like a lift somewhere to let them simmer down . . . Yes?' He called into the lounge: 'Mr Collier's leaving with me – he'll be back in a couple of hours.'

They drove away into the night. Collier dozed in the back seat but woke when the car began to slow down.

'But surely we're not in Brichester now! Haven't you come the wrong way?'

'Oh, no,' Bond said, stopping the car at the edge of a quarry. 'I assure you this is the right way.'

Two weeks later, Terence Brooke arrived at the lawyer's house in Almshouse Gardens, and found the owner at work in the greenhouse.

'Why, hello,' Bond greeted him. 'Any word about Collier yet?'

'No, none,' said Brooke. 'Nobody seems to know what to do about it.'

'Well, as I told the police at the time,' Bond went on, 'I took him to my office and told him how generally hated he'd be if he did you all out of your legacies, and he left, and that was the last I saw of him.'

'Somehow,' Brooke mused, 'I have the feeling he won't be back . . . But anyway, I didn't really come here about that – what – ?'

'Bloody worms,' said Bond, driving his spade down again and again while something pale writhed. 'I can't stand the things . . . Oh, sorry. Go on.'

'I was going to say that my car's broken down just at the end of the road,' continued Brooke, looking away from the still descending spade, 'and I was wondering if you had a spanner I could borrow.'

'Well, I've got a heavy one in the back of the car,' began the lawyer, '. . . oh – oh, no, I'm afraid I lost it some time ago.'

'Never mind,' Brooke said, 'I'll have it towed to the nearest garage. But you ought to get yourself a new spanner, you know.'

'Oh, it doesn't really matter,' Bond assured him, wrenching his spade at last out of the ground. 'I never use it except in an emergency.'

THE MOON-LENS

Sitting in his office in Mercy Hill hospital, Dr James Linwood read the headline again:

PROMINENT BRICHESTER SURGEON TO
ADVOCATE EUTHANASIA AT CONVENTION

. . . *Prominent*, eh? And on the front page too! But it was the *Brichester Weekly News*, of course, and anything local had automatic preference.

He glanced at his watch and saw that it showed five past midnight. Out of habit, he changed his desk calendar from April 2 to April 3, 1961. He leaned back in his desk and considered: should he go home to bed or stay to work on his convention speech? He decided on the latter, and switched on the tape-recorder.

At that moment there came a tap on the door – someone else working late, no doubt. He called out 'Good night,' but the shadow on the frosted glass panel did not move. Dr Linwood stood up and opened the door.

A man he had never seen before was standing outside. The doctor felt somehow instinctively repelled; whether by the man's dirty, ridiculously baggy trousers and long raincoat, or by a faint reptilian odour which he caught, he could not say. The other did not speak – and the silence began to unnerve Dr Linwood.

'Visiting time's over, I'm afraid,' he finally said.

'I'm not a visitor,' said the other in an abnormally deep and slow voice.

'Well, if you're a patient, you want the other side of the building.'

'No, I don't,' contradicted the visitor. 'I want to see you, Dr Linwood – you are *the* Dr Linwood? The one who's in favour of mercy killing?'

'That's correct,' confirmed the doctor, 'but at this time of night – '

'I want you to kill me,' the other said.

The doctor regarded him carefully, and decided he was not joking. 'I'm sorry – I *advocate* it, I don't carry it out – not yet, anyway. And I must say that you don't look like a euthanasia case.'

'But surely – if you thought somebody really needed it, you might . . . do it privately so nobody would know? I'd do it myself, but the thought of pain . . . I thought maybe an overdose of chloroform – '

'I'm sorry,' repeated the doctor more coldly, 'it's impossible at the moment, and anyway I do *not* intend it to make suicide legal.'

'But I need it,' insisted the man. 'I have a condition which makes living completely unbearable.'

'Maybe if I examined you – ' suggested Dr Linwood.

The visitor shrank away from the doctor's hand. 'You mustn't see – it'd be too much . . . But perhaps I could convince you. If I can just tell you what's happened to me – '

'I don't really have the time – ' protested the doctor, but the other had already pushed into the office and sat down before the desk. Well, perhaps he could use this in his speech to stress his aversion to legalized suicide. He sat down and motioned for the man to begin.

'My name is Roy Leakey,' began the other . . .

On April 1, 1961, Roy Leakey had set out for Exham. He had already visited all of Brichester's antiquarian bookshops; and, hearing that many fruitful second-hand shops existed in Exham, he decided to explore the town. Few people went there, and there was no direct railway line between the two towns, and no bus route whatever. He disliked train journeys, especially when changing trains was necessary, but here this seemed unavoidable. At the station he learned that only one train left for Exham that day, at 11:30; he would have to change at Goatswood at approximately 12:10 and wait perhaps twenty minutes for the connection,

The train left Lower Brichester station five minutes late and rushed to keep to schedule. Leakey jolted uncomfortably in his seat, staring uninterestedly out of the window. He found nothing interesting in the red-brick houses which rocked by below, advertisements painted in crude white letters on their railway-facing walls, nor even the gentle Cotswold hills which surrounded the line once it escaped the dismal cuttings. Soon the grass on the hills gave way to trees; close bare trunks which huddled closer until the entire landscape was wooded. He saw no houses among the trees, and sensed no life in the woods. Once he thought for a second that he saw a strange grey cone far off in the forest; then it was gone, but the sight filled him with an odd disquiet.

This far the line had been almost straight, except for the slight curves round the hills. Then, about half-an-hour out of Brichester, the train slowed to take a more pronounced bend in the track. Leakey's carriage reached the bend. The left-hand side, where he was sitting, was on the inside of the curve; and as he looked out, for the first time he saw Goatswood.

The impression he got from that first glimpse was of furtiveness. The close-set dull-red roofs, the narrow streets, the encircling forests – all seemed somehow furtive. Then his carriage passed the bend, and the train plunged down again through the bleak woods.

Five minutes later, Leakey watched the last carriage dwindle up the line, then looked about the platform.

Nobody else had alighted at Goatswood, and he could see why. The platform consisted of bare slippery boards, the waiting-room windows were dirty and inscribed with obscenities, the hard wooden seats were unpainted; the whole place seemed dead. Out of habit Leakey approached the stationmaster's office to ask when the connecting train would arrive. The man who appeared repelled him at once; he wore a grotesquely voluminous uniform, and his face was revoltingly goat-like – resembling some medieval woodcut of a satyr, Leakey thought.

'Train won't be along fer quarter of an 'our yet,' said the stationmaster, and went back into his office.

Leakey sat on an unpainted seat and stared over the wooden railing at the street a few yards below. Occasionally a passer-by would glance up, but most merely strolled past without seeing him. It struck Leakey that they were preoccupied; with what he could not know, but everybody who went by had an expectant air.

He grew tired of watching after a few minutes, and looked away over the roofs – to where something towered at the centre of town, between the station and a large hill, bare of trees, which rose behind the town. Leakey could not make it out, for the sunlight reflected dazzlingly from it; but it was shaped rather like a flagpole, with a round object atop it.

Still watching, he was vaguely aware of the stationmaster answering his office telephone, listening and then coming towards him.

''Fraid there won't be a train t'Exham t'day,' the man said behind him. 'Tree's fell an' blocked the line.'

Disappointed, Leakey did not look forward to a sojourn in Goatswood. 'What time's the next one back to Brichester, then?'

'Oh, there's only one t'day, an' that went about 'alf an 'our ago.'

Leakey did not recall passing a train on the opposite line, but at that moment he could only think of being stranded. 'But then – what am I going to do?'

'Only one thing y' *can* do – Stay at an 'otel in town fer the night.'

To give himself time to think, Leakey left the station and went for a meal at the Station Café opposite. The meal – sausage, egg and chips, all over-raw – was barely palatable, but he would not have enjoyed a better meal. The faces of the other customers were too grotesque, and he felt under the bulky suits and long dresses might lie the most revolting deformities. More, for the first time he was served by a waiter wearing gloves – and by what he could make out of the hands under them Leakey thought they were deservingly worn.

At the cash-desk, he asked for directions to a hotel where he could spend the night.

'We've only one good hotel in town,' the cashier replied. 'That's in Central Place. No, you wouldn't know where that is; well, it's a square with an island in the middle, and a p – Anyway, you go along Blakedon Street – '

Leakey followed the cashier's directions and approached the town centre. He saw offices, department stores, public houses, cinemas, parked cars, all the attributes of any town centre; but he felt something unusual here – perhaps merely a strengthening of that expectancy he had remarked at the station.

Eventually he reached a large square, read the street

sign and saw the neon *Central Hotel* at the other side. But his attention was immediately drawn to the metal pylon, fifty feet high, which rose from the centre of the square. At the top he saw a large convex lens surrounded by an arrangement of mirrors, and all hinged on a pivot attached to the ground by taut ropes.

Leakey stared at the object for so long that he caught someone watching him. He turned to the watcher and remarked: 'I'm curious because I'm from out of town – do you happen to know what that thing is?'

But the other merely peered at him wordlessly until Leakey glanced away in embarrassment; then hurried away. Baffled, Leakey made for the nearby hotel.

Once inside he felt relieved. The reception desk, the large foyer, the wide red-carpeted staircase, all seemed welcoming. He crossed to the reception desk and rang the bell.

'A room for the night?' repeated the middle-aged man who answered it. 'Yes, we do have one or two – I'm afraid they look out on the square, so you may be a bit troubled by noise. Twenty-seven and six bed and break-fast, is that all right?'

'Yes, that's fine,' Leakey replied, signing the book. He followed the manager upstairs.

On the landing, he asked: 'What's that thing in the square outside?'

'What? – oh, that? Just a local relic. You'll probably find out about it tonight.'

He opened a door marked *no 7* and ushered Leakey into a thick-carpeted room furnished with a bed, dressing-table, bedside table with a framed photograph in the middle, and two wardrobes. Leakey entered and turned to ask the meaning of his remark, but the manager was already heading for the stairs. Shrugging, he went to the window and watched the crowd below. Strange, he thought – he had brought no luggage, yet the manager had not asked him to pay in advance.

He heard a train whistle, and idly looked towards the pillar of smoke. Then he threw up the window as he realized – the train had just left the station, and was speeding *towards Brichester*!

He ran for the door, but in his hurry knocked the table to the floor, and he delayed to right it. His foot crunched on glass. It was the framed photograph, the glass smashed but the picture intact. He picked it up, turned it upright, and recoiled.

The thing in the picture was standing in a doorway. He could not believe it was alive – that pillar of white flesh supported on many-jointed bony legs tipped with great circular pads could never move about, let alone think. It had no arms, merely three spines which dug into the ground. But the head was worst – formed of thick coils of white jelly, covered with grey watery eyes, and at the centre was a huge toothed beak. And the thing that most troubled Leakey was none of these details, but only the idea that he had recently seen the doorway; not open as in the picture, but closed.

He threw open the bedroom door and thudded down-stairs. The manager was standing by the reception desk, talking to a younger man behind it.

'There's a picture in my room! Did you put it there?' Leakey demanded.

'Why, no,' answered the manager. 'What sort of picture is this? I'd better have a look.'

He examined the photograph. 'This *is* peculiar, I must admit, but I didn't put it there. I wonder what it's supposed to be . . . Well, if it's getting on your nerves, I'll take it away.'

'No – no, don't do that,' Leakey told him. 'I'd like to examine it a bit more closely.'

When the manager had left, Leakey crossed again to the window. Looking out, he had the odd feeling that the crowd below were not passing through the square; more milling about to give that impression, but really awaiting something – and watching covertly. He noticed suddenly that all of them avoided the road opposite his window; a road which he saw was unusually wide and bordered by obviously disused buildings. Raising his gaze, Leakey discovered that the road connected the square to the large bare hill behind the town. There was a trail of faint marks on that road, but he could not make out any shape.

He looked towards the hill again, and saw the railway stretching into the distance. Then he remembered, and turned angrily to leave for the station.

At that moment the door slammed and a key turned in the lock.

Leakey threw his weight against the door, but he could hear at the same time something heavy being shoved against it from the outside. Nobody answered his irate shouts, and he ran for the window. Looking down he saw the wall below was smooth, devoid of handholds, and escape upward was just as difficult. He drew back at the thought of jumping to the street, and wondered frantically how he could escape. What lunatic had imprisoned him, and why? But the people of Goatswood were surely not *all* lunatics – perhaps he could attract the attention of someone in the street.

'Do you know how Goatswood got its name?' said a voice behind him.

Leakey whirled. Nobody was in the room with him.

'Did you ever hear of the Goat of Mendes?' continued

the voice slowly, he realized, from beyond the door. 'Do you know what used to appear at the witches' sabbaths? Do you know about the Land of the Goat in the Pyrenees, or the Great God Pan? What about the Protean God? *And the Black Goat of the Woods with a Thousand Young?*'

Leakey battered the door again, then hurried back to the window. He yelled to the people below, and one looked up. Even at that distance Leakey saw his expressionless face – and the surreptitious movement of his hand. When a crowd began to form directly below the window and stare at him expressionlessly, Leakey threw himself back trembling and glancing wildly round the room.

'The goat's been there all through the ages, you know,' went on the voice. 'The black goat which appeared in the circle of the sects in Spain – the Meadow of the Goat where the Basque magicians used to meet – and always the devil appears as a hybrid animal . . . Why do you think the priests of Jupiter offered a white goat on the Ides? – but you wouldn't know of the cosmic complements . . . And you've no idea of the basis of the Haitian goat-girl ritual, or what horror lies behind the myth of the Golden Fleece . . .'

'What's all this you're saying?' screamed Leakey. 'Let me out, will you!' but when no answer came he subsided and collapsed on the bed.

'Oh, you won't understand it all yet – not yet . . . All I'm trying to tell you is that *he* is here, very near at this moment – he has been here since before the human race . . . Maybe he has always been here, or maybe he came from *out there*, but the Others – those from Glyu'uho – imprisoned him within the star-signs, and only on nights of the moon can his body come out inside their boundary.

But he goes forth if you call through the reversed angles, though then he's only partly corporeal – that's what'd appear at the sabbaths.

'They wouldn't tell all that happened at the Black Mass, of course. *He* came, but not in his real shape – that'd be too much even for the worshippers – but he retained certain portions of his real form. I suppose you've heard how they used to kiss his arse? Well, that wasn't just to be dirty – he's not built like a goat, and from there he puts things forth to draw off blood. But you'll know more about that tonight.

'You may get a bit of a shock tonight when you see us naked, though. We've gone down below his *place*, to a region I won't describe to you, and to live longer we've had to . . . to change. You've probably heard about it in a different way, though – the young of the Black Goat? *Gof'nn hupadgh Shub-Niggurath?* But the dryads and fauns and satyrs are a lot different from the classical descriptions, so don't think you're prepared – '

As suddenly as it had begun, the voice ceased. Leakey stared out of the window; the sun had almost set. He glared at the door, the window, the walls, but could see no avenue of escape. The crowd still waited below; an unintelligible muttering drifted up. Suddenly he felt very tired, and sank back on the bed.

When he awoke, the moon had risen.

It shone whitely on the street below as he craned out the window. The crowd below were passive no longer; they were standing in a stiff semi-circle around that central pylon, staring towards the hill opposite. He raised the window-frame more, and it rattled – but nobody looked up. He could hear a chorused murmur from below, a chant whose words were inaudible, and he began to realize just how serious his position was. Were they all insane? Was he trapped after dark in a town of lunatics? Clutched by sudden terror, he pushed the wardrobe against the door, and reinforced it with the bed.

What had the man who had imprisoned him said – 'you'll know more about that tonight'? Surely the whole town couldn't be caught up by this mad belief. A god that came into the town on moonlit nights – and that wasn't all. If he was right, there was a cult of Satanists in this town – and they were supposed to make a sacrifice to Satan on ritual nights. A human sacrifice – was *that* what they wanted him for?

At a shout from below, Leakey rushed to the window and looked down. A figure in black robes was standing by the pylon with his back to Leakey. He was adjusting the ropes tied to the pivot, and as he did so the lens and mirrors shifted, and a concentrated beam of moonlight moved up the road towards the hill. This must be the lunatic who had imprisoned him – but *who* . . . ?

Then the figure turned. The man was wearing a robe covered with phallic designs, and round his neck hung a necklace of small pink cylinders – whose identity Leakey sickly suspected – but he was still recognizable as the manager of the Central Hotel.

'*He* is coming! *She* is coming!' he shouted in that slow, thick voice. 'Make the way easy!'

Then, to Leakey's horror, the crowd began to chant: 'Astarte – Ashtaroth – Magna Mater . . . *Ia! Shub-Niggurath!* Gorgo, Mormo, thousand-faced moon, look favourably on our sacrifices . . . Ram with a Thousand Ewes, fill us with thy seed that more may come to worship at thy shrine . . . *Gof'n hupadgh Shub-Niggurath* . . .'

The disc of concentrated moonlight was now steadily creeping up the hill as the robed priest manipulated the ropes. Suddenly it wavered and stopped, the priest gave an inarticulate cry, and the crowd fell silent. In that silence Leakey heard a faint restless stirring, as of something distant – and vast.

Then the hill burst open.

That was how it seemed to Leakey. Almost at once he realized that a door had opened in it; a door which occupied the whole side of the hill. The little moonlight that shone beyond the gaping hole revealed the beginning of an immense passage. Back in the darkness, something pale and enormous shifted and glistened with reflected light.

Suddenly Leakey turned and ran for the door. He did not want to see what would come forth from that passage. He wanted to escape from this room and into the street, even if the crowd killed him. He struggled to move the bed, but it would not shift. He had only just managed to heave it into position – escape that way was impossible.

At that moment the crowd in the square cried out hysterically. Slowly, reluctantly, Leakey turned to look out of the window.

Something was standing in the doorway of the hill. It was the thing in the photograph; but that photograph had been too small to show all the details, and it had not been alive or moving. The head was worst of all, for those great yellow eyes peered in different directions, and all the coils were twisting and jerking, sometimes transparent so that he could see into the head.

The thing moved out of the doorway, and the three spines moved with a grotesque rowing motion to heave the body forward. The beak opened, and from it a voice issued – sibilant and high-pitched, it spoke to its worshippers who now swayed back and forth in the square to the chant. They were becoming frenzied – here

and there one would feverishly strip, but Leakey turned
nauseated from these sights.

Suddenly his numb composure broke, and he screamed
and battered the door, tore at the immovable bed, and
looked vainly around for some weapon. Outside he heard
the priest yelling incomprehensibly, and a whistling voice
answering him.

The priest yelled: *'Ia! Shub-Niggurath!* The Goat
accepts our sacrifice!'

Leakey knew instinctively what he meant. He risked a
glance out of the window – and stared straight into those
yellow eyes, far above the rooftops, watching him avidly.
It stood swaying at the other side of the square, and was
even now moving towards the hotel . . .

He looked down. The worshippers had approached the
being, and directly below was an empty strip of ground.
With terrified desperation, Leakey climbed over the sill,
hung by his fingers for a moment, and let himself fall.

The creature must have been capable of great speed.
Leakey heard a slithering sound; then fell straight on to
the squirming coils of the thing's head.

He struggled desperately, but the gelatinous coils
dragged him down, and he was enveloped. He was held
inside transparent walls which pulsed and gripped him
firmly, but not tightly enough to injure him. His hands
slipped off the jelly when he clawed at the walls, and
when he kicked out the gelatin only gave and returned to
position. He could move his head, and straining to look
upward he realized that he was imprisoned in a pocket of
air, which he did not doubt was intentional. So he was
not to die yet – but then what worse thing was to happen
to him?

The landscape he glimpsed dimly through the transparent coils was jolting now; the colossus was moving

forward, towards the hill. It reached the enormous doorway and passed within. Leakey heard a dull crash of stone, then he was jolted on through half-darkness.

The passage seemed to plunge downward for miles, but at last the creature swayed to a standstill. Leakey sank towards the ground, the prisoning coils oozed away, and hands grabbed him. He was pushed forward towards an immense archway. He glanced round frantically, but had time only to glimpse a gigantic cavern, hexagonal in shape, with droplets of moisture streaming down the walls and gleaming on carvings which stared from the shadows. And the pallid colossus was still swaying after him. Then he was hustled under the archway.

After that he stumbled down an interminable staircase, twilit from some source he could not see. The stairway did not turn from its downward path, but the twilight was too dim to show him the bottom.

'The Romans built this, you know,' said a voice at his ear in a horribly conversational tone. 'They built the lens, too, when they came here and recognized their Magna Mater . . . But these stairs lead much further down, perhaps to the place *he* came from originally – '

Leakey had an inkling what sort of place they were approaching when the light began to strengthen and they continued to walk downward *though no steps were visible*. Terrifying sounds rose from below – bass trumpetings and hollow ululations – but a flickering mist hid the region from above.

Then they were standing on solid ground – at least, it felt like solid ground, but to Leakey it appeared as if they were standing on empty air. The region was no longer hidden, and what he could see was not reassuring. Distances were variable, and he was never sure whether an object was large and far off, or small and close at hand.

The more recognizable living bodies were dissociated alarmingly without any noticeable injury, while some others were composed of parts of varying familiarity, together with portions that did not seem to belong at all. A few feet away he noticed an isolated path of glistening metal leading to a distant flight of upward-heading stairs.

'This is where we come to gain immortality,' whispered the priest, 'and now you will become like us – '

They moved back, still encircling him. Above him he heard the monstrosity ululate, and the coils began to descend towards him.

Abruptly Leakey smashed his fist into the priest's throat and leapt for the metal path.

The unnatural properties of the place, for once, aided him. Almost at once he was standing at the foot of the steps, while behind him the pursuers were struggling dissociatedly amid a mass of strangely angled walls which had suddenly appeared. He clattered up the stairs into half-darkness, listening for sounds behind him. A few hundred stairs up, he stumbled over a line of star-shaped bas-reliefs.

A little further up, he heard something huge and ponderous squelching up the stairs after him.

He ran faster, though he was gasping for breath, and his hands were cut from falls. He looked back and whimpered in horror, for a shape was swaying dimly upward not six hundred feet below. He tried to take three steps at a time, slipped – and began to tumble back down the staircase.

He grabbed at the slick stone and managed to check his fall about fifty stairs down. There was no sound from below, but when he turned his head to look, a baffled whistling broke out. The being was swaying back and forth two hundred feet below, as if fighting an invisible opponent. It was, Leakey saw, at the line of bas-reliefs; and he abruptly remembered something the priest had said – about 'star-signs' . . .

He fled upward again, stopping only five hundred yards up when there was no sign of pursuit. He struggled upward for what seemed – and may have been – hours, and finally reached a high-arched passage which ended, he could see, in the open. He ran down it and emerged in daylight.

Then he looked down at his body.

'And what did you see?' Dr Linwood prompted.

'I'd become like them, you see,' Leakey told him. 'Not altogether, but it was already taking effect – I think I can still die, though. In fact, immortality is the worst thing that could happen to me this way . . .'

'Well,' the doctor said, 'let me take a look.'

'Are you out of your mind? The only reason *I* didn't go mad was because my mind must have changed as well!'

'Listen,' Dr Linwood said, 'I've seen a great many horrible things in my time, things that would turn your stomach. I once saw a cyclist whose head had been run over by a lorry and burst open . . . I'm not easily revolted, and if you don't let me examine you I certainly won't believe your story – you'll admit it's not very credible – and I won't be able to do anything for you.'

Leakey was silent for a long time.

'All right,' he replied at last. 'But first – ' And he switched the tape-recorder off.

At 3:17 on April 3, 1961, everybody in Mercy Hill Hospital was startled by a hysterical screaming from the office block. The cries were so shocking that even the patients on the other side of the building were awoken, and all those who heard it were troubled by nightmares long after. Such was the terror in those cries that practically all the nurses ran to find the cause, leaving the wards almost unattended.

When they broke into Dr Linwood's office, he was lying on the floor with his hands over his eyes. He was alone, and there were no signs that he had been attacked. Under sedation he stopped screaming, but said nothing that revealed the cause of his insanity. He seemed to be obsessed with something that had happened in his office, but what he imagined he had seen is not clear. All he could say was that something about the patient he had examined – who, from the tape of the interview, was dangerously obsessed, and has not been caught yet – was 'horribly changed,' and seemed to be connected with the 'Great God Pan,' 'a rebirth in the vagina of Shub-Niggurath,' 'a fluctuation of form,' and something which was 'half a dryad.' The popular opinion is that Dr Linwood had been unbalanced by the strain of his work, together with the stress of preparing his speech for the coming convention, and had been affected by a species of contagious hallucination.

If the testimony of Dr Whitaker, the house surgeon, is to be believed, this hallucination may have had some basis in fact. He had been on his way to consult Dr Linwood over a medical matter when the screams broke out, and thus reached the office before anyone else. As he entered the corridor he saw someone opening the exit door – someone who must have been the patient whom Dr Linwood examined. Dr Whitaker did not see the man's face, but he particularly noticed the hand as the patient opened the door.

'It was black, shiny black,' he told the others, 'covered with lines – shaped like a bird's claw made out of wood. In fact, it didn't look like a human hand at all.'

BEFORE THE STORM

Above the town the sun strained behind grey blankness; thunder rumbled wakefully on the horizon. Along Walton Street the flocking crowds escaped into the open to catch their breaths, tried vainly to avoid their own throbbing heat. A blinding stasis held the buildings.

He knew suddenly that before the storm broke, the heat would release the life which even now he felt stirring in the darkness. Where could he hide? Not beyond the plodding shoppers, whose lightest touch released a twist of pain in him; but then how could he leave the burning street? He turned to stare at the blurred buildings, and managed to focus an entrance to the left. He plunged, kicking the tin of money to spill across the newspapers, through a low vestibule, into an elevator on the right.

The walls were featureless except for a row of buttons before his face. Instinctively he pressed the highest, with a finger through which pain blazed. The doors met and the lift jerked upward, and the man's hands moved unoccupied at his sides. His streaming eyes bent the ceiling; he thought something small and round ran up against the roof. He was crawling through a cavern whose roof pressed down less than a foot above him. The place was lightless, but somehow he could see the spiders which swarmed overhead, covering the entire roof, at intervals falling softly on him. Then the end of the cave appeared: a pitted wall from floor to ceiling, cutting off all escape. There came a vast rustling. He turned on his back and saw the globular bodies dropping, rushing across the cavern towards him, biting. He hit out in black despair as they prised their way into his mouth.

His flailing hand struck the opening elevator door. He fell out into an empty vestibule. Windows shone ahead of him, but at least the sun's rays turned down beyond the panes. A pointing finger with, to him, illegible words above it on the wall directed him. This was better than the street – there was even the suggestion of a breeze through one open window. He obeyed the finger and limped down a short passage, at whose end he followed a second digital instruction. The latter brought him into what seemed to be a waiting-room.

A door faced him, on his right a second invited. A partition slammed left of him, and a face bobbed in the opening. Was there any shelter in that direction? No, the opening was too high for access, and he turned, a coil of vertigo twisting up, and stumbled through the right-hand doorway.

He had no clear picture of the room beyond, nor did he care. He had an impression of cabinets close to him, a long high room, at a great distance a murmur as of conversation, muted. There was only one thing of importance: the chair ahead of him, by a table. He staggered sickly forward and painfully lowered himself into the chair. Then he closed his eyes. He remembered at once and snapped them open; yet in that instant he had been sucked downward to a pitted plain of crumbling spires, out of which groped tentative hands. Feverish heat burned through him. He blinked about him in despair and discovered a young man seated nearby at a desk, perhaps the closest of many. He called out as best he could, and saw the young man look enquiringly towards him, stand up slowly, approach, emerging gradually from the liquid haze.

'Who's that? Oh, sorry,' Joan added as she realized

Bob was answering the phone. He confirmed something and replaced the receiver, signalled to her that he was open to remarks. 'It's just that someone odd seems to want an interview,' she said. 'Down by the interviewing table. He looks really ill.'

'Yes, the switchboard told me. Seems he ignored the girl at the enquiry window and came straight in. Sounds like a difficult taxpayer. Better not be one of mine. If he is, I'm not taking the interview.'

'Well, you can't expect me to do this one! Anyway,' she pointed out, 'it looks as if he's roped in Bernie.'

This was going to be difficult and unpleasant, thought Bernard Cohen as he sat down across the table. At least that was a barrier between him and the man opposite. Bernard had seen him come in; it would have been impossible not to notice the arrival, with his boots awkwardly thumping the floor in a ridiculously bowlegged walk. Up close, Bernard's dislike hardened. There were unshaven men scattered across the town, but surely more shaven than this; the newcomer's coat was filthy; his whole form was pale and greasily swollen, with almost the fatness of a drowned corpse, and the bulging eyes were cracked by crimson veins. He seemed in the last stages of some foul disease.

'Do you have a query about your income tax?' enquired Bernard.

And he saw that the interview would be worse than he had anticipated. The man's hand came up and flapped loosely at his nearest ear; the mouth opened and hung that way. Bernard wondered with a shock of revulsion whether the other was mentally defective. Then the mouth moved and loud petulant sounds issued from it. Down the office people looked up or around. 'Wa-uh . . . eer,' throbbed through the office, and Bernard did not understand.

He tried again. 'Would you like to give me your name? That'd be a help.'

But now the corners of the mouth turned downward and the hands fluttered flabbily, wildly. The sounds came again, thick, more petulant. Bernard cleared his throat. 'Excuse me,' he said, and hurried away down the room.

Alone again, isolated by walls of optical fog, the man rested his chin on his hands; even this action pricked his elbows. His clothes had shrunk to a second skin, and pulled free stickily whenever he moved. He looked about, straining at the vagueness. Ahead of him, on the left, was the recently vacated form-strewn desk; beside which closed curtains hung wearily. His head wavered right; his eyes managed to isolate a metal cabinet with high double doors. High double doors – like those in that house . . .

He had believed when first he had been drawn into the Society, one night in a pub; all scepticism vanished when, outside one of the small nearby towns, they led him down steps into a pit; by the time he came up from that pit, from the touch and the whispers of unseen inhabitants of black pools down there, he was insulated from any kind of mundane knowledge. So when he walked down South Street that night and came to the house beyond the road, he accepted as truth the tales hinted by the local people, of vast faces that peered from the windows of that house, of shapes seen on the roof by moonlight – for this had been the residence of a witch, a witch who had run screaming from it one night decades ago, screaming and clawing at the shapes that swarmed on her body as she vanished into the nearby woods. But if he had gone with doubts in his mind, such doubts would have disappeared at the sight of the house. The distortedly peaked roof and tottering chimney loomed against the blackened sky, the front door leaned open on twisted hinges, the windows peered at the sky; all bespoke the gateway the building was.

He entered under an oddly carved overhang, and it was as if he had turned over a stone in some dark moist place; he felt things come alive and retreat into the dark. He was engulfed by a fear overcome only by knowledge of the bargain he was here to make. The place was alive – he sensed that life pulsed and watched from every unlit room. As he passed the iron balustrade of the stair, something moved above him in the filtered moonlight, and he thought he saw an object like the tail of something huge drawn quickly round the bend of the staircase. The doors in the hall beyond the balustrade were closed; perhaps they had only just been closed, for from one room there came a flapping as of wings straining for release. The door of the last room gaped lightlessly; he hastened past it, but could not avoid glimpsing a bed in the depths of the room and a pale motionless figure propped up in that bed. Now he was facing the high double doors at the end of the hall. He hesitated, and as he did so, he heard something heavy begin to rumble down the stairs. He pulled open the doors and plunged beyond.

He fell into total darkness, screamed as his foot went down to avoid a tumble and found no floor to hold it. He fell until it seemed he would never stop, vainly trying to catch his breath as unseen gusts howled over him, down tunnels lined with a soft substance whose nature he did not care to consider. But he hit bottom at last: a circular area of some rubber material, away from which he crawled down a passage, feeling shapes in the dark which throbbed and recoiled from his hands. He emerged in a great vault with an arched ceiling; countless passages entered the vault and converged on a dark well in the floor. He went cold at the sight of that well, and while he yet wavered he saw the bobbing white things stream out of the passages to the cavern rim and felt those which pushed him from his refuge. Then came pale movement in the wall, and something clambered up from the dark – a bloated blanched oval supported on myriad fleshless legs. Eyes formed in the gelatinous oval and stared at him. And he prostrated himself as he had been told, and called the horror's name – Eihort – and under the arched roof amid the nighted tunnels, the bargain was sealed.

He became aware once more of the table before him, the seat under him, the voices that ebbed and the heat that pricked – and as suddenly as all these retreated. He tried to hold on, but this was no memory like the well and the tunnels – this was *real*.

He was clawing his way up a spiral ramp of some gleaming metal, to what end he did not know. He levered himself to the edge, his body responding with unfamiliar movements, and looked over for one vertiginous second. The ramp climbed the interior of a tower which extended downward and upward further than he could see. At the limit of his downward vision, a shape was rushing with appalling speed around the spiral, gaining on him as he watched. He pulled himself upward in blind terror. No window broke the walls, and he was somehow glad not to see what lay outside, for in his flight he passed murals depicting a city of towers which rose from a marsh – a city in whose streets walked tall skeletal figures whose faces were always obscured. A faint hope pushed him again to the edge to peer upward, but the roof was not in sight, and as he turned back, the climbing ramp reflected both what he was and what now stood one step behind him. He shrieked.

Bernard looked up from complaining to Joan and Robert. 'We've got a nut on our hands.'

Mr Weedall hurried over to them. 'What on earth is wrong with that fellow? Who's dealing with him?'

'I was, but I found him impossible to deal with,' Bernard said.

'Well, somebody must be able to deal with him! My God!' Mr Weedall hissed. 'What must the taxpayers at the other interview table think? Whose taxpayer is he anyway?'

'I didn't even find that out – or rather, I couldn't – '

'Surely you've been in the department long enough to master that much procedure. Very well, I'll conduct the interview.' He strode on down the room, glancing back until the group dispersed, and reached the table. But the eyes of the seated man were glazed and did not fill with awareness. This was a very sick man, Mr Weedall decided, and touched the other's wrist to recall him – but he drew back his hand in dismay, for the man's skin throbbed as though all the nerves and muscles had come alive.

The night sky was not that of Earth. The black city around him was ruined; its pillars lay on stone stairways, its walls with their minute windows were jagged against the glacial void. Whatever his mission had been, he should not have entered these labyrinthine streets; for the more dead a city the more life it conceals. Something peered around a pillar; there was a rustle of debris behind him, and he whirled to see a hooded ragged figure in pursuit. While he stood helpless it skimmed nearer, the hood half open and revealing a head of flying cobwebs. He had no chance to scream as the head pressed into his face.

The hand on his wrist created the table and chair. Opposite him a figure swam on his vision; it enquired something of him. It was not like his earlier questioner; its manner was purposefully official. It leaned closer and asked in a whisper that sliced through him: 'What seems to be the trouble, please?'

Could this be a minion of Eihort or perhaps a member of some cult? If so, it might turn him out of his shade into the sun – he must play for time. Explain. But his throat had thickened and no word bubbled up. He twisted dizzily in the chair and found a desk, scraps of paper, scattered ballpoint pens. With a hand that twinged like a plucked tooth he groped at them, so desperately that eventually they were placed in front of him.

His flesh was crawling, but he dared not scratch. Sensation in his hand had subsided into a pounding ache. He fumbled with the pen and tried to think, to select items from his memory that would help describe his plight. But other images crowded in, things he had seen, places he had visited: the colossi guarding black canals on Yuggoth – the whistling heads – the horn-notes which pursued through the forests of Tond – the giant eye which peered between trees – the face which mouthed in the gulf beyond the rim – the dead things in orbit around the worlds beyond Shaggai – the shuttered storehouses hidden in a dockland town – the last revelation by the lake of Glaaki – the sun-bleached buildings of a forgotten city whose walls throbbed a word T R A K and in whose corners white shapes shifted feebly –

Mr Weedall was uncomprehendingly disturbed. The man before him would begin to write, his face twisted with exertion – then his eyes would dim and he would stiffen with panic. This became almost a rhythm as the pen struggled over the paper, slowly forming words:

Made bargain with Eihort God of the Labyrinth Gave me other lives Life selling papers didnt matter because i could go into other bodies leave mine behind to sell papers But people told me i didnt know all about the bargein Nobody made it any more and when they did years after

*Hed use them to send His children into the world Now i
cant control places i go When His servants die they come
into my body and make me go into theirs and die in thier
place Got no controllers His children will come through if
you dont let me stay*

The pen faltered; there was nothing more to be said,
and the swollen hand laid it down on the table. Mr
Weedall reread the tottering letters, which dimmed under
the onrushing storm outside, and found no sense among
them. He was sure that the man was both physically and
mentally in need of medical attention, and that he should
be escorted from the office, one way or another, in early
course. He leaned down and said 'I think I understand
now. Hold on, and I'll contact someone who can help
you.'

So he *was* one of the servants of Eihort, and calling
others to close in for the breakthrough. The man lurched
to his feet, feeling as if pain were slashing open his limbs.
He must escape, find another shelter. The room was
growing darker, as though someone was engulfing the
walls. He reeled to the door and threw it open, swayed
sickly through the waiting-room, into the vestibule. A
voice called behind him. Which way? The lifts would
take time to respond. He saw a door on the right, rushed
at it, his legs leaden and boiling.

'Not that way!' Mr Weedall shouted.

Emerging from the office with a file, Robert saw what
happened. He did not faint, but threw himself back into
the waiting-room and wrenched open the office door.
Joan was on her way out, but he pushed her back and
somehow managed to persuade her and the rest not to
approach the door. At last Mr Weedall appeared, very
pale, attempting calmness as he told them he had called
an ambulance. He would let nobody leave the room.

But before long he motioned Robert outside and suggested vaguely that they search the open rooms, staircases and halls of the building for something he did not specify. Strings of rain writhed on the windows as they searched; the storm exploded triumphantly overhead. They found nothing. Nevertheless, Mr Weedall arranged himself a transfer to another office, and Robert persuaded him to obtain transfers for himself and Joan. For the others in the office, who had not even glimpsed the object from which the ambulance men turned their eyes as they lifted it from the vestibule floor, nothing could be done. Robert does not like to think of what may threaten those working in that high office building, especially after dark.

For the crippled visitor had swung open the door despite Mr Weedall's warning – and been confronted by the roofs beyond the fire escape. Stagnant air pressed in through the opening, and a last pure ray of sunlight had struck in, so accurate in its aim as to seem deliberate. It caught the man, who let out a dreadful glutinous howl and staggered round to confront them, his head shaking insanely. Then Mr Weedall went sick, and Robert fled back to sanity and what he had once accepted as the everyday.

Perhaps he had not seen what he spent the rest of his life trying to forget: the man's face tearing, a rent appearing from temple to jaw, opening the cheek to hang revealed; for there had been no blood – only something pale as things that had never seen the sun, something that poured down the man's body, which collapsed like a balloon. Surely Robert could not have had time to see the flood separate into moving objects that rolled away down the stairs into the depths of the building, but that was the memory he always shrank from focusing; for some instinct told him that if he ever remembered clearly what he had seen, it would be something even worse than a swarm of enormous fat white spiders.

COLD PRINT

'. . . for even the minions of Cthulhu dare not speak of
Y'golonac; yet the time will come when Y'golonac strides
forth from the loneliness of aeons to walk once more among
men . . .'

Revelations of Glaaki, vol. 12

Sam Strutt licked his fingers and wiped them on his
handkerchief; his fingertips were grey with snow from the
pole on the bus platform. Then he coaxed his book out of
the polythene bag on the seat beside him, withdrew the
bus-ticket from between the pages, held it against the
cover to protect the latter from his fingers, and began to
read. As often happened the conductor assumed that the
ticket authorized Strutt's present journey; Strutt did not
enlighten him. Outside, the snow whirled down the side
streets and slipped beneath the wheels of cautious cars.

The slush splashed into his boots as he stepped down
outside Brichester Central and, snuggling the bag beneath
his coat for extra safety, pushed his way towards the
bookstall, treading on the settling snowflakes. The glass
panels of the stall were not quite closed; snow had filtered
through and dulled the glossy paperbacks. 'Look at that!'
Strutt complained to a young man who stood next to him
and anxiously surveyed the crowd, drawing his neck down
inside his collar like a tortoise. 'Isn't that disgusting?
These people just don't care!' The young man, still
searching the wet faces, agreed abstractedly. Strutt strode
to the other counter of the stall, where the assistant
was handing out newspapers. 'I say!' called Strutt. The

assistant, sorting change for a customer, gestured him to
wait. Over the paperbacks, through the steaming glass,
Strutt watched the young man rush forward and embrace
a girl, then gently dry her face with a handkerchief. Strutt
glanced at the newspaper held by the man awaiting
change. *Brutal Murder in Ruined Church*, he read; the
previous night a body had been found inside the roofless
walls of a church in Lower Brichester; when the snow
had been cleared from this marble image, frightful mutilations had been revealed covering the corpse, oval mutilations which resembled – The man took the paper and
his change away into the station. The assistant turned to
Strutt with a smile: 'Sorry to keep you waiting.' 'Yes,'
said Strutt. 'Do you realize those books are getting
snowed on? People may want to buy them, you know.'
'Do *you*?' the assistant replied. Strutt tightened his lips
and turned back into the snow-filled gusts. Behind him
he heard the ring of glass pane meeting pane.

Good Books on The Highway provided shelter; he
closed out the lashing sleet and stood taking stock. On
the shelves the current titles showed their faces while the
others turned their backs. Girls were giggling over comic
Christmas cards; an unshaven man was swept in on a
flake-edged blast and halted, staring around uneasily.
Strutt clucked his tongue; tramps shouldn't be allowed in
bookshops to soil the books. Glancing sideways to
observe whether the man would bend back the covers or
break the spines, Strutt moved among the shelves, but
could not find what he sought. Chatting with the cashier,
however, was the assistant who had praised *Last Exit to
Brooklyn* to him when he had bought it last week, and
had listened patiently to a list of Strutt's recent reading,
though he had not seemed to recognize the titles. Strutt
approached him and enquired: 'Hello – any more exciting
books this week?'

The man faced him, puzzled. 'Any more – ?'

'You know, books like this?' Strutt held up his poly-thene bag to show the grey Ultimate Press cover of *The Caning-Master* by Hector Q.

'Ah, no. I don't think we have.' He tapped his lip. 'Except – Jean Genet?'

'Who? Oh, you mean *Jennet*. No, thanks, he's dull as dishwater.'

'Well, I'm sorry, sir, I'm afraid I can't help you.'

'Oh.' Strutt felt rebuffed. The man seemed not to recognize him, or perhaps he was pretending. Strutt had met his kind before and had them mutely patronize his reading. He scanned the shelves again, but no cover caught his eye. At the door he furtively unbuttoned his shirt to protect his book still further, and a hand fell on his arm. Lined with grime, the hand slid down to his and touched his bag. Strutt shook it off angrily and confronted the tramp.

'Wait a minute!' the man hissed. 'Are you after more books like that? I know where we can get some.'

This approach offended Strutt's self-righteous sense of reading books which had no right to be suppressed. He snatched the bag out of the fingers closing on it. 'So you like them too, do you?'

'Oh, yes, I've got lots.'

Strutt sprang his trap. 'Such as?'

'Oh, *Adam and Evan, Take Me How You Like*, all the Harrison adventures, you know, there's lots.'

Strutt grudgingly admitted that the man's offer seemed genuine. The assistant at the cash-desk was eyeing them; Strutt stared back. 'All right,' he said. 'Where's this place you're talking about?'

The other took his arm and pulled him eagerly into the slanting snow. Clutching shut their collars, pedestrians were slipping between cars as they waited for a skidded bus ahead to be removed; flakes were crushed into the corners of the windscreens by the wipers. The man dragged Strutt amid the horns which brayed and honked, then between two store windows from which girls watched smugly as they dressed headless figures, and down an alley. Strutt recognized the area as one which he vainly combed for back-street bookshops; disappointing alcoves of men's magazines, occasional hot pungent breaths from kitchens, cars fitted with caps of snow, loud pubs warm against the weather. Strutt's guide dodged into the doorway of a public bar to shake his coat; the white glaze cracked and fell from him. Strutt joined the man and adjusted the book in its bag, snuggled beneath his shirt. He stamped the crust loose from his boots, stopping when the other followed suit; he did not wish to be connected with the man even by such a trivial action. He looked with distaste at his companion, at his swollen nose through which he was now snorting back snot, at the stubble shifting on the cheeks as they inflated and the man blew on his trembling hands. Strutt had a horror of touching anyone who was not fastidious. Beyond the doorway flakes were already obscuring their footprints, and the man said: 'I get terrible thirsty walking fast like this.'

'So that's the game, is it?' But the bookshop lay ahead. Strutt led the way into the bar and bought two pints from a colossal barmaid, her bosom bristling with ruffles, who billowed back and forth with glasses and worked the pumps with gusto. Old men sucked at pipes in vague alcoves, a radio blared marches, men clutching tankards aimed with jovial inaccuracy at dart-board or spittoon. Strutt flapped his overcoat and hung it next to him; the other retained his and stared into his beer. Determined not to talk, Strutt surveyed the murky mirrors which reflected gesticulating parties around littered tables not directly visible. But he was gradually surprised by the taciturnity of his table mate; surely these people (he thought) were remarkably loquacious, in fact virtually impossible to silence? This was intolerable; sitting idly in an airless backstreet bar when he could be on the move or reading – something must be done. He gulped down his beer and thumped the glass upon its mat. The other started. Then, visibly abashed, he began to sip, seeming oddly nervous. At last it was obvious that he was dawdling over the froth, and he set down his glass and stared at it. 'It looks as if it's time to go,' said Strutt.

The man looked up; fear widened his eyes. 'Christ, I'm wet,' he muttered. 'I'll take you again when the snow goes off.'

'That's the game, is it?' Strutt shouted. In the mirrors, eyes sought him. 'You don't get that drink out of me for nothing! I haven't come this far – !!'

The man swung round and back, trapped. 'All right, all right, only maybe I won't find it in this weather.'

Strutt found this remark too inane to comment. He rose, and buttoning his coat strode into the arcs of snow, glaring behind to ensure he was followed.

The last few shop-fronts, behind them pyramids of tins marked with misspelt placards, were cast out by lines of furtively curtained windows set in unrelieved vistas of red brick; behind the panes Christmas decorations hung like wreaths. Across the road, framed in a bedroom window, a middle-aged woman drew the curtains and hid the teenage boy at her shoulder. 'Hel-*lo*, there they go,' Strutt did not say; he felt he could control the figure ahead without speaking to him, and indeed had no desire to speak to the man as he halted trembling, no doubt from the cold, and hurried onward as Strutt, an inch taller than his five-and-a-half feet and better built, loomed behind him. For an instant, as a body of snow drove towards him down the street, flakes over-exposing the

landscape and cutting his cheeks like transitory razors of
ice, Strutt yearned to speak, to tell of nights when he lay
awake in his room, hearing the landlady's daughter being
beaten by her father in the attic bedroom above, straining
to catch muffled sounds through the creak of bed-springs,
perhaps from the couple below. But the moment passed,
swept away by the snow; the end of the street had
opened, split by a traffic-island into two roads thickly
draped with snow, one curling away to hide between the
houses, the other short, attached to a roundabout. Now
Strutt knew where he was. From a bus earlier in the
week he had noticed the *Keep Left* sign lying helpless on
its back on the traffic island, its face kicked in.

They crossed the roundabout, negotiated the crumbling
lips of ruts full of deceptively glazed pools collecting
behind the bulldozer treads of a redevelopment scheme,
and onward through the whirling white to a patch of
waste ground where a lone fireplace drank the snow.
Strutt's guide scuttled into an alley and Strutt followed,
intent on keeping close to the other as he knocked
powdered snow from dustbin lids and flinched from back-
yard doors at which dogs clawed and snarled. The man
dodged left, then right, between the close labyrinthine
walls, among houses whose cruel edges of jagged window-
panes and thrusting askew doors even the snow, kinder
to buildings than to their occupants, could not soften. A
last turning, and the man slithered on to a pavement
beside the remnants of a store, its front gaping emptily to
frame wine-bottles abandoned beneath a *Hein 57 Variet*
poster. A dollop of snow fell from the awning's skeleton
to be swallowed by the drift below. The man shook, but
as Strutt confronted him, pointed fearfully to the opposite
pavement: 'That's it. I've brought you here.'

The tracks of slush splashed up Strutt's trouser legs as
he ran across, checking mentally that while the man had

tried to disorient him he had deduced which main road lay some five hundred yards away, then read the inscription over the shop: *American Books Bought and Sold*. He touched a railing which protected an opaque window below street level, wet rust gritting beneath his nails, and surveyed the display in the window facing him; *History of the Rod* – a book he had found monotonous – thrusting out its shoulders among science-fiction novels by Aldiss, Tubb and Harrison, which hid shamefacedly behind lurid covers; *Le Sadisme au Cinema;* Robbe-Grillet's *Voyeur* looking lost; *The Naked Lunch* – nothing worth his journey there, Strutt thought. 'All right, it's about time we went in,' he urged the man inside, and with a glance up the eroded red brick at the first-floor window, the back of a dressing-table mirror shoved against it to replace one pane, entered also. The other had halted again, and for an unpleasant second Strutt's fingers brushed the man's musty overcoat. 'Come on, where's the books?' he demanded, shoving past into the shop.

The yellow daylight was made murkier by the window display and the pin-up magazines hanging on the inside of the glass-panelled door; dust hung lazily in the stray beams. Strutt stopped to read the covers of paperbacks stuffed into cardboard boxes on one table, but the boxes contained only Westerns, fantasies and American erotica, selling at half price. Grimacing at the books which stretched wide their corners like flowering petals, Strutt bypassed the hardcovers and squinted behind the counter, slightly preoccupied; as he had closed the door beneath its tongueless bell, he had imagined he had heard a cry somewhere near, quickly cut off. No doubt round here you hear that sort of thing all the time, he thought, and turned on the other: 'Well, I don't see what I came for. Doesn't anybody work in this place?'

Wide-eyed, the man gazed past Strutt's shoulder; Strutt

looked back and saw the frosted glass panel of a door, one corner of the glass repaired with cardboard, black against a dim yellow light which filtered through the panel. The bookseller's office, presumably – had he heard Strutt's remark? Strutt confronted the door, ready to face impertinence. Then the man pushed by him, searching distractedly behind the counter, fumbling open a glass-fronted bookcase full of volumes in brown paper jackets and finally extracting a parcel in grey paper from its hiding-place in one corner of a shelf. He thrust it at Strutt, muttering 'This is one, this is one,' and watched, the skin beneath his eyes twitching, as Strutt tore off the paper.

The Secret Life of Wackford Squeers – 'Ah, that's fine,' Strutt approved, forgetting himself momentarily, and reached for his wallet; but greasy fingers clawed at his wrist. 'Pay next time,' the man pleaded. Strutt hesitated; could he get away with the book without paying? At that moment, a shadow rippled across the frosted glass: a headless man dragging something heavy. Decapitated by the frosted glass and by his hunched position, Strutt decided, then realized that the shopkeeper must be in contact with Ultimate Press; he must not prejudice this contact by stealing a book. He knocked away the frantic fingers and counted out two pounds; but the other backed away, stretching out his fingers in stark fear, and crouched against the office door, from whose pane the silhouette had disappeared, before flinching almost into Strutt's arms. Strutt pushed him back and laid the notes in the space left on the shelf by *Wackford Squeers*, then turned on him: 'Don't you intend to wrap it up? No, on second thoughts I'll do it myself.'

The roller on the counter rumbled forth a streamer of brown paper; Strutt sought an undiscoloured stretch. As he parcelled the book, disentangling his feet from the

rejected coil, something crashed to the floor. The other
had retreated towards the street door until one dangling
cuff-button had hooked the corner of a carton full of
paperbacks; he froze above the scattered books, mouth
and hands gaping wide, one foot atop an open novel like
a broken moth, and around him motes floated into beams
of light mottled by the sifting snow. Somewhere a lock
clicked. Strutt breathed hard, taped the package and
circling the man in distaste, opened the door. The cold
attacked his legs. He began to mount the steps and the
other flurried in pursuit. The man's foot was on the
doorstep when a heavy tread approached across the
boards. The man spun about and below Strutt the door
slammed. Strutt waited; then it occurred to him that he
could hurry and shake off his guide. He reached the
street and a powdered breeze pecked at his cheeks,
cleaning away the stale dust of the shop. He turned away
his face and kicking the rind of snow from the headline of
a sodden newspaper, made for the main road which he
knew to pass close by.

Strutt woke shivering. The neon sign outside the window
of his flat, a cliché but relentless as toothache, was
garishly defined against the night every five seconds, and
by this and the shafts of cold Strutt knew that it was early
morning. He closed his eyes again, but though his lids
were hot and heavy his mind would not be lulled. Beyond
the limits of his memory lurked the dream which had
awoken him; he moved uneasily. For some reason he
thought of a passage from the previous evening's reading:
'As Adam reached the door he felt Evan's hand grip his,
twisting his arm behind his back, forcing him to the
floor – ' His eyes opened and sought the bookcase as if
for reassurance; yes, there was the book, secure within
its covers, carefully aligned with its fellows. He recalled

returning home one evening to find *Miss Whippe, Old-Style Governess*, thrust inside *Prefects and Fags*, straddled by *Prefects and Fags*; the landlady had explained that she must have replaced them wrongly after dusting, but Strutt knew that she had damaged them vindictively. He had bought a case that locked, and when she asked him for the key had replied: 'Thanks, I think I can do them justice.' You couldn't make friends nowadays. He closed his eyes again; the room and bookcase, created in five seconds by the neon and destroyed wth equal regularity, filled him with their emptiness, reminding him that weeks lay ahead before the beginning of next term, when he would confront the first class of the morning and add 'You know me by now' to his usual introduction 'You play fair with me and I'll play fair with you,' a warning which somebody would be sure to test, and Strutt would have him; he saw the expanse of white gym-shorts seat stretched tight down on which he would bring a gym-shoe with satisfying force – Strutt relaxed; soothed by an overwhelming echo of the pounding feet on the wooden gymnasium floor, the fevered shaking of the wallbars as the boys swarmed ceilingwards and he stared up from below, he slept.

Panting, he drove himself through his morning exercises, then tossed off the fruit juice which was always his first call on the tray brought up by the landlady's daughter. Viciously he banged the glass back on the tray; the glass splintered (he'd say it was an accident; he paid enough rent to cover, he might as well get a little satisfaction for his money). 'Bet you have a fab Christmas,' the girl had said, surveying the room. He'd made to grab her round the waist and curb her pert femininity – but she'd already gone, her skirt's pleats whirling, leaving his stomach hotly knotted in anticipation.

Later he trudged to the supermarket. From several front gardens came the teeth-grinding scrape of spades clearing snow; these faded and were answered by the crushed squeak of snow engulfing boots. When he emerged from the supermarket clutching an armful of cans, a snowball whipped by his face to thud against the window, a translucent beard spreading down the pane like that fluid from the noses of those boys who felt Strutt's wrath most often, for he was determined to beat this ugliness, this revoltingness out of them. Strutt glared about him for the marksman – a seven-year-old, boarding his tricycle for a quick retreat; Strutt moved involuntarily as if to pull the boy across his knee. But the street was not deserted; even now the child's mother, in slacks and curlers peeking from beneath a headscarf, was slapping her son's hand: 'I've told you, *don't* do that. – Sorry,' she called to Strutt. 'Yes, I'm sure,' he snarled, and tramped back to his flat. His heart pumped uncontrollably. He wished fervently that he could talk to someone as he had talked to the bookseller on the edge of Goatswood who had shared his urges; when the man had died earlier that year Strutt had felt abandoned in a tacitly conspiring, hostile world. Perhaps the new shop's owner might prove similarly sympathetic? Strutt hoped that the man who had conducted him there yesterday would not be in attendance, but if he were, surely he could be got rid of – a bookseller dealing with Ultimate Press must be a man after Strutt's own heart, who would be as opposed as he to that other's presence while they were talking frankly. As well as this discussion, Strutt needed books to read over Christmas, and *Squeers* would not last him long; the shop would scarcely be closed on Christmas Eve. Thus reassured, he unloaded the cans on the kitchen table and ran downstairs.

Strutt stepped from the bus in silence; the engine's

throb was quickly muffled among the laden houses. The piled snow waited for some sound. He splashed through the tracks of cars to the pavement, its dull coat depressed by countless overlapping footprints. The road twisted slyly; as soon as the main road was out of sight the side street revealed its real character. The snow laid over the house-fronts became threadbare; rusty protrusions poked through. One or two windows showed Christmas trees, their ageing needles falling out, their branches tipped with luridly sputtering lights. Strutt, however, had no eye for this but kept his gaze on the pavement, seeking to avoid stains circled by dogs' pawmarks. Once he met the gaze of an old woman staring down at a point below her window which was perhaps the extent of her outside world. Momentarily chilled, he hurried on, pursued by a woman who, on the evidence within her pram, had given birth to a litter of newspapers, and halted before the shop.

Though the orange sky could scarcely have illuminated the interior, no electric gleam was visible through the magazines, and the torn notice hanging behind the grime might read CLOSED. Slowly Strutt descended the steps. The pram squealed by, the latest flakes spreading across the newspapers. Strutt stared at its inquisitive proprietor, turned and almost fell into sudden darkness. The door had opened and a figure blocked the doorway.

'You're not shut, surely?' Strutt's tongue tangled.

'Perhaps not. Can I help you?'

'I was here yesterday. Ultimate Press book,' Strutt replied to the face level with his own and uncomfortably close.

'Of course you were, yes, I recall.' The other swayed incessantly like an athlete limbering up, and his voice wavered constantly from bass to falsetto, dismaying Strutt. 'Well, come in before the snow gets to you,' the other said and slammed the door behind them, evoking a note from the ghost of the bell's tongue.

The bookseller – this was he, Strutt presumed – loomed behind him, a head taller; down in the half-light, among the vague vindictive corners of the tables, Strutt felt an obscure compulsion to assert himself somehow, and remarked: 'I hope you found the money for the book. Your man didn't seem to want me to pay. Some people would have taken him at his word.'

'He's not with us today.' The bookseller switched on the light inside his office. As his lined pouched face was lit up it seemed to grow; the eyes were sunk in sagging stars of wrinkles; the cheeks and forehead bulged from furrows; the head floated like a half-inflated balloon above the stuffed tweed suit. Beneath the unshaded bulb the walls pressed close, surrounding a battered desk from which overflowed fingerprinted copies of *The Bookseller* thrust aside by a black typewriter clogged with dirt, beside which lay a stub of sealing-wax and an open box of matches. Two chairs faced each other across the desk, and behind it was a closed door. Strutt seated himself before the desk, brushing dust to the floor. The bookseller paced round him and suddenly, as if struck by the question, demanded: 'Tell me, why d'you read these books?'

This was a question often aimed at Strutt by the English master in the staffroom until he had ceased to read his novels in the breaks. Its sudden reappearance caught him off guard, and he could only call on his old riposte: 'How d'you mean, why? Why not?'

'I wasn't being critical,' the other hurried on, moving restlessly around the desk. 'I'm genuinely interested. I was going to make the point that don't you want what you read about to happen, in a sense?'

'Well, maybe.' Strutt was suspicious of the trend of this

discussion, and wished that he could dominate; his words seemed to plunge into the snow-cloaked silence inside the dusty walls to vanish immediately, leaving no impression.

'I mean this: when you read a book don't you make it happen before you, in your mind? Particularly if you consciously attempt to visualize, but that's not essential. You might cast the book away from you, of course. I knew a bookseller who worked on this theory; you don't get much time to be yourself in this sort of area, but when he could he worked on it, though he never quite formulated – Wait a minute, I'll show you something.'

He leapt away from the desk and into the shop. Strutt wondered what was beyond the door behind the desk. He half-rose but, peering back, saw the bookseller already returning through the drifting shadows with a volume extracted from among the Lovecrafts and Derleths.

'This ties in with your Ultimate Press books, really,' the other said, banging the office door to as he entered. 'They're publishing a book by Johannes Henricus Pott next year, so we hear, and that's concerned with forbidden lore as well, like this one; you'll no doubt be amazed to hear that they think they may have to leave some of Pott in the original Latin. This here should interest you, though; the only copy. You probably won't know the *Revelations of Glaaki*; it's a sort of Bible written under supernatural guidance. There were only eleven volumes – but this is the twelfth, written by a man at the top of Mercy Hill guided through his dreams.' His voice grew unsteadier as he continued. 'I don't know how it got out; I suppose the man's family may have found it in some attic after his death and thought it worth a few coppers, who knows? My bookseller – well, he knew of the *Revelations*, but he realized this was priceless; but he didn't want the seller to realize he had a find and perhaps take it to the library or the University, so he took it off his hands as part of a job lot and said he might use it for scribbling. When he read it – Well, there was one passage that for testing his theory looked like a godsend. Look.'

The bookseller circled Strutt again and placed the book in his lap, his arms resting on Strutt's shoulders. Strutt compressed his lips and glanced up at the other's face; but some strength weakened, refusing to support his disapproval, and he opened the book. It was an old ledger, its hinges cracking, its yellowed pages covered by irregular lines of scrawny handwriting. Through the introductory monologue Strutt had been baffled; now the book was before him, it vaguely recalled those bundles of duplicated typewritten sheets which had been passed around the toilets in his adolescence. 'Revelations' suggested the forbidden. Thus intrigued, he read at random. Up here in Lower Brichester the bare bulb defined each scrap of flaking paint on the door opposite, and hands moved on his shoulders, but somewhere down below he would be pursued through darkness by vast soft footsteps; when he turned to look a swollen finger was upon him – What was all this about? A hand gripped his left shoulder and the right hand turned pages; finally one finger underlined a phrase:

'Beyond a gulf in the subterranean night a passage leads to a wall of massive bricks, and beyond the wall rises Y'golonac to be served by the tattered eyeless figures of the dark. Long has he slept beyond the wall, and those which crawl over the bricks scuttle across his body never knowing it to be Y'golonac; but when his name is spoken or read he comes forth to be worshipped or to feed and take on the shape and soul of those he feeds upon. For those who read of evil and search for its form within their minds call forth evil, and so may Y'golonac return to walk among men and await that time when the earth is cleared off and Cthulhu rises from his tomb among the weeds, Glaaki thrusts open the crystal trapdoor, the brood of Eihort are born into daylight, Shub-Niggurath strides forth to smash the moon-lens, Byatis bursts forth from his prison, Daoloth tears away illusion to expose the reality concealed behind.'

The hands on his shoulders shifted constantly, slackening and tightening. The voice fluctuated: 'What did you think of that?'

Strutt thought it was rubbish, but somewhere his courage had slipped; he replied unevenly: 'Well, it's – not the sort of thing you see on sale.'

'You mean you found it interesting?' The voice was deepening; now it was an overwhelming bass. The other swung round behind the desk; he seemed taller – his head struck the bulb, setting shadows peering from the corners and withdrawing, and peering again. 'You're interested?' His expression was intense, as far as it could be made out; for the light moved darkness in the hollows of his face, as if the bone structure were melting visibly.

In the murk in Strutt's mind appeared a suspicion; had he not heard from his dear dead friend the Goatswood bookseller that a black magic cult existed in Brichester, a circle of young men dominated by somebody Franklin or Franklyn? Was he being interviewed for this? 'I wouldn't say that,' he countered.

'Listen. There was a bookseller who read this, and I told him you may be the high priest of Y'golonac. You will call down the shapes of night to worship him at the times of year; you will prostrate yourself before him and in return you will survive when the earth is cleared off for the Great Old Ones; you will go beyond the rim to what stirs out of the light . . .'

Before he could consider Strutt blurted: 'Are you talking about me?' He had realized he was alone in a room with a madman.

'No, no, I meant the bookseller. But the offer now is for you.'

'Well, I'm sorry, I've got other things to do.' Strutt prepared to stand up.

'He refused also.' The timbre of the voice grated in Strutt's ears. 'I had to kill him.'

Strutt froze. How did one treat the insane? Pacify them. 'Now, now, hold on a minute . . .'

'How can it benefit you to doubt? I have more proof at my disposal than you could bear. You will be my high priest, or you will never leave this room.'

For the first time in his life, as the shadows between the harsh oppressive walls moved slower as if anticipating, Strutt battled to control an emotion; he subdued his mingled fear and ire with calm. 'If you don't mind, I've got to meet somebody.'

'Not when your fulfilment lies here between these walls.' The voice was thickening. 'You know I killed the bookseller – it was in your papers. He fled into the ruined church, but I caught him with my hands . . . Then I left the book in the shop to be read, but the only one who picked it up by mistake was the man who brought you here . . . Fool! He went mad and cowered in the corner when he saw the mouths! I kept him because I thought he might bring some of his friends who wallow in physical taboos and lose the true experiences, those places forbidden to the spirit. But he only contacted you and brought you here while I was feeding. There is food occasionally; young boys who come here for books in secret; they make sure nobody knows what they read! – and can be persuaded to look at the *Revelations*. Imbecile! He can no longer betray me with his fumbling – but I knew you would return. Now you will be mine.'

Strutt's teeth ground together silently until he thought his jaws would break; he stood up, nodding, and handed the volume of the *Revelations* towards the figure; he was poised, and when the hand closed on the ledger he would dart for the office door.

'You can't get out, you know; it's locked.' The bookseller rocked on his feet, but did not start towards him; the shadows now were mercilessly clear and dust hung in the silence. 'You're not afraid – you look too calculating. Is it possible that you still do not believe? All right – ' he laid his hands on the doorknob behind the desk: ' – do you want to see what is left of my food?'

A door opened in Strutt's mind, and he recoiled from what might lie beyond. 'No! No!' he shrieked. Fury followed his involuntary display of fear; he wished he had a cane to subjugate the figure taunting him. Judging by the face, he thought, the bulges filling the tweed suit must be of fat; if they should struggle, Strutt would win. 'Let's get this clear,' he shouted, 'we've played games long enough! You'll let me out of here or I – ' but he found himself glaring about for a weapon. Suddenly he thought of the book still in his hand. He snatched the matchbox from the desk, behind which the figure watched, ominously impassive. Strutt struck a match, then pinched the boards between finger and thumb and shook out the pages. 'I'll burn this book!' he threatened.

The figure tensed, and Strutt went cold with fear of his next move. He touched the flame to paper, and the pages curled and were consumed so swiftly that Strutt had only the impression of bright fire and shadows growing unsteadily massive on the walls before he was shaking ashes to the floor. For a moment they faced each other, immobile. After the flames a darkness had rushed into Strutt's eyes. Through it he saw the tweed tear loudly as the figure expanded.

Strutt threw himself against the office door, which resisted. He drew back his fist, and watched with an odd timeless detachment as it shattered the frosted glass; the act seemed to isolate him, as if suspending all action outside himself. Through the knives of glass, on which gleamed drops of blood, he saw the snowflakes settle through the amber light, infinitely far; too far to call for help. A horror filled him of being overpowered from behind. From the back of the office came a sound; Strutt spun and as he did so closed his eyes, terrified to face the source of such a sound – but when he opened them he saw why the shadow on the frosted pane yesterday had been headless, and he screamed. As the desk was thrust aside by the towering naked figure, on whose surface still hung rags of the tweed suit, Strutt's last thought was an unbelieving conviction that this was happening because he had read the *Revelations*; somewhere, someone had *wanted* this to happen to him. It wasn't playing fair, he hadn't done anything to deserve this – but before he could scream out his protest his breath was cut off, as the hands descended on his face and the wet red mouths opened in their palms.

Among the pictures are these:

A void. Against it stand several cut-out figures, representing men. One feels they give a glimpse of an infinite series. They are completely featureless except for a small slit in the region of the heart. Below them, half obscuring the undivided legs of one, is a small figure, formed of dust; it is impossible to discern its slit. Above, a hand protrudes from a cylinder and manipulates a puppet, which wears a crude crown and brandishes a stick tipped with a pointed stone or jewel. Near the hobbling unequal feet of the puppet, a mouth hangs in the void. Within it a record-player balances on the lower lip.

An undistinguished stone landscape. A single tuft of grass sprouts from a rock, a river rushes by. Against a lone cloud stretched to a point, a landed spaceship smokes. A rubber simulacrum of a tree bears a single apple, and a naked man with abnormally short legs, perhaps the pilot of the spaceship, reaches for the fruit.

A cave. Several creatures – a one-eyed chinless humanoid with one arm considerably longer than the other, a figure with a long thin head and eyes on stalks, a small snarling pot-bellied dinosaur, a disquieted lizard – regard a fragment tied to the wall of the cave. The fragment depicts a spaceship which has crashed among rocks. A man wearing a jacket and shrunken checked trousers, and with rudimentary hands and gun, steps forward from it. One foot rests on the floor of the cave.

A title page: *Ye Anciente Marinere*. Web envelops the capital letters. A one-eyed grinning snake with bared fangs curls about the margin. Above a bow and arrow floats a contented skull. A bird with horns, bat-wings and a small penis stands on a rock in the sea. A zephyr who has lost one eye rests his head on the skull of an animal and blows in unison with a furious dog-headed creature with webbed feet. The sea's crest of foam contains three skulls.

A crossroads at midnight, deserted except for a faceless witch kneeling in a pentagram. From the flames in the pot before her rises the head of a demon, its face rather like that of a sleepy cat. One word is visible on the signpost: EXHAM.

A plain. In the middle stands a thumb-shaped rock, seen through (or contained in) a drinking-glass. A head like a malformed potato grips the top joint of the thumb with eleven spidery legs. The head glares skyward with its one eye and bares a single fang. Below, tiny figures kneel and worship, and one stands with a fuming cup in its hand. Outside the glass, more distant, another head unattended by worshippers clings to its rock and gazes sadly at the sky.

A landscape of high thin peaks and spears of rock. A comet with the face of a skull rushes over the horizon. Nearer and higher, a second comet drifts. Its neck and shoulders solidify into the head, whose face is that of a blind horse with long eyelashes, while from the shoulders hang claws on arms like fragile pipes. In the foreground a grimoire is held open by two long-fingered hands, clearly not those of one person. From the pages fumes a flattened cloud, containing a plain broken by mountains and, above the plain, a snarling bat-winged demon with fangs, horns, and moustache. Behind the cloud hovers a figure with a single webbed wing and the stump of another. It has the face of a grasshopper, and its proboscis reaches down to the tips of its pendulous breasts. From its waist curls a thin trail of dust.

Night under a full moon, outside the mouth of a cave. On the ground two figures copulate. The female lies in an attitude of submission, her arms splayed limply. Her face and pointed ears are huge, and her upper lip is extremely prominent. Her mouth gapes, showing pointed teeth, and her glazed eyes gaze upwards; she may be hypnotized or dead. The male's head is smaller, but his ears cover most of the side of his head. His jaw opens wide enough to touch his throat, and he bites into the female's armpit, drawing streams of blood. His arms appear to be boneless; one curls around his mate's body, while his other hand is poised above his head, its pointed fingers aimed at her face. Within the cave, a shadow with a conical head frowns down.

A void. Nearest, a lugubrious face whose mouth has grown down into the chin on the left side. The backs of two hands with pointed nails beat a tuned drum. Beneath a bed a naked man lies smirking; against the bed rests a large wheel with a cutting edge. A living bust with a terrified face floats above the footboard, staring at a vibrating stick thrust into a plank. Outside an askew window, a disembodied face stares in from the night. The cross-pieces of the window obscure both the eyes and the mouth of the face completely.

An avenue of wild bare trees on a plain. Several display raw stumps. Some way down the avenue, six figures join hands and dance around a corpse. From their midst rises a wraith, passing across the moon with pointed arms outstretched. At the near end of the avenue stands a figure; one breast, the chin, an ear and the other side of the face have melted. A hand reaches towards it, its nails liquefying.

A title page: *Alethia Phrikodes*. Webbed capitals. A cross formed of tentacles stands gesturing at the foot of a hill. From the tower of a melted church a tree waves, and above it a glove is veined by black lightning.

A finger beckons, pointing to a figure with malformed fragile arms, almost nude except for a loincloth. The face is covered by a hood of sacking, and only the pointed chin is visible. Pan-pipes shriek a discord, and behind them appears an eye and a mouth overhung by a blood-tipped fang. A hand, within whose insubstantial wrist can be seen the silhouette of a hanging, points to a gibbet. From the gibbet swings a skeleton. The skull is oval; the teeth protrude, and the lower jaw is missing.

A naked man with abnormally short legs climbs a rock face. Legless birds with flattened heads and long beaks torment him. There is a large open wound beneath his left shoulderblade. At the top of the rock face lies a corpse wearing a jacket or sweater. Its limp fingers hang over the edge, and from near them falls a rock. Further along the edge stands a tree like a flash of lightning stylized in wood.

An explosion in an abyss. Portions of wall fly out of the smoke, some framing shattered windows. An arm is hurled out, and more distant, a tattered torso still bearing its head and one arm. Highest against the fish-shaped clouds rise a leg and, still calmly smoking, a chimney.

Caption: 'Once I beheld . . . a thing I saw not clearly, yet from glimpsing, fled.' A man wearing a short jacket and trousers stares horrified at a slab before a cave. Behind him a hand with four digits gropes from a pool. On the slab a chinless head, tufted like a pineapple, grips the stone with eleven short legs and stares at the sky with a look of dismayed resignation. Beside it hover three faceless bats. A shadow kneels before the slab.

A mountainous landscape. Against the moon hangs the askew silhouette of a horned man with bat-wings. Nearer, on a rock, another stands. He has long hair and a pugnacious Neanderthal face. His wings rise from his shoulders; he has no arms, and instead of buttocks a wistful face with a snub nose surmounts his thighs. His toes grip the rock. Ropes and claws of dust drift past him, across the sky.

An operating theatre. From beneath a sheet protrudes the head and arm of an unconscious man. The sheet is drawn so tight that it appears there is no body beneath it; in any case, the table is by no means long enough to accommodate a body in proportion to the head. Within a stain on the sheet can be seen disembodied eyes and a sneering face with a cowl pulled down over its eyes. A surgeon, his eyes masked, stares away from the table. His eyes and mouth are rudimentary, and he holds a knife perhaps a foot long. About him drift clouds containing affrighted faces, one with a knife in its throat; a huge shadowy skull; a howling fanged mouth with flaring nostrils, thrusting out a hand which holds a glass globe; the head of a man on the table, pouring blood, with a disembodied arm flourishing a dagger above it, and beside it a sorrowful naked figure with a chinless phallic head, kneeling and declaiming.

A plain. A few gravestones stand or lean. Against one sits a skeleton, one hand caressing its pelvis. From its mouth drifts the legless body of a vampire, her mouth and shroud daubed with blood. Nearby a figure holds a bone to its fanged mouth, its stance reminiscent both of gnawing and of playing a flute. Its pointed head rises straight from its chest through the V of its jacket, emerging only from the ears upwards. Above a single sketchy tree on the horizon, a dismayed face floats. Its hair is plastered blackly to its long head, and its eyes are drawn vertically into thin rectangles. Its arms and shoulders withdraw to huddle behind the head, and together with the rest of it are stretched to a ragged ectoplasmic point above the tree. As it gazes down, its whole attitude recalls that of a distressed priest.

A plateau broken by erect clubs of rock. A figure wearing a loincloth stands with one hand on a cracked skull. Its hair is long and its nose hooked; its breasts are rudimentary, but although the loincloth has slipped it is impossible to determine the figure's sex. One foot presses on a small snake with an eye missing. The figure's right hand holds a book, one finger marking a place. From that page streams a sparkling mist, forming into a head and arms with long hands. The conical reptilian face frowns, and one hand displays a globe containing a silhouette of a gibbet. Near the skull a shattered hourglass drifts, while in the sky oval bat-winged heads flutter.

A mountainous area. Narrow veils of a distorting mist rise from the ground. On a short length of railway line stands an engine. Its boiler is tilted far to the left, and from the tilted funnel flies an animal's skull. A face with fangs, lacking ears and one eye, grimaces from within the circle of the front of the boiler. A figure dressed in sacking, malformed by decay and the mist, stretches out an undecayed hand towards the engine. Skulls hover or streak skyward. Near one, a broken crystal ball contains a bedstead. A huge gun shoots liquid at the engine. Above the gun, a crescent moon lies on its back, sliced by the mist and imperfectly reassembled, and beside the moon appears a great eye set in dust.

Caption: 'All this he bade – but my soul . . . fled without aim or knowledge, shrieking in silence through the gibbering deeps.' An inverted mountain landscape hangs over a void. A head with upswept hair clings to the mountains with eight thick tufted legs. The head has one eye, two fangs and a cleft chin. A watery hand points away across the void, while beneath it two hands whose wrists trail off into dust cover a terrified face.

An extinguished candle smoulders. Behind it, a slightly taller figure is completely hooded, and the hood rises to a high point at the back of the head. Closer, a woman fingers one of her breasts, which press together on the left side of her body. Beneath her hair, her face is a shadow containing one eye, the socket of another, and a painted mouth. A figure, whose head may be hooded or faceless, stands with hands on hips; its arms appear to be sewn to the body. A man wearing a hat and cape leaps from a pinnacle into the sea. A door opens, revealing a shadow. Near the top half of a corpse lying in a pool of blood hangs a dripping knife, while above the corpse hovers a cluster of terrified masks. Several of the masks, however, are smiling.

In 1973 I came across some notebooks full of drawings I'd made twelve years previously. Their technique was minimal, but their effect on me was too disconcerting not to share. Influences on them include Lovecraft as well as surrealism and Weird Tales *covers. I've tried to describe what's here as objectively as possible.*

THE TUGGING

I

When Ingels awoke he knew at once he'd been dreaming
again. There was an image, a memory clamouring faintly
but urgently at the edge of his mind; he snatched at it,
but it was gone. He swung himself off the crumpled bed.
Hilary must have gone to do her research in the library
hours ago, leaving him a cold breakfast. Outside hung a
chill glazed blue sky, and frost was fading from the
window pane.

The dream continued to nag at his mind. He let it
pluck at him, hoping that the nagging would turn by itself
into memory. He slowed himself down, dressing slowly,
eating slowly, to allow the memory to catch up. But there
was only the insistence, like a distant recollection of a
plucked tooth. Through the wall he could hear a radio
announcer's voice in the next flat, a blurred cadence
rising as if to leap a barrier that obscured its words
completely. It buzzed at his mind, bumbling. He washed
up quickly, irritably, and hurried out.

And found that he couldn't look up at the sky.

The feeling seized his neck like a violent cramp, forcing
his head down. Around him women were wheeling prams
in which babies and groceries fought for space, dogs were
playing together in the alleys, buses quaked at bus stops,
farting. But on Ingels, pressing down from a clear rather
watery blue expanse to which he couldn't even raise his
eyes, weighed a sense of intolerable stress, as if the calm

sky were stretched to splitting: as if it were about to split and to let his unformed fear through at him.

A bus braked, a long tortured scraping squeal. When Ingels recovered from his heart-clutching start he'd jolted off the fear. He ran for the bus as the last of the queue shuffled on. Scared of the sky indeed, he thought. I've got to get more sleep. Pill myself to sleep if I have to. His eyes felt as if floating in quicklime.

He sat among the coughing shoppers. Across the aisle a man shook his head at the tobacco-smoke, snorting like a horse. A woman threw herself and three carrier bags on to a seat, patting them reassuringly, and slammed her predecessor's open window. Ingels rummaged in his briefcase. He'd left one notebook at his own flat, he discovered, muttering. He flicked through the notes for his column, holding them flat on his briefcase. Wonder if the fellow whose knee I'm fighting recognizes my style. World's champion egotist, he rebuked himself, hiding the notes with his forearm. Don't worry, he won't steal the copyright, he scoffed, pulling his arm back. He put the notes away. They looked as bleary as he felt.

He gazed around the bus, at the flat stagnant smoke, at the ranks of heads like wig-blocks, and settled on head-lines over the shoulder in front of him:

IS THE SOLAR SYSTEM ON TOW?

Six months ago an amateur astronomer wrote to us, warning that a planet might pass dangerously close to Earth.

THE ASTRONOMER ROYAL'S COMMENT: '*UTTER TWADDLE*'.

Now the world's leading astronomers have agreed to let us have the facts.

TODAY WE TELL ALL.

In an exclusive interview.

But he'd turned over, to the smaller print of the story. Ingels sat back again, remembering how the *Herald* had received a copy of that letter six months ago. They hadn't published it, and the letters editor had gazed at Ingels pityingly when he'd suggested they might at least follow it up. 'I suppose you arts people need imagination,' he'd said. Ingels grimaced wryly, wondering how they would handle the story in tonight's edition. He leaned forward, but the man had reached the editorial comment: 'Even if his aim was to prevent panic, are we paying the Astronomer Royal to tell us what too many people are now suggesting was a lie?'

Ingels glanced out of the window. Offices flashed past, glazed displays of figures at desks, the abrupt flight of perspective down alleys with a shock like a fall in a dream, more displays. The offices thinned out and aged as the bus gathered speed towards the edge of Brichester. Nearly there, Ingels thought, then realized with a leap from his seat that he'd passed the *Herald* building three stops back. For a second he knew where he'd been heading. So what? he thought savagely, the rims of his eyes rusty and burning, as he clattered downstairs. But once he was on the street he wished that he'd thought to remember: now he couldn't imagine where he could have been going in that direction.

BRICHESTER HERALD: BRICHESTER'S EVENING VOICE. The iron poem (two-thirds of a haiku, he'd thought until he grew used to it) clung to the bricks above him. The foyer was quiet. He wondered how long it would be before the presses began to thump heartily, disproving the soundproofing. Not long, and he had to write his column.

His mind felt flat and empty as the elevator. He drifted numbly through the hundred-yard open-plan office, past the glancing heads behind glass personalized in plastic.

Some looked away quickly, some stared, some smiled. My God, I don't even know his name, Ingels thought of several. 'Hello, Moira,' he said. 'How's it going, Bert.' Telephones shrilled, were answered, their calls leapt prankishly across the floor. Reporters sidestepped through the aisles. Smells of deodorant and sweat, tang of ink, brandished paper, scurrying typewriters, hasty agitated conferences.

Bert had been following him to his desk. 'Don't wait for your personal bulletin,' Bert said, throwing a telex sheet on the desk. 'The latest on your wandering planet.'

'Don't tell me I've convinced you at last.'

'No chance,' Bert said, retreating. 'Just so you don't start turning the place upside down for it.'

Ingels read the sheet, thinking: I could have told them this six months ago. The Americans had admitted that an unmanned probe was well on its way to photograph the wanderer. He rested his elbow on the desk and covered his eyes. Against the restless patches of light he almost glimpsed what he'd dreamed. He started, bewildered; the noise of the newspaper poured into him. Enough, he thought, sorting out his notes.

He typed the television review – a good play from Birmingham, when are we going to see a studio in Brichester – and passed it to Bert. Then he pawed desultorily at the day's accumulation on his desk. Must go and see my folks this week. Might drain my tension a little. He turned over a brown envelope. A press ticket, elaborately pretty lettering: exhibition of associational painting – the new primitivism and surrealism. Ugh, he thought, and whatever you say to surrealists. Private view this afternoon. Which means now. 'You can have a local arts review tomorrow,' he said, showing the ticket to Bert, and went out.

Once out of the building his mind teetered like a

dislocated compass. Again the sky seemed brittle glass, ready to crack, and when he moved to shake off the obsession he found himself urged towards the edge of Brichester. A woman flinched from him as he snarled himself to a halt. 'Sorry,' he called after her. Whatever's in that direction, it isn't the show I've been invited to. But there must be something there. Maybe I went there when I was young. Have a look when I can. Before I sleepwalk there.

Although he could have taken a bus into Lower Brichester, where the exhibition was, he walked. Clear my head, perhaps, if I don't get high on petrol first. The sky was thin and blue; nothing more, now. He swung his briefcase. Haven't heard of these artists before. Who knows, they could be good.

He hadn't been through Lower Brichester for months, and was taken aback by its dereliction. Dogs scrabbled clattering in gouged shop-fronts, an uprooted streetlamp lay across a road, humped earth was scattered with disembowelled mattresses, their entrails fluttering feebly. He passed houses where one window was blinded with brick, the next still open and filmy with a drooping curtain. He examined his ticket. Believe it or not, I'm on the right track.

Soon whole streets were derelict. There was nothing but Ingels, the gaping houses and uneven pavements, the discreet sky, his footsteps alone; the rush of the city was subdued, quiescent. The houses went by, shoulder to shoulder, ribs open to the sky, red-brick fronts revealing their jumble of shattered walls and staircases. Ingels felt a lurking sympathy for the area in its abandonment, its indifference to time. He slowed down, strolling. Let myself go a bit. The private view's open for hours yet. Relax. He did, and felt an irrational impulse pleading with him.

And why not, he thought. He glanced about: nobody. Then he began to lope through the deserted streets, arms hanging, fingers almost touching the road. Unga bunga, he thought. One way to prepare myself for the primitives, I suppose.

He found his behaviour touched a memory; perhaps the memory was its source. A figure running crouched through ruins, somewhere nearby. A kind of proof of virility. But they hadn't been deserted city streets, he thought, loping. Just flat blocks of black rock in which square windows gaped. Abandoned long before but hardly affected by time. A figure running along a narrow path through the stone, not looking at the windows.

Clouds were creeping into the sky; darkness was suffusing the streets around him. Ingels ran, not looking at the houses, allowing them to merge with the memory they touched. It was coming clearer. You had to run all the way along one of the stone paths. Any path at all, for there were no intersections, just a straight unbroken run. You had to run fast, before something within the windows became aware of you, rather as a carnivorous plant becomes aware of a fly. The last part of the run was the worst, because you knew that at any moment something would appear in all the windows at once: things that, although they had mouths, were not faces –

Ingels stumbled wildly as he halted, glaring up at the empty windows of the houses. What on earth was that? he thought distractedly. Like one of those dreams I used to have, the ones that were so vivid. Of course, that's what it must have been. These streets reminded me of one of them. Though the memory felt much older, somehow. From the womb, no doubt, he shouted angrily at his pounding heart.

When he reached the exhibition he walked straight past it. Returning, he peered at the address on the ticket.

My God, this is it. Two of a street of dingy but tenanted terraced houses had been run together; on the front door of one, in lettering he'd taken for graffiti, were the words LOWER BRICHESTER ARTS LAB. He recalled how, when it had opened last year, the invitations to the opening had arrived two days later. The project he'd described after a hurried telephone interview hadn't looked at all like this. Oh well, he thought, and went in.

In the hall, by the reception desk, two clowns were crawling about with children on their backs. One of the children ran behind the desk and gazed up at Ingels. 'Do you know where the exhibition is?' he said. 'Up your arse,' she said, giggling. 'First floor up,' said one of the clowns, who Ingels now realized was a made-up local poet, and chased the children into a playroom full of inflatables.

The first floor was a maze of plywood partitions in metal frames. On the partitions hung paintings and sketches. As Ingels entered, half-a-dozen people converged on him, all the artists save one, who was trying to relight a refractory cone of incense. Feeling outnumbered, Ingels wished he'd made it to the maze. 'You've just missed the guy from Radio Brichester,' one said, 'Are you going to talk to all of us, like him?' another asked. 'Do you like modern art?' 'Do you want coffee?'

'Now leave him be,' said Annabel Pringle, as Ingels recognized her from her picture on the cover of the catalogue. 'They're new to exhibiting, you see, you can't blame them. I mean, this whole show is my idea but their enthusiasm. Now, I can explain the principles as you go round if you like, or you can read them in the catalogue.'

'The latter, thanks,' Ingels hurried into the maze, opening the typed catalogue. A baby with an ear-trumpet, which was 2: Untitled. 3 was a man throwing his nose into a wastebasket, and Untitled. 4: Untitled. 5, 6, 7 –

Well, their paintings are certainly better than their prose, Ingels thought. The incense unravelled ahead of him. A child playing half-submerged in a lake. A blackened green-tinged city shouldering up from the sea. A winged top hat gliding over a jungle. Suddenly Ingels stopped short and turned back to the previous painting. He was sure he had seen it before.

22: Atlantis. But it wasn't like any Atlantis he'd seen pictured. The technique was crude and rather banal, obviously one of the primitives, yet Ingels found that it touched images buried somewhere in him. Its leaning slabs of rock felt vast, the sea poured from its surfaces as if it had just exploded triumphantly into sight. Drawn closer, Ingels peered into the darkness within a slab of rock, beyond what might be an open doorway. If there were the outline of a pale face staring featurelessly up from within the rock, its owner must be immense. If there were, Ingels thought, withdrawing: but why should he feel there ought to be?

When he'd hurried around the rest of the exhibition he tried to ask about the painting, but Annabel Pringle headed him off. 'You understand what we mean by associational painting?' she demanded. 'Let me tell you. We select an initial idea by aleatory means.'

'Eh?' Ingels said, scribbling.

'Based on chance. We use the I Ching, like John Cage. The American composer, he originated it. Once we have the idea we silently associate from it until each of us has an idea they feel they must communicate. This exhibition is based on six initial ideas. You can see the diversity.'

'Indeed,' Ingels said. 'When I said "eh" I was being an average reader of our paper, you understand. Listen, the one that particularly interested me was number 22. I'd like to know how that came about.'

'That's mine,' one young man said, leaping up as if it were House.

'The point of our method,' Annabel Pringle said, gazing at the painter, 'is to erase all the associational steps from your mind, leaving only the image you paint. Of course Clive here wouldn't remember what led up to that painting.'

'No, of course,' Ingels said numbly. 'It doesn't matter. Thank you. Thanks all very much.' He hurried downstairs, past a sodden clown, and into the street. In fact it didn't matter. A memory had torn its way through his insomnia. For the second time that day he realized why something had looked familiar, but this time more disturbingly. Decades ago he had himself dreamed the city in the painting.

II

Ingels switched off the television. As the point of light dwindled into darkness it touched off the image in him of a gleam shooting away into space. Then he saw that the light hadn't sunk into darkness but into Hilary's reflection, leaning forward from the cane rocking-chair next to him, about to speak. 'Give me fifteen minutes,' he said, scribbling notes for his review.

The programme had shown the perturbations which the wandering planet had caused in the orbits of Pluto, Neptune, and Uranus, and had begun and ended by pointing out that the planet was now swinging away from the Solar System; its effect on Earth's orbit would be negligible. Photographs from the space-probe were promised within days. Despite its cold scientific clarity (Ingels wrote) and perhaps without meaning to, the programme managed to communicate a sense of foreboding, of the intrusion into and interference with our familiar skies. 'Not to me it didn't,' Hilary said, reading over his shoulder.

'That's sad,' he said. 'I was going to tell you about my dreams.'

'Don't if I wouldn't understand them either. Aren't I allowed to criticize now?'

'Sorry. Let's start again. Just let me tell you a few of the things that have happened to me. I was thinking of them all today. Some of them even you'll have to admit are strange. Make some coffee and I'll tell you about them.

When she'd brought the coffee he waited until she sat forward, ready to be engrossed, long soft black hooks of hair angling for her jawbone. 'I used to dream a lot when I was young,' he said. 'Not your average childhood dream, if there is such a thing. There was one I remember, about these enormous clouds of matter floating in outer space, forming very slowly into something. I mean *very* slowly . . . I woke up long before they got there, yet while I was dreaming I knew whatever it was would have a face, and that made me very anxious to wake up. Then there was another where I was being carried through a kind of network of light, on and on across intersections for what felt like days, until I ended up on the edge of this gigantic web of paths of light. And I was fighting to stop myself going in, because I knew that hiding behind the light there was something old and dark and shapeless, something dried-up and evil that I couldn't make out. I could hear it rustling like an old dry spider. You know what I suddenly realized that web was? My brain, I'd been chasing along my nervous system to my brain. Well, leave that one to the psychologists. But there were odd things about these dreams – I mean, apart from all that.

They always used to begin the same way, and always about the same time of the month.'

'The night of the full moon?' Hilary said, slurping coffee.

'Funnily enough, yes. Don't worry, I didn't sprout midnight shadow or anything. But some people are sensitive to the full moon, that's well enough documented. And I always used to begin by dreaming I could see the full moon over the sea, way out in the middle of the ocean. I could see the reflection resting on the water, and after a while I'd always find myself thinking it wasn't the moon at all but a great pale face peering up out of the ocean, and I'd panic. Then I wouldn't be able to move and I'd know that the full moon was pulling at something deep in the ocean, waking up. I'd feel my panic swelling up in me, and all of a sudden it would burst and I'd be in the next dream. That's how it happened, every time.'

'Didn't your parents know? Didn't they try to find out what was wrong?'

'I don't know what you mean by wrong. But yes, they knew eventually, when I told them. That was after I had the idea my father might be able to explain. I was eleven then and I'd had strange feelings sometimes, intuitions and premonitions and so forth, and sometimes I'd discovered they'd been my father's feelings too.'

'I know all about your father's feelings,' Hilary said. 'More than he knows about mine.'

Soon after they'd met Ingels had taken her to see his parents. She'd felt his father had been too stiffly polite to her, and when she'd cross-examined Ingels he'd eventually admitted that his father had felt she was wrong for him, unsympathetic to him. 'You were going to let me tell you about my dreams,' he said. 'I told my father about the sea dream and I could see there was something he wasn't saying. My mother had to make him tell me.

Her attitude to the whole thing was rather what yours would have been, but she told him to get it over with, he'd have to tell me sometime. So he told me he'd sometimes shared his father's dreams without either of them ever knowing why. And he'd had several of my dreams when he'd been young, until one night in the mid-twenties – early 1925, I think he said. Then he'd dreamed a city had risen out of the sea. After that he'd never dreamed again. Well, maybe hearing that was some kind of release for me, because the next time I dreamed of the city too.'

'You dreamed of a city,' Hilary said.

'The same one. I told him about it next morning, details of it he hadn't told me, that were the same in both our dreams. I was watching the sea, the same place as always. Don't ask me how I knew it was always the same. I knew. One moment I was watching the moon on the water, then I saw it was trembling. The next moment an island rose out of the ocean with a roaring like a waterfall, louder than that, louder than anything I've ever heard while awake; I could actually feel my ears hurting. There was a city on the island, all huge greenish blocks with sea and seaweed pouring off them. And the mud was boiling with stranded creatures, panting and bursting. Right in front of me and above me and below me there was a door. Mud was trickling down from it, and I knew that the great pale face I was terrified of was behind the door, getting ready to come out, opening its eyes in the dark. I woke up then, and that was the end of the dreams. Say they were only dreams if you like. You might find it easiest to believe my father and I were sharing them by telepathy.'

'You know perfectly well,' Hilary said, 'that I'd find nothing of the sort.'

'No? Then try this,' he said sharply. 'At the exhibition

I visited today there was a painting of our dream. And not by either of us.'

'So what does that mean?' she cried. 'What on earth is that supposed to mean?'

'Well, a dream I can recall so vividly after all this time is worth a thought. And that painting suggests it's a good deal more objectively real.'

'So your father read about the island in a story,' she said. 'So did you, so did the painter. What else can you possibly be suggesting?'

'Nothing,' he said at last.

'So what were the other strange things you were going to tell me?'

'That's all,' he said. 'Just the painting. Nothing else. Really.' She was looking miserable, a little ashamed. 'Don't you believe me?' he said. 'Come here.'

As the sheepskin rug joined their caresses she said 'I don't really need to be psychic for you, do I?' 'No,' he said, probing her ear with his tongue, triggering her ready. Switching off the gooseneck steel lamps as she went, she led him through the flat as if wheeling a basket behind her; they began laughing as a car's beam shone up from Mercy Hill and seized for a moment on her hand, his handle. They reached the crisp bed and suddenly, urgently, couldn't prolong their play. She was all around him, working to draw him deeper and out, he was lapped softly, thrusting roughly at her grip on him to urge it to return redoubled. They were rising above everything but each other, gasping. He felt himself rushing to a height, and closed his eyes.

And was falling into a maelstrom of flesh, into a vast almost lightless cave whose roof seemed as far above him as the sky. He had a long way still to fall, and beneath him he could make out the movements of huge bubbles and ropes of flesh, of eyes swelling and splitting of flesh, of gigantic dark green masses climbing sluggishly over one another. 'No, Christ no,' he cried, gripped helpless.

He slumped on Hilary. 'Oh God,' she said. 'What is it now?'

He lay beside her. Above them the ceiling shivered with reflected light. It looked as he felt. He closed his eyes and found dark calm, but couldn't bear to keep them closed for long. 'All right,' he said. 'There's more I haven't told you. I know you've been worried about how I've looked lately. I told you it was lack of sleep, and so it is, but it's because I've begun dreaming again. It started about nine months ago, just before I met you, and it's becoming more frequent, once or twice a week now. Only this time I can never remember what it is, perhaps because I haven't dreamed for so long. I think it has something to do with the sky, maybe this planet we've been hearing about. The last time was this morning, after you went to the library. For some reason I don't have them when I'm with you.'

'Of course if you want to go back to your place, go ahead,' Hilary said, gazing at the ceiling.

'In one way I don't,' he said. 'That's just the trouble. Whenever I try to dream I find I don't want to sleep, as if I'm fighting the dream. But today I'm tired enough just to drift off and have it anyway. I've been getting hallucinations all day that I think are coming from the dream. And it feels more urgent, somehow. I've got to have it. I knew it was important before, but that painting's made me sure it's more than a dream. I wish you could understand this. It's not easy for me.'

'Suppose I did believe you?' she said. 'What on earth would you do then? Stand on the street warning people? Or would you try to sell it to your paper? I don't want to believe you, how can you think they would?'

'That's exactly the sort of thing I don't need to hear,'

Ingels said. 'I want to talk to my father about it. I think he may be able to help. Maybe you wouldn't mind not coming with me.

'I wouldn't want to,' she said. 'You go and have your dream and your chat with your father if you want. But as far as I'm concerned that means you don't want me.'

Ingels walked to his flat, further up Mercy Hill. Newspapers clung to bushes, flapping; cars hissed through nearby streets, luminous waves. Only the houses stood between him and the sky, their walls seeming low and thin. Even in the pools of lamplight he felt the night gaping overhead.

The building where he lived was silent. The stereo that usually thumped like an electronic heart was quiet. Ingels climbed to the third floor, his footsteps dropping wooden blocks into the silence, nudging him awake. He fumbled in his entrance hall for the coathook on the back of the door, which wasn't where Hilary kept hers. Beneath the window in the main room he saw her desk spread with her syndicated cartoon strip – except that when he switched on the light it was his own desk, scattered with television schedules. He peered blearily at the rumpled bed. Around him the room felt and moved like muddy water. He sagged on the bed and was asleep at once.

The darkness drew him out, coaxing him forward, swimming softly through his eyes. A great silent darkness surrounded him. He sailed through it, sleeping yet aware. He sensed energy flowering far out in the darkness, vast soundless explosions that cooled and congealed. He sensed immense weights slowly rolling at the edge of his blindness.

Then he could see, though the darkness persisted almost unchanged. Across its furthest distances a few points of light shone like tiny flaws. He began to sail towards them, faster. They parted and fled to the edge of his vision as he approached. He was rushing between them, towards others that now swooped minutely out of the boundless night, carrying cooler grains of congealed dust around them. They were multiplying, his vision was filling with sprinkled light and its attendant parasites. He was turning, imprinting each silently blazing vista on his mind. His mind felt enormous. He felt it take each pattern of light and store it easily as it returned alert for the next.

It was so long before he came to rest he had no conscious memory of starting out. Somehow the path he'd followed had brought him back to his point of origin. Now he sailed in equilibrium with the entire system of light and dust that surrounded him, boundless. His mind locked on everything he'd seen.

He found that part of his mind had fastened telescopically on details of the worlds he'd passed: cities of globes acrawl with black winged insects; mountains carved or otherwise formed into heads within whose hollow sockets worshippers squirmed; a sea from whose depths rose a jointed arm, reaching miles inland and a filmy web of skin to net itself food. One tiny world in particular seemed to teem with life that was aware of him.

Deep in one of its seas a city slept, and he shared the dreams of its sleepers: of an infancy spent in a vast almost lightless cave, tended by a thin rustling shape so tall its head was lost to sight; of flight to this minute but fecund planet; of dancing hugely and clumsily beneath the light of a fragment they'd torn free of this world and flung into space; of dormancy in the submarine basalt tombs. Dormant, they waited and shared the lives of other similar beings active on the surface; for a moment he was the inhabitant of a black city deserted by its builders, coming alert and groping lazily forth as a pale grub fled along a path between the buildings.

Later, as the active ones on the surface had to hide from the multiplying grubs, those in the submarine city stilled, waiting. Ingels felt their thoughts searching sleepily, ranging the surface, touching and sampling the minds of the grubs, vastly patient and purposeful. He felt the womb of the sea lapping his cell. His huge flesh quivered, anticipating rebirth.

Without warning he was in a room, gazing through a telescope at the sky. He seemed to have been gazing for hours; his eyes burned. He was referring to a chart, adjusting the mounting of the telescope. A pool of light from an oil-lamp roved, snatching at books in cases against the walls, spilling over the charts at his feet. Then he was outside the room, hurrying through a darkened theatre; cowls of darkness peered down from the boxes. Outside the theatre he glanced up towards the speckled sky, towards the roof, where he knew one slate hid the upturned telescope. He hurried away through the gas-lit streets, out of Ingels' dream.

He awoke and knew at once where the theatre was: at the edge of Brichester, where his mind had been tugging him all day.

III

He rose at dawn, feeling purged and refreshed. He washed, shaved, dressed, made himself breakfast. In his lightened state the preamble of his dream seemed not to matter: he had had his inclination towards the edge of Brichester explained, the rest seemed external to him, perhaps elaborately symbolic. He knew Hilary regarded his dreams as symptoms of disturbance, and perhaps she was right. Maybe, he thought, they all meant the theatre was trying to get up through my mind. A lot of fuss, but that's what dreams are like. Especially when they're having to fight their way, no doubt. Can't wait to see what the theatre means to me.

When he went out the dawn clutched him as if he hadn't shaken off his dreams. The dull laden light settled about him, ambiguous shapes hurried by. The air felt suffocated by imminence, not keen as the cold should make it. That'll teach me to get up at cockcrow, he thought. Feels like insomnia. Can't imagine what they find to crow about. The queues of commuters moved forward like the tickings of doom.

Someone had left a sheet from the telex on his desk. Photographs from the space probe were expected any hour. He wrote his reviews hurriedly, glancing up to dispel a sense that the floor was alive with pale grubs, teeming through the aisles. Must have needed more sleep than I thought. Maybe catch a nap later.

Although his dream had reverted the streets, replacing the electric lamps with gas, he knew exactly where the theatre should be. He hurried along the edge of Lower Brichester, past champing steam-shovels, roaring skeletons of burning houses. He strode straight to the street of his dream.

One side was razed, a jagged strip of brown earth extending cracks into the pavement and into the fields beyond. But the theatre was on the other side. Ingels hurried past the red-brick houses, past the wind-whipped gardens and broken flowers, towards the patched gouge in the road where he knew a gas-lamp had used to guard the theatre. He stood arrested on it, cars sweeping past, and stared at the houses before him, safe from his glare in their sameness. The theatre was not there.

Only the shout of an overtaking car roused him. He

wandered along, feeling sheepish and absurd. He remembered vaguely having walked this way with his parents
once, on the way to a picnic. The gas-lamp had been
standing then; he'd gazed at it and at the theatre, which
by then was possessed by a cinema, until they'd coaxed
him away. Which explained the dream, the insomnia,
everything. And I never used to be convinced by *Citizen
Kane*. Rosebud to me too, with knobs on. In fact he'd
even mistaken the location of the lamp; there it was, a
hundred yards ahead of him. Suddenly he began to run.
Already he could see the theatre, now renamed as a
furniture warehouse.

He was almost through the double doors and into the
first aisle of suites when he realized that he didn't know
what he was going to say. Excuse me, I'd like to look
under your rafters. Sorry to bother you, but I believe you
have a secret room here. For God's sake, he said,
blushing, hurrying down the steps as a salesman came
forward to open the doors for him. I know what the
dream was now. I've made sure I won't have it again.
Forget the rest.

He threw himself down at his desk. Now sit there and
behave. What a piddling reason for falling out with
Hilary. At least I can admit that to her. Call her now. He
was reaching for the telephone when Bert tramped up,
waving Ingels' review of the astronomical television programme. 'I know you'd like to rewrite this,' he said.

'Sorry about that.'

'We'll call off the men in white this time. Thought
you'd gone the same way as this fellow,' Bert said,
throwing a cutting on the desk.

'Just lack of sleep,' Ingels said, not looking. 'As our
Methuselah, tell me something. When the warehouse on
Fieldview was a theatre, what was it called?'

'The Variety, you mean?' Bert said, dashing for his

phone. 'Remind me to tell you about the time I saw Beaumont and Fletcher performing there. Great double act.'

Ingels turned the cutting over, smiling half at Bert, half at himself for the way he had still not let go of his dream. Go on, look through the files in your lunch-hour, he told himself satirically. Bet the Variety never made a headline in its life.

LSD CAUSES ATTEMPTED SUICIDE, said the cutting. American student claims that in LSD 'vision' he was told that the planet now passing through our solar system heralded the rising of Atlantis. Threw himself from second-storey window. Insists that the rising of Atlantis means the end of humanity. Says the Atlanteans are ready to awaken. Ingels gazed at the cutting; the sounds of the newspaper surged against his ears like blood. Suddenly he thrust back his chair and ran upstairs, to the morgue of the *Herald*.

Beneath the ceiling pressed low by the roof, a fluorescent tube fluttered and buzzed. Ingels hugged the bound newspapers to his chest, each volume an armful, and hefted them to a table, where they puffed out dust. 1900 was the first that came to hand. The streets would have been gas-lit then. Dust trickled into his nostrils and frowned over him, the phone next to Hilary was mute, his television review plucked at his mind, anxious to be rewritten. Scanning and blinking, he tried to shake them off with his doubts.

But it didn't take him long, though his gaze was tired of ranging up and down, up and down, by the time he saw the headline:

ATTEMPTED THEFT AT 'THE VARIETY.'
TRADESMEN IN THE DOCK.

Francis Wareing, a draper pursuing his trade in Brichester,

Donald Norden, a butcher [and so on, Ingels snarled, sweeping past impatiently] were charged before the Brichester stipendiary magistrates with forcibly entering 'The Variety' theatre, on Fieldview, in attempted commission of robbery. Mr Radcliffe, the owner and manager of this establishment

It looked good, Ingels thought wearily, abandoning the report, tearing onward. But two issues later the sequel's headline stopped him short:

ACCUSATION AND COUNTER-ACCUSATION
IN COURT.
A BLASPHEMOUS CULT REVEALED.

And there it was, halfway down the column:

Examined by Mr Kirby for the prosecution, Mr Radcliffe affirmed that he had been busily engaged in preparing his accounts when, overhearing sounds of stealth outside his office, he summoned his courage and ventured forth. In the auditorium he beheld several men

Get on with it, Ingels urged, and saw that there had been impatience in the court too:

Mr Radcliffe's narrative was rudely interrupted by Wareing, who accused him of having let a room in his theatre to the accused four. This privilege having been summarily withdrawn, Wareing alleged, the four had entered the building in a bid to reclaim such possessions as were rightfully theirs. He pursued:
'Mr Radcliffe is aware of this. He has been one of our number for years, and still would be, if he had the courage.'
Mr Radcliffe replied: 'That is a wicked untruth. However, I am not surprised by the depths of your iniquity. I have evidence of it here.'
So saying, he produced for the Court's inspection a notebook containing, as he said, matter of a blasphemous and sacrilegious nature. This which he had found beneath a seat in his theatre, he indicated to be the prize sought by the unsuccessful robbers. The book, which Mr Radcliffe described as 'the journal of a cult

dedicated to preparing themselves for a blasphemous travesty of the Second coming,' was handed to Mr Poole, the magistrate, who swiftly pronounced it to conform to this description.

Mr Kirby adduced as evidence of the corruption which this cult wrought, its bringing of four respectable tradesmen to the state of common robbers. Had they not felt the shame of the beliefs they professed, he continued, they had but to petition Mr Radcliffe for the return of their mislaid property.

But what beliefs? Ingels demanded. He riffled onward, crumbling yellow fragments from the pages. The tube buzzed like a bright trapped insect. He almost missed the page.

FOILED ROBBERS AT 'THE VARIETY.'
FIFTH MAN YIELDS HIMSELF TO JUSTICE.

What fifth man? Ingels searched:

Mr Poole condemned the cult of which the accused were adherents as conclusive proof of the iniquity of those religions which presume to rival Christianity. He described the cult as 'unworthy of the lowest breed of mulatto.'

At this juncture a commotion ensued, as a man entered precipitately and begged leave to address the Court. Some few minutes later Mr Radcliffe also entered, wearing a resolute expression. When he saw the latecomer, however, he appeared to relinquish his purpose, and took a place in the gallery. The man, meanwhile, sought to throw himself on the Court's mercy, declaring himself to be the fifth of the robbers. He had been prompted to confess, he affirmed, by a sense of his injustice in allowing his friends to take full blame. His name, he said, was Joseph Ingels.

Who had received a lighter sentence in acknowledgement of his gesture, Ingels saw in a blur at the foot of the column. He hardly noticed. He was still staring at his grandfather's name.

'Nice of you to come,' his father said ambiguously. They'd finished decorating, Ingels saw; the flowers on the hall wallpaper had grown and turned bright orange. But the light was still dim, and the walls settled about his eyes like night around a feeble lamp. Next to the coat-rack he saw the mirror in which he'd made sure of himself before teenage dates, the crack in one corner where he'd driven his fist, caged by fury and by their incomprehension of his adolescent restlessness. An ugly socket of plaster gaped through the wallpaper next to the supporting nail's less treacherous home. 'I could have hung the mirror for you,' Ingels said, not meaning to disparage his father, who frowned and said 'No need.' They went into the dining-room, where his mother was setting out the best tablecloth and cutlery. 'Wash hands,' she said. 'Tea's nearly ready.'

They ate and talked. Ingels watched the conversation as if it were a pocket maze into which he had to slip a ball when the opening tilted towards him. 'How's your girl friend?' his mother said. Don't you know her name? Ingels didn't say. 'Fine,' he said. They didn't mention Hilary again. His mother produced infant photographs of him they'd discovered in the sideboard drawer. 'You were a lovely little boy,' she said. 'Speaking of memories,' Ingels said, 'do you remember the old Variety theatre?'

His father was moving his shirt along the fireguard to give himself a glimpse of the fire, his back to Ingels. 'The old Variety,' his mother said. 'We wanted to take you to a pantomime there once. But,' she glanced at her husband's back, 'when your father got there all the tickets were sold. Then there was the Gaiety,' and she produced a list of theatres and anecdotes.

Ingels sat opposite his father, whose pipe-smoke was pouring up the chimney. 'I was looking through our old newspapers,' he said, 'I came across a case that involved the Variety.'

'Don't you ever work at that paper?' his father said.

'This was research. It seems there was a robbery at the theatre. Before you were born, it was, but I wonder if you remember hearing about it.'

'Now, we aren't all as clever as you,' his mother said. 'We don't remember what we heard in our cradle.'

Ingles laughed, tightening inside; the opening was turning away from him. 'You might have heard about it when you were older,' he told his father. 'Your father was involved.'

'No,' his father said. 'He was not.'

'He was in the paper.'

'His name was,' his father said, facing Ingels with a blank stare in his eyes. 'It was another man. Your grandfather took years to live that down. The newspapers wouldn't publish an apology or say it wasn't him. And you wonder why we didn't want you to work for a paper. You wouldn't be a decent shopkeeper, you let our shop go out of the family, and now here you are, raking up old dirt and lies. That's what you chose for yourself.'

'I didn't mean to be offensive,' Ingels said, holding himself down. 'But it was an interesting case, that's all. I'm going to follow it up tomorrow, at the theatre.'

'If you go there you'll be rubbing our name in the dirt. Don't bother coming here again.'

'Now hold on,' Ingels said. 'If your father wasn't involved you can't very well mean that. My God,' he cried, flooded with a memory, 'you do know something! You told me about it once, when I was a child! I'd just started dreaming and you told it to me so I wouldn't be frightened, to show me you had these dreams too. You were in a room with a telescope, waiting to see something. You told me because I'd dreamed it too! That's the second time I've had that dream! It's the room at the Variety, it has to be!'

'I don't know what you mean,' his father said. 'I never dreamed that.'

'You told me you had.'

'I must have told you that to calm you down. Go on, say I shouldn't have lied to you. It must have been for your own good.'

He'd blanked out his eyes with an unblinking stare. Ingels gazed at him and knew at once there was more behind the blank than the lie about his childhood. 'You've been dreaming again,' he said. 'You've been having the dream I had last night, I know you have. And I think you know what it means.'

The stare shifted almost imperceptibly, then returned strengthened. 'What do you know?' his father said. 'You live in the same town as us and visit us once a week, if that. Yet you know I've been dreaming? Sometimes we wonder if you even know we're here!'

'I know. I'm sorry,' Ingels said. 'But these dreams – you used to have them. The ones we used to share, remember?'

'We shared everything when you were a little boy. But that's over,' his father said. 'Dreams and all.'

'That's nothing to do with it!' Ingels shouted. 'You still have the ability! I know you must have been having these dreams! It's been in your eyes for months!' He trailed off, trying to remember whether that was true. He turned to his mother, pleading. 'Hasn't he been dreaming?'

'What do I know about it?' she said. 'It's nothing to do with me.' She was clearing the table in the dim rationed light beyond the fire, not looking at either of them. Suddenly Ingels saw her as he never had before: bewildered by her husband's dreams and intuitions, further excluded from the disturbingly incomprehensible bond between him and her son. All at once Ingels knew why he'd always felt she had been happy to see him leave home: it was only then that she'd been able to start reclaiming her husband. He took his coat from the hall and looked into the dining-room. They hadn't moved: his father was staring at the fire, his mother at the table. 'I'll see you,' he said, but the only sound was the crinkling of the fire as it crumbled, breaking open pinkish embers.

IV

He watched television. Movement of light and colours, forming shapes. Outside the window the sky drew his gaze, stretched taut, heavily imminent as thunder. He wrote words.

Later, he was sailing through enormous darkness; glinting globes turned slowly around him, one wearing an attenuated band of light; ahead, the darkness was scattered with dust and chunks of rock. A piece of metal was circling him like a timid needle, poking towards him, now spitting flame and swinging away. He felt a contempt so profound it was simply vast indifference. He closed his eyes as he might have blinked away a speck of dust.

In the morning he wrote his review at the flat. He knew he wouldn't be able to bear the teeming aisles for long. Blindly shouldering his way across the floor, he found Bert. He had to gaze at him for a minute or so; he couldn't remember immediately what he should look like. 'That rewrite you did on the TV review wasn't your best,' Bert said. 'Ah well,' Ingels said, snatching his copy of last night's *Herald* automatically from his desk, and hurried for the door.

He'd nearly reached it when he heard the news editor

shouting into the telephone. 'But it can't affect Saturn and Jupiter! I mean, it can't change its mass, can it? . . . I'm sorry, sir. Obviously I didn't mean to imply I knew more about your field than you. But is it possible for its mass to change? . . . What, trajectory as well?' Ingels grinned at the crowd around the editor's desk, at their rapt expressions. They'd be more rapt when he returned. He strode out.

Through the writhing crowds, up the steps, into a vista of beds and dressing-tables like a street of cramped bedrooms whose walls had been tricked away. 'Can I speak to the manager, please,' he said to the man who stepped forward. '*Brichester Herald*.'

The manager was a young man in a pale streamlined suit, longish clipped hair, a smile which he held forward as if for inspection. 'I'm following a story,' Ingels said, displaying his press card. 'It seems that when your warehouse was a theatre a room was leased to an astronomical group. We think their records are still here, and if they can be found they're of enormous historical interest.'

'That's interesting,' the manager said. 'Where are they supposed to be?'

'In a room at the top of the building somewhere.'

'I'd like to help, of course.' Four men passed, carrying pieces of a dismembered bed to a van. 'There were some offices at the top of the building once, I believe. But we don't use them now, they're boarded up. It would be a good deal of trouble to open them now. If you'd phoned I might have been able to free some men.'

'I've been out of town,' Ingels said, improvising hastily now his plans were going awry. 'Found this story on my desk when I got back. I tried to phone earlier but couldn't get through. Must be a tribute to the business you're doing.' An old man, one of the loaders, was sitting on a chair nearby, listening; Ingels wished he would move, he couldn't bear an audience as well. 'These records really would be important,' he said wildly. 'Great historical value.'

'In any case I can't think they'd still be here. If they were in one of the top rooms they would have been cleared out long ago.'

'I think you're a bit wrong there,' the old man said from his chair.

'Have you nothing to do?' the manager demanded.

'We've done loading,' the man said. 'Driver's not been here yet. Mother's sick. It's not for me to say you're wrong, but I remember when they were mending the roof after the war. Men who were doing it said they could see a room full of books, they looked like, all covered up. But we couldn't find it from down here and nobody wanted to break their necks trying to get in from the roof. Must be there still, though.'

'That has to be the one,' Ingels said. 'Whereabouts was it?'

'Round about there,' the old man said, pointing above a Scandinavian four-poster. 'Behind one of the offices, we used to reckon.'

'Could you help find it?' Ingels said. 'Maybe your workmates could give you a hand while they're waiting. That's of course if this gentleman doesn't mind. We'd make a point of your cooperation,' he told the manager. 'Might even be able to give you a special advertising rate, if you wanted to run an ad on that day.'

The five of them climbed a rusty spiral staircase, tastefully screened by a partition, to the first floor. The manager, still frowning, had left one loader watching for the driver. 'Call us as soon as he comes,' he said. 'Whatever the reason, time lost loses money.' Across the first floor, which was a maze of crated and cartoned furniture, Ingels glimpsed reminiscences of his dream:

the outline of theatre boxes in the walls, almost erased by
bricks; a hook that had supported a chandelier. They
seemed to protrude from the mundane, beckoning him
on.

The staircase continued upward, more rustily. 'I'll go
first,' the manager said, taking the flashlight one of the
loaders had brought. 'We don't want accidents,' and his
legs drew up like a tail through a trapdoor. They heard
him stamping about, challenging the floor. 'All right,' he
called, and Ingels thrust his face through drifting dust
into a bare plank corridor.

'Here, you said?' the manager asked the old man,
pointing to some of the boards that formed a wall. 'That's
it,' the old man said, already ripping out nails with his
hammer, aided by his workmates. A door peeked dully
through. Ingels felt a smile wrenching at his face. He
controlled himself. Wait until they've gone.

As soon as they'd prised open the office door he ran
forward. A glum green room, a ruined desk in whose
splintered innards squatted a dust-furred typewriter. 'I'm
afraid it's as I thought,' the manager said. 'There's no
way through. You can't expect us to knock down a wall,
obviously. Not without a good deal of consultation.'

'But there must have been an entrance,' Ingels said.
'Beyond this other wall. It must have been sealed up
before you got the building. Surely we can look for it.'

'You won't have to,' the old man said. He was kicking
at the wall nearest the supposed location of the room.
Plaster crumbled along a crack, then they heard the shifting of brick. 'Thought as much,' he said. 'The war did
this, shook the building. The boards are all right but the
mortar's done for.' He kicked again and whipped back
his foot. He'd dislodged two bricks, and at once part of
the wall collapsed, leaving an opening four feet high.

'That'll be enough!' the manager said. Ingels was stooping, peering through the dust-curtained gap. Bare boards, rafters and slates above, what must be bookcases draped with cloth around the walls, something in the centre of the room wholly covered by a frame hung with heavy material, perhaps velvet. Dust crawled on his hot face, prickling like fever. 'If the wall would have collapsed anyway it's a good job you were here when it did,' he told the manager. 'Now it's done I'm sure you won't object if I have a look around. If I'm injured I promise not to claim. I'll sign a waiver if you like.'

'I think you'd better,' the manager said, and waited while Ingels struggled with his briefcase, last night's *Herald*, a pen and sheet from his notebook, brushing at his eyebrows where dust and sweat had become a trickle of mud, rubbing his trembling fingers together to clean them. The men had clambered over the heap of bricks and were lifting the velvety frame. Beneath it was a reflector telescope almost a foot long, mounted on a high sturdy stand. One of the men bent to the eyepiece, touching the focus. 'Don't!' Ingels screamed. 'The setting may be extremely important,' he explained, trying to laugh.

The manager was peering at him. 'What did you say you do at the *Herald*?' he said.

'Astronomy correspondent,' Ingels said, immediately dreading that the man might read the paper regularly. 'I don't get too much work,' he blundered on. 'This is a scoop. If I could I'd like to spend a few hours looking at the books.'

He heard them descending the spiral staircase. Squirm away, he thought. He lifted the covers from the bookcases gingerly, anxious to keep dust away from the telescope, as the velvety cover had for decades. Suddenly he hurried back to the corridor. Its walls bobbed about him as the flashlight swung. He selected a plank and hefting it over the bricks, poked it at the rafters above the telescope, shielding the latter with his arm. After a minute the slate above slid away, and a moment later he heard a distant crash.

He squatted down to look through the eyepiece. No doubt a chair had been provided once. All he could see was a blurred twilit sky. Soon be night, he thought, and turned the flashlight on the books. He remembered the light from the oil-lamp lapping at his feet in the dream.

Much of the material was devoted to astronomy. As many of the books and charts were astrological, he found, some in Oriental script. But there were others, on shelves in the corner furthest from the sealed-off door: *The Story of Atlantis and the Lost Lemuria, Image du Monde, Liber Investigationis, Revelations of Glaaki*. There were nine volumes of the last. He pulled them out, curious, and dust rose about his face like clouds of sleep.

Voices trickled tinily up the staircase, selling beds. In the close room dimmed by the dust that crowded at the hole in the roof, towards which the telescope patiently gazed, Ingels felt as if he were sinking back into his dream. Cracked fragments of the pages clung beneath his nails. He read on like an incantation, like voices muttering in sleep, melting into another style, jerking clumsily into another. Sketches and paintings were tipped into the books, some childishly crude, some startlingly detailed: M'nagalah, a tentacled mass of what looked like bloated raw entrails and eyes; Glaaki, a half-submerged spongy face peering stalk-eyed from a lake; R'lyeh, an island city towering triumphant above the sea, a vast door ajar. This he recognized, calmly accepting the information. He felt now as if he could never have had reason to doubt his dream.

The early winter night had blocked up the hole in the

roof. Ingels stooped to the eyepiece again. Now there was only darkness through the telescope. It felt blurred by distance; he felt the distance drawing him vertiginously down the tube of darkness, out into a boundless emptiness no amount of matter could fill. Not yet, he thought, withdrawing swiftly. Soon.

Someone was staring at him. A girl. She was frowning up at the hole in the roof. A saleswoman. 'We're closing soon,' she said.

'All right,' Ingels said, returning to the book, lying face upward in the splayed light. It had settled into a more comfortable position, revealing a new page to him, and an underlined phrase: 'when the stars are right.' He stared at it, trying to connect. It should mean something. The dim books hemmed him in. He shook his head and turned the pages swiftly, searching for underlining. Here it was repeated in the next volume, no, augmented: 'when the stars are right again.' He glanced sharply at the insistent gap of night above him. In a minute, he snarled. Here was a whole passage underlined:

'Though the universe may feign the semblance of fickleness, its soul has always known its masters. The sleep of its masters is but the largest cycle of all life, for as the defiance and forgetfulness of winter is rendered vain by summer, so the defiance and forgetfulness of man, and of those others who have assumed stewardship, shall be cast aside by the reawakened masters. When these hibernal times are over, and the time for reawakening is near, the universe itself shall send forth the Harbinger and Maker, Ghroth. Who shall urge the stars and worlds to rightness. Who shall raise the sleeping masters from their burrows and drowned tombs; who shall raise the tombs themselves. Who shall be attentive to those worlds where worshippers presume themselves stewards.

Who shall bring those worlds under sway, until all acknowledge their presumption, and bow down.'

Ghroth, Ingels thought, gazing up at the gap in the roof. They even had a name for it then, despite the superstitious language. Not that that was so surprising, he thought. Man used to look upon comets that way, this is the same sort of thing. An omen that becomes almost a god.

But an omen of what? he thought suddenly. What exactly was supposed to happen when the stars were right again? He knelt in the dust and flurried through the books. No more underlining. He rushed back to the telescope. His thighs twinged as he squatted. Something had entered the field of view.

It was the outer edge of the wandering planet, creeping into the telescope's field. As it came it blurred, occasionally sharpening almost into focus for a moment. Ingels felt as if the void were making sudden feeble snatches at him. Now the planet was only a spreading reddish smudge. He reached for the focus, altering it minutely. 'We're closing now,' said the manager behind him.

'I won't be long,' Ingels said, feeling the focus sharpen, sharpen –

'We're waiting to close the doors,' the manager said. 'And I'm afraid I'm in a hurry.'

'Not long!' Ingels screamed, tearing his gaze from the eyepiece to glare.

When the man had gone Ingels switched off the flashlight. Now he could see nothing but the tiny dim gap in the roof. He let the room settle on his eyes. At last he made out the immobile uplifted telescope. He groped towards it and squatted down.

As soon as he touched the eyepiece the night rushed through the telescope and clutched him. He was sailing through the void, yet he was motionless; everything moved with him. Through the vast silence he heard the ring of a lifted telephone, a voice saying 'Give me the chief editor of the *Herald*, please,' back there across the void. He could hear the pale grubs squeaking tinily, back all that way. He remembered the way they moved, soft, uncarapaced. Before him, suspended in the dark and facing him, was Ghroth.

It was red as rust, featureless except for bulbous protrusions like hills. Except that of course they weren't hills if he could see them at that distance; they must be immense. A rusty globe covered with lumps, then. That was all, but that couldn't explain why he felt as if the whole of him were magnetized to it through his eyes. It seemed to hang ponderously, communicating a thunderous sense of imminence, of power. But that was just its unfamiliarity, Ingels thought, struggling against the suction of boundless space; just the sense of its intrusion. It's only a planet, after all. Pain was blazing along his thighs. Just a red warty globe.

Then it moved.

Ingels was trying to remember how to move his body to get his face away from the eyepiece; he was throwing his weight against the telescope mounting to sweep away what he could see. It was blurring, that was it, although it was a cold windless day air movements must be causing the image to blur, the surface of a planet doesn't move, it's only a planet, the surface of a planet doesn't crack, it doesn't roll back like that, it doesn't peel back for thousands of miles so you can see what's underneath, pale and glistening. When he tried to scream air whooped into his lungs as if space had exploded a vacuum within him.

He'd tripped over the bricks, fallen agonizingly down the stairs, smashed the manager out of the way with his shoulder and was at the *Herald* building before he knew that was where he intended to go. He couldn't speak, only make the whooping sound as he sucked in air; he threw his briefcase and last night's paper on his desk and sat there clutching himself, shaking. The floor seemed to have been in turmoil before he arrived, but they were crowding around him, asking him impatiently what was wrong.

But he was staring at the headline in his last night's newspaper: SURFACE ACTIVITY ON WANDERER 'MORE APPARENT THAN REAL' SAY SCIEN-TISTS. Photographs of the planet from the space-probe: one showing an area like a great round pale glistening sea, the next circuit recording only mountains and rock plains. 'Don't you see?' Ingels shouted at Bert among the packed faces. 'It closed its eye when it saw us coming!'

Hilary came at once when they telephoned her, and took Ingels back to her flat. But he wouldn't sleep, laughed at the doctor and the tranquillizers, though he swallowed the tablets indifferently enough. Hilary unplugged the television, went out as little as possible, bought no newspapers, threw away her contributor's copies unopened, talked to him while she worked, stroked him soothingly, slept with him. Neither of them felt the earth begin to shift.

THE FACES AT PINE DUNES

I

When his parents began arguing Michael went outside. He could still hear them through the thin wall of the trailer. 'We needn't stop yet,' his mother was pleading.

'We're stopping,' his father said. 'It's time to stop wandering.'

But why should she want to leave here? Michael gazed about the trailer park – the Pine Dunes Caravanserai. The metal village of trailers surrounded him, cold and bright in the November afternoon. Beyond the dunes ahead he heard the dozing of the sea. On the three remaining sides a forest stood: remnants of autumn, ghosts of colour, were scattered over the trees; distant branches displayed a last golden mist of leaves. He inhaled the calm. Already he felt at home.

His mother was persisting. 'You're still young,' she told his father.

She's kidding! Michael thought. Perhaps she was trying flattery. 'There are places we haven't seen,' she said wistfully.

'We don't need to. We need to be here.'

The slowness of the argument, the voices muffled by the metal wall, frustrated Michael; he wanted to be sure that he was staying here. He hurried into the trailer. 'I want to stay here. Why do we have to keep moving all the time?'

'Don't come in here talking to your mother like that,' his father shouted.

He should have stayed out. The argument seemed to cramp the already crowded space within the trailer; it made his father's presence yet more overwhelming. The man's enormous wheezing body sat plumped on the couch, which sagged beneath his weight; his small frail wife was perched on what little of the couch was unoccupied, as though she'd been squeezed tiny to fit. Gazing at them, Michael felt suffocated. 'I'm going out,' he said.

'Don't go out,' his mother said anxiously; he couldn't see why. 'We won't argue any more. You stay in and do something. Study.'

'Let him be. The sooner he meets people here, the better.'

Michael resented the implication that by going out he was obeying his father. 'I'm just going out for a walk,' he said. The reassurance might help her; he knew how it felt to be overborne by the man.

At the door he glanced back. His mother had opened her mouth, but his father said 'We're staying. I've made my decision.' And he'd lie in it, Michael thought, still resentful. All the man could do was lie there, he thought spitefully; that was all he was fat for. He went out, sniggering. The way his father had gained weight during the past year, his coming to rest in this trailer park reminded Michael of an elephant's arrival at its graveyard.

It was colder now. Michael turned up the hood of his anorak. Curtains were closing and glowing. Trees stood, intricately precise, against a sky like translucent papery jade. He began to climb the dunes towards the sea. But over there the sky was blackened; a sea dark as mud tossed nervously and flopped across the bleak beach. He turned towards the forest. Behind him sand hissed through grass.

The forest shifted in the wind. Shoals of leaves swam in the air, at the tips of webs of twigs. He followed a path

which led from the Caravanserai's approach road. Shortly
the diversity of trees gave way to thousands of pines.
Pine cones lay like wattled eggs on beds of fallen needles.
The spread of needles glowed deep orange in the early
evening, an orange tapestry displaying rank upon rank of
slender pines, dwindling into twilight.

The path led him on. The pines were shouldered
out by stouter trees, which reached overhead, tangling.
Beyond the tangle the blue of the sky grew deeper; a
crescent moon slid from branch to branch. Bushes massed
among the trunks; they grew higher and closer as he
pushed through. The curve of the path would take him
back towards the road.

The ground was turning softer underfoot. It sucked his
feet in the dark. The shrubs had closed over him now; he
could hardly see. He struggled between them, pursuing
the curve. Leaves rubbed together rustling at his ear, like
desiccated lips; their dry dead tongues rattled. All at
once the roof of the wooden tunnel dropped sharply. To
go further he would have to crawl.

He turned with difficulty. On both sides thorns caught
his sleeves; his dark was hemmed in by two ranks of dim
captors. It was as though midnight had already fallen
here, beneath the tangled arches; but the dark was solid
and clawed. Overhead, netted fragments of night sky
illuminated the tunnel hardly at all.

He managed to extricate himself, and hurried back.
But he had taken only a few steps when his way was
blocked by hulking spiky darkness. He dodged to the left
of the shrub, then to the right, trying irritably to calm his
heart. But there was no path. He had lost his way in the
dark. Around him dimness rustled, chattering.

He began to curse himself. What had possessed him to
come in here? Why on earth had he chosen to explore so
late in the day? How could the woods be so interminable?

He groped for openings between masses of thorns. Sometimes he found them, though often they would not admit his body. The darkness was a maze of false paths.

Eventually he had to return to the mouth of the tunnel and crawl. Unseen moisture welled up from the ground, between his fingers. Shrubs leaned closer as he advanced, poking him with thorns. His skin felt fragile, and nervously unstable; he burned but his heat often seemed to break, flooding him with the chill of the night.

There was something even less pleasant. As he crawled, the leaning darkness – or part of it – seemed to move beside him. It was as though someone were pacing him, perhaps on all fours, outside the tunnel. When he halted, so did the pacing. It would reach the end of the tunnel just as he did.

Nothing but imagination, helped by the closely looming treetrunks beyond the shrubs. Apart from the creaking of wood and the rattling sway of leaves, there was no sound beyond the tunnel – certainly none of pacing. He crawled. The cumbersome moist sounds that accompanied the pacing were those of his own progress. But he crawled more slowly, and the darkness imitated him. Wasn't the thorny tunnel dwindling ahead? It would trap him. Suddenly panicking, he began to scrabble backwards.

The thorns hardly hindered his retreat. He must have broken them down. He emerged gasping, glad of the tiny gain in light. Around him shrubs pressed close as ever. He stamped his way back along what he'd thought was his original path. When he reached the hindrance he smashed his way between the shrubs, struggling and snarling, savage with panic, determined not to yield. His hands were torn; he heard cloth rip. Well, the thorns could have that.

When at last he reached an open space his panic sighed loudly out of him. He began to walk as rapidly as seemed safe, towards where he remembered the road to be. Overhead black nets of branches turned, momentarily catching stars. Once, amid the enormous threshing of the woods, he thought he heard a heavy body shoving through the nearby bushes. Good luck to whoever it was. Ahead, in the barred dark, hung little lighted windows. He had found the trailer park, but only by losing his way.

He was home. He hurried into the light, smiling. In the metal alleys pegged shirts hung neck down, dripping; they flapped desperately on the wind. The trailer was dark. In the main room, lying on the couch like someone's abandoned reading, was a note: OUT, BACK LATER. His mother had added DON'T GO TO BED TOO LATE.

He'd been looking forward to companionship. Now the trailer seemed too brightly lit, and false: a furnished tin can. He made himself coffee, leafed desultorily through his floppy paperbacks, opened and closed a pocket chess set. He poked through his box of souvenirs: shells, smooth stones; a minute Bible; a globe of synthetic snow within which a huge vague figure, presumably meant to be a snowman, loomed outside a house; a dead flashlight fitted with a set of clip-on Halloween faces; a dull grey ring whose metal swelled into a bulge over which colours crawled slowly, changing. The cardboard box was full of memories: the Severn valley, the Welsh hills, the garishly glittering mile of Blackpool: he couldn't remember where the ring had come from. But the memories were dim tonight, uninvolving.

He wandered into his parents' room. It looked to him like a second-hand store for clothes and toiletries. He found his father's large metal box, but it was locked as usual. Well, Michael didn't want to read his old books anyway. He searched for contraceptives, but as he'd expected, there were none. If he wasn't mistaken, his parents had no need for them. Poor buggers. He'd never been able to imagine how, out of proportion as they seemed to be, they had begot him.

Eventually he went out. The incessant rocking of the trailer, its hollow booming in the wind, had begun to infuriate him. He hurried along the road between the pines; wind sifted through needles. On the main road buses ran to Liverpool. But he'd already been there several times. He caught a bus to the opposite terminus.

The bus was almost empty. A few passengers rattled in their lighted pod over the bumpy country roads. Darkness streamed by, sometimes becoming dim hedges. The scoop of the headlamps set light to moths, and once to a squirrel. Ahead the sky glowed, as if with a localized dawn. Lights began to emerge from behind silhouetted houses; streets opened, brightening.

The bus halted in a square, beside a village cross. The passengers hurried away, snuggling into their collars. Almost at once the street was deserted, the bus extinguished. Folded awnings clattered, tugged by the wind. Perhaps after all he should have gone into the city. He was stranded here for – he read the timetable: God, two hours until the last bus.

He wandered among the grey stone houses. Streetlamps glared silver; the light coated shop windows, behind whose flowering of frost he could see faint ghosts of merchandise. Curtains shone warmly, chimneys smoked. His heels clanked mechanically on the cobbles. Streets, streets, empty streets. Then the streets became crowded, with gleaming parked cars. Ahead, on the wall of a building, was a plaque of coloured light. FOUR IN THE MORNING. A club.

He hesitated, then he descended the steps. Maybe he wouldn't fit in with the brand-new sports car set, but anything was better than wandering the icy streets. At the bottom of the stone flight, a desk stood beside a door to coloured dimness. A broken-nosed man wearing evening dress sat behind the desk. 'Are you a member, sir?' he said in an accent that was almost as convincing as his suit.

Inside was worse than Michael had feared. On a dance-floor couples turned lethargically, glittering and changing colour like toy dancers. Clumps of people stood shouting at each other in county accents, swaying and laughing; some stared at him as they laughed. He heard their talk: motor-boats, bloody bolshies, someone's third abortion. He didn't mind meeting new people – he'd had to learn not to mind – but he could tell these people preferred, now they'd stared, to ignore him.

His three pounds' membership fee included a free drink. I should think so too, he thought. He ordered a beer, to the barman's faint contempt. As he carried the tankard to one of the low bare tables he was conscious of his boots, tramping the floorboards. There was nothing wrong with them, he'd wiped them. He sipped, making the drink last, and gazed into the beer's dim glow.

When someone else sat at the table he didn't look at her. He had to glance up at last, because she was staring. What was the matter with her, was he on show? Often in groups he felt alien, but he'd never felt more of a freak than here. His large-boned arms huddled protectively around him, his gawky legs drew up.

But she was smiling. Her stare was wide-eyed, inno-cent, if somehow odd. 'I haven't seen you before,' she said. 'What's your name?'

'Michael.' It sounded like phlegm; he cleared his throat. 'Michael. What's yours?'

'June.' She made a face as though it tasted like medicine.

'Nothing wrong with that.' Her hint of dissatisfaction with herself had emboldened him.

'You haven't moved here, have you? Are you visiting?'

There was something strange about her: about her eyes, about the way she seemed to search for questions. 'My parents have a caravan,' he said. 'We're in the Pine Dunes Caravanserai. We docked just last week.'

'Yeah.' She drew the word out like a sigh. 'Like a ship. That must be fantastic. I wish I had that. Just to be able to see new things all the time, new places. The only way you can see new things here is taking acid. I'm tripping now.'

His eyebrows lifted slightly; his faint smile shrugged.

'That's what I mean,' she said, smiling. 'These people here would be really shocked. They're so provincial. You aren't.'

In fact he hadn't been sure how to react. The pupils of her eyes were expanding and contracting rapidly, independently of each other. But her small face was attractive, her small body had large firm breasts.

'I saw the moon dancing before,' she said. 'I'm beginning to come down now. I thought I'd like to look at people. You wouldn't know I was tripping, would you? I can control it when I want to.'

She wasn't really talking to him, he thought; she just wanted an audience to trip to. He'd heard things about LSD. 'Aren't you afraid of starting to trip when you don't mean to?'

'Flashbacks, you mean. I never have them. I shouldn't like that.' She gazed at his scepticism. 'There's no need to be afraid of drugs,' she said. 'All sorts of people used to trip. Witches used to. Look, it tells you about it in here.'

She fumbled a book out of her handbag; she seemed to have difficulty in wielding her fingers. *Witchcraft in*

England. 'You can have that,' she said. 'Have you got a job?'

It took him a moment to realize that she'd changed the subject. 'No,' he said. 'I haven't left school long. I had to have extra school because of all the moving. I'm twenty. I expect I'll get a job soon. I think we're staying here.'

'That could be a good job,' she said, pointing at a notice behind the bar: TRAINEE BARMAN REQUIRED. 'I think they want to get rid of that guy there. People don't like him. I know a lot of people would come here if they got someone friendly like you.'

Was it just her trip talking? Two girls said goodbye to a group, and came over. 'We're going now, June. See you shortly.'

'Right. Hey, this is Michael.'

'Nice to meet you, Michael.'

'Hope we'll see you again.'

Perhaps they might. These people didn't seem so bad after all. He drank his beer and bought another, wincing at the price and gazing at the job notice. June refused a drink: 'It's a downer.' They talked about his travels, her dissatisfactions and her lack of cash to pay for moving. When he had to leave she said, 'I'm glad I met you. I like you.' And she called after him, 'If you got that job I'd come here.'

II

Darkness blinded him. It was heavy on him, and moved. It was more than darkness: it was flesh. Beneath him and around him and above him, somnolent bodies crawled blindly. They were huge; so was he. As they shifted incessantly he heard sounds of mud or flesh.

He was shifting too. It was more than restlessness. His whole body felt unstable; he couldn't make out his own form – whenever he seemed to perceive it, it changed. And his mind; it felt too full, of alien chunks that ground harshly together. Memories or fantasies floated vaguely through him. Stone circles. Honeycombed mountains; glimmering faces like a cluster of bubbles in a cave mouth. Enormous dreaming eyes beneath stone and sea. A labyrinth of thorns. His own face. But why was his own face only a memory?

He woke. Dawn suffocated him like grey gas; he lay panting. It was all right. It hadn't been his own face that he'd seemed to remember in the dream. His body hadn't grown huge. His large bones were still lanky. But there was a huge figure, nonetheless. It loomed above him at the window, its spread of face staring down at him.

He woke, and had to grab the dark before he could find the light-switch. He twisted himself to sit on the edge of the couch, legs tangled in the blankets, so as not to fall asleep again. Around him the trailer was flat and bright, and empty. Beyond the ajar door of his parents' room he could see that their bed was smooth and deserted.

He was sure he'd had that dream before – the figure at the window. Somehow he associated it with a windmill, a childhood memory he couldn't locate. Had he been staying with his grandparents? The dream was fading in the light. He glanced at his clock: two in the morning. He didn't want to sleep again until the dream had gone.

He stood outside the trailer. A wind was rising; a loud whisper passed through the forest, unlit trailers rocked and creaked a little at their moorings; behind everything, vast and constant, the sea rushed vaguely. Scraps of cloud slid over the filling moon; light caught at them, but they slipped away. His parents hadn't taken the car. Where had they gone? Irrationally, he felt he knew, if only he could remember. Why did they go out at night so much?

A sound interrupted his musing. The wind carried it to him only to snatch it away. It seemed distant, and therefore must be loud. Did it contain words? Was someone being violently ill, and trying to shout? The moon's light flapped between a procession of dark clouds. A drunk, no doubt, shouting incoherently. Michael gazed at the edge of the forest and wondered about his parents. Light and wind shifted the foliage. Then he shrugged. He ought to be used to his parents' nocturnal behaviour by now.

He slammed the door. His dream was still clinging to him. There had been something odd about the head at the window, besides its size. Something about it had reminded him unpleasantly of a bubble. Hadn't that happened the first time he'd had the dream? But he was grinning at himself: never mind dreams, or his parents. Think of June.

She had been in the club almost every evening since he'd taken the job, a month ago. He had dithered for a week, then he'd returned and asked about the notice. Frowning, the barman had called the manager – to throw Michael out? But June had told them her parents knew Michael well. 'All right. We'll give you six weeks and see how you do.' The barman had trained him, always faintly snooty and quick to criticize. But the customers had begun to prefer Michael to serve them. They accepted him, and he found he could be friendly. He'd never felt less like an outsider.

So long as the manager didn't question June's parents. June had invited Michael to the cottage a couple of times. Her parents had been polite, cold, fascinated, contemptuous. He'd tried to fit his lanky legs beneath his chair, so that the flares of his trousers would cover up his boots – and all the while he'd felt superior to these people in some way, if only he could think of it. 'They aren't my kind of people either,' June had told him, walking to the club. 'When can we go to your caravan?'

He didn't know. He hadn't yet told his parents about her; the reaction to the news of his job hadn't been what he'd hoped. His mother had gazed at him sadly, and he'd felt she was holding more of her feelings hidden, as they all had to in the cramped trailer. 'Why don't you go to the city? They'll have better jobs there.'

'But I feel at home here.'

'That's right,' his father had said. 'That's right.' He'd stared at Michael strangely, with a kind of uneasy joy. Michael had felt oppressed, engulfed by the stare. Of course there was nothing wrong, his father had become uneasy on hearing of his son's first job, his first step in the world, that was all.

'Can I borrow the car to get to the club?'

His father had become dogmatic at once; his shell had snapped tight. 'Not yet. You'll get the key soon enough.'

It hadn't seemed worth arguing. Though his parents rarely used the car at night, Michael was never given the key. Where *did* they go at night? 'When you're older' had never seemed much of an explanation. But surely their nocturnal excursions were more frequent now they'd docked at Pine Dunes? And why was his mother so anxious to persuade him to leave?

It didn't matter. Sometimes he was glad that they went out; it gave him a chance to be alone, the trailer seemed less cramped, he could breathe freely. He could relax, safe from the threat of his father's overwhelming presence. And if they hadn't gone out that night he would never have met June.

Because of the wanderings of the trailer he had never had time for close friendships. He had felt more attached to this latest berth than to any person – until he'd met June. She was the first girl to arouse him. Her small slim body, her bright quick eyes, her handfuls of breast – he felt his body stirring as he thought of her.

For years he'd feared he was impotent. Once, in a village school, a boy had shown him an erotic novel. He'd read about the gasps of pleasure, the creaking of the bed. Gradually he'd realized why that troubled him. The walls of the trailer were thin; he could always hear his father snoring or wheezing, like a huge fish stranded on the shore of a dream. But he had never heard his parents copulating.

Their sexual impulse must have faded quickly, soon after he was born – as soon, he thought, as it had served its purpose. Would his own be as feeble? Would it work at all. Yes, he'd gasped over June, the first night his parents were out. 'I think it'd be good to make love on acid,' she'd said as they lay embraced. 'That way you really become one, united together.' But he thought he would be terrified to take LSD, even though what she'd said appealed deeply to him.

He wished she were here now. The trailer rocked; his parents' door swung creaking, imitated by the bathroom door, which often sprang open. He slammed them irritably. The dream of the bubbling head at the window – if that had been what was wrong with it – was drifting away. Soon he'd sleep. He picked up *Witchcraft in England*. It looked dull enough to help him sleep. And it was June's.

Naked witches danced about on the cover, and on many of the pages. They danced obscenely. They danced lewdly. They chanted obscenely. And so on. They used poisonous drugs, such as belladonna. No doubt that had interested June. He leafed idly onward; his gaze flickered impatiently.

Suddenly he halted, at a name: Severnford. Now that

was interesting. We can imagine, the book insisted, the witches rowing out to the island in the middle of the dark river, and committing unspeakable acts before the pallid stone in the moonlight; but Michael couldn't imagine anything of the kind, nor did he intend to try. Witches are still reputed to visit the island, the book told him before he interrupted it and riffled on. But a few pages later his gaze was caught again.

He stared at his new name. Then reluctantly he turned to the index. At once words stood out from the columns, eager to be seen. They slipped into his mind as if their slots had been ready for years. Exham. Whitminster. The Old Horns. Holihaven. Dilham. Severnford. His father had halted the trailer at all of them, and his parents had gone out at night.

He was still staring numbly at the list when the door snapped open. His father glanced sharply at him, then went into the bedroom. 'Come on,' he told Michael's mother, and sat heavily on the bed, which squealed. To Michael's bewildered mind his father's body seemed to spread as he sat down, like a dropped jelly. His mother sat obediently; her gaze dodged timidly, she looked pale and shrunken – by fear, Michael knew at once. 'Go to bed,' his father told him, raising one foot effortfully to kick the door shut. Almost until dawn Michael lay in the creaking unstable dark, thinking.

III

'You must have seen all sorts of places,' June said.

'We've seen a few,' said Michael's mother. Her eyes moved uneasily. She seemed nervously resentful, perhaps at being reminded of something she wanted desperately to forget. At last, as if she'd struggled and found courage, she managed to say 'We may see a few more.'

'Oh no we won't,' her husband said. He sat slumped on the couch, as though his body were a burden he'd had to drop there. Now that there were four people in the trailer he seemed to take up even more room; his presence overwhelmed all the spaces between them.

Michael refused to be overwhelmed. He stared at his father. 'What made you choose the places we've lived?' he demanded.

'I had my reasons.'

'What reasons?'

'I'll tell you sometime. Not now, son. You don't want us arguing in front of your girlfriend, do you?'

Into the embarrassed silence June said, 'I really envy you, being able to go everywhere.'

'You'd like to, would you?' Michael's mother said.

'Oh yes. I'd love to see the world.'

His mother turned from the stove. 'You ought to. You're the right age for it. It wouldn't do Michael any harm, either.'

For a moment her eyes were less dull. Michael was glad: he'd thought she would approve of June's wanderlust – that was one reason why he'd given in to June's pleas to meet his parents. Then his father was speaking, and his mother dulled again.

'Best to stay where you're born,' his father told June. 'You won't find a better place than here. I know what I'm talking about.'

'You should try living where I do. It'd kill your head in no time.'

'Mike feels at home here. That's right, isn't it, son? You tell her.'

'I like it here,' Michael said. Words blocked his throat. 'I mean, I met you,' he hawked at June.

His mother chopped vegetables: chop, chop, chop – the sound was harsh, trapped within the metal walls. 'Can I do anything?' June said.

'No thank you. It's all right,' she said indifferently. She hadn't accepted June yet, after all.

'If you're so keen on seeing the world,' his father demanded, 'what's stopping you?'

'I can't afford it, not yet. I work in a boutique, I'm saving the money I'd have spent on clothes. And then I can't drive. I'd need to go with someone who can.'

'Good luck to you. But I don't see Mikey going with you.'

Well, ask *me*! Michael shouted at her, gagged (by unsureness: she mightn't have had him in mind at all). But she only said 'When I travel I'm going to have things from everywhere.'

'I've got some,' he said. 'I've kept some things.' He carried the cardboard box to her, and displayed his souvenirs. 'You can have them if you like,' he said impulsively; if she accepted he would be more sure of her. 'The flashlight only needs batteries.'

But she pushed the plastic faces aside, and picked up the ring. 'I'd like that,' she said, turning it so that its colours spilled slowly over one another, merging and separating. She whispered. 'It's like tripping.'

'There you are. I'm giving it to you.'

His father stared at the ring, then a smile spread his mouth. 'Yes, you give her that. It's as good as an engagement, that ring.'

Michael slid the ring on to her finger before she could change her mind; she had begun to look embarrassed. 'It's lovely,' she said. 'Have we time for Mike to take me for a walk before dinner?'

'You can stay out for an hour if you like,' his mother

said, then anxiously: 'Go down to the beach. You might get lost in the woods, in the fog.'

The fog was ambiguous: perhaps thinning, perhaps gathering again. Inside a caravan a radio sang Christmas carols. A sharp-edged bronze sun hung close to the sea. Sea and fog had merged, and might be advancing over the beach. June took Michael's hand as they climbed the slithering dunes.'I just wanted to come out to talk,' she explained.

So had he. He wanted to tell her what he'd discovered. That was his main reason for inviting her: he needed her support in confronting his parents, he would be too disturbed to confront them alone – he'd needed it earlier when he'd tried to interrogate his father. But what could he tell her? I've found out my parents are witches? You know that book you lent me –

'No, I didn't really want to talk,' she said. 'There were just too many bad vibes in there. I'll be all right, we'll go back soon. But they're strange, your parents, aren't they? I didn't realize your father was so heavy.'

'He used to be like me. He's been getting fatter for the last few months.' After a pause he voiced his worst secret fear: 'I hope I never get like him.'

'You'll have to get lots of exercise. Let's walk as far as the point.'

Ahead along the beach, the grey that stretched on the sea was land, not fog. They trudged towards it. Sand splashed from his boots; June slid, and gripped his hand. He strained to tell her what he'd found out, but each phrase he prepared sounded more absurd: his voice echoed hollowly, closed into his mind. He'd tell her – but not today. He relaxed, and felt enormously relieved; he enjoyed her hand small in his. 'I like fog,' she said. 'There are always surprises in it.'

The bronze sun paced them, sinking. The sea shifted

restlessly, muffled. To their left, above the dunes, trees were a flat mass of prickly fog. They were nearly at the point now. It pulled free of the grey, darkening and sharpening. It looked safe enough for them to climb the path.

But when they reached the top it seemed hardly worth the effort. A drab patch of beach and dunes, an indistinct fragment of sea scattered with glitterings of dull brass, surrounded them in a soft unstable frame of fog. Otherwise the view was featureless, except for a tree growing beside the far dunes. Was it a tree? Its branches seeemed too straight, its trunk too thick. Suddenly troubled, Michael picked his way over the point as far as he dared. The fog withdrew a little. It wasn't a tree. It was a windmill.

A windmill by the sea! 'My grandparents lived here,' he blurted.

'Oh, did they?'

'You don't understand. They lived near that windmill. It's the same one, I know it is.'

He still wasn't sure whether she felt his confusion. Memories rushed him, as if all at once afloat: he'd been lying on the couch in his grandparents' decrepit trailer, the huge head had loomed at the window, vague with dawn. It must have been a dream then too.

He followed June down the path. Chill fog trailed them, lapping the point. His thoughts drifted, swirling. What did his discovery mean? He couldn't remember his grandparents at all, not even what they'd looked like. They had been his father's parents – why had the man never mentioned them? Why hadn't he remarked that they'd lived here? The sun slid along the rim of the sea, swollen as though with glowing blood. Had his grandparents also been witches?

'Did Mike's grandparents live here, then?' June said.

His mother stared at her. The spoon and saucepan she was holding chattered like nervous teeth, he was sure she was going to scream and throw everything away – the utensils, her self control, the mask behind which she'd hidden to protect him: for how long? For the whole of his childhood? But she stammered 'How did you know that?'

'Mike told me. The windmill just reminded him.'

'Is dinner ready?' Michael interrupted. He wanted to think everything out before questioning his father. But June was opening her mouth to continue. The trailer was crowded, suffocating. Shut up! he screamed at her. Get out! 'Were they born here, then?' June said.

'No, I don't think so.' His mother had turned away and was washing vegetables. June went to hold the dishes. 'So why did they come here?' she said.

His mother frowned, turning back; with her frown she was searching. 'To retire,' she said abruptly.

His father nodded and smiled to himself, squeezing forward his ruff of chins. 'You could retire from the human race here,' June said sourly, and he wheezed like a punctured balloon.

As the four ate dinner, their constraint grew. Michael and June made most of the conversation; his parents replied shortly when at all, and watched. His mother observed June uneasily; he read dislike in her eyes, or pity. He felt irritably resentful, her uneasiness made his skin nervous. Night edged closer to the windows, blank-faced.

His father leaned back as if his weight had toppled the chair, which creaked loudly. He patted his quaking stomach. 'Just storing it up for the winter,' he said, winking at June.

His arms flopped around her shoulders and Michael's. 'You two go well together. Don't they, eh?'

But his wife said only 'I'm going to bed now. I'm very

tired. Perhaps we'll see you again,' which sounded like dutiful politeness.

'I hope so,' June said.

'I know we will,' Michael's father said expansively.

Michael walked June to the bus-stop. 'I'll see you at the club,' she said through a kiss. Smouldering cones of yellow light led the bus away, and were engulfed. As he walked back, twisted shapes of fog bulked between the trees. Nearby in the dark, something shifted moistly.

He halted. What had it been? Blurred trees creaked with a deadened sound, thin trails of fog reached out for him from branches. He'd heard a shifting, deep in the dark. A vague memory plucked at him. He shivered as if to shake it free, into the chill clinging night. A restless moist shifting. He felt as though the depths of the forest were reaching for his mind with ambiguous tatters of grey. He strode rapidly towards the invisible light. Again he heard the slow moist shifting. Only the sea, he told himself. Only the sea.

IV

As he emerged into the open, the clouds parted and the moon rolled free. The enormous shape in the open space glistened with moonlight. The unstable head turned its crawling face towards him.

The dream trailed him to Liverpool, to the central library, although the space and the head had faded before he could make them out – if indeed he had wanted to. A rush of rain, and the bright lights of the library, washed the dream away. He hurried up the wide green stairs to the Religion and Philosophy section.

He pulled books from the shelves. *Lancashire Witches*.

North-West Hauntings. Ghostly Lancashire. The banality of their covers was reassuring; it seemed absurd that his parents could be mixed up in such things. Yet he couldn't quite laugh. Even if they were, what could he do? He slammed the books angrily on the table, startling echoes.

As he read he began to feel safer. Pine Dunes wasn't indexed in *North-West Hauntings*. His attention strayed fascinated into irrelevances. The hanged man's ghost in Everton Library. The poltergeist of the Palace Hotel, Birkdale. Jokey ghost stories in Lancashire dialect, ee lad. Rain and wind shook the windows, fluorescent light lay flat on the tables. Beyond a glass partition people sat studying, library staff clattered up and down open staircases, carrying scraps of paper. Reassured, he turned to *Lancashire Witches*. Pine Dunes. It was there, on three pages.

When he made himself search the pages they didn't say much. Over the centuries, witches had been rumoured to gather in the Pine Dunes forest. Was that surprising? Wouldn't they naturally have done so, for concealment? Besides, these were only rumours; few people would have bothered struggling through the undergrowth. He opened *Ghostly Lancashire*, expecting irrelevances. But the index showed that Pine Dunes covered several pages.

The author had interviewed a group the other books ignored: the travellers. Their stories were unreliable, he warned, but fascinating. Few travellers would walk the Pine Dunes road after dark; they kept their children out of the woods even by day. A superstitious people, the author pointed out. The book had been written thirty years ago, Michael reminded himself. And the travellers gave no reason for their nervousness except vague tales of something unpleasantly large glimpsed moving beyond the most distant trees. Surely distance must have formed the trees into a solid wall; how could anyone have seen beyond?

One traveller, senile and often incoherent, told a story. A long time ago he, or someone else – the author couldn't tell – had wandered back to the travellers' camp, very drunk. The author didn't believe the story, but included it because it was vivid and unusual. Straying from the road, the man had become lost in the forest. Blinded by angry panic, he'd fought his way towards an open space. But it wasn't the camp, as he'd thought. He had lost his footing on the slippery earth and had gone skidding into a pit.

Had it been a pit, or the mouth of a tunnel? As he'd scrabbled, bruised but otherwise unhurt, for a foothold on the mud at the bottom, he'd seen an opening that led deeper into darkness. The darkness had begun moving slowly and enormously towards him, with a sound like that of a huge shifting beneath mud – darkness which had parted loudly, resolving itself into several sluggish forms that glistened dimly as they advanced to surround him. Terror had hurled him in a leap halfway up the pit; his hands had clamped on rock, and he'd wrenched himself up the rest of the way. He'd run blindly. In the morning he'd found himself full of thorns on a sprung bed of undergrowth.

So what did all that prove? Michael argued with himself on the bus to Pine Dunes. The man had been drunk. All right, so there were other tales about Pine Dunes, but nothing very evil. Why shouldn't his parents go out at night? Maybe they were ghost-hunters, witch-hunters. Maybe they were going to write a book about their observations. How else could such books be written? His mind was becoming desperate as he kept remembering his mother's masked fear.

His parents were asleep. His father lay beached on the

bed, snoring flabbily; beyond his stomach his wife could hardly be seen. Michael was glad, for he hadn't known what to say to them. He wheeled out the bicycle he'd bought from his first month's wages.

He cycled to the Four in the Morning. His knees protruded on either side of him, jerking up and down. Hedges sailed by slowly; their colours faded and dimmed into twilight. The whirr of his dynamo caught among the leaves. He struggled uphill, standing on the pedals. Dim countryside opened below him, the sea glinted dully. As he poised on the edge of the downhill rush he knew how he could unburden himself, or begin to. Tonight he would tell June everything.

But she didn't come to the club. People crowded in; the lights painted them carelessly monochrome. Discotheque records snarled and thumped, swirls of tobacco-smoke glared red, pink, purple. Michael hurried about, serving. Dim wet discoloured faces jostled to reach him, shouting 'Mike! Mike!' Faces rose obsessively to the surface of the jostling: June's, who wasn't there; his mother's, her eyes trying to dodge fear. He was suffocating. His frustration gathered within him; he felt swollen, encumbered. He stared at the luridly pink smoke while voices called. 'I've got to go home,' he told the barman.

'Had enough, have you?'

'My parents aren't well. I'm worried.'

'Strange you didn't say so when you came in. Well, I've managed by myself before.' He turned away, dismissing Michael. 'You'll have to make do with me tonight,' he told the shouting.

The last of the lit streets faded behind Michael. The moon was full, but blurred by unkempt fields of cloud; it showed him only a faint windy swaying that surrounded him for miles. When he confronted his father, what would his mother do? Would she break down? If she admitted to witchcraft and said it was time Michael knew, the scene would be easier – if she did. The moon struggled among plump clouds, and was engulfed.

He cycled fast up the Pine Dunes road. Get there, don't delay to reconsider. Gravel ground together squeaking beneath his wheels; his yellow light wobbled, plucking at trees. The depths of the forest creaked, distant tree trunks were pushed apart to let a huge unstable face peer through. He was overtired – of course there was nothing among the far trees but dark. He sped into the Caravanserai; random patches of unlit trailers bobbed up and faded by. His trailer was unlit too.

Perhaps his parents weren't there. He realized furiously that he felt relieved. They were in there all right, they'd be asleep. He would wake his father, the man might betray himself while still half-asleep. He'd dazzle his father awake, like an interrogator. But his parents' bed was empty.

He punched the wall, which rang flatly. His father had outwitted him again. He stared around the room, enraged. His father's huge suits dangled emptily, like sloughed skin; his mother's clothes hid in drawers. His father's metal box of books sat on top of the wardrobe. Michael glanced resentfully at it, then stared. It was unlocked.

He lifted it down and made to sit on his parents' bed. That made him feel uneasy; he carried the box into the main room. Let his father come in and find him reading. Michael hoped he would. He tugged at the lid, which resisted then sprang open with a loud clang.

He remembered that sound. He'd heard it when he was quite young, and his mother's voice, pleading: 'Let him at least have a normal childhood.' After a moment he'd heard the box closed again. 'All right. He'll find out when it's time,' he'd heard his father say.

The box contained no printed books, but several note-books. They had been written in by numerous people; the inks in the oldest notebook, whose spine had given way, were brown as old bloodstains. Some of the writing in the latest book was his mother's. Odd pages showed rough maps: The Old Horns, Exham, Whitminster, though none of Pine Dunes. These he recognized; but he couldn't understand a word of the text.

Most of it was in English, but might as well not have been. It consisted largely of quotations copied from books; sometimes the source was indicated – *Necro, Revelations Glaaki, Garimiaz, Vermis, Theobald*, whatever they were. The whole thing reminded him of pamphlets issued by cranky cults – like the people who gave all their worldly goods to a man in America, or the others who'd once lured Michael into a seedy hotel for a personality profile, which they'd lied would be fun. He read, baffled.

After a while he gave up. Even the entries his mother had written made no sense. Some of the words he couldn't even pronounce. Kuthullhoo? Kuthoolhew? And what was supposed to be so Great about it, whatever it was?

He shrugged, sniggering a little. He didn't feel so worried now. If this was all his parents were involved in, it seemed silly and harmless. The fact that they'd concealed it from him so successfully for so long seemed to prove as much. They were so convincingly normal, it couldn't be anything very bad. After all, many business-men belonged to secret societies with jargon nobody else could understand. Maybe his father had been initiated into this society as part of one of the jobs he'd taken in his wanderings!

One thing still troubled Michael: his mother's fear. He couldn't see what there was to fear in the blurred language of the notebooks. He made a last effort, and let the books fall open where they would – at the pages that had been read most frequently.

What a waste of time! He strained his mind, but the pages became more bewildering still; he began to laugh. What on earth was 'the millennial gestation'? Something to do with 'the fosterling of the Great Old Ones'? 'The hereditary rebirth'? 'Each of Its rebirths comes closer to incarnation'? 'When the mind opens to all the dimensions will come the incarnation. Upon the incarnation all minds will become one.' Ah, that explains it! Michael sniggered wildly. But there was more: 'the ingestion,' 'the mating beyond marriage,' 'the melting and merging' –

He threw the book angrily into the box. The skin of his eyes crawled hotly; he could hardly keep them open, yet he was wasting his time reading this. The trailer rocked as something huge tugged at it: the wind. The oldest, spineless, notebook began to disintegrate. As he knocked it square, an envelope slipped out.

It was addressed in his father's large handwriting; the last word had had to be cramped. TO MICHAEL: NOT TO BE OPENED UNTIL AFTER I AM GONE. He turned it over and began to tear, but his hand faltered. He'd been unreasonable enough to his father for one day. After a moment he put the envelope unopened in his pocket, feeling sly and ashamed. He replaced the box, then he prepared to sleep. In the dark he tried to arrange his limbs on the sagging couch. Rocking, the trailer sounded like a rusty cradle.

He slept. He wasn't sure whether he was asleep when he heard his mother's low voice. He must be awake, for he could feel her breath on his face. 'Don't stay here.' Her voice trembled. 'Your girlfriend's got the right idea. Go away with her if that's what you want. Just get away from here.'

His father's voice reached for her out of the dark. 'That's enough. He's asleep. You come to bed.'

Silence and darkness settled down for the night. But in the night, or in Michael's dream, there were noises: the stealthy departure of a car from the park; heavy footsteps trying not to disturb the trailer; the gingerly closing of his parents' door. Sleep seemed more important.

His father's voice woke him, shouting into the bedroom. 'Wake up. The car's gone. It's been stolen.'

Daylight blazed through Michael's eyelids. He was sure at once what had happened. His father had hidden the car, so that nobody could get away. Michael lay paralysed, waiting for his mother's cry of panic. Her silence held time immobile. He squeezed his eyelids tighter, filling his eyes with red.

'Oh,' his mother said at last, dully. 'Oh dear.'

There was more in her voice than resignation: she sounded lethargic, indifferent. Suddenly Michael remembered what he'd read in June's book. Witches used drugs. His eyes sprang wide. He was sure that his father was drugging his mother.

V

It didn't take the police long to find the car, abandoned and burnt out, near the windmill. 'Kids, probably,' one of the policemen said. 'We may be in touch with you again.' Michael's father shook his head sadly, and they left.

'I must have dropped the car keys while we were out.' Michael thought his father hardly bothered to sound convincing. Why couldn't he tell the man so, confront him? Because he wasn't sure; he might have dreamed the sounds last night – He raged at his own cowardice, staring at his mother. If only he could be certain of her support! She wandered desultorily, determinedly cleaning the trailer, as though she were ill but expecting company.

When his gagged rage found words at last it weakened immediately. 'Are you all right?' he demanded of her, but then could only stammer 'Do you think you'd better see a doctor?'

Neither of his parents responded. His unsureness grew, and fed his frustration. He felt lethargic, unable to act, engulfed by his father's presence. Surely June would be at the club tonight. He had to talk to someone, to hear another interpretation; perhaps she would prove that he'd imagined everything.

He washed and shaved. He was glad to retreat, even into the cramped bathroom; he and his parents had been edging uneasily around one another all day – the trailer made him think unpleasantly of a tin can full of squirming. As he shaved, the bathroom door sprang open, as it often did. His father appeared behind him in the mirror, staring at him.

Steam coated the mirror again. Beneath the steam, his father's face seemed to writhe like a plastic mask on fire. Michael reached to clear the mirror, but already his father and the man's emotions were upon him. Before Michael could turn his father was hugging him violently, his flesh quivering as though it would burst. Michael held himself stiff, refusing to be engulfed. What are you doing? Get away! In a moment his father turned clumsily and plodded out. The trailer rumbled, shaking.

Michael sighed loudly. God, he was glad that was over. He finished shaving and hurried out. Neither of his parents looked at him; his father pretended to read a book, and whistled tunelessly; his mother turned vaguely as he passed. He cycled to the club.

'Parents all right?' the barman said indifferently.

'I'm not sure.'

'Good of you to come.' Perhaps that was sarcasm. 'There's some things for you to wash.'

Michael could still feel his father's clinging embrace; he kept trying to wriggle it away. He welcomed the press of bodies at the bar, shouting 'Mike!' – even though June wasn't among them. He welcomed the companionship of ordinary people. He strode expertly about, serving, as the crowd grew, as smoke gathered. He could still feel swollen flesh pressed hotly against his back. He won't do that to me again, he thought furiously. He'll never – A tankard dropped from his hand, beneath a beertap. 'Oh my God,' he said.

'What's up with you now?' the barman demanded.

When his father had embraced him, Michael hd thought of nothing but escape. Now at last he realized how final his father's gesture had been. 'My parents,' he said. 'They're, they're worse.'

'Just sent you a message, did they? Off home again now, I suppose? You'd better see the manager, or I will – Will you watch that bloody beer you're spilling!'

Michael slammed shut the tap and struggled through the crowd. People grimaced sympathetically at him, or stared. It didn't matter, his job didn't matter. He must hurry back to head off whatever was going to happen. Someone bumped into him in the doorway, and hindered him when he tried to push them aside. 'What's the matter with you?' he shouted. 'Get out of the way!' It was June.

'I'm really sorry I didn't come last night,' she said. 'My parents dragged me out to dinner.'

'All right. Okay. Don't worry.'

'You're angry. I really am sorry, I wanted to see you – You're not going, are you?'

'Yes, I've got to. Look, my parents aren't well.'

'I'll come back with you. We can talk on the way. I'll help you look after them.' She caught at his shoulder as he tried to run upstairs. 'Please, Mike. I'll feel bad if you just leave me. We can catch the last bus in five minutes if we run. It'll be quicker than your bike.'

God! She was worse than his father! 'Listen,' he snarled, having clambered to street level. 'It isn't ill, they aren't ill,' he said, letting words tumble wildly as he tried to flee. 'I've found out what they do at night. They're witches.'

'Oh no!' She sounded shocked but delighted.

'My mother's terrified. My father's been drugging her.' Now that he was able to say so, his urgency diminished a little; he wanted to release all he knew. 'Something's going to happen tonight,' he said.

'Are you going to try and stop it? Let me come too. I know about it. I showed you my book.' When he looked doubtful she said: 'They'll have to stop when they see me.'

Perhaps she could look after his mother while he confronted his father. They ran to the bus, which sat unlit in the square for minutes, then dawdled along the country roads, hoping for passengers who never appeared. Michael's frustration coiled tighter again. He explained to June what he'd discovered: 'Yeah,' she kept saying, excited and fascinated. Once she began giggling uncontrollably. 'Wouldn't it be weird if we saw your father dancing naked?' He stared at her until she said 'Sorry.' Her pupils were expanding and contracting slightly, randomly.

As they ran along the Pine Dunes road the trees leaned closer, creaking and nodding. Suppose his parents hadn't left the trailer yet? What could he say? He'd be tongue-tied again by his unsureness, and June would probably make things worse. He gasped with relief when he saw that the windows were dark, but went inside to make sure. 'I know where they've gone,' he told June.

Moonlight and unbroken cloud spread the sky with dim milk; dark smoky breaths drifted across the glow. He heard the incessant restlessness of the sea. Bare black silhouettes crowded beside the road, thinly intricate against the sky. He hurried June towards the path.

Why should his parents have gone that way? Something told him they had – perhaps the maze he remembered, the tunnel of undergrowth: that was a secret place. The path wound deeper into the woods, glinting faintly; trees rapidly shuttered the glow of the moon. 'Isn't this fantastic,' June said, hurrying behind him.

The pines gave out, but other trees meshed thickly overhead. The glimpses of flat whitish sky, smouldering with darker cloud, dwindled. In the forest everything was black or blanched, and looked chill, although the night was unseasonably mild. Webs of shadow lay on the path, tangling Michael's feet; tough grass seized him. Bushes massed around him, towering, choking the gaps between trees. The glimpses of sky were fewer and smaller. 'What's that?' June said uneasily.

For a moment he thought it was the sound of someone's foot, unplugging itself from the soft ground: it sounded like a loud slow gulp of mud. But no, it wasn't that. Someone coughing? It didn't sound much like a human cough. Moreover, it sounded as though it were straining to produce a sound, a single sound; and he felt inexplicably that he ought to know what that was.

The bushes stirred, rattling. The muddy sound faded, somewhere ahead. There was no point in telling June his vague thoughts. 'It'll be an animal,' he said. 'Probably something's caught it.'

Soon they reached the tunnel. He knelt at once and began to crawl. Twigs scraped beside his ears, a clawed dry chorus. He found the experience less disturbing now, less oppressive; the tunnel seemed wider, as though someone stout had recently pushed his way through. But behind him June was breathing heavily, and her voice fluttered in the dark. 'There's something following us outside the tunnel,' she said tightly, nervously.

He crawled quickly to the end and stood up. 'There's nothing here now. It must have been an animal.'

He felt odd: calm, safe, yet slyly and elusively excited. His eyes had grown equal to the dark. The trees were stouter, and even closer; they squeezed out masses of shrub between them. Overhead, a few pale scraps of sky were caught in branches. The ground squelched underfoot, and he heard another sound ahead: similar, but not the same.

June emerged panting. 'I thought I'd finished tripping. Where are we going?' she said unevenly. 'I can't see.'

'This way.' He headed at once for a low opening in the tangled growth. As he'd somehow expected, the passage twisted several times, closing almost impenetrably, then widened. Perhaps he'd noticed that someone before him had thrust the bushes apart.

'Don't go so fast,' June said in the dark, almost weeping. 'Wait for me.'

Her slowness annoyed him. His indefinable excitement seemed to affect his skin, which crawled with nervousness like interference on the surface of a bubble. Yet he felt strangely powerful, ready for anything. Wait until he saw his father! He stood impatiently, stamping the mushy ground, while June caught up with him. She gripped his arm. 'There it is again,' she gasped.

'What?' The sound? It was only his feet, squelching. But there was another sound, ahead in the tangled creaking dark. It was the gurgling of mud, perhaps of a muddy stream gargling ceaselessly into the earth. No: it was growing louder, more violent, as though the mud were straining to spew out an obstruction. The sound was repeated, again and again, becoming gradually clearer: a single syllable. All at once he knew what it was. Somewhere ahead in the close dark maze, a thick muddy voice was struggling to shout his name.

June had recognized the sound too, and was tugging at his arm. 'Let's go back,' she pleaded.'I don't like it. Please.'

'God,' he scoffed. 'I thought you were going to help me.' The muddy sounds blurred into a mumble, and were gone. Twigs shook in the oppressive dark, squeaking hollowly together. Suddenly, ahead of him, he heard his father's voice; then, after a long silence, his mother's. Both were oddly strained and muffled. As though this were a game of hide and seek, each had called his name.

'There,' he said to June. 'I haven't got time to take you back now.' His excitement was mounting, his nervous skin felt light as a dream. 'Don't you want to look after my mother?' he blurted.

He shouldered onward. After a while he heard June following him timidly. A wind blundered through the forest, dragging at the bushes. Thorns struggled overhead, clawing at the air; the ground gulped his feet, sounding to his strained ears almost like words. Twice the walls of the passage tried to close, but someone had broken them apart. Ahead the passage broadened. He was approaching an open space.

He began to run. Bushes applauded like joyful bones. The thick smoky sky rushed on, fighting the moonlight. The vociferous ground was slippery; he stumbled as he ran, and almost tripped over a dark huddle. It was his parents' clothes. Some of them, as he glanced back impatiently, looked torn. He heard June fall slithering against bushes. 'Don't!' she cried. But he had reached the space.

It was enclosed by trees. Ivy thickened the trunks, and had climbed to mat the tangle overhead; bushes crowded the cramped gaps between the trees. In the interstices of the tangle, dark sky smouldered.

Slowly his eyes found the meagre light; outlines gathered in the clearing, dimmer than mist. Bared wooden limbs groped into the space, creaking. The dimness sketched them. He could see now that the clearing was about thirty feet wide, and roughly circular. Dimness crawled on it, as though it were an infested pond. At the far side, a dark bulk stood between him and the trees.

He squinted painfully, but its shape persisted in eluding him. Was it very large, or was the dark lying? Across the clearing mud coughed and gurgled thickly, or something did. Dimness massed on the glistening shape. Suddenly he saw that the shape was moving lethargically, and alive.

June had hung back; now she ran forward, only to slip at the edge of the clearing. She clutched his arm to steady herself, then she gazed beyond him, trembling. 'What is it?' she cried.

'Shut up,' he said savagely.

Apart from her interruption, he felt more calm than he had ever felt before. He knew he was gazing at the source of his dreams. The dreams returned peacefully to his mind and waited to be understood. For a moment he wondered whether this was like June's LSD. Something had been added to his mind, which seemed to be expanding awesomely. Memories floated free, as though they had been coded deep in him: wombs of stone and submarine depths; hovering in a medium that wasn't space, somehow linked to a stone circle on a hill; being drawn closer to the circle, towards terrified faces that stared up through the night; a pregnant woman held writhing at the centre of the circle, screaming as he hovered closer and reached for her. He felt primed with centuries of memories. Inherited memories, or shared; but whose?

He waited. All was about to be clarified. The huge bulk shifted, glistening. Its voice, uncontrollably loud and uneven, struggled muddily to speak. The trees creaked ponderously, the squashed bushes writhed, the sky fled incessantly. Suddenly, touched by an instinct he couldn't define, Michael realized how he and June must look from the far side of the clearing. He took her arm, though she struggled briefly, and they stood waiting: bride and bridegroom of the dark.

After a long muddy convulsion in the dimness, words coughed free. The voice seemed unable to speak more than a phrase at a time; then it would blur, gurgling. Sometimes his father's voice, and occasionally his mother's – high-pitched, trembling – seemed to help. Yet the effect was disturbing, for it sounded as though the muddy voice were attempting muffled imitations of his parents. He held himself calm, trusting that this too would be clarified in due course.

The Great Old Ones still lived, the halting voice gurgled loudly. Their dreams could reach out. When the human race was young and strayed near the Old Ones the dreams could reach into the womb and make the unborn in their image. Something like his mother's voice spoke the last words, wavering fearfully. June struggled, but he gripped her arm.

Though the words were veiled and allusive, he understood instinctively what was being said. His new memories were ready to explain. When he read the notebooks again he would understand consciously. He listened and gazed, fascinated. He was in awe of the size of the speaking bulk. And what was strange about the head? Something moved there, rapid as the whirl of colours on a bubble.

In the dark the face seemed to strain epileptically, perhaps to form words.

The Old Ones could wait, the voice or voices told him. The stars would come right. The people the Old Ones touched before birth did not take on their image all at once but gradually, down the centuries. Instead of dying, they took on the form that the Old Ones had placed in the womb of an ancestor. Each generation came closer to the perfect image.

The bulk glistened as though flayed; in the dimness it looked pale pink, and oddly unstable. Michael stared uneasily at the head. Swift clouds dragged darknesses over the clearing and snatched them away. The face looked so huge, and seemed to spread. Wasn't it like his father's face? But the eyes were swimming apart, the features slid uncontrollably across the head. All this was nothing but the antics of shadows. A tear in the clouds crept towards the dimmed moon. June was trying to pull away. 'Keep still,' he snarled, tightening his grip.

They would serve the Old Ones, the voice shouted thickly, faltering. That was why they had been made: to be ready when the time came. They shared the memories of the Old Ones and at the change their bodies were transformed into the stuff of the Old Ones. They mated with ordinary people in the human way, and later in the way the Old Ones had decreed. That way was

June screamed. The tear in the clouds had unveiled the moon. Her cry seemed harsh enough to tear her throat. He turned furiously to silence her; but she dragged herself free, eyes gaping, and fled down the path. The shadow of a cloud rushed towards the clearing. About to pursue June, he turned to see what the moon had revealed.

The shadow reached the clearing as he turned. For a moment he saw the huge head, a swollen bulb which, though blanched by moonlight, reminded him of a mass dug from within a body. The glistening lumpy forehead was almost bare, except for a few strands that groped restlessly over it – strands of hair, surely, though they looked like strings of livid flesh.

On the head, seeming even smaller amid the width of flesh, he saw his mother's face. It was appallingly dwarfed, and terrified. The strands flickered over it, faster, faster. Her mouth strained wordlessly, gurgling.

Before he could see the rest of the figure, a vague gigantic squatting sack, the shadow flooded the clearing. As it did so, he thought he saw his mother's face sucked into the head, as though by a whirlpool of flesh. Did her features float up again, newly arranged? Were there other, plumper, features jostling among them? He could be sure of nothing in the dark.

June cried out. She'd stumbled; he heard her fall, and the thud of her head against something: then silence. The figure was lumbering towards him, its bulk quaking. For a moment he was sure that it intended to embrace him. But it had reached a pit, almost concealed by undergrowth. It slid into the earth, like slow jelly. The undergrowth sprang back rustling.

He stood gazing at June, who was still unconscious. He knew what he would tell her: she had had a bad LSD experience, that had been what she'd seen. LSD reminded him of something. Slowly he began to smile.

He went to the pit and peered down. Faint sluggish muddy sounds retreated deep into the earth. He knew he wouldn't see his parents for a long time. He touched his pocket, where the envelope waited. That would contain his father's explanation of their disappearance, which he could show to people, to June.

Moonlight and shadows raced nervously over the pit. As he stared at the dark mouth he felt full of awe, yet calm. Now he must wait until it was time to come back here, to go into the earth and join the others. He remembered that now; he had always known, deep in himself, that this was home. One day he and June would return. He gazed at her unconscious body, smiling. Perhaps she had been right; they might take LSD together, when it was time. It might help them to become one.

BLACKED OUT

Once out of the Munich traffic, Lamb drove leisurely. Painted giants, elaborate and luminous as frescoes, adorned the walls of houses, which looked as though you had only to lift their roofs to make them chime. Flowers blazed on a multitude of balconies. Between village cows wandered, gently jangling with bells, in fields near barns. August sunlight glided over chalky lakes. Here and there he glimpsed crucifixes in wayside shrines like wooden alcoves on stalks.

He'd neglected to buy a road map. He ought to buy one before dark, at the latest. But he was enchanted with Bavaria. Occasionally, outside houses, he saw tree stumps or even entire trunks carved with grotesque faces. Sometimes they bunched together like a knot of gnarled and incomplete old men, grimacing at him. He drove by, smiling.

While the landscape around Munich had been absolutely flat, mountains were rising now. They bristled with pines. Gazing ahead, he distinguished layer on layer of peaks, which grew paler with mist and distance. Were the furthest shapes mountains or clouds? In squinting to be certain, he passed the signpost. When he failed to make it out by craning he had to creep irritably back to it in reverse.

Yes, something was odd. The direction in which he had been heading was erased by a slash of black paint. A warning, or vandalism? The pointer to the side road indicated Munich. He didn't want to backtrack if it could be avoided. Besides, there was a church ahead: he could see the tip of its spire, a pointed onion which glinted green, beyond a rise. Surely the road was safe.

As he neared the church, the priest came out to meet him. At least, that was how it looked; certainly the man appeared to be gesturing to him – though Lamb found it difficult to be sure, for the light of late afternoon which barred the road with the shadow of the spire also submerged the porch in dimness. The approach of twilight had taken Lamb unawares; it seemed at least an hour earlier than in England. British Summer Time must be the explanation – and of course the days were dwindling. Was the priest beckoning, or gesturing him away?

Before Lamb could tell, the priest was engulfed by his congregation. Movements in the dim porch developed into people, who emerged and stood outside the church: a man like a barrel for the beer that rouged his face, which drooped as though melting in the sullen heat; a thin man whose hands clambered incessantly over each other, spider-like; a young buxom blonde. Of the gazes which fastened on Lamb, and which multiplied as more of the worshippers emerged, only hers was timid. Lamb felt absurd; the priest had withdrawn into the church; the dawdling car panted fumes at the watchers. He drove on.

As it occurred to him that the congregation must come from somewhere nearby, he glimpsed the village. Its lights – or, considering the time of day, more likely reflections of sunlight on windows – gleamed through trees at the foot of the hill. Perhaps he could stay in the village, and gain experience of making himself understood.

Outside the village, horned heads stared over a gate at him. Their eyes were stagnant, but their jaws shifted, chewing. Why did the eyes look ringed by mascara? He wound down the window in order to lean out; then, faintly dismayed, he accelerated into the village. The eye-sockets were crawling with flies.

He had in fact glimpsed lights. All along the narrow clean street they hovered, pale but steady, in their globes. Perhaps a fault refused to let them be extinguished. They were dazzled not only by the daylight but by flowers which crowded the verges of lawns and swarmed on tiers of wooden balconies. Scents roamed the streets.

The village felt oddly artificial, dream-like: an exhibit constructed for tourists. Only when he had halted the car and was searching his phrasebook for aid – 'Helfen Sie mir, bite' meant 'Help me, please,' which seemed an excessively melodramatic way to ask for directions – did he realize what was odd: the street was deserted. Every window was brightly blank; flowers alone leaned out from the balconies. Nothing moved, for even the lawns were weighed down by the hot still air.

All at once the stillness was unnerving. Light clung to the village as though paralysed by the heat. The place seemed too perfect, its cleanliness oppressive. The rustling of pages was close and nerve-racking – besides being pointless: it looked as though he wouldn't need phrases. He stowed the book beneath the dashboard and drove on.

The Gasthaus sign halted him. He understood that word without referring to the book. He couldn't afford to drive past the chance of a meal and a room. Ahead there might be only ski resorts, their hotels full. With its balconies that made it resemble a chest of ajar drawers, the building seemed too attractive to pass.

But it was empty. Heat lent the emptiness a presence which swallowed the ring of the bell on the counter, like fog. The low beams troubled him; he felt caged by dark wood. The bright lights only made them more solid and heavy. He couldn't bring himself to call 'Anyone here?' –

even assuming he might be understood. He hurried back to the car.

Houses sailed by. The sense of unreality intensified; had he allowed his concentration to falter, he might have imagined himself to be coasting through a dream of a model village grown man-size. Still, he had almost reached the end. The road curved, to reveal a house whose windows were crowded with large unlit candles. Presumably it was a candle-maker's, though there was no sign. Beyond it, at the limit of the village, stood a small church.

What kind of church might belong to so silent a village? Though his curiosity was not altogether enjoyable, he left the car. On some of the graves which surrounded the church, candles flickered within glass, in the Bavarian tradition. He climbed the path, which was uneven and pitted as a bad road, and pushed open the door beneath the pointed arch. There he halted, taken aback.

Once, to judge by the onion spire, this had been a typical Bavarian church. What remained of the frescoes – a spotless feathered wing here, there the tatters of a face and its halo – suggested that it had been worth admiring. But only these fragments clung to the scaling walls, and most of the roof was gone. Pews leaned against one another for support; they looked merged by their crust of fallen plaster. The inner door lay within the porch, splintered into several pieces.

That door looked more recent than the building. What had broken it outward? A stray, perhaps dormant, bomb? Momentarily Lamb suffered a twinge of vague historical guilt. Systematic desecration could not have ruined the church more thoroughly, nor have made it feel less like a church.

Late afternoon light seeped through the grimy windows. Once that light must have ignited a gilded altar.

Now it groped over flakes and wounds of raw plaster. As clouds chased across the sun, the tattered discoloured patch of wall appeared to writhe stealthily, to crawl.

Where the altar had stood was a jagged hole in stone. If what Lamb could hear was plaster sifting over the edge, disturbed presumably by his entering the church, then the hole sounded deep as a pit. He didn't intend to check. The floor might well be unsafe, and the church must certainly be damp, for its chill had reached him; he suppressed a shiver. There was a stench of mould – of something growing, anyway.

He ought to be moving on, to make sure of accommodation before dark. Or should he head back a few miles, to that hotel overlooking the lake? He was still hesitating within the porch when he heard footsteps behind him.

For a moment, as he turned, the waking dream of the village toppled into nightmare. He knew all the several faces in the street; yet equally he knew he had met none of them. Then everything fitted together. He'd seen them emerging from the previous church. That was why the village had been deserted. Even the superfluous lighting of the streets seemed explained, just as you might leave lights burning while you went out of the house for a few minutes, to show you would return shortly. Of course that was nonsense, but its absurdity expressed his surge of relief. And mightn't there be someone in the Gasthaus now? As he hurried past the nervous flames to his car, he saw the thin man with the restless hands entering the candle-maker's. Perhaps those hands were calmed by making candles.

What else could the barrel-shaped man have been except the innkeeper? Yes, he could give Lamb *ein Zimmer* for the night. His spaniel jowls drooped beneath the dark beams; the lights made his face vivid as an

elaborately melted candle. He seemed morosely preoccupied, and hardly interested in Lamb. Was he distracted
by the heat? But as Lamb hefted his suitcase upstairs, he
caught the man gazing sidelong at him. Perhaps he was
too proud to welcome Lamb openly. To judge by the
silence of the Gasthaus, Lamb might be the only guest.

In that case he ought to refuse the room. When he
arrived, having panted up three flights of steep dark
wood, he found that it was cramped beneath the eaves.
At least the window in the slanting wall was low enough
for him to look down on the street. He wondered where
the shapely blonde might be.

In a fit of resentful frustration, he took from his case
the magazines he'd bought in Munich. Weren't they the
next best thing? But the explicit photographs seemed
clinical rather than erotic. They succeeded only in making
him feel alone at the top of the house. Abruptly he strode
downstairs to demand another room.

He couldn't make himself understood. The phrasebook
allowed him to say 'No, I don't like it' – but not to name
his dislike. 'Es ist zu – ' Cold/hot/dark/small/noisy? He
couldn't find the words for 'lonely' or 'misshapen' or
'depressing', even assuming that he could have made
himself say such things. The small dim preoccupied eyes
watched him from beneath the dark beams with a spaniel's
glum patience. At last Lamb desisted, feeling stupid and
inept, and turned aside into the restaurant.

The waitress seemed aloof, almost loath to serve him.
If only she had been the blonde! Was he expected to buy
a meal to justify his beer? Too bad; he didn't intend to
eat dinner too early – he would have little else to use up
his evening, except a stroll afterwards. He emptied his
stein quickly, for the restaurant was too bright, hostile to
the vague gloomy haze of beer he craved. Hardly a corner
was left alone with its shadows.

Perhaps his room was preferable, at least for a while. He could lock himself in with the magazines – though however he restrained himself, they would occupy too little time. His shadow humped like a segmented larva over the stairs before him; it looked alone amid the brightness. The upper reaches of the building sounded hollow. But as he reached the top landing, the door of his room opened. As he faltered, one foot dangling, the blonde emerged.

His emotions collided and almost overbalanced him: delight, embarrassment, disbelief, suspicion. He pretended that his gasp had been a prelude to a cough. What had she been doing in his room? Her sidelong glance at him seemed less timid than slyly enticing, for she smiled.

Whether or not that was meant to attract him, it allowed him to stride forward. As she stood aside in the narrow passage, the strong light rendered all of her intensely vivid: her large firm breasts, her wide blue eyes, her skin that looked both sculpted and tanned, her gradual shy smile. What were her eyes telling him? Before he could judge, she was heading for the stairs. Was she swaying her round bottom beneath the tight black uniform just for him?

Of course, she was a chambermaid. Anything beyond that was a fantasy. He saw that as soon as he glimpsed the towel draped over the end of his bed. But he had hardly stepped into the room when he and his thoughts froze. His magazines, which he had left closed on the floor, lay side by side on the bed, and open.

How dare she pry! What he read was his business! By God, if he caught her he would – Suddenly he realized how carefully the magazines were arranged on the bed, open to the most explicit pages. At once he realized what her smile and her gaze had meant to tell him.

By the time he'd hurried out on to the landing, the

staircase was empty, even of shadows. Nor could he hear her. He must be meant to wait. He lay on his bed and dreamed of her – or tried to, but the harsh light kept interrupting. Where on earth was the switch? Not in the room, apparently. He could unscrew the light, except that the junction of bulb and socket was bandaged with insulating tape. Perhaps it was unsafe. No doubt the girl would know how to switch out the light – supposing that he had any time for sleep.

He lay with her on the bed. Darkness and their warmth cradled them. It took her footsteps in the street to start him from his dream of her. He stumbled to the window. The sky was muddy with clouds; the street, perhaps by contrast, looked even brighter. Yes, it was the blonde whose footsteps he'd heard. She was talking to the thin man with the scrambling hands.

Lamb tried to open the window stealthily, in the hope of hearing words which he could understand. But the window rattled in its frame, and the man looked up. His face seemed to pinch into an expression of puritanical contempt, though at that distance Lamb could well have been mistaken. He turned curtly to the girl, and Lamb heard their discussion, incomprehensible save for one reassuring word: she called the man 'father'. All seemed well, and could hardly have been better, for as she hurried after her father the girl glanced up at Lamb and, unmistakably, smiled.

So there was to be a plot between her and Lamb. If she was going home to cook her father's dinner, then Lamb had best eat now. Yet this strategy was so rooted in the banal that it made him hesitate. Could all this really be happening? Was he making a fool of himself? At the same time, the day's adventures seemed to promise further surprises. He felt as though not knowing where he was, not even the name of the town, freed him to explore new possibilities.

Still, in the restaurant the unreality grew threatening. Beneath the multitude of lights, faces surrounded him, clinically detailed. He recognized every one, but understood not a word of their chatter. Under the circumstances, it seemed just as well that nobody sat at his table or spoke to him. But that left him alone with a mounting paranoia: how many of them knew about him and the girl? Some of them kept glancing at him as they talked; most of them seemed nervously restless, no doubt because of the heat.

Of course he must simply be imposing his own doubts on them. He ate dinner, a rich unfamiliar spiced meat. It was surely not what he had ordered, but it gave him no other cause to complain. He would have liked to savour it, but felt that he ought not to dawdle here; the girl was unlikely to come to him except in his room.

He was glad to retreat upstairs, even to the dwarf room. Above the naked bulb a blazing patch hovered on the canted ceiling,which looked prepared to descend on him. He wished he had complained that the room was too small – but he mustn't change his room now.

He lay waiting. Night gathered in the window; the brightness of the village made it look more like fog. How long had he been waiting? It was impossible to tell; his watch had stopped – it must have done so during the meal. Had the girl's father forbidden her to meet him? Surely she couldn't have discussed the plan, surely that hadn't been the reason for the man's hostile glare, the glances of the diners. Lamb's loneliness was talking nonsense. Just relax, don't nag at the dream, just let things happen. He drifted through clumps of grimacing faces; their eyes were unequal knotholes. Before he could reach the church beyond their branches, darkness swallowed him. He woke, and saw that the door of his room was open.

Had she visited him and been afraid to wake him? He stumbled to the window. The street was theatrically bright, and quite empty. His mouth tasted sour with awakening and with disappointment. Had he been tricked, or had he tricked himself? As much to waken himself thoroughly as in any hope, he trudged on to the landing. Movement made him peer down, and the girl turned at the foot of the staircase to smile timidly at him.

At once she slipped out of sight. She must be leaving the inn. Fumbling in his pocket to make sure he had the key, Lamb slammed the door and hurried down. Dark wood thundered beneath him. Good God, he sounded like a stampede all by himself. She could hardly want to attract attention.

Had his noise scared her off? The street looked clean as bone, cleared even of shadows. It looked like a dream of perfection, in which his car outside the Gasthaus provided incongruity. Had her face at the foot of the stairs been the remnant of a dream? No, for he glimpsed her black dress vanishing beyond the curve of the street.

He strode in pursuit, not yet wondering where she meant to lead him. The heat and the lingering numbness of sleep closed him into himself, dulled his thoughts; he felt feverish. She seemed to have chosen her time well, for the street remained deserted, though here and there another window lit up. Of course she would know when the villagers would be occupied in their houses or in the Gasthaus.

The street was too short to give him time for many doubts. But the silence, the isolation of his steps and hers, seemed dauntingly unreal, as though he had been lured into miming a sexual chase. Scents wafted at him, enticing him onward. He quickened his pace, frustrated that the curve blocked his view of her. He heard her pace increase too. She was nearly at her father's house.

Was her father away from home – or was he expecting them both? Lamb wasn't about to perform for an audience. Adventure was one thing, perversion which he didn't enjoy quite another. But as he rounded the curve he saw her clearly. Passing the house without a glance, she marched stiffly towards the church.

Apparently she meant to lead him into the fields. That had a certain primitive appeal, but was hardly alluring. He had no time to reflect, for the church had seized his attention. Was the building on fire?

Venturing forward, he saw the flames. He had the impression that they numbered thousands; their glass jars stood not only on the graves but on the paths between. The entire churchyard blazed with a multitude of candles.

The restless light made the church appear to stir on its foundations. Had someone propped a tree trunk in the porch? The glimpse must be a trick of the light, for momentarily he thought that the object was carved with a writhing face as long and thin as the doorway. When he squinted, his eyes only grew more dazzled, unable to make out the interior of the porch.

Nor could he distinguish the girl at first. As he peered into the dark beyond the village, a stench came welling up from somewhere. Was it fertilizer, or over-ripe crops? Good Lord, how long did they leave things to rot? If the girl had gone into that dark, he was no longer so anxious to follow her.

Then he saw her. She was stealing along the outer edge of the churchyard. Only the fluttering oval of her face was visible above the dance of the railings; her clothes merged with the dark. Still, there was enough light on her path to make him feel safe.

When he trod on the path, it stirred sluggishly beneath

its pelt of grass. He spent time gingerly ensuring that it was firm enough. Along the railings he heard the clash of a metal gate, and a quick rattling. The girl was out of sight now. Good Lord, what was he dawdling for? He ran past the dazzling graveyard, to the end of the railing. There was the gate, and beyond it a narrow path between hedges – but the gate was chained and padlocked.

So she was a teaser, was she? Before his anger could gather momentum it subsided, cowed. Something more was wrong than sexual trickery, though he couldn't yet tell how he knew. What was troubling him? The sharp points on the railings and on the gate, which imprisoned him in the dark? The bright street locked into itself? The desertion? By the church, something moved.

His hand clenched convulsively on a railing. Then he relaxed a little. The movement had only been a leap of darkness: a few adjacent candles, closest to the porch, had gone out. But before he had time to look away, the next flames were engulfed.

That was the only word. It was as though a shadow had fallen on them, a shadow composed of mud: he saw the flames sputter, shrink, die. Above them, at the edge of his dazzled vision, a shape tall as the doorway seemed to lean out of the porch. The stench of growth or decay flooded over Lamb, choking him. He remembered the smell of the church. A clammy chill, like the cold he had felt in the church, reached for him and set his body trembling.

When the third rank of candles was doused, he ran. Before he reached the churchyard gate, the stain of darkness had spread across half the graves. Was a shape advancing beyond the dazzle? He moaned, though air had to strugggle through his constricted throat to his shaking lips, and ran.

All seemed inevitable as a nightmare. Everything was

planned. He was hardly surprised to see, as he ran stumbling into the village, that every window was lit. The blaze showed him the girl in the act of retreating into her father's house.

Perhaps she had been forced to entice him. Might she shelter him now? Please, for God's sake, let her help – for behind him the entire graveyard was dark. He might not have time to reach his car, if the lights of the village failed to protect him. The stench rushed at him, the chill embraced him. The silence of the graveyard seemed altogether dreadful. He staggered towards her. 'Help me,' he cried.

She turned in the doorway. Her face was unreadable, though certainly not timid. 'Helfen Sie mir,' he managed to pronounce. It sounded absolutely unconvincing, and absurd. 'Bitte!' he cried. 'Bitte!' The sound chattered in his mouth, and would have seemed comic if its unimpressiveness had not been terrifying.

All at once Lamb saw that behind the girl stood her father. Avoiding Lamb's gaze, she reached back and grabbed – Lamb flinched away, but it wasn't a weapon, only a wide pan and a wooden spoon. At once she began to clatter them together. Still unable to look at Lamb, she kicked the door shut in his face. As though her noise had been a signal – which no doubt it was – the locked houses came alive with an uproar of utensils.

The row was deafening. It tumbled his thoughts in disarray. He couldn't plan, only run wildly as he realized that the street had dimmed behind him. The first lamps had been swallowed. The violent clamour must be meant to keep the pursuit away from the houses, in the middle of the street – Lamb and the other.

He ran, moaning desperately to himself. His chest felt raw, unable to grasp breath. His ankles gave way, pierced with pain, and tried to throw him headlong. How short

the street had appeared before! The metal uproar drove
him onward, mindlessly terrified.

When he came in sight of the Gasthaus and saw that
his car was gone, he cried out inarticulately. He stumbled
to the Gasthaus door, though he knew it would be locked,
and pounded on it, sobbing. From the edge of his eye he
glimpsed darkness flooding the street. The clattering
urged it towards him.

As his fist thumped the door, no longer in the hope of
entry but because the whole of his arm was shivering, he
saw a glow ahead, beyond the village. It was pale, and
looked gnawed. He limped in that direction, for there
was nowhere else to go. Then he realized that it was
moonlight rising over mountains. The gnawing was silhouettes of pines.

Surely nothing could douse that light. He forced himself
to run, rasping air into his lungs. But at the edge of the
village he faltered. There were several hundred yards to
run through darkness before he reached the crest of the
road, where the glow might be waiting for him. But – he
squinted from the edge of the light of the village, not
daring yet to risk the dark – the crest was not deserted. A
car was parked there, which must be his.

Perhaps he had a chance. He sucked air into his lungs
until they throbbed – then, with a gasp of pure panic, he
drove himself forward, into the dark. Behind him the
village dimmed to an ember, and went out.

There was only the distant toothed glow. But almost at
once the village sprang alight, and the metal clamour
dwindled jaggedly into silence. At once he knew that
whatever had emerged from the broken church was out
here in the dark with him, barring him from the village.

In any case, the insidious chill and the advancing stench
would have told him so. Why had the villagers pushed his
car to the hill? In case he managed to reach the Gasthaus

or in order to lure him onward? He wished that the silence had not allowed these thoughts to form. He ran, trying to stumble faster and to deafen himself and his thoughts with his panting – for behind him in the dark he could hear a leisurely creaking which could be both the sound of limbs and, worse, a kind of laughter.

THE VOICE OF THE BEACH

I

I met Neal at the station.

Of course I can't describe it, I have only to go up the road and look, but there is no need. That isn't what I have to get out of me. It isn't me, it's out there, it can be described. I need all my energy for that, all my concentration, but perhaps it will help if I can remember before that, when everything looked manageable, expressible, familiar enough – when I could bear to look out of the window.

Neal was standing alone on the small platform, and now I see that I dare not go up the road after all, or out of the house. It doesn't matter, my memories are clear, they will help me hold on. Neal must have rebuffed the station-master, who was happy to chat to anyone. He was gazing at the bare tracks, sharpened by June light, as they cut their way through the forest – gazing at them as a suicide might gaze at a razor. He saw me and swept his hair back from his face, over his shoulders. Suffering had pared his face down, stretched the skin tighter and paler over the skull. I can remember exactly how he looked before.

'I thought I'd missed the station,' he said, though surely the station's name was visible enough, despite the flowers that scaled the board. If only he had! 'I had to make so many changes. Never mind. Christ, it's good to see you. You look marvellous. I expect you can thank the sea for that.' His eyes had brightened, and he sounded so full of life that it was spilling out of him in a tumble of words, but his handshake felt like cold bone.

I hurried him along the road that led home and to the He was beginning to screw up his eyes at the sunlight, and I thought I should get him inside; presumably headaches were among his symptoms. At first the road is gravel, fragments of which always succeed in working their way into your shoes. Where the trees fade out as though stifled by sand, a concrete path turns aside. Sand sifts over the gravel; you can hear the gritty conflict underfoot, and the musing of the sea. Beyond the path stands this crescent of bungalows. Surely all this is still true. But I remember now that the bungalows looked unreal against the burning blue sky and the dunes like embryo hills; they looked like a dream set down in the piercing light of June.

'You must be doing well to afford this.' Neal sounded listless, envious only because he felt it was expected. If only he had stayed that way! But once inside the bungalow he seemed pleased by everything – the view, my books on show in the living-room bookcase, my typewriter displaying a token page that bore a token phrase, the Breughel prints that used to remind me of humanity. Abruptly, with a moody eagerness that I hardly remarked at the time, he said 'Shall we have a look at the beach?'

There, I've written the word. I can describe the beach, I must describe it, it is all that's in my head. I have my notebook which I took with me that day. Neal led the way along the gravel path. Beyond the concrete turn-off to the bungalows the gravel was engulfed almost at once by sand, despite the thick ranks of low bushes that had been planted to keep back the sand. We squeezed between the bushes, which were determined to close their ranks across the gravel.

Once through, we felt the breeze whose waves passed

through the marram grass that spiked the dunes. Neal's hair streamed back, pale as the grass. The trudged dunes were slowing him down, eager as he was. We slithered down to the beach, and the sound of the unfurling sea leapt closer, as though we'd awakened it from dreaming. The wind fluttered trapped in my ears, leafed through my notebook as I scribbled the image of wakening and thought with an appalling innocence: perhaps I can use that image. Now we were walled off from the rest of the world by the dunes, faceless mounds with unkempt green wigs, mounds almost as white as the sun.

Even then I felt that the beach was somehow separate from its surroundings: introverted, I remember thinking. I put it down to the shifting haze which hovered above the sea, the haze which I could never focus, whose distance I could never quite judge. From the self-contained stage of the beach the bungalows looked absurdly intrusive, anachronisms rejected by the geomorphological time of sand and sea. Even the skeletal car and the other debris, half engulfed by the beach near the coast road, looked less alien. These are my memories, the most stable things left to me, and I must go on. I found today that I cannot go back any further.

Neal was staring, eyes narrowed against the glare, along the waste of beach that stretched in the opposite direction from the coast road and curved out of sight. 'Doesn't anyone come down here? There's no pollution, is there?'

'It depends on who you believe.' Often the beach seemed to give me a headache, even when there was no glare – and then there was the way the beach looked at night. 'Still, I think most folk go up the coast to the resorts. That's the only reason I can think of.'

We were walking. Beside us the edge of the glittering sea moved in several directions simultaneously. Moist sand, sleek as satin, displayed shells which appeared to flash patterns, faster than my mind could grasp. Pinpoint mirrors of sand gleamed, rapid as Morse. My notes say this is how it seemed.

'Don't your neighbours ever come down?'

Neal's voice made me start. I had been engrossed in the designs of shell and sand. Momentarily I was unable to judge the width of the beach: a few paces, or miles? I grasped my sense of perspective, but a headache was starting, a dull impalpable grip that encircled my cranium. Now I know what all this meant, but I want to remember how I felt before I knew.

'Very seldom,' I said. 'Some of them think there's quicksand.' One old lady, sitting in her garden to glare at the dunes like Canute versus sand, had told me that warning notices kept sinking. I'd never encountered quicksand, but I always brought my stick to help me trudge.

'So I'll have the beach to myself.'

I took that to be a hint. At least he would leave me alone if I wanted to work. 'The bungalow people are mostly retired,' I said. 'Those who aren't in wheelchairs go driving. I imagine they've had enough of sand, even if they aren't past walking on it.' Once, further up the beach, I'd encountered nudists censoring themselves with towels or straw hats as they ventured down to the sea, but Neal could find out about them for himself. I wonder now if I ever saw them at all, or simply felt that I should.

Was he listening? His head was cocked, but not towards me. He'd slowed, and was staring at the ridges and furrows of the beach, at which the sea was lapping. All at once the ridges reminded me of convolutions of the brain, and I took out my notebook as the grip on my skull tightened. The beach as a subconscious, my notes say: the horizon as the imagination – sunlight set a ship ablaze on the edge of the world, an image that impressed me as vividly yet indefinably symbolic – the debris as memories, half-buried, half-comprehensible. But then what were the bungalows, perched above the dunes like boxes carved of dazzling bone?

I glanced up. A cloud had leaned towards me. No, it had been more as though the cloud were rushing at the beach from the horizon, dauntingly fast. Had it been a cloud? It had seemed more massive than a ship. The sky was empty now, and I told myself that it had been an effect of the haze – the magnified shadow of a gull, perhaps.

My start had enlivened Neal, who began to chatter like a television wakened by a kick. 'It'll be good for me to be alone here, to get used to being alone. Mary and the children found themselves another home, you see. He earns more money than I'll ever see, if that's what they want. He's the head of the house type, if that's what they want. I couldn't be that now if I tried, not with the way my nerves are now.' I can still hear everything he said, and I suppose that I knew what had been wrong with him. Now they are just words.

'That's why I'm talking so much,' he said, and picked up a spiral shell, I thought to quiet himself.

'That's much too small. You'll never hear anything in that.'

Minutes passed before he took it away from his ear and handed it to me. 'No?' he said.

I put it to my ear and wasn't sure what I was hearing. No, I didn't throw the shell away, I didn't crush it underfoot; in any case, how could I have done that to the rest of the beach? I was straining to hear, straining to make out how the sound differed from the usual whisper of a shell. Was it that it seemed to have a rhythm that I couldn't define, or that it sounded shrunken by distance rather than cramped by the shell? I felt expectant, entranced – precisely the feeling I'd tried so often to communicate in my fiction, I believe. Something stooped towards me from the horizon. I jerked, and dropped the shell.

There was nothing but the dazzle of sunlight that leapt at me from the waves. The haze above the sea had darkened, staining the light, and I told myself that was what I'd seen. But when Neal picked up another shell I felt uneasy. The grip on my skull was very tight now. As I regarded the vistas of empty sea and sky and beach my expectancy grew oppressive, too imminent, no longer enjoyable.

'I think I'll head back now. Maybe you should as well,' I said, rummaging for an uncontrived reason, 'just in case there is quicksand.'

'All right. It's in all of them,' he said, displaying an even smaller shell to which he'd just listened. I remember thinking that his observation was so self-evident as to be meaningless.

As I turned towards the bungalows the glitter of the sea clung to my eyes. After-images crowded among the debris. They were moving; I strained to make out their shape. What did they resemble? Symbols – hieroglyphs? Limbs writhing rapidly, as if in a ritual dance? They made the debris appear to shift, to crumble. The herd of faceless dunes seemed to edge forward; an image leaned towards me out of the sky. I closed my eyes, to calm their antics, and wondered if I should take the warnings of pollution more seriously.

We walked towards the confusion of footprints that climbed the dunes. Neal glanced about at the sparkling of sand. Never before had the beach so impressed me as a complex of patterns, and perhaps that means it was already too late. Spotlighted by the sun, it looked so artificial that I came close to doubting how it felt underfoot.

The bungalows looked unconvincing too. Still, when we'd slumped in our chairs for a while, letting the relative dimness soothe our eyes while our bodies guzzled every hint of coolness, I forgot about the beach. We shared two litres of wine and talked about my work, about his lack of any since graduating.

Later I prepared melon, salads, water ices. Neal watched, obviously embarrassed that he couldn't help. He seemed lost without Mary. One more reason not to marry, I thought, congratulating myself.

As we ate he kept staring out at the beach. A ship was caught in the amber sunset: a dream of escape. I felt the image less deeply than I'd experienced the metaphors of the beach; it was less oppressive. The band around my head had faded.

When it grew dark Neal pressed close to the pane. 'What's that?' he demanded.

I switched out the light so that he could see. Beyond the dim humps of the dunes the beach was glowing, a dull pallor like moonlight stifled by fog. Do all beaches glow at night? 'That's what makes people say there's pollution,' I said.

'Not the light,' he said impatiently. 'The other things. What's moving?'

I squinted through the pane. For minutes I could see nothing but the muffled glow. At last, when my eyes were smarting, I began to see forms thin and stiff as scarecrows, jerking into various contorted poses. Gazing for so long was bound to produce something of the kind, and I took them to be after-images of the tangle, barely visible, of bushes.

'I think I'll go and see.'

'I shouldn't go down there at night,' I said, having

realized that I'd never gone to the beach at night and that I felt a definite, though irrational, aversion to doing so.

Eventually he went to bed. Despite all his travelling, he'd needed to drink to make himself sleepy. I heard him open his bedroom window, which overlooked the beach. There is so much still to write, so much to struggle through, and what good can it do me now?

II

I had taken the bungalow, one of the few entries in my diary says, to give myself the chance to write about being distracted by city life – the cries of the telephone, the tolling of the doorbell, the omnipresent clamour – only to discover, once I'd left it behind, that city life was my theme. But I was a compulsive writer: if I failed to write for more than a few days I became depressed. Writing was the way I overcame the depression of not writing. Now writing seems to be my only way of hanging on to what remains of myself, of delaying the end.

The day after Neal arrived, I typed a few lines of a sample chapter. It wasn't a technique I enjoyed – tearing a chapter out of the context of a novel that didn't yet exist. In any case, I was distracted by the beach, compelled to scribble notes about it, trying to define the images it suggested. I hoped these notes might build into a story. I was picking at the notes in search of their story when Neal said 'Maybe I can lose myself for a bit in the countryside.'

'Mm,' I said curtly, not looking up.

'Didn't you say there was a deserted village?'

By the time I directed him I would have lost the thread of my thoughts. The thread had been frayed and tangled, anyway. As long as I was compelled to think about the beach I might just as well be down there. I can still write as if I don't know the end, it helps me not to think of 'I'll come with you,' I said.

The weather was nervous. Archipelagos of cloud floated low on the hazy sky, above the sea; great Rorschach blots rose from behind the slate hills, like dissolved stone. As we squeezed through the bushes, a shadow came hunching over the dunes to meet us. When my foot touched the beach a moist shadowy chill seized me, as though the sand disguised a lurking marsh. Then sunlight spilled over the beach, which leapt into clarity.

I strode, though Neal appeared to want to dawdle. I wasn't anxious to linger; after all, I told myself, it might rain. Glinting mosaics of grains of sand changed restlessly around me, never quite achieving a pattern. Patches of sand, flat shapeless elongated ghosts, glided over the beach and faltered, waiting for another breeze. Neal kept peering at them as though to make out their shapes.

Half a mile along the beach the dunes began to sag, to level out. The slate hills were closing in. Were they the source of the insidious chill? Perhaps I was feeling the damp; a penumbra of moisture welled up around each of my footprints. The large wet shapes seemed quite unrelated to my prints, an effect which I found unnerving. When I glanced back, it looked as though something enormous was imitating my walk.

The humidity was almost suffocating. My head felt clamped by tension. Wind blundered booming in my ears, even when I could feel no breeze. Its jerky rhythm was distracting because indefinable. Grey cloud had flooded the sky; together with the hills and the thickening haze above the sea, it caged the beach. At the edge of my eye the convolutions of the beach seemed to writhe, to struggle to form patterns. The insistent sparkling nagged at my mind.

I'd begun to wonder whether I had been blaming imagined pollution for the effects of heat and humidity – I was debating whether to turn back before I grew dizzy or nauseous – when Neal said 'Is that it?'

I peered ahead, trying to squint the dazzle of waves from my eyes. A quarter of a mile away the hills ousted the dunes completely. Beneath the spiky slate a few uprights of rock protruded from the beach like standing stones. They glowed sullenly as copper through the haze; they were encrusted with sand. Surely that wasn't the village.

'Yes, that's it,' Neal said, and strode forward.

I followed him, because the village must be further on. The veil of haze drew back, the vertical rocks gleamed unobscured, and I halted bewildered. The rocks weren't encrusted at all; they were slate, grey as the table of rock on which they stood above the beach. Though the slate was jagged, some of its gaps were regular: windows, doorways. Here and there walls still formed corners. How could the haze have distorted my view so spectacularly?

Neal was climbing rough steps carved out of the slate table. Without warning, as I stood confused by my misperception, I felt utterly alone. A bowl of dull haze trapped me on the bare sand. Slate, or something more massive and vague, loomed over me. The kaleidoscope of shells was about to shift; the beach was ready to squirm, to reveal its pattern, shake off its artificiality. The massive looming would reach down, and

My start felt like a convulsive awakening. The table was deserted except for the fragments of buildings. I could hear only the wind, baying as though its mouth was vast and uncontrollable. 'Neal,' I called. Dismayed by the smallness of my voice, I shouted 'Neal!'

I heard what sounded like scales of armour chafing
together – slate, of course. The grey walls shone lifelessly,
cavitied as skulls; gaping windows displayed an absence
of faces, of room. Then Neal's head poked out of half a
wall. 'Yes, come on,' he said. 'It's strange.'

As I climbed the steps, sand gritted underfoot like
sugar. Low drifts of sand were piled against the walls;
patches glinted on the small plateau. Could that sand
have made the whole place look encrusted and half-
buried? I told myself that it had been an effect of the
heat.

Broken walls surrounded me. They glared like storm-
clouds in lightning. They formed a maze whose centre
was desertion. That image stirred another, too deep in
my mind to be definable. The place was – not a maze,
but a puzzle whose solution would clarify a pattern, a
larger mystery. I realized that then; why couldn't I have
fled?

I suppose I was held by the enigma of the village. I
knew there were quarries in the hills above, but I'd never
learned why the village had been abandoned. Perhaps its
meagreness had killed it – I saw traces of less than a
dozen buildings. It seemed further dwarfed by the beach;
the sole visible trace of humanity, it dwindled beneath
the gnawing of sand and the elements. I found it enervating, its lifelessness infectious. Should I stay with Neal, or
risk leaving him there? Before I could decide, I heard
him say amid a rattle of slate 'This is interesting.'

In what way? He was clambering about an exposed
cellar, among shards of slate. Whatever the building had
been, it had stood furthest from the sea. 'I don't mean
the cellar,' Neal said. 'I mean that.'

Reluctantly I peered where he was pointing. In the
cellar wall furthest from the beach, a rough alcove had
been chipped out of the slate. It was perhaps a yard

deep, but barely high enough to accommodate a huddled man. Neal was already crawling in. I heard slate crack beneath him; his feet protruded from the darkness. Of course they weren't about to jerk convulsively – but my nervousness made me back away when his muffled voice said 'What's this?'

He backed out like a terrier with his prize. It was an old notebook, its pages stuck together in a moist wad. 'Someone covered it up with slate,' he said as though that should tempt my interest.

Before I could prevent him he was sitting at the edge of the beach and peeling the pages gingerly apart. Not that I was worried that he might be destroying a fragment of history – I simply wasn't sure that I wanted to read whatever had been hidden in the cellar. Why couldn't I have followed my instincts?

He disengaged the first page carefully, then frowned. 'This begins in the middle of something. There must be another book.'

Handing me the notebook, he stalked away to scrabble in the cellar. I sat on the edge of the slate table, and glanced at the page. It is before me now on my desk. The pages have crumbled since then – the yellowing paper looks more and more like sand – but the large writing is still legible, unsteady capitals in a hand that might once have been literate before it grew senile. No punctuation separates the words, though blotches sometimes do. Beneath the relentless light at the deserted village the faded ink looked unreal, scarcely present at all.

FROM THE BEACH EVERYONE GONE NOW BUT ME ITS NOT SO BAD IN DAYTIME EXCEPT I CANT GO BUT AT NIGHT I CAN HEAR IT REACHING FOR (a blot of fungus had consumed a word here) AND THE VOICES ITS VOICE AND THE GLOWING AT LEAST IT HELPS ME SEE DOWN HERE WHEN IT COMES

I left it at that; my suddenly unsteady fingers might have torn the page. I wish to God they had. I was on edge with the struggle between humidity and the chill of slate and beach; I felt feverish. As I stared at the words they touched impressions, half-memories. If I looked up, would the beach have changed?

I heard Neal slithering on slate, turning over fragments. In my experience, stones were best not turned over. Eventually he returned. I was dully fascinated by the shimmering of the beach; my fingers pinched the notebook shut.

'I can't find anything,' he said. 'I'll have to come back.' He took the notebook from me and began to read, muttering 'What? Jesus!' Gently he separated the next page from the wad. 'This gets stranger,' he murmured. 'What kind of guy was this? Imagine what it must have been like to live inside his head.'

How did he know it had been a man? I stared at the pages, to prevent Neal from reading them aloud. At least it saved me from having to watch the antics of the beach, which moved like slow flames, but the introverted meandering of words made me nervous.

IT CANT REACH DOWN HERE NOT YET BUT OUTSIDE IS CHANGING OUTSIDES PART OF THE PATTERN I READ THE PATTERN THATS WHY I CANT GO SAW THEM DANCING THE PATTERN IT WANTS ME TO DANCE ITS ALIVE BUT ITS ONLY THE IMAGE BEING PUT TOGETHER

Neal was wide-eyed, fascinated. Feverish disorientation gripped my skull; I felt too unwell to move. The heat-haze must be closing in: at the edge of my vision, everything was shifting.

WHEN THE PATTERNS DONE IT CAN COME BACK AND GROW ITS HUNGRY TO BE EVERYTHING I KNOW HOW IT WORKS THE SAND MOVES AT NIGHT

AND SUCKS YOU DOWN OR MAKES YOU GO WHERE
IT WANTS TO MAKE (a blotch had eaten several words)
WHEN THEY BUILT LEWIS THERE WERE OLD STONES
THAT THEY MOVED MAYBE THE STONES KEPT IT
SMALL NOW ITS THE BEACH AT LEAST

On the next page the letters are much larger, and
wavery. Had the light begun to fail, or had the writer
been retreating from the light – from the entrance to the
cellar? I didn't know which alternative I disliked more.

GOT TO WRITE HANDS SHAKY FROM CHIPPING
TUNNEL AND NO FOOD THEYRE SINGING NOW HELP-
ING IT REACH CHANTING WITH NO MOUTHS THEY
SING AND DANCE THE PATTERN FOR IT TO REACH
THROUGH

Now there are very few words to the page. The letters
are jagged, as though the writer's hand kept twitching
violently.

GLOW COMING ITS OUT THERE NOW ITS LOOKING
IN AT ME IT CANT GET HOLD IF I KEEP WRITING
THEY WANT ME TO DANCE SO ITLL GROW WANT ME
TO BE

There it ends. 'Ah, the influence of Joyce,' I com-
mented sourly. The remaining pages are blank except for
fungus. I managed to stand up; my head felt like a
balloon pumped full of gas. 'I'd like to go back now. I
think I've a touch of sunstroke.'

A hundred yards away I glancd back at the remnants
of the village – Lewis, I assumed it had been called. The
stone remains wavered as though striving to achieve a
new shape; the haze made them look coppery, fat with a
crust of sand. I was desperate to get out of the heat.

Closer to the sea I felt slightly less oppressed – but the
whispering of sand, the liquid murmur of the waves, the

bumbling of the wind, all chanted together insistently. Everywhere on the beach were patterns, demanding to be read.

Neal clutched the notebook under his arm. 'What do you make of it?' he said eagerly.

His indifference to my health annoyed me, and hence so did the question. 'He was mad,' I said. 'Living here – is it any wonder? Maybe he moved there after the place was abandoned. The beach must glow there too. That must have finished him. You saw how he tried to dig himself a refuge. That's all there is to it.'

'Do you think so? I wonder,' Neal said, and picked up a shell.

As he held the shell to his ear, his expression became so withdrawn and unreadable that I felt a pang of dismay. Was I seeing a symptom of his nervous trouble? He stood like a fragment of the village – as though the shell was holding him, rather than the reverse.

Eventually he mumbled 'That's it, that's what he meant. Chanting with no mouths.'

I took the shell only very reluctantly; my head was pounding. I pressed the shell to my ear, though I was deafened by the storm of my blood. If the shell was muttering, I couldn't bear the jaggedness of its rhythm. I seemed less to hear it than to feel it deep in my skull.

'Nothing like it,' I said, almost snarling, and thrust the shell at him.

Now that I'd had to strain to hear it, I couldn't rid myself of the muttering; it seemed to underlie the sounds of wind and sea. I trudged onward, eyes half shut. Moisture sprang up around my feet; the glistening shapes around my prints looked larger and more definite. I had to cling to my sense of my own size and shape.

When we neared home I couldn't see the bungalows.

There appeared to be only the beach, grown huge and blinding. At last Neal heard a car leaving the crescent, and led me up the path of collapsed footprints.

In the bungalow I lay willing the lights and patterns to fade from my closed eyes. Neal's presence didn't soothe me, even though he was only poring over the notebook. He'd brought a handful of shells indoors. Occasionally he held one to his ear, muttering 'It's still there, you know. It does sound like chanting.' At least, I thought peevishly, *I* knew when something was a symptom of illness – but the trouble was that in my delirium I was tempted to agree with him. I felt I had almost heard what the sound was trying to be.

III

Next day Neal returned to the deserted village. He was gone for so long that even amid the clamour of my disordered senses, I grew anxious. I couldn't watch for him; whenever I tried, the white-hot beach began to judder, to quake, and set me shivering.

At last he returned, having failed to find another notebook. I hoped that would be the end of it, but his failure had simply frustrated him. His irritability chafed against mine. He managed to prepare a bedraggled salad, of which I ate little. As the tide of twilight rolled in from the horizon he sat by the window, gazing alternately at the beach and at the notebook.

Without warning he said 'I'm going for a stroll. Can I borrow your stick?'

I guessed that he meant to go to the beach. Should he be trapped by darkness and sea, I was in no condition to go to his aid. 'I'd rather you didn't,' I said feebly.

'Don't worry, I won't lose it.'

My lassitude suffocated my arguments. I lolled in my chair and through the open window heard him padding away, his footsteps muffled by sand. Soon there was only the vague slack rumble of the sea, blundering back and forth, and the faint hiss of sand in the bushes.

After half an hour I made myself stand up, though the ache in my head surged and surged, and gaze out at the whitish beach. The whole expanse appeared to flicker like hints of lightning. I strained my eyes. The beach looked crowded with debris, all of which danced to the flickering. I had to peer at every movement, but there was no sign of Neal.

I went out and stood between the bushes. The closer I approached the beach, the more crowded with obscure activity it seemed to be – but I suspected that much, if not all, of this could be blamed on my condition, for within five minutes my head felt so tight and unbalanced that I had to retreat indoors, away from the heat.

Though I'd meant to stay awake, I was dozing when Neal returned. I woke to find him gazing from the window. As I opened my eyes the beach lurched forward, shining. It didn't look crowded now, presumably because my eyes had had a rest. What could Neal see to preoccupy him so? 'Enjoy your stroll?' I said sleepily.

He turned, and I felt a twinge of disquiet. His face looked stiff with doubt; his eyes were uneasy, a frown dug its ruts in his forehead. 'It doesn't glow,' he said.

Assuming I knew what he was talking about, I could only wonder how badly his nerves were affecting his perceptions. If anything, the beach looked brighter. 'How do you mean?'

'The beach down by the village – it doesn't glow. Not any more.'

'Oh, I see.'

He looked offended, almost contemptuous, though I couldn't understand why he'd expected me to be less indifferent. He withdrew into a scrutiny of the notebook. He might have been trying to solve an urgent problem.

Perhaps if I hadn't been ill I would have been able to divert Neal from his obsession, but I could hardly venture outside without growing dizzy; I could only wait in the bungalow for my state to improve. Neither Neal nor I had had sunstroke before, but he seemed to know how to treat it. 'Keep drinking water. Cover yourself if you start shivering.' He didn't mind my staying in – he seemed almost too eager to go out alone. Did that matter? Next day he was bound only for the library.

My state was crippling my thoughts, yet even if I'd been healthy I couldn't have imagined how he would look when he returned: excited, conspiratorial, smug. 'I've got a story for you,' he said at once.

Most such offers proved to be prolonged and dull. 'Oh yes?' I said warily.

He sat forward as though to infect me with suspense. 'That village we went to – it isn't called Lewis. It's called Strand.'

Was he pausing to give me a chance to gasp or applaud? 'Oh yes,' I said without enthusiasm.

'Lewis was another village, further up the coast. It's deserted too.'

That seemed to be his punch line. The antics of patterns within my eyelids had made me irritable. 'It doesn't seem much of a story,' I complained.

'Well, that's only the beginning.' When his pause had forced me to open my eyes, he said 'I read a book about your local unexplained mysteries.'

'Why?'

'Look, if you don't want to hear – '

'Go on, go on, now you've started.' Not to know might be even more nerve-racking.

'There wasn't much about Lewis,' he said eventually, perhaps to give himself more time to improvise.

'Was there much at all?'

'Yes, certainly. It may not sound like much. Nobody knows why Lewis was abandoned, but then nobody knows that about Strand either.' My impatience must have showed, for he added hastily 'What I mean is, the people who left Strand wouldn't say why.'

'Someone asked them?'

'The woman who wrote the book. She managed to track some of them down. They'd moved as far inland as they could, that was one thing she noticed. And they always had some kind of nervous disorder. Talking about Strand always made them more nervous, as though they felt that talking might make something happen, or something might hear.'

'That's what the author said.'

'Right.'

'What was her name?'

Could he hear my suspicion? 'Jesus *Christ*,' he snarled, 'I don't know. What does it matter?'

In fact it didn't, not to me. His story had made me feel worse. The noose had tightened round my skull, the twilit beach was swarming and vibrating. I closed my eyes. Shut up, I roared at him. Go away.

'There was one thing,' he persisted. 'One man said that kids kept going on the beach at night. Their parents tried all ways to stop them. Some of them questioned their kids, but it was as though the kids couldn't stop themselves. Why was that, do you think?' When I refused to answer he said irrelevantly 'All this was in the 1930s.'

I couldn't stand hearing the children called kids. The recurring word had made me squirm: drips of slang, like water torture. And I'd never heard such a feeble punch line. His clumsiness as a storyteller enraged me; he couldn't even recognize his material. I was sure he hadn't read any such book.

After a while I peered out from beneath my eyelids, hoping he'd decided that I was asleep. He was poring over the notebook again, and looked rapt. I only wished that people and reviewers would read my books as carefully. He kept rubbing his forehead, as though to enliven his brain.

I dozed. When I opened my eyes he was waiting for me. He shoved the notebook at me to demonstrate something. 'Look, I'm sorry,' I said without much effort to sound so. 'I'm not in the mood.'

He stalked into his room, emerging without the book but with my stick. 'I'm going for a walk,' he announced sulkily, like a spouse after a quarrel.

I dozed gratefully, for I felt more delirious; my head felt packed with grains of sand that gritted together. In fact, the whole of me was made of sand. Of course it was true that I was composed of particles, and I thought my delirium had found a metaphor for that. But the grains that floated through my inner vision were neither sand nor atoms. A member, dark and vague, was reaching for them. I struggled to awaken; I didn't want to distinguish its shape, and still less did I want to learn what it meant to do with the grains – for as the member sucked them into itself, engulfing them in a way that I refused to perceive, I saw that the grains were worlds and stars.

I woke shivering. My body felt uncontrollable and unfamiliar. I let it shake itself to rest – not that I had a choice, but I was concentrating on the problem of why I'd woken head raised, like a watchdog. What had I heard?

Perhaps only wind and sea: both seemed louder, more

intense. My thoughts became entangled in their rhythm. I felt there had been another sound. The bushes threshed, sounding parched with sand. Had I heard Neal returning? I stumbled into his room. It was empty.

As I stood by his open window, straining my ears, I thought I heard his voice, blurred by the dull tumult of waves. I peered out. Beyond the low heads of the bushes, the glow of the beach shuddered towards me. I had to close my eyes, for I couldn't tell whether the restless scrawny shapes were crowding my eyeballs or the beach; it felt, somehow, like both. When I looked again, I seemed to see Neal.

Or was it Neal? The unsteady stifled glow aggravated the distortions of my vision. Was the object just a new piece of debris? I found its shape bewildering; my mind kept apprehending it as a symbol printed on the whitish expanse. The luminosity made it seem to shift, tentatively and jerkily, as though it was learning to pose. The light, or my eyes, surrounded it with dancing.

Had my sense of perspective left me? I was misjudging size, either of the beach or of the figure. Yes, it was a figure, however large it seemed. It was moving its arms like a limp puppet. And it was half-buried in the sand.

I staggered outside, shouting to Neal, and then I recoiled. The sky must be thick with a stormcloud; it felt suffocatingly massive, solid as rock, and close enough to crush me. I forced myself towards the bushes, though my head was pounding, squeezed into a lump of pain.

Almost at once I heard plodding on the dunes. My blood half deafened me; the footsteps sounded vague and immense. I peered along the dim path. At the edge of my vision the beach flickered repetitively. Immense darkness hovered over me. Unnervingly close to me, swollen by the glow, a head rose into view. For a moment my tension seemed likely to crack my skull. Then Neal spoke.

His words were incomprehensible amid the wind, but it was his voice.

As we trudged back towards the lights the threat of a storm seemed to withdraw, and I blamed it on my tension. 'Of course I'm all right,' he muttered irritably. 'I fell and that made me shout, that's all.' Once we were inside I saw the evidence of his fall; his trousers were covered with sand up to his knees.

IV

Next day he hardly spoke to me. He went down early to the beach, and stayed there. I didn't know if he was obsessed or displaying pique. Perhaps he couldn't bear to be near me; invalids can find each other unbearable.

Often I glimpsed him, wandering beyond the dunes. He walked as though in an elaborate maze and scrutinized the beach. Was he searching for the key to the notebook? Was he looking for pollution? By the time he found it, I thought sourly, it would have infected him.

I felt too enervated to intervene. As I watched, Neal appeared to vanish intermittently; if I looked away, I couldn't locate him again for minutes. The beach blazed like bone, and was never still. I couldn't blame the aberrations of my vision solely on heat and haze.

When Neal returned, late that afternoon, I asked him to phone for a doctor. He looked taken aback, but eventually said 'There's a box by the station, isn't there?'

'One of the neighbours would let you phone.'

'No, I'll walk down. They're probably all wondering why you've let some long-haired freak squat in your house, as it is.'

He went out, rubbing his forehead gingerly. He often

did that now. That, and his preoccupation with the demented notebook, were additional reasons why I wanted a doctor: I felt Neal needed examining too.

By the time he returned, it was dusk. On the horizon, embers dulled in the sea. The glow of the beach was already stirring; it seemed to have intensified during the last few days. I told myself I had grown hypersensitive.

'Dr Lewis. He's coming tomorrow.' Neal hesitated, then went on 'I think I'll just have a stroll on the beach. Want to come?'

'Good God no. I'm ill, can't you see?'

'I know that.' His impatience was barely controlled. 'A stroll might do you good. There isn't any sunlight now.'

'I'll stay in until I've seen the doctor.'

He looked disposed to argue, but his restlessness overcame him. As he left, his bearing seemed to curse me. Was his illness making him intolerant of mine, or did he feel that I'd rebuffed a gesture of reconciliation?

I felt too ill to watch from the window. When I looked I could seldom distinguish him or make out which movements were his. He appeared to be walking slowly, poking at the beach with my stick. I wondered if he'd found quicksand. Again his path made me think of a maze.

I dozed, far longer than I'd intended. The doctor loomed over me. Peering into my eyes, he reached down. I began to struggle, as best I could: I'd glimpsed the depths of his eye-sockets, empty and dry as interstellar space. I didn't need his treatment, I would be fine if he left me alone, just let me go. But he had reached deep into me. As though I was a bladder that had burst, I felt myself flood into him; I felt vast emptiness absorb my substance and my self. Dimly I understood that it was nothing like emptiness – that my mind refused to perceive what it was, so alien and frightful was it teeming.

It was dawn. The muffled light teemed. The beach glowed fitfully. I gasped: someone was down on the beach, so huddled that he looked shapeless. He rose, levering himself up with my stick, and began to pace haphazardly. I knew at once that he'd spent the night on the beach.

After that I stayed awake. I couldn't imagine the state of his mind, and I was a little afraid of being asleep when he returned. But when, hours later, he came in to raid the kitchen for a piece of cheese, he seemed hardly to see me. He was muttering repetitively under his breath. His eyes looked dazzled by the beach, sunk in his obsession.

'When did the doctor say he was coming?'

'Later,' he mumbled, and hurried down to the beach.

I hoped he would stay there until the doctor came. Occasionally I glimpsed him at his intricate pacing. Ripples of heat deformed him; his blurred flesh looked unstable. Whenever I glanced at the beach it leapt forward, dauntingly vivid. Cracks of light appeared in the sea. Clumps of grass seemed to rise twitching, as though the dunes were craning to watch Neal. Five minutes' vigil at the window was as much as I could bear.

The afternoon consumed time. It felt lethargic and enervating as four in the morning. There was no sign of the doctor. I kept gazing from the front door. Nothing moved on the crescent except windborne hints of the beach.

Eventually I tried to phone. Though I could feel the heat of the pavement through the soles of my shoes, the day seemed bearable; only threats of pain plucked at my skull. But nobody was at home. The bungalows stood smugly in the evening light. When I attempted to walk to the phone box, the noose closed on my skull at once.

In my hall I halted startled, for Neal had thrown open

the living-room door as I entered the house. He looked flushed and angry. 'Where were you?' he demanded.

'I'm not a hospital case yet, you know. I was trying to phone the doctor.'

Unfathomably, he looked relieved. 'I'll go down now and call him.'

While he was away I watched the beach sink into twilight. At the moment, this seemed to be the only time of day I could endure watching – the time at which shapes become obscure, most capable of metamorphosis. Perhaps this made the antics of the shore acceptable, more apparently natural. Now the beach resembled clouds in front of the moon; it drifted slowly and variously. If I gazed for long it looked nervous with lightning. The immense bulk of the night edged up from the horizon.

I didn't hear Neal return; I must have been fascinated by the view. I turned to find him watching me. Again he looked relieved – because I was still here? 'He's coming soon,' he said.

'Tonight, do you mean?'

'Yes, tonight. Why not?'

I didn't know many doctors who would come out at night to treat what was, however unpleasant for me, a relatively minor illness. Perhaps attitudes were different here in the country. Neal was heading for the back door, for the beach. 'Do you think you could wait until he comes?' I said, groping for an excuse to detain him. 'Just in case I feel worse.'

'Yes, you're right.' His gaze was opaque. 'I'd better stay with you.'

We waited. The dark mass closed over beach and bungalows. The nocturnal glow fluttered at the edge of my vision. When I glanced at the beach, the dim shapes were hectic. I seemed to be paying for my earlier fascination, for now the walls of the room looked active with faint patterns.

Where was the doctor? Neal seemed impatient too. The only sounds were the repetitive ticking of his footsteps and the irregular chant of the sea. He kept staring at me as if he wanted to speak; occasionally his mouth twitched. He resembled a child both eager to confess and afraid to do so.

Though he made me uneasy I tried to look encouraging, interested in whatever he might have to say. His pacing took him closer and closer to the beach door. Yes, I nodded, tell me, talk to me.

His eyes narrowed. Behind his eyelids he was pondering. Abruptly he sat opposite me. A kind of smile, tweaked awry, plucked at his lips. 'I've got another story for you,' he said.

'Really?' I sounded as intrigued as I could.

He picked up the notebook. 'I worked it out from this.'

So we'd returned to his obsession. As he twitched pages over, his feet shifted constantly. His lips moved as though whispering the text. I heard the vast mumbling of the sea.

'Suppose this,' he said all at once. 'I only said suppose, mind you. This guy was living all alone in Strand. It must have affected his mind, you said that yourself – having to watch the beach every night. But just suppose it didn't send him mad? Suppose it affected his mind so that he saw things more clearly?'

I hid my impatience. 'What things?'

'The beach.' His tone reminded me of something – a particular kind of simplicity I couldn't quite place. 'Of course we're only supposing. But from things you've read, don't you feel there are places that are closer to another sort of reality, another plane or dimension or whatever?'

'You mean the beach at Strand was like that?' I suggested, to encourage him.

'That's right. Did you feel it too?'

His eagerness startled me. 'I felt ill, that's all. I still do.'

'Sure. Yes, of course. I mean, we were only supposing. But look at what he says.' He seemed glad to retreat into the notebook. 'It started at Lewis where the old stones were, then it moved on up the coast to Strand. Doesn't that prove that what he was talking about is unlike anything we know?'

His mouth hung open, awaiting my agreement; it looked empty, robbed of sense. I glanced away, distracted by the fluttering glow beyond him. 'I don't know what you mean.'

'That's because you haven't read this properly.' His impatience had turned harsh. 'Look here,' he demanded, poking his fingers at a group of words as if they were a Bible's oracle.

WHEN THE PATTERNS READY IT CAN COME BACK. 'So what is that supposed to mean?'

'I'll tell you what I think it means – what he meant.' His low voice seemed to stumble among the rhythms of the beach. 'You see how he keeps mentioning patterns. Suppose this other reality was once all there was? Then ours came into being and occupied some of its space. We didn't destroy it – it can't be destroyed. Maybe it withdrew a little, to bide its time. But it left a kind of imprint of itself, a kind of coded image of itself in our reality. And yet that image is itself in embryo, growing. You see, he says it's alive but it's only the image being put together. Things become part of its image, and that's how it grows. I'm sure that's what he meant.'

I felt mentally exhausted and dismayed by all this. How much in need of a doctor was he? I couldn't help sounding a little derisive. 'I don't see how you could have put all that together from that book.'

'Who says I did?'

His vehemence was shocking. I had to break the tension, for the glare in his eyes looked as unnatural and nervous as the glow of the beach. I went to gaze from the front window, but there was no sign of the doctor. 'Don't worry,' Neal said. 'He's coming.'

I stood staring out at the lightless road until he said fretfully 'Don't you want to hear the rest?'

He waited until I sat down. His tension was oppressive as the hovering sky. He gazed at me for what seemed minutes; the noose dug into my skull. At last he said 'Does this beach feel like anywhere else to you?'

'It feels like a beach.'

He shrugged that aside. 'You see, he worked out whatever came from the old stones kept moving towards the inhabited areas. That's how it added to itself. That's why it moved on from Lewis and then Strand.'

'All nonsense, of course. Ravings.'

'No. It isn't.' There was no mistaking the fury that lurked, barely restrained, beneath his low voice. That fury seemed loose in the roaring night, in the wind and violent sea and looming sky. The beach trembled wakefully. 'The next place it would move to would be here,' he muttered. 'It has to be.'

'If you accepted the idea in the first place.'

A hint of a grimace twitched his cheek; my comment might have been an annoying fly – certainly as trivial. 'You can read the pattern out there if you try,' he mumbled. 'It takes all day. You begin to get a sense of what might be there. It's alive, though nothing like life as we recognize it.'

I could only say whatever came into my head, to detain him until the doctor arrived. 'Then how do you?'

He avoided the question, but only to betray the depths of his obsession. 'Would an insect recognize us as a kind of life?'

Suddenly I realized that he intoned 'the beach' as a priest might name his god. We must get away from the beach. Never mind the doctor now. 'Look, Neal, I think we'd better – '

He interrupted me, eyes glaring spasmodically. 'It's the strongest at night. I think it soaks up energy during the day. Remember, he said that the quicksands only come out at night. They move, you know – they make you follow the pattern. And the sea is different at night. Things come out of it. They're like symbols and yet they're alive. I think the sea creates them. They help make the pattern live.'

Appalled, I could only return to the front window and search for the lights of the doctor's car – for any lights at all.

'Yes, yes,' Neal said, sounding less impatient than soothing. 'He's coming.' But as he spoke I glimpsed, reflected in the window, his secret triumphant grin.

Eventually I managed to say to his reflection 'You didn't call a doctor, did you?'

'No.' A smile made his lips tremble like quicksand. 'But he's coming.'

My stomach had begun to churn slowly; so had my head, and the room. Now I was afraid to stand with my back to Neal, but when I turned I was more afraid to ask the question. 'Who?'

For a moment I thought he disdained to answer; he turned his back on me and gazed towards the beach – but I can't write any longer as if I have doubts, as if I don't know the end. The beach was his answer, its awesome transformation was, even if I wasn't sure what I was seeing. Was the beach swollen, puffed up as if by the irregular gasping of the sea? Was it swarming with indistinct shapes, parasites that scuttled dancing over it, sank into it, floated writhing to its surface? Did it quiver along the whole of its length like luminous gelatin? I tried to believe that all this was an effect of the brooding dark – but the dark had closed down so thickly that there might have been no light in the world outside except the fitful glow.

He craned his head back over his shoulder. The gleam in his eyes looked very like the glimmering outside. A web of saliva stretched between his bared teeth. He grinned with a frightful generosity; he'd decided to answer my question more directly. His lips moved as they had when he was reading. At last I heard what I'd tried not to suspect. He was making the sound that I'd tried not to hear in the shells.

Was it meant to be an invocation, or the name I'd asked for? I knew only that the sound, so liquid and inhuman that I could almost think it was shapeless, nauseated me, so much so that I couldn't separate it from the huge loose voices of wind and sea. It seemed to fill the room. The pounding of my skull tried to imitate its rhythm, which I found impossible to grasp, unbearable. I began to slide along the wall towards the front door.

His body turned jerkily, as if dangling from his neck. His head laughed, if a sound like struggles in mud is laughter. 'You're not going to try to get away?' he cried. 'It was getting hold of you before I came, he was. You haven't a chance now, not since we brought him into the house,' and he picked up a shell.

As he levelled the mouth of the shell at me my dizziness flooded my skull, hurling me forward. The walls seemed to glare and shake and break out in swarms; I thought that a dark bulk loomed at the window, filling it. Neal's mouth was working, but the nauseating sound might have been roaring deep in a cavern, or a shell. It sounded distant and huge, but coming closer and growing more definite – the voice of something vast and liquid that was gradually taking shape. Perhaps that was because I was listening, but I had no choice.

All at once Neal's free hand clamped his forehead. It looked like a pincer desperate to tear something out of his skull. 'It's growing,' he cried, somewhere between sobbing and ecstasy. As he spoke, the liquid chant seemed to abate not at all. Before I knew what he meant to do, he'd wrenched open the back door and was gone. In a nightmarish way, his nervous elaborate movements resembled dancing.

As the door crashed open, the roar of the night rushed in. Its leap in volume sounded eager, voracious. I stood paralysed, listening, and couldn't tell how like his chant it sounded. I heard his footsteps, soft and loose, running unevenly over the dunes. Minutes later I thought I heard a faint cry, which sounded immediately engulfed.

I slumped against a chair. I felt relieved, drained, uncaring. The sounds had returned to the beach, where they ought to be; the room looked stable now. Then I grew disgusted with myself. Suppose Neal was injured, or caught in quicksand? I'd allowed his hysteria to gain a temporary hold on my sick perceptions, I told myself – was I going to use that as an excuse not to try to save him?

At last I forced myself outside. All the bungalows were dark. The beach was glimmering, but not violently. I could see nothing wrong with the sky. Only my dizziness, and the throbbing of my head, threatened to distort my perceptions.

I made myself edge between the bushes, which hissed

like snakes, mouths full of sand. The tangle of footprints made me stumble frequently. Sand rattled the spikes of marram grass. At the edge of the dunes, the path felt ready to slide me down to the beach.

The beach was crowded. I had to squint at many of the vague pieces of debris. My eyes grew used to the dimness, but I could see no sign of Neal. Then I peered closer. Was that a pair of sandals, half buried? Before my giddiness could hurl me to the beach, I slithered down.

Yes, they were Neal's, and a path of bare footprints led away towards the crowd of debris. I poked gingerly at the sandals, and wished I had my stick to test for quicksand – but the sand in which they were partially engulfed was quite solid. Why had he tried to bury them?

I followed his prints, my eyes still adjusting. I refused to imitate his path, for it looped back on itself in intricate patterns which made me dizzy and wouldn't fade from my mind. His paces were irregular, a cripple's dance. He must be a puppet of his nerves, I thought. I was a little afraid to confront him, but I felt a duty to try.

His twistings led me among the debris. Low obscure shapes surrounded me: a jagged stump bristling with metal tendrils that groped in the air as I came near; half a car so rusty and misshapen that it looked like a child's fuzzy sketch; the hood of a pram within which glimmered a bald lump of sand. I was glad to emerge from that maze, for the dim objects seemed to shift; I'd even thought the bald lump was opening a crumbling mouth.

But on the open beach there were other distractions. The ripples and patterns of sand were clearer, and appeared to vibrate restlessly. I kept glancing towards the sea, not because its chant was troubling me – though, with its insistent loose rhythm, it was – but because I had a persistent impression that the waves were slowing, sluggish as treacle.

I stumbled, and had to turn back to see what had tripped me. The glow of the beach showed me Neal's shirt, the little of it that was left unburied. There was no mistaking it; I recognized its pattern. The glow made the nylon seem luminous, lit from within.

His prints danced back among the debris. Even then, God help me, I wondered if he was playing a sick joke – if he was waiting somewhere to leap out, to scare me into admitting I'd been impressed. I trudged angrily into the midst of the debris, and wished at once that I hadn't. All the objects were luminous, without shadows.

There was no question now: the glow of the beach was increasing. It made Neal's tracks look larger; their outlines shifted as I squinted at them. I stumbled hastily towards the deserted stretch of beach, and brushed against the half-engulfed car.

That was the moment at which the nightmare became real. I might have told myself that rust had eaten away the car until it was thin as a shell, but I was past deluding myself. All at once I knew that nothing on this beach was as it seemed, for as my hand collided with the car roof, which should have been painfully solid, I felt the roof crumble – and the entire structure flopped on the sand, from which it was at once indistinguishable.

I fled towards the open beach. But there was no relief, for the entire beach was glowing luridly, like mud struggling to suffocate a moon. Among the debris I glimpsed the rest of Neal's clothes, half absorbed by the beach. As I staggered into the open, I saw his tracks ahead – saw how they appeared to grow, to alter until they became unrecognizable, and then to peter out at a large dark shapeless patch on the sand.

I glared about, terrified. I couldn't see the bungalows. After minutes I succeeded in glimpsing the path, the mess of footprints cluttering the dune. I began to pace towards it, very slowly and quietly, so as not to be noticed by the beach and the looming sky.

But the dunes were receding. I think I began to scream then, scream almost in a whisper, for the faster I hurried, the further the dunes withdrew. The nightmare had overtaken perspective. Now I was running wildly, though I felt I was standing still. I'd run only a few steps when I had to recoil from the sand that seized my feet so eagerly I almost heard it smack its lips. Minutes ago there had been no quicksand, for I could see my earlier prints embedded in that patch. I stood trapped, shivering uncontrollably, as the glow intensified and the lightless sky seemed to descend – and I felt the beach change.

Simultaneously I experienced something which, in a sense, was worse: I felt myself change. My dizziness whirled out of me. I felt light-headed but stable. At last I realized that I had never had sunstroke. Perhaps it had been my inner conflict – being forced to stay yet at the same time not daring to venture on to the beach, because of what my subconscious knew would happen.

And now it was happening. The beach had won. Perhaps Neal had given it the strength. Though I dared not look, I knew that the sea had stopped. Stranded objects, elaborate symbols composed of something like flesh, writhed on its paralysed margin. The clamour which surrounded me, chanting and gurgling, was not that of the sea: it was far too articulate, however repetitive. It was underfoot too – the voice of the beach, a whisper pronounced by so many sources that it was deafening.

I felt ridges of sand squirm beneath me. They were firm enough to bear my weight, but they felt nothing like sand. They were forcing me to shift my balance. In a moment I would have to dance, to imitate the jerking shapes that had ceased to pretend they were only debris, to join in the ritual of the objects that swarmed up from the congealed sea. Everything glistened in the quivering glow. I thought my flesh had begun to glow too.

Then, with a lurch of vertigo worse than any I'd experienced, I found myself momentarily detached from the nightmare. I seemed to be observing myself, a figure tiny and trivial as an insect, making a timid hysterical attempt to join in the dance of a teeming beach. The moment was brief, yet felt like eternity. Then I was back in my clumsy flesh, struggling to prance on the beach.

At once I was cold with terror. I shook like a victim of electricity, for I knew what viewpoint I'd shared. It was still watching me, indifferent as outer space – and it filled the sky. If I looked up I would see its eyes, or eye, if it had anything that I would recognize as such. My neck shivered as I held my head down. But I would have to look up in a moment, for I could feel the face, or whatever was up there, leaning closer – reaching down for me.

If I hadn't broken through my suffocating panic I would have been crushed to nothing. But my teeth tore my lip, and allowed me to scream. Released, I ran desperately, heedless of quicksand. The dunes crept back from me, the squirming beach glowed, the light flickered in the rhythm of the chanting. I was spared being engulfed – but when at last I reached the dunes, or was allowed to reach them, the dark massive presence still hovered overhead.

I clambered scrabbling up the path. My sobbing gasps filled my mouth with sand. My wild flight was from nothing that I'd seen. I was fleeing the knowledge, deep-rooted and undeniable, that what I perceived blotting out the sky was nothing but an acceptable metaphor. Appalling though the presence was, it was only my mind's version of what was there – a way of letting me glimpse it without going mad at once.

V

I have not seen Neal since – at least, not in a form that anyone else would recognize.

Next day, after a night during which I drank all the liquor I could find to douse my appalled thoughts and insights, I discovered that I couldn't leave. I pretended to myself that I was going to the beach to search for Neal. But the movements began at once; the patterns stirred. As I gazed, dully entranced, I felt something grow less dormant in my head, as though my skull had turned into a shell.

Perhaps I stood engrossed by the beach for hours. Movement distracted me: the skimming of a windblown patch of sand. As I glanced at it I saw that it resembled a giant mask, its features ragged and crumbling. Though its eyes and mouth couldn't keep their shape, it kept trying to resemble Neal's face. As it slithered whispering towards me I fled towards the path, moaning.

That night he came into the bungalow. I hadn't dared go to bed; I dozed in a chair, and frequently woke trembling. Was I awake when I saw his huge face squirming and transforming as it crawled out of the wall? Certainly I could hear his words, though his voice was the inhuman chorus I'd experienced on the beach. Worse, when I opened my eyes to glimpse what might have been only a shadow, not a large unstable form fading back into the substance of the wall, for a few seconds I could still hear that voice.

Each night, once the face had sunk back into the wall as into quicksand, the voice remained longer – and each night, struggling to break loose from the prison of my chair, I understood more of its revelations. I tried to believe all this was my imagination, and so, in a sense, it was. The glimpses of Neal were nothing more than acceptable metaphors for what Neal had become, and what I was becoming. My mind refused to perceive the truth more directly, yet I was possessed by a temptation, vertiginous and sickening, to learn what the truth might be.

For a while I struggled. I couldn't leave, but perhaps I could write. When I found that however bitterly I fought I could think of nothing but the beach, I wrote this. I hoped that writing about it might release me, but of course the more one thinks of the beach, the stronger its hold becomes.

Now I spend most of my time on the beach. It has taken me months to write this. Sometimes I see people staring at me from the bungalows. Do they wonder what I'm doing? They will find out when their time comes – everyone will. Neal must have satisfied it for a while; for the moment it is slower. But that means little. Its time is not like ours.

Each day the pattern is clearer. My pacing helps. Once you have glimpsed the pattern you must go back to read it, over and over. I can feel it growing in my mind. The sense of expectancy is overwhelming. Of course that sense was never mine. It was the hunger of the beach.

My time is near. The large moist prints that surround mine are more pronounced – the prints of what I am becoming. Its substance is everywhere, stealthy and insidious. Today, as I looked at the bungalows, I saw them change; they grew like fossils of themselves. They looked like dreams of the beach, and that is what they will become.

The voice is always with me now. Sometimes the congealing haze seems to mouth at me. At twilight the dunes edge forward to guard the beach. When the beach is dimmest I see other figures pacing out the pattern. Only those whom the beach has touched would see them; their outlines are unstable – some look more like coral than flesh. The quicksands make us trace the pattern, and he stoops from the depths beyond the sky to watch. The sea feeds me.

Often now I have what may be a dream. I glimpse what Neal has become, and how that is merely a fragment of the imprint which it will use to return to our world. Each time I come closer to recalling the insight when I wake. As my mind changes, it tries to prepare me for the end. Soon I shall be what Neal is. I tremble uncontrollably, I feel deathly sick, my mind struggles desperately not to know. Yet in a way I am resigned. After all, even if I managed to flee the beach, I could never escape the growth. I have understood enough to know that it would absorb me in time, when it becomes the world.

The most chilling horror stories – now available in paperback from Grafton Books

Robert Bloch
The Night of the Ripper   £2.50 ☐
Richard Haigh
The Farm   £1.75 ☐
The City   £1.95 ☐
Michael Shea
The Colour out of Time   £1.95 ☐
Mendal Johnson
Let's Go Play at the Adams'   £2.50 ☐
H P Lovecraft
Omnibus 1: At the Mountains of Madness   £2.95 ☐
Omnibus 2: Dagon and other macabre tales   £2.95 ☐
Omnibus 3: The Haunter of the Dark   £2.95 ☐
Brian Lumley
Psychomech   £1.95 ☐
Psychosphere   £1.95 ☐
Psychamok   £2.50 ☐
Necroscope   £3.50 ☐
Whitley Strieber
Black Magic   £1.95 ☐
The Night Church   £1.95 ☐
Miles Gibson
The Sandman   £1.95 ☐
Ramsey Campbell
The Nameless   £1.95 ☐
The Parasite   £2.50 ☐
Incarnate   £2.50 ☐
Obsession   £2.50 ☐

To order direct from the publisher just tick the titles you want
and fill in the order form.   **GF3181**

All these books are available at your local bookshop or newsagent, or can be ordered direct from the publisher.

To order direct from the publishers just tick the titles you want and fill in the form below.

Name _____

Address _____

_____

Send to:
Grafton Cash Sales
PO Box 11, Falmouth, Cornwall TR10 9EN.

Please enclose remittance to the value of the cover price plus:

UK 60p for the first book, 25p for the second book plus 15p per copy for each additional book ordered to a maximum charge of £1.90.

BFPO 60p for the first book, 25p for the second book plus 15p per copy for the next 7 books, thereafter 9p per book.

Overseas including Eire £1.25 for the first book, 75p for second book and 28p for each additional book.

Grafton Books reserve the right to show new retail prices on covers, which may differ from those previously advertised in the text or elsewhere.